THE HOUSE ON THE HILL

By the same author

Fiction

Awaydays
Powder
Leisure
Outlaws
Clubland
Freshers
Stars Are Stars
The Killing Pool

Non-fiction

Extra Time

KEVIN SAMPSON

THE HOUSE ON THE HILL

JONATHAN CAPE
LONDON

Published by Jonathan Cape 2014

2 4 6 8 10 9 7 5 3 1

Copyright © Kevin Sampson 2014

First published in Great Britain in 2014 by
Jonathan Cape
Random House, 20 Vauxhall Bridge Road,
London SW1V 2SA

www.vintage-books.co.uk

Addresses for companies within The Random House Group Limited can be found at:
www.randomhouse.co.uk/offices.htm

The Random House Group Limited Reg. No. 954009

A CIP catalogue record for this book
is available from the British Library

ISBN 9780224097178

The Random House Group Limited supports the Forest Stewardship Council®
(FSC®), the leading international forest-certification organisation. Our books
carrying the FSC label are printed on FSC®-certified paper. FSC is the only
forest-certification scheme supported by the leading environmental organisations,
including Greenpeace. Our paper procurement policy can be found at
www.randomhouse.co.uk/environment

Typeset in Perpetua by Palimpsest Book Production Limited,
Falkirk, Stirlingshire
Printed and bound in Great Britain by
CPI Group (UK) Ltd, Croydon CR0 4YY

For Dan Franklin. It's been wild.

Part One

The Glass House

June 1990

Hamilton was late. It was unlike him. The Prince stepped back out onto the hull of the yacht, walked to its prow and surveyed the marina, left and right. This was definitely the right boat; but no sign of John-John Hamilton, yet. No sign of the goods. He'd give it until the hour, just in case the infidel was working to British time. Any longer could be dangerous.

Jamal was always warning him to be on full alert, at all times. The Unit had come to the attention of the FBI of late – a nuisance, so close to the fourth of July fireworks they'd been planning. Still, Europe was rich with possibilities. In truth, the Prince was even more excited by the Jabal Tariq initiative than the Independence Day blitz they'd had to scrap. That was another of Jamal's traits he had come to admire: no matter how well laid a plan – no matter how late in the day – at the first sign of compromise, Jamal would abort the entire operation. Shame about the Boston Tea Party; but this new assault was going to be spectacular. He'd given Hamilton the pills – served him right, the degenerate. All they needed was for JJ to come up with his side of the bargain now. All they needed was the Semtex; and Hamilton, if nothing else, was good for the Semtex.

Footsteps. At last! He glanced at his Rolex Oyster. OK, benefit of the doubt. If he was going by their Greenwich Mean

Time, then Hamilton was absolutely punctual to the minute. He picked his way over the ropes and railings to go and greet his guest when a voice from behind startled him.

'Ali!'

He hadn't heard it in quite some time, but this was a voice he knew immediately, and knew well. He turned, a smile on his lips, an excited chuckle already halfway out. It was to be the penultimate sound the Prince would utter. His last word was the name of his killer.

The previous week . . .

McCartney couldn't help himself. He hated football; he wasn't that keen on New Order; but whenever 'World in Motion' came on he could not resist turning it up and belting it out, a big fat grin on his face as he sang along. Especially the John Barnes bit. One on one. Respect yourself. Too right!

At this time of day, on a bank holiday Monday, there was hardly a car on the road. He accelerated down Vauxhall Bridge Road, keen to get there, now, and find out what this was all about. As early as it was, even with the roof down, the day was heating up. It was going to be another scorcher, after yesterday's record highs. There was a brief but welcome gust as he crossed the bridge and swung the XR2 left onto the Albert Embankment. The streets were deserted; not even a rootless tramp or an early jogger on the riverside path. Still, he checked all three mirrors and lurched left suddenly, without indicating, as had always been his practice when visiting Kenneth Shanley at his place of work. He headed down the ramp and into the cool of the underground car park.

The call had come first thing, on the work line. He sat up in bed, instinctively clearing his throat so he'd sound right, and scooped up the handset on the fifth ring. The workaholic Scot got straight down to business.

'Mac. Sorry for the alarm call, so to speak. I'll tell you more when you get here . . .'

'Where are you?'

'The main place.' A pause. He could almost hear the shifts of gear as Shanley thought out loud. 'Did you happen to attend Spike Island, ultimately?'

He enunciated 'Spike' and 'Island' with a self-conscious overemphasis, as though he were translating from an ancient tongue – with a pronounced pause between each word as oldies will, when flagging up their lack of cool and their wholehearted satisfaction with that state of affairs.

'No, sir. I didn't go . . .'

'Oh . . .'

'If you recall, sir, I had to go back to Dorset . . .'

'Quite so. You did appraise us. I hope you gave your father my best?'

'I did, sir. Thank you.'

A lengthy silence; one of Shanley's stock-in-trades. Mac spoke first.

'So. Spike Island. Did something occur?'

A pause.

'Can you come in, Billy? Now?'

'On my way, sir. HQ?'

'HQ. Bunty will give you the numbers.'

Mac was still on leave – technically – but Shanley was one of the very few people for whom he would drop everything and do anything. It was in no small part down to Shanley that he could belt across town in T-shirt, white Levi's and Gazelles, dressed for work, doing the job he was born to do. He parked up in one of the unnumbered bays and got out, enjoying the stillness and the shade. Still checking around and about, half enjoying the role play, he strode to the lift and punched the code he'd been given into the number pad. This lift only went to one floor.

Shanley was there to greet him as he stepped out.

'Good of you to come at such wretched short notice, Billy.'

The rolling Dundonian *r* was less prominent these days, but there was still no mistaking Shanley's roots. He beckoned towards the long corridor with a bowling motion, and they set off.

'I'm aware you're not due back yet, but this has somewhat blown up overnight. It could be big . . .'

'Consider me intrigued, sir . . .'

Shanley hooked an arm around McCartney's shoulder.

'This club music, Billy – Ibiza . . .' He wrinkled his nose. 'Acid house and suchlike. It's your thing, yes?'

'It pretty much comes with the territory, sir. Occupational hazard . . .'

He tried a knowing smile, which Shanley chose to ignore.

'Aye, for sure, for sure. But away from the job . . . you know your way round the, the *scene*?'

Shanley was staring at him, hopeful. Did he want a crash course in Balearic? A quick trip to Zoom? He looked serious. Mac shrugged.

'Well, yeah, I do. I like some of it . . . especially the slower stuff . . .'

'Stuff. Not a word I've ever embraced . . .'

Amm-brrrrraced. McCartney slowed as they approached Shanley's office, but the compact little Scot steered him on – past the Xerox machines, past the water cooler and the kitchenette. McCartney had never been this far along before.

The office windows and glass divides were blacked out now. Mac could see his own cropped, blond hair – £25 plus tip at Cuts of Soho – and his puzzled face staring back from successive black surfaces as they passed unit after secret unit. At the furthest end of the corridor, Shanley slotted a big, toy-like grey plastic key into a white veneer door and stepped aside to allow Mac in first. A man was there with his back to them, looking out of the huge windows.

'Come,' he said, without turning round. Even on the single, one-syllable word Mac detected a Southern European inflection. 'Look . . .'

McCartney stood beside him. The view out over the river was staggering; to their right, on the opposite bank but close enough to touch, Big Ben and the Houses of Parliament looked like huge Lego models. To the left, Battersea Power Station and, seemingly in its back garden, fields of green that must have been, what? Clapham Common and Richmond Park? Snaking through the middle yet in perfect stasis was the River Thames, just as it appeared on the *EastEnders* credits – one long, writhing sigma, making its way from country, to town, to the seven seas beyond.

'See?'

'What am I looking at?'

The man turned to face McCartney. He had a look of De Niro about him; wise. Playful. He'd oiled his thinning hair, which made it look as though it was melting in the heat – but he was handsome. Mid-thirties, well built, with appraising, bird-like black eyes.

'The world. It can be so good, no? So *pura*. Pure.'

Shanley stepped between them, smiling.

'Billy, I'd like you to meet my long-time collaborator and friend, Jus . . .' He put a friendly arm around him and pulled him close, just once, before letting him loose again. 'Inspector Juan Sebastien Roig from Madrid –'

'*Based* out of Madrid . . .'

'Of course. Jus is a proud Catalan –'

'Andorran, but yes . . .' He smiled again. 'And am now Inspector *Jefe* . . .'

Shanley bowed his head in apology. 'Of course. I think I knew that. Anyway – happy new pay rise!'

'Thank you, Kenneth. We take these guys down – I pay for dinner!'

The two men laughed. Roig's eyes twinkled, and his face creased up into a dozen deep lines. McCartney liked him straight away.

'Jus and I worked on the Harlow Boys case. Remember? The Estepona stake-out . . .?'

McCartney nodded. He remembered every case like that – even the ones he didn't work on.

'Inspector Jefe Roig is part of the SNP's elite squad, dealing almost entirely with the drugs and organised crime side of things over there. That fair to say, Jus?'

Roig inclined his head but didn't commit to a full, affirmative nod. 'Is national security, yes. If my bosses tell Roig to jump, I jump!' He grinned. 'But sure – drug, gun, bomb . . . for us is equal.'

'Like I say, Billy. Pretty much what we do – but with guns . . .'

Roig gave a silent laugh, shook his head and sent Shanley a little look – 'May I?'

Shanley gave a slight nod back.

'The boss and me, we have been sharing the information about certain – how you say – rogues . . .'

He pronounced it rog-ez. McCartney nodded.

'OK. So these people, they are not, you know – unidad. Not a gang. But there is connection, yes? We don't know what the connection is . . . this is the problem.'

'What sort of, well, rogues are we talking about? Drugs?'

Shanley stepped forward. 'The whole sideshow, potentially, Billy. Guns, money laundering, drugs, terrorism . . .'

Terrorism?, thought Mac. Interesting.

'With one or two of these characters there are very visible links, for sure. But there's the problem. We can't join it all up. We don't actually know what the link is –'

'Or if there is any link at all,' smiled Roig.

'But as of last night, with the Ecstasy death –'

Mac went to say something; Shanley silenced him with a hand. *In a minute.*

'– with that very sad death, the UK now has licence as well as cause to join our colleagues in Spain in looking at some of these characters a lot more closely . . .'

McCartney tried to strangle his hopes. Please, please, please – a JV with the Spanish! This was what he was born for! This would make all that training worthwhile; the language schools, the environmental conditioning, the psychological profiling. *Please!* Shanley picked up a remote control, pointed at the windows and zapped. Blinds came down on five of the six windows. One of the two central blinds became jammed, billowing back upon itself as it unravelled. Roig pursed his lips – intimidating, all of a sudden. McCartney stepped over, slipped the middle three fingers of each hand underneath and gently manoeuvred the sickly blind down to the window ledge, from whose grille the chill wheeze of the air conditioning seeped.

Shanley beckoned towards the plastic bucket chairs laid out in a shallow crescent. Even though he was wearing jeans, Mac automatically pulled them up at the knee as he sat. Roig perched side-saddle, cross-legged on the end chair, while Shanley remained standing.

'When did you last see John-John Hamilton, Mac?'

McCartney let out a silent whistle. 'Let's see. That would be about four weeks ago. Milk Bar, off Charing Cross Road. Is he back?'

'No. No, he's still out in Ibiza. I merely wondered whether we ever established the purpose of his visit . . .'

A disappointment, that one. The Milk Bar was a small, intimate scene. Lots of people, some of them semi-famous, loose and languid on E and guarana, all sat around on scatter cushions, massaging one another's shoulders. Tiny dance floor and a laid-back soundtrack in defiant opposition to the high-energy acid house still fuelling the raves and warehouse parties up and down the country. It was easy enough to insinuate yourself into clubs like Monkey Drum and the Milk Bar, but it was difficult to get close to your targets. JJ Hamilton – notorious Scouse dealer, latterly based in Ibiza – had been tagged meeting the Irish arms dealer Davey Lane in a Heathrow hotel. There'd been mooted links between the IRA and main-land drug dealing but they'd been struggling even to prove Lane's Sinn Fein connections, let alone tie him to Hamilton. Davey Lane was a lone wolf, it seemed, with few qualms – certainly nothing ideological – as to who he dealt with. Mac was on a watching brief, tailing the pair, hoping to get some context and some pictures.

That night, a month ago, Mac had found himself at the bar, right next to Davey Lane, buying beers and vodka jellies. Close up, he seemed boyish with his short, reddish-blond curls, yet his attitude was at odds with the cosy vibe of the club. He was cold, remote; the barmaid might as well flirt with herself – there'd be no eye contact, let alone any tip from the Irishman.

The remix of the next Mondays single came on and Lane turned away from the bar, nodding to the track as though the band was actually there, onstage.

'Love that line!' smiled Mac. Lane turned sharply as though surprised, but immediately turned away again and carried on nodding to the track. Mac tried again. 'Cracks me up . . .'

Lane grinned to himself, squeezed lime into his Corona and turned back to the bar. That was that. Mac knew from experi-ence it'd be hopeless trying to force the issue. He bought a

Corona too, overtipped the girl and drifted away from the bar, gently swaying to the music, trying to keep a subtle eye out for John-John and Lane.

At one point Hamilton had been sat cross-legged on a cushion, scratching Patsy Kensit's scalp. There was no denying, JJ Hamilton was a good-looking man. He must have been thirty, at least, to have got that far up the ladder, but with his gypsy-black hair and those blue eyes framed by lashes thick as kohl, he could have easily passed for twenty. Patsy certainly seemed to go for him, and if it wasn't her, it was her twin sister. Davey Lane had been lying to their left, propped up on his elbow, smiling, smiling, smiling . . . If Mac had started snapping away, no matter how much he looked the part, he'd have stood out a mile. They'd have taken his film, and asked him to leave.

He spotted a freelance taking pictures of Flowered Up onstage later on. Mac took her card. Next day he'd gone down to her studio off Curtain Road posing as a fanzine editor, but none of her pictures gave a clear image of Lane and Hamilton together. He purchased a couple nonetheless – best practice in terms of maintaining his legend – but the photographs were next to useless. He could connect the two villains anecdotally, but so what? No crime there. Other than getting close up in the club, the job had been a damp squib. He could barely look Shanley in the eye.

'No, sir. We did manage to get sight of the pictures available, but –'

'It doesn't matter. He was there, they were together –'

'Undoubtedly. Why? What's happened?'

Shanley dropped his head. 'Where to start . . .'

He mugged up an expression that was intended to give off a hint of honesty, or humility – a slight self-censure. In spite of himself, though, Shanley just looked like a battle-weary veteran who found it hard to trust anyone. He let out a long hiss of despair.

'OK. So we had, we believe, Ecstasy-related deaths yesterday. Last night, to be precise . . .'

McCartney sat up; sat forward. 'At Spike Island?'

'In a sense – but not exactly . . .'

'Right . . .'

'Let me start at the start . . .'

Shanley dimmed the lights, stumbled slightly as he went to operate the VCR, and froze the first image with another remote control. A map of Ibiza, with little balloon motifs marking certain spots. Again, McCartney's spine tingled. Ibiza. This was beginning to make sense. If it was an Ibiza job, there could be *no one* better equipped than him . . .

'When I say Ecstasy deaths, I'm talking *here*, mainland UK. The holiday season hasn't even started over there yet, but we've already had reports of two drug-related deaths in Ibiza, too. Jus can fill us in on that.'

'Sure, and sad to say it could get worse. The Swedish girl and a German boy, they both died, and there is also Brits girl in the hospital, not waking up yet. All had been out in same club –'

'And all had taken Ecstasy?'

'Correct. Yes . . .'

'And those drugs would have been supplied, we presume, by John-John Hamilton's firm?'

'We don't have that as absolute fact – but everyone's working on the basis they're Hamilton's pills, yes. Although until last night this was primarily a matter for the Guardia Local out there on Ibiza . . .'

Roig grimaced. 'Who are, you know . . . happy to keep this whole thing off front-page news . . .' Roig smiled to himself. '*Not* good story for the holiday business, yes? Kind of a *Jaws* affair . . .'

He shrugged and held his hands out, inviting them to draw their own conclusions. McCartney shifted in his seat so he was facing Roig now.

'So. What about here? What's the link?'

Roig gave the slightest nod back at Shanley.

'Car crash. Nottinghamshire, not long after midnight. The survivors say the driver just seemed to lose control of the vehicle. Car veered across the central reservation, and . . . well. Two dead, another two in hospital . . .'

'And we think this is related to JJ Hamilton?'

'We are almost certain, sadly, Billy. We can be even more precise. We're something like 99.9 per cent sure that the tablet that caused the driver of that car to have a seizure comes from the same rogue batch that's done for the kids in Ibiza . . .'

Mac couldn't help himself; his spirits sagged before he could put himself in check. Forget Ibiza. Forget any fanciful notions of a possible JV with the Spanish. There was a bad batch of pills over here – *that's* what they were going to ask him to investigate.

'And these bad tablets are now about to go native here in the UK?'

'There's one compelling reason to hope not . . .'

It was only one word, but McCartney could barely keep the hopeful quiver out of his voice.

'Oh?'

'The driver's surname. He was called Colin Macmillan. One of our survivors mentioned in his statement last night that Colin only received his tablets a few days ago. His sister sent them. She's working in Ibiza. The girl in a coma out there is called Abi Macmillan . . .'

'Right, right – I hear you . . .'

Shanley fixed him with his unblinking, always appraising gaze. 'Our people are working round the clock to confirm the link . . .' He let out another of his world-weary sighs. 'But – and with all due respect to the dead, if that's what has come to pass, and their families . . .' He scratched his head, trying to find the right form of words. 'Look. The fact is that this agency has bigger fish to fry, if you will, than the tragic, if isolated, deaths of club-goers . . .'

'That's assuming they do indeed remain isolated, sir . . .'

Roig shot Shanley a look. The boss held up both hands, pleading for Mac to just shut up and listen. He flicked at the controller in his hand, and the video resumed. In place of the Ibiza map, a poorly graded video image flickered on the screen, its jerky, CCTV image shifting focus repeatedly, as though culled from multiple sources.

'This is where it really does start to get troublesome . . .'

The backdrop of the footage – a yacht, moored at a marina or typical harbour boardwalk – was almost bleached by a dazzling sunshine that kept the camera's subject as a silhouette for most of its minute-long duration. When he did eventually step out of the sunlight, a young man of Arabic appearance came into shot, studious, searching for something – or someone. For a moment, his face filled the screen, narrowing his eyes against the sun.

'What we really would like to know is what Hamilton's link is with *this* guy . . .' Shanley paused the video, leaving the Arab kid squinting comically. Mac leaned forward, scrutinising the grainy image.

'Who is he?'

Shanley turned to his dapper colleague. 'Jus?'

Roig stood up, any trace of levity now gone from his face. He fixed his tiny eyes on McCartney.

'The kid goes by name of the Prince. Is familiar, this?'

McCartney stuck his lower lip out and shook his head.

'No. For us this is new as well. But the Prince is also known as Ali El Glaoui, youngest son of big mafioso Moroccan drug family. *Now* you know him!' Roig smiled, his eyes glittering. 'You hear this name – El Glaoui, yes?' Mac nodded – of course. '*Very* powerful in the world of drugs, familia El Glaoui. Big, big hashish family for many decades. But Ali? No. Ali is not involved in the family business. No, no, no . . .' He wagged his forefinger in the classic 'telling-off' mode. 'No. Ali is . . . what is the word? . . . he is a *privileged* boy. All the hopes of the family go into this boy. They send him to school in Princeton. He's a quiet, hard-working boy and he goes on to study the molecular technologies at the world-famous MIT . . .'

McCartney nodded once, impressed, but Roig expanded nonetheless.

'The Massachussets Institute of Technologies, yes? Best in all world. Ali is a so-so student – certainly not bad – but not outstanding, either; not special. For his first two years, Ali is just a model student. Quiet, makes his grades, but nothing spectacular. He has no *duende, sí?*'

McCartney nodded. *Duende.* The Muse.

'No feel for the subject, eh?'

'*Exactly* . . .'

'So. What then? After those first two years . . .'

Roig clapped his hands together.

'OK, so then it becomes serious. The world is Ali's world to do what Ali want do, then *ban*! He drops out from course. He disappears from the world-famous MIT . . .' Jus made a 'pfft!' sound and held his hands out wide. 'Gone. Vanished. And then, suddenly, our friends in the Bureau, they begin hear of "the Prince". Yes? He is no longer Ali El Glaoui, he is *the Prince*. But he is very no-careful, OK? Speak often of the revolution, the jihad, the evil Uncle Sam. Big Satan . . .'

McCartney nodded, brain still whirring. Waiting for them to get to the bit where he came in. The drugs.

'Our friends in Boston, they start to show a big interest in the Prince. Now the Prince has his *unidad*, yes? His gang. They're only kids. Students. But they call this gang the Young Umayyad. Among themselves, members of this gang they call themselves "the Unit". And the FBI begins to take a very big interest in this Unit. They think the Unit has a big plan for Boston. They think Young Umayyad is planning a bomb . . .'

Roig stopped dead still; stared at McCartney, then Shanley, then back to McCartney. To Mac's slight consternation, Roig put his hands together and dipped his fingers down, as though trying to imitate a rat, scurrying. He opened his eyes wide. 'The boys from the Bureau, they decide to take a closer look at the Unit.' Roig began sneaking towards the window, then went on his tiptoes, peeping at an imaginary target. He turned sharply. Mac stifled a giggle. 'They look. They gather the information. They learn of a big explosion, right there in Boston . . .' Roig dropped his hands and shrugged. 'But then, out of nothing, the Prince goes quiet. Then he buys a flight to Madrid . . .'

'When was this?'

'One month – maybe six weeks . . .'

'And that was it? No arrests?'

'No explosion. No bomb. No arrest. Our friends from the Boston Bureau refer the Prince to us . . .'

'This is the FBI, yes?'

Shanley stepped in. 'Precisely. They categorise the Prince as high risk. Very slim file, but his particular pattern of . . .'

'Radical . . .'

'Exactly. His radicalisation. It's not so unusual in a boy of his age. Meets some kids of a similar mindset, they egg each other on . . . you know how it goes. He's almost beholden to prove himself. It looks very much as though they had something cooking for the fourth of July, but then . . .'

He fired the showreel back into action – Ali walking along the marina promenade. Lots of yachts moored along the harbour front, bars and cafes on the other side of the walkway. Ali's head was craning right as he walked, seemingly looking for a particular bar or restaurant. He turned sharply, as though someone had shouted his name. Jus paused the video and walked right up to the screen; pointed to a young man in a dark shirt, his hand held above his head.

'See? Who is this please, gentlemen?' Mac leaned forward again, but couldn't make out any clear detail. Roig continued pointing to the screen. 'No? You don't see? Look closely . . .'

McCartney strained his eyes.

'Looks like it could be –'

'*Sí*. It is!' He stabbed his finger at the man in black. '*This* is your good friend John-John Hamilton.'

'Are we certain it's him?'

Shanley stepped in again. 'Yes. We know it's him.' He turned to face Mac. 'I agree with you, Billy. It's not irrefutably apparent from the footage. But Jus's team have backed all this up with photographs and so on, placing this Prince kid from the moment he touched down in Madrid. We can track both him and Hamilton arriving, where they parked, the paths each of them took to the marina, where they went immediately after their meeting. It's John-John Hamilton, all right.'

'When was this taken?'

Roig froze the image again and pointed at the time code burnt into the bottom right-hand corner.

'See? The meeting took place one month ago. Five weeks. But we took this from the port authority's security cameras only three days ago. And now, on top of this, the Ecstasy deaths –'

'Jesus. What the fuck, hey?'

Roig crouched down so his nose was almost touching McCartney's chin.

'Yes, Billy Mac. Kids dead in Ibiza. John-John Hamilton, the island's *numero uno*, having a happy lunch with this so-called Prince. Ali El Glaoui, model student, now wanted by the FBI. What the fuck is correct! What the fuck? You tell me, Billy Mac, because Jus Roig also wants to know this thing.'

Shanley touched Roig on the shoulder. He got up and stepped away to the window, leaving Shanley to close the deal. McCartney tried to slow himself down, regulate his breathing. He knew what was coming now – but it didn't stop him swooning when the boss came out with it.

'We need to sort you a legend, Mac. Pronto. We need to get you out there.'

'Ibiza?'

'Ibiza . . .'

John-John Hamilton had his work cut out. Clubbers were dying. The season hadn't even started yet, and kids were keeling over, poisoned. As the biggest dealer on the White Island, JJ was as good as certain the iffy pills had come from his batch. There were the gypsies from Barcelona doing their little thing round Ibiza Town. There were the old boys, the cockneys who'd been here years, doing small scale round and about. But no one was working on the scale the Liverpool boys were operating. With their pedigree, their reputation, their connections with Dublin and Amsterdam as well as back home, JJ and his firm were the boys out here, and that was that – but that was the problem, too. He was dealing on licence, basically – more or less running a franchise – and Molina could make that go away just as easily as he'd helped make it happen. So it gave him something of a headache when, on the eve of the three big months of the year that made the other nine easy, the club kids had started dropping like flies, and the vomit trail led directly to his door.

It was all very well tracking down the kid brother – the Prince, for fuck's sake! Fuck did he think he was? Grandmaster Flash? Those brothers though, they'd be chocker with their Ali, course they would – but JJ knew what the Arabs were like. They'd wrap him up. If there was going to be any reprisal, they'd keep it in-house. Much as JJ wanted to steam over there, give him a hiding and get his money back, there was a bigger picture: much, much bigger. He could not remotely afford to alienate the El Glaoui brothers.

So, how to keep a lid on these moody pills? He could go and see the kid in hospital. Pay her whatever to keep her mouth shut – say she'd had a dodgy paella or something. Or he could do nothing and hope the whole mad episode fizzled out. Either way, he'd have to recall the tablets that were already out there. He'd only done a couple of hundred of the tabs so far – but he'd taken thousands from Ali El Glaoui, hundreds of thousands. Whichever way you looked at it, it was a fucking mess. He could hear his old fella's rough Bootle voice in his ear:

'If a deal seems too good to be true, lad, add it up on your fingers. It'll be too good to be true.'

Had he listened? No. He'd betrayed his own golden rules; the careful, sensible principles that had got him to the top of this trade. Softly-softly. Let the others take the fast route. Let the hard men take their fill. Chip away on the fringes, John-John. Keep on smiling. Pay what you owe, and pay it on time. Pick up the tab, but don't be a mug. Never fall out with anyone unless you're left with no choice. If you do have to dish out a slap, make sure people are there to see it. 'That JJ Hammo – ruthless when he has to be, so just don't cross him.' That would be him – hard, but fair. Good to work for. Good to know. John-John Hamilton – everyone's a winner. Everyone gets paid.

He wasn't just on his way up, he was there – but this time he'd been greedy. He'd only said he'd go and meet the El Glaoui kid because of who he was; but the proposition, well, it was – sorry, Dad, but it really was just too good to be true.

Shanley left McCartney to construct the legend he felt best suited the op, only popping in occasionally to check on progress. Mac looked at a few strong personas but, in the end, there was only one real contender for this particular role. Bunty brought up a stack of silhouettes from archive – guys who had made fortunes breeding carp, inventing high-power, hand-held vacuum cleaners or overseeing a soft-porn empire in which everyday people were the stars and the stories. She also gave him a file on Charlie Innes, a young businessman from Reading who had become a millionaire pulping and recycling newspaper. It was perfect. Mac took Innes's basic story, honed it and created Rob Martindale, an upbeat, up-for-it, good-time guy from Southampton who'd made a fortune recycling paper into toilet tissue. Southampton he knew from university days, the rest was pure backstory. Mac's instinct was that Martindale, and toilet tissue, was so uninspiring, so utterly unglamorous that not even the nosiest inquisitor would pry beyond the first few layers. Rob had worked hard throughout his teens and twenties, building up his business while the rest of the city partied. Thirty-three now, he was a multimillionaire – out in Ibiza with an open mind and a big wallet, making up for lost time. Shanley had cut him a decent budget to live the life and make the legend 3-D – clothes, villa, all-terrain vehicle and plenty of spends to spread around the clubs and dealers. Shanley had also understood the need for Millie.

'Hamilton's big thing – the thing that will get us into him – is women,' Mac told him. 'I'll qualify that. He's into beautiful, refined, sophisticated, educated . . . call them posh, call them what you will, but that Sloaney type of upper-crust lady is John-John Hamilton's *raison d'être*. Get someone like that up close to him . . .'

Shanley nodded. 'Very well. We're fortunate in this department to have many talented officers who could potentially fulfil that role . . .' He fixed his eyes firmly on McCartney. 'But, Mac, this is *your* op. It's your responsibility. Be careful. Hear me? Be very bloody careful . . .'

Mac held his stare, then nodded back. They held preliminary talks with Roberta Hebburn from the Foreign Office. Shanley suggested his chief researcher, Bunty Soames; but when DS Camilla Baker walked into the operations room, McCartney felt a pang in his abdomen that he knew would send Hamilton flying, too. Going right back to those first days at Hope Street with Alfie Manners and Dooley, Mac had long despised the term *classy*. For him, it reeked of that macho locker-room badinage that made his teeth grate. Yet, statuesque Millie Baker, with her clear-eyed gaze, her dressed-down elegance, her long neck and that perfectly golden hair, exuded class. She was a heart-stopper; he couldn't stop staring at her.

So the decision was made there and then – it was going to be Mac and Millie; Rob Martindale and his high-class paramour, Sophia Yorke.

'It *has* to be a place, at the very least,' smiled Millie. 'An ancient and venerable place, like Lancaster or Warwick . . . if not an entire county. York! I should be Sophia Yorke!'

She flicked her golden hair and smiled with her eyes; joking at the role play, yet serious underneath. Shanley was right – Mac was going to have to be very, very careful. He found himself stealing glances at Sophia – Millie. Her supernaturally blue eyes kept finding him, somehow, and McCartney had to look away. It was like a first crush. It was stupid. Since Rebecca, there'd been no one of any great significance. Billy was more than used to being on his own; being the way he was. He'd ride the attraction out, no problem. He'd get used to her. He smiled back at Millie.

'Pronounced Suff-eye-ah, no doubt?'

'No doubt,' she winked. 'I shall be the justified and ancient Sophia Yorke from . . . where?' A knowing smile. 'Canterbury! I shall be Sophia from Canterbury.'

'Canterbury it is, then. You know the place well?'

'No.'

'Know it at all?'

'Er . . .'

They laughed, immediately at ease with one another.

'Always best to choose a place you can bullshit about with at least a degree of conviction . . .'

'Sure.' Millie went silent and fiddled with her fingertips. 'So. When does this, like . . . *happen?*'

'Your guess is as good as mine. But soon, I think.'

JJ knew he couldn't put this on Mustapha. He'd got to know the old man well, and what shone through was that his youngest was his pride and joy. 'My son at Oxford,' he'd say. Wrong college, wrong fucking country – but who was counting? It would be counterproductive, running crying to Muzzy El Glaoui, bursting his illusions about Ali in academia – but he couldn't let it go. Hamilton decided he'd have to speak to the brothers – certainly Hassan, effectively the boss these days anyway. And if he was going to tell Hassan, then, out of respect, he'd tell Yousef, too. Yousef was soft – he wouldn't want to believe it – but it was Hassan's opinion that counted.

He mulled it over, as he mulled everything, but his feeling

was that the Moroccans would want to know about the stunt their youngest brother had pulled – and he was spot on. They were horrified. They were like him – they'd rather take a hit than fall out and fuck up a long-term proposition. But above and beyond that, Hassan was troubled by the Davey Lane connection. He knew who Davey was. He knew what he did. And the idea that his cherished, protected little brother – the anointed one who was going to take future generations of the El Glaoui family legit – was associating with arms dealers and terrorists and gangsters, as good as broke his heart. JJ neglected to add that he himself had been the go-between.

'Ali is making business with the *IRA*? Why? *Why?!*'

'Well, Davey's freelance, but yeah, same difference. I take your point . . .'

'Why, John-John? Ali is grade-A student. *Why?*' He could barely believe it – yet he knew that Hamilton would not lie. 'It is not like my brother needs money or something . . .'

JJ could hear it in Hassan's voice; the dismay. The fear. But there was anger there, too; there was a note of vexation – perhaps even a quiver of envy – that came as relief to JJ's ears. Ali El Glaoui had worked the head on all three of them, and the family was embarrassed. When Ali – the Prince – had first come to see him, the implication was always there that he had the family's blessing. He hadn't said so explicitly, but he'd intimated they were giving him his own little start. But the brothers knew nothing about Ali's private enterprise – and he certainly hadn't mentioned the Davey thing. It was a mess, and Hassan could not apologise enough.

'John, I know you long time. Yes? I know like my brother. If this needs attention, please – you know that you only have to ask.'

So there it was. Business as usual. Even though they didn't have to spell it out to one another, Hassan had made it perfectly clear to him; if JJ had to do something to bring the kid back in line, him and Yousef were OK with it.

Whichever way you looked at it, though, it was a train wreck. Davey had already ordered in what he'd asked for from the Irish. He was on his way with the pyro and that was that. JJ was going to have to wear it – pay the Paddies, take delivery, take it on the chin. But no way was he taking it up the arse, too. If that little Moroccan ponce wanted the loud gear, he was going to have to pay for the hassle he'd brought on them. He'd always preferred to go about his business with a minimum of fuss, JJ had. He was almost pathologically low-key, but he could do things the other way, too. If there had to be a scene, there'd be a scene.

Hassan held the phone out so his brother was in no doubt.

'No answer?'

'Again. It's ringing, but he won't pick up.'

'Little fucker! Why didn't Hamilton phone us straight away, huh? Check out what the little bastard's been telling him?'

'I know, kid. I know. But think of it from his side . . . Ali can be very persuasive –'

'Fuck, man! He's a *kid*! He's a student. He can't be getting himself into all that.'

'I'm going out there.'

'Ibiza?'

'Ibiza.'

'The shit don't come down until Wednesday.'

'I know this.'

'So?'

'So? *You* bring it! Yes? You bring it in, like normal. But this time I shall be there on the beach . . .' His face dissolved into a rapturous smile. 'Waiting with the English to welcome you ashore . . .'

'What does Father say?'

'Yousef, I'm not sure you're hearing this. Ali has crossed the wrong people. I have to get to him before they do.'

'I *do* hear you. I do . . .' Yousef stroked his long chin. 'I hear you. And I thank you – as our brother should, too.' He winked at his big brother. 'Save a canary for me.'

They hugged, closely. Brothers.

Roig stepped forward to give them their final notes.

'So, it is important that you know some rules about how things work in Ibiza. It's true my outfit have overall control of this operation. But Guardia Civil in Ibiza have overall control of . . .' He narrowed his eyes. 'They control the territory, yes? Control the island. So it is *very* important that you don't piss off Chief Molina, OK?'

He zapped up a good, sharp head shot of a lugubrious uniformed officer, his decorated epaulettes only eclipsed by his outstanding moustache.

'Rodolfo Molina. He's an OK guy. Had his gun licence taken away . . .' Roig shrugged and popped his lip out as though to tell them this was a trifle. 'Molina can be difficult. He likes to be in charge; wants to do things his way. He won't be happy if you English come onto his *campo*, try to tell him how things are going to be. I think the best is if you go direct to Molina, no? Go to Rodolfo Molina and make your introductions. Act, you know . . . like *this*, yes?' He stooped and made a beggarly face. 'Be *humble*. Respect, respect, respect – please, sir, we request your assistance. Please, if it is possible, can you help us? Yes? Give him a *little* story, tell him why you're there. Something trivial, I don't know this . . . you are looking for a man who don't pay his tax, something like this. Better to have Molina with you, so his officers don't pull you in for the speeding, or the trespass, you know? Tell him you are here in Ibiza for, I don't know . . .' Another shoulder shrug, arms stiff, stuck to his sides. 'For apprehend a car thief, something like that. No glory for Molina, some car thief. He has no interest in this small matter. He give you the free pass for come and go, so long as you don't take the, the . . . *glory*, yes?' He beamed at them. 'For Molina, it is very important to take the glory!'

Mac and Millie nodded, eager to get going now. They still had to get to Gatwick and, travelling civilian, they'd have to clear security like everybody else.

'Good. Myself, I too will come and go. Yes? I have the same walkie-talkie as you. We will use only the frequency we discussed . . .' His tiny eyes sparkled as he looked at Mac, then Camilla, then back to Mac. 'So. Good luck. Without the luck – and I beg your pardon – we are fucked.'

McCartney laughed out loud – a little too loudly, betraying his anxiety to get this show on the road, at last. Shanley stood up.

'OK. That's it. That's everything. You've done your training, you know what you're doing. Just . . . *be* your legend. Be that person. Live that life. Don't go looking for the bad guys – they will come to you. Sit there long enough, and that will happen. They will come. When they do, be aware of what this is, and what we need. We need *evidence*. OK? Real evidence . . .'

Millie gave a cowgirl whoop and high-fived all three of them, shouting 'All right!' McCartney just sat there, smiling to himself. OK, he thought. Very OK.

Sitting outside his all-glass villa, high in the hills above Saint Agnes, JJ took a call on his chunky satellite phone.

'John!' It was Mustapha, as he knew it would be. 'John, my friend.' His rasping chuckle. 'Mr John-John Hamilton . . .'

He tailed off, his laughter turning into a hacking cough. JJ cranked as much bonhomie into his voice as he could muster.

'Mustapha! All good, my friend?'

Any other time, he would be certain of the answer. All would be very good. The hash would have made its way down from their plant, high in the mountains; crates of it, brought down to the fort on a train of donkeys, all pressed and sealed with the El Glaoui hallmark. A call to JJ from the old man meant that the boys would soon be coming over with the season's first load; and their arrival had come to signal the start of the season proper. The El Glaoui brothers' first shipment meant parties, wild, crazy parties; champagne, cocaine and the hottest ladies he could conjure. They were animals, the El Glaoui boys. They were proper men. They'd look you in the eye and shake your hand and you knew you had a deal. With the Moroccans, their word and their hand really was their bond. A handshake from Hassan was worth ten of any paper contract he'd ever signed. His deal was your deal, and when the deal was done, fulfilled on both sides to the satisfaction of everyone – then the El Glaoui would party. Hassan and Yousef loved to party; they always wanted women, always wanted blondes. And they sometimes asked for one to take back for their father, too. JJ cranked extra levity into his telephone voice.

'What's the word from the Rif, *amigo*?'

'Ah, John, John, John. I don't know. I don't think a man he understand this until he is father. My son . . .'

'Hassan?'

'No. No Hassan. No Yousef. The baby . . .'

This presented JJ with a problem. Did he play dumb? Act like he hadn't discussed Ali with the other two? No. Instinctively, he knew that that would not play. The El Glaoui boys – the older two – might be the sophisticated face of the family business these days, but their father commanded – and demanded – absolute respect. Mustapha was a mountain man, a goatherd – but he was nobody's fool.

'Ah, young Ali. Yes. Fine boy. I met him for the first time, only a few weeks ago . . .'

'I know this, John.'

'Very bright boy.'

'Very.' A pause. 'Perhaps too bright for his own benefit, no?'

At any time of year a call like this would be unwelcome. But for Rodolfo Molina, coming, as it did, on the eve of the club season's first big weekend and with all the other issues that entailed, the timing was particularly bad. But there was only ever one man who called him on that line, and the message was always the same. Go and sort this out. This is what we pay you for. He replaced the handset, reached into his bottom drawer and dug out the keys, the set he'd had made for himself, for instances just like this.

He kept his thumb over the bottom of the ID card in case his name triggered any vague recollections. Word would have gone round about his firearm ban, but it was mainly a topic for the top brass. Bastards. One lousy foul-up – the kid didn't even die – and they make an example of him. Make a fool of him. Too bad for them, anyway. He'd lost some privileges, yes – but he'd gained a reputation.

This rankled, though – this latest from Hamilton. He'd do it, because he had no choice now. He'd made his bed. But his stomach was in knots as he swept past the desk sergeant and made his way down the long, cool corridor, down three stone steps to the lower level then, turning right, the short walk to the armoury. He checked left and right – no one coming. No one *would* be coming, obviously – not here. He slotted the five-bar into the keyhole, let himself in, locked the door behind him. Straight to the cabinet. Fished out the keys, opened it up. His heart soared at the sight of all that hardware. Magnificent. But this was no time to stroke and stare. He knew exactly what he'd need for this brief. He located the Glock, wrapped it in the handkerchief, stowed it in his pocket, locked the cabinet. Went to the ammo store, found the right drawer, helped himself. He'd only need one bullet – but he took six, for good measure; good method. Sharpshooters always like six.

Shanley had insisted on driving McCartney down to Gatwick himself. Millie didn't even raise an eyebrow; a quick nod, more of a sharp ducking of the head to show her swift and absolute comprehension, followed by a tight handshake.

'I'll see you down there. Iberia?'

'Yep. Iberia. See you at the gate?'

'Sorted.'

And off she went, without another word. As the staff car crawled through the south London traffic, they made small talk about the heatwave; the travesty of Scotland being drawn in the same World Cup group as Brazil again; then, once they hit the A23 proper, Shanley came to the point.

'So. Roig. Jus is a good guy . . .'

'But?'

'Precisely. With Jus Roig there is often a "but". He's in overall charge out there. But don't let him dominate you.'

'OK . . .'

'What I mean by that, Billy, is that you are a British operative, working in Ibiza on UK targets and priorities.' He checked to make sure the road ahead was clear, then turned to face Mac. 'Jus might not see things quite the same way.'

'I understand, sir. I think I understand . . .'

'Good. I knew you would.' His eyes were fixed straight

ahead again now. He gripped the leather steering wheel tight. 'This terrorism angle is all well and good, but our unwavering gaze is trained on the druggies. Understood?' Mac nodded, irked. What's not to understand? His boss shook his head as he spoke. 'Hamilton may well be based out there, but he's sending no end of his shite back here. And that has to stop.'

'John-John Hamilton is my absolute priority, sir. Be in no doubt whatsoever about that.'

Shanley threw his head back and laughed, showing yellowish, nicotine-stained teeth.

'Excellent. You go and bloody well get him, then! And, Billy – you keep an eye on Baker. Hear? She's new to all this.'

Molina parked away from the marina, in the shadows of one of the new apartment blocks; just as cheap and ugly as their predecessors but, under the new ruling, at least they couldn't go above four storeys.

He stood back, surveyed the scene. Barely anything, coming or going. A moped passed at speed; another, off in the distance, possibly heading this way. There was not a soul to be seen on foot, the late-afternoon heat still too squalid to bring the crowds back out. He crossed the dual carriageway and, quickly checking his notes one last time, set off across the first foot-bridge and onto the boardwalk, glancing left and right for the yacht in question.

Mac sat back, feet propped up on the whitewashed wall, and closed his eyes against the mellow, waning sun. Out on the bay below, the distant whirr of speedboats; mopeds beginning to make the climb back up from the bumpy beach path; the evening getting gently into gear. He could hear Millie in the kitchen, levering the caps off bottles of beer they'd bought en route. That was step one in the flying of their kite, pulling up outside the little mercado in Sant Miguel and producing a big wad – a thick, chunky brick of banknotes – to pay for their goods. It was minor – as much to do with easing themselves into their Ibiza selves as banging out those first tentative beats on the jungle drum. Yet, over months and years of training for operations like this one, successive mentors had assured them both that basic, method-style actions and routines would be the making of a credible persona. Flashing the cash was a crude but necessary opening salvo.

Mac could picture the beer bottles, their brown glass misted over with a chilly dew from the hour they'd been stashed in the freeze box. He could picture Millie in her denim cut-offs; could hear her flip-flops, now, slapping across the terracotta tiles, out of the side door and over the terrace.

'Yo!'

He sat up. The setting sun cast a crimson sheen over Cap Bernat, the Sphinx-like rock staring out to sea, bathed in shades of red.

'. . . budge up, Roberto . . .'

Millie placed the dripping bottles and a vinyl file on the wall and dragged a wooden chair across, backwards. Sat down. Passed Mac a beer and picked up the file.

'Cheers.' They clinked bottles. 'This is the life . . .'

Mac nodded at the file. 'What's that?'

'Oh, just general background. Hamilton's routine, likely habitat, up-to-date photos and so forth.'

'And?'

She jerked her head down towards the beach below. 'He's as likely to be down there as anywhere, this time of day. Fancies himself as the spiritual type.'

'Anything to help him pull, eh?'

'Precisely.' She tapped the file with a fingernail. 'There's always a certain type of lady who'll fall for the psychic soul-brother bollocks.'

'Do we think that's a possible way in?'

'What? The lady thing?' She shrugged. 'Can't harm us, can it?'

Mac smiled, raised his bottle, downed a throat-full. By God this was good beer! Cold and cutting, with a biting mineral aftertaste – heaven. Millie placed the file on her thigh and raised her face to the sun.

'So. Should we?'

'What?'

'Show our faces. Benirras Beach . . .'

'Bit late now, isn't it?'

'How come?'

'Thought it was like, you know – bit of a sunset scene?'

'Well, yeah . . . people do go there for the sunset. But they'll stay on, too – people come and go all night. There's the drummers and what have you. The bars are supposed to do this amazing fresh-grilled fish.'

'Someone *has* been doing their homework!'

'So?'

Mac sat up and faced her.

'Shanley did say nice and easy does it . . .'

Even in the twilight, the sea was a pellucid green. Mac took a sip of Estrella and tilted his head back, eyeing the pine-clad rocky headland across the shallow bay. He raised his bottle.

'To work!'

She laughed, held her beer bottle up without clinking.

'Work . . .'

The drummers were gradually turning up the volume and, in twos and threes, girls stumbled down from the beach bars to dance. There were boys, too, tanned, toned, lithe as they writhed to the hypnotic throb of the skins – but it was mainly girls, fingering their hair as they danced, self-conscious, not yet abandoned to the night.

'Come on!' grinned Millie.

'What?'

'We're supposed to be going au naturel – let's dance!'

Mac winced. 'To *this*?'

'Come on!'

She slammed her bottle down, jumped to her feet and grabbed his wrist, tugging him to get up. Mac sat firm.

'No. Come on. It'll look phoney if we're too in-your-face. Hey? Let's just . . .' He pushed his flat hands down on an imaginary gushing geyser. 'You know? Let them come to us . . .'

She shrugged. 'Suit yourself.' She tottered down the three stone steps, stumbling on the last of them. She looked back at Billy over her shoulder – a film star, in slow motion. 'You big bore!' She winked and carried on down to the throng, effortlessly insinuating herself into the ebb and flow of tanned, flailing limbs.

Mac couldn't stop staring at her. Once again, that gnawing spasm in his guts as he watched her small bottom bump and jerk, her face lit up. A good-looking kid slowly danced towards her, wild curly hair, no top on, chevrons of rutted muscle glistening as he swayed. He smiled at Millie – she smiled back – and began swivelling his hips in a slow, sexual grind. Millie moved closer, tossing her hair, eyes closed – and the pang in Mac's abdomen was supplanted by something more savage. He fixed his eyes on her, willing her to look up, and, when she did, jerked his head for her to return. She looked chastened, a little scared – but tried to talk it out of her voice.

'What's up, Mac?'

'Time we made a move.'

Whatever she was going to say, she swallowed it. She gave a curt nod and followed him back to the Shogun.

She stole a glance at him as he drove, trying to gauge the situation. Had she done something wrong? She was just fatigued. She was imagining it. She swept her hair out of her eyes and clapped her hands.

'So – what's the plan, then?'

Mac stared straight ahead as he drove.

'Well – I should probably check in with Molina. And you should probably head down to the infirmary.'

'You think she'll be OK for a visit?'

Mac nodded, indicating and piloting the big vehicle down the unmade lane.

'Latest on Abi Macmillan is that she's sitting up, perfectly compos mentis.'

'They're not going to just let me in, though, are they?'

He pulled up outside the villa, still irritable.

'Jesus, Sofe! Use this . . .' He tapped his temple, smiling to show he wasn't cross. 'Just . . . tell them you're her sister. Cousin. Best friend . . .'

'Sure. Sorry.'

'*De nada*. You OK on that moped?'

She undid her seat belt and nodded, smiling curtly with her cheeks.

'Sure. All good.'

She opened the passenger door but didn't get out. He'd have to learn to manage the boss dynamics much more subtly. Millie was stung, and it was all down to him. He clapped his hands together and tried to wash over it.

'Good stuff. Let's liaise at the Rock Bar at, say . . . eleven. Yes?'

She sent him another cheek-smile and got out.

'Date. Over.'

A moment later the moped's tinny engine fired up and, with a melodramatic triple rev of the accelerator, she was off – a red light burning into the night.

Rodolfo Molina had got back to base as quickly as possible, knowing the call would be coming. A murder was a rarity in Ibiza and, as the chief, he'd be expected to attend. He locked up the Glock and replaced the unused bullets, scurrying back to his office unnoticed. It was already the talk of the building. Theories rang around the walls and corridors as different names from rival gangs were placed in the frame. Everybody had a good idea who was behind the killing. None of them had a clue.

McCartney recognised Molina straight away, striding towards the thick glass doors when a young officer stopped him. He looked tense, serious – more troubled or irritated than down-right angry. Mac picked up the word *inglés* and *comisario*, then Molina turned to him. He held out a hand and squeezed McCartney's hard, holding it without shaking.

'I'm sorry, Mr McCartney. You had better come with me. We can talk in the car.'

'By all means. Has there been an incident?'

'There has been a shooting.'

'Serious?'

'Fatal.'

'I see . . .'

Thoughts running amok, he followed the bristling commander to his car.

Millie took a sharp breath when she saw the girl. Abi was not much older than her, but she looked ancient. Her face was grey and clammy, her eyes sunken, her blonde hair lank and dull. She sat up and attempted a smile.

'Let me guess – Old Bill?'

Millie laughed and made a thing of checking around and about.

'Damn! This disguise was supposed to get me into all the best parties.'

Abi laughed too, and visibly relaxed. Millie pulled up a chair.

'So, you're close. I am on the snoop, sort of. But not Old Bill. I'm looking for my sister . . .'

'Oh?' Abi pushed herself up the bed so she was sitting up straight, now. 'Not sure what that's got to do with me . . .'

'No, me neither. I'm just chasing any possible lead, really. A few of the girls she knew told me she'd been knocking round with a guy called Hamilton. John-John Hamilton . . .'

Abi's face tensed. 'Oh. Him. Right . . .'

'Not a fan?'

'Most definitely not a fan. It's him that's done this to me.'

She doesn't know about her brother yet, thought Millie. Maybe her parents are on their way. Maybe they blame her. She snuffed out the train of thought and strived for the right note of sympathy.

'You know him well?'

'I hardly know the bastard at all. Only by rep . . .'

'Treat me as stupid. What's his rep?'

'You know. Mr Ibiza. Party king. That's where he give us the bad tablet, isn't it?'

'Where?'

'The party, you div!' She hesitated, looking Millie up and down. 'Supposed to be this big dealer, isn't he? Everyone goes silly for an invite to one of his after-clubs.'

'Right. Sounds like Jenny's sort of thing – more fool her . . .'

'Who's Jenny?'

'Sister. It's not like she's the best at keeping in touch anyway, but we're all just a bit, you know . . .' She let her head drop down, let out a long sigh of resignation. 'We haven't heard from her in a while.'

Abi forced a smile. 'You got a photo?'

Millie nodded. She pulled out her purse, showed Abi a picture of herself and her real-life younger sister, Jennifer.

'Cute. Definitely Hamilton's type.'

Millie folded up the purse and sat back.

'Tell me about this party then . . .'

The glare of Forensics arc lamps framed the pier in shrill white light. Mac hung back behind the tape while Molina went to inspect the corpse. The victim was young, dark; possibly North African – but very, very dead. If it wasn't a professional hit then it was a very lucky strike. The body lay sideways on the wooden jetty. One small entry wound right between the eyes and, even from where Mac was standing, one very evident exit point, taking half the skull with it. The usual melange of brain and blood spattered the side of the nearest cruiser: *La Bandera Verde*. You could add *rojo* to that now, too; with a spray of egg-yolk *amarillo*. An impact like that could only have been caused by dumdum bullets. It was a professional strike, all right – no doubt about that. Molina returned, his eyes and his attention elsewhere. Mac stepped forward, held the tape up for Molina to duck under.

'Look, sir – I can see this is . . .' He trailed off. No response from Molina. 'If you prefer to see me some other time . . .'

Molina snapped back to attention.

'No, no. My apologies. No – let us talk as we walk.'

He indicated that McCartney should follow him down the gangway, and away towards the marina's main quayside. They walked, but Molina said nothing.

'Who is it? *Was* it . . .?'

Molina fluttered a hand at thin air. 'Oh. Nobody . . .'

'Looked North African?'

'Arab. *Sí*. I think Maroc . . .'

OK, thought Mac. Know your place. Stick to the script.

'So – my car ring. I'd like to carry out my investigations with a minimum amount of disruption to your –'

'Just you?'

'Sorry?'

'No team?'

'Oh, right, I see . . . no. Not at this stage. I'm sure you're in the exact same situation here, budget-wise.'

'Too true, my friend. This part is all too true. Take this . . .'

He handed him a small, creased, laminated card. Balearic emblem top right, lettering barely discernible. *Permiso?* Probably.

'Anyone give you any shit, say my name. Is OK. Mention Molina and the problem will disappear . . .'

'That's great, sir. Señor . . .' He tried a smile on the down-beat detective. No response. Nothing. 'Thank you. So . . .'

Molina waved a fluttering hand at the rows upon rows of yachts, cruisers and powerboats. 'Too much wealth on this island.' He heaved a sad sigh and shook his head. 'Not sufficient quality . . .'

Now he turned to look McCartney in the eye.

'If you can get some of these bastards, you get them. *Sí?*'

Mac nodded his thanks. He held out his hand and, once again, Molina squeezed hard; this time he shook, too.

'If Molina can help, you only have to ask. Otherwise, I know you understand that I am a very busy man. OK?'

'OK. Thanks. I appreciate it.'

'*De nada. Buena suerte.*'

*　　*　　*

Hassan El Glaoui tore back to the glass house, biting his tongue as he raced over the cattle grid, almost putting his back out, he was driving so fast. He ditched the moped on the gravel and ran inside. Two young lads he hadn't seen before were sitting there, playing cards. Dark-skinned. Looked like brothers. Both in black shirts and black trousers, feet up on the table as they surveyed their hand. Hassan stood over them.

'Where is he?'

The bigger of the two, the one who looked the older, gave the younger kid a look. They carried on playing. Hassan gave the big lad a kick in the calf. He jumped up. The two of them snarled at one another.

'I said – where is John-John?'

The younger lad got up, very casually, and walked behind Hassan. He carried on staring straight ahead at the older brother.

'He's out. On business. Who the fuck are you?'

Hassan turned round. The younger kid had a knife.

'I *am* business . . .'

He pulled out the piece. The kid stepped back. Hassan turned to the big brother. Held it up, so both could fully appreciate its long, sleek barrel. He walked right up to him, so his forehead was touching his chin.

'Tell your boss that Hassan called by . . .' He waited for the name to register. It registered. The brothers cast one another panicked looks. 'Tell him that we need to meet. I am sure he knows why . . .'

He took one step back, bored his eyes into the big lad's face, turned and walked out.

The sulphuric flood lighting bathed the seaward side of the fort a lambent yellow. It was near midnight and the outdoor tables at the street cafes and restaurants below were only just beginning to fill up. Millie leaned her head back and took in the winking lights of the boats in the harbour below.

'I'm sorry, sir . . .' She smiled, acknowledging her mistake. 'Rob. But if this is work, give me more of it . . .'

'I hear you.' He knocked back the last of the Viña Sol; carefully placed his wine glass back upon the damp ring its base had cut into the paper table cover. Picked up his spoon and turned it round and round in his fingers. 'Try the dorado next time.'

'Only if you try the *sardinhas*.'

'Done deal, Sofe. I'm in. So . . .' Mac put the spoon down again; wiped his mouth with the thick linen napkin. Picked a tiny bone from between his front teeth. He was glad they were fine with each other again. He aimed to keep it that way – and he'd do that by keeping things businesslike. 'The bad tablet definitely came from Hamilton?'

'Yah, I mean, that's what she said . . .'

'OK. Just go through everything she told you, one more time. Where they met, club, bar, everything . . .'

'Everything?'

'Please. I need to try and visualise it. It's how I like to do this stuff.' He looked her in the eye. 'Just go through it all, from the start. Everything Abi told you . . .'

'O-K . . .'

'How she came to meet JJ Hamilton, for starters.'

'That's the only area she was at all clear about. Remembers Hamilton sweeping into the City Café, shaking hands with the waiters and so on, like he owned the place. He invited Abi and a gang of her mates up to this big party in the hills. She said there was a convoy of them driving up there, loads of Jeeps and trucks. And one thing she *clearly* remembers is the house itself . . .' Millie paused for maximum effect. 'She said it was like a huge glass beetle squatting on the side of the mountain.'

McCartney picked up the spoon again, closed his eyes as Millie spoke, bringing the scene to life.

'But that's about it. Abi can't really remember too much about the party itself. She said there was this . . .' Millie smiled and shook her head. 'Poor kid was trying *so* hard not to be racist, but I took it as her telling me there was this black guy hassling her.'

Mac felt the surge – the impulsive rush he always got on these jobs, when his gut told him something mattered. He leaned forward, eyes wide open again.

'A black guy? Could she have meant Arab, do we think?'

'I'm not sure . . . I can go back and absolutely double-check with Abi, if you –'

'No, no, it's fine, for now. It'll keep.'

'What are you thinking?'

'I'm thinking . . . the local police find a guy of Arab appearance with half his head blown off down at the marina, earlier this evening. Looked like a proper hit . . .'

'Wow!'

'Yep. So . . .' He stopped fiddling with his spoon. Placed it carefully on the table now, at a quarter past three. 'Just go with me on this, right . . . OK – known international drug dealer John-John Hamilton is caught in flagrante with Ali El Glaoui, youngest son of Moroccan drug-dealing dynasty. What on earth could they possibly be discussing, do we think?'

'OK, that part I see. New boy joins the family firm . . .'

'Then Abi Macmillan's at a big, lavish party up at JJ Hamilton's place – and so is Ali El Glaoui. We *think* . . .'

'Go on . . .'

'Abi ends up in hospital. Ali ends up dead.'

He picked up the spoon again, began twiddling.

'Whats the connection, Rob?'

He shook his head. 'Honest answer? I have not got the foggiest, Madame Sophia. But there's *something* there . . .'

'I think you're right. But what? What's our next move?'

He shrugged. Placed the spoon back on the table with finality, and sat back.

'Maybe young Ali's been given a rite of passage. Go and negotiate a price with John-John Hamilton . . .'

Millie wrinkled her nose. 'I mean, stupid question, probably, given his line of trade, but . . . is John-John Hamilton a killer?'

'Pass. For now. But I'll find out. I promise you, Millie . . .' He grinned, gave a subtle bow with his head. '*Sophia*. I shall join the dots and I will work this thing out . . .'

She looked directly into his eyes. He saw trust, yes; respect, yes; there was an element of something akin to awe that was not entirely unexpected, either. Millie was an officer who researched her cases thoroughly and, no matter how much he downplayed himself, McCartney was a cop with an up-and-coming reputation. For Millie, working with Billy McCartney was a Big Gig. Yet, no matter how much he downplayed this, too, there was an element of something akin to desire in her look – and he didn't know what to do about that. He dropped his eyeline to the table. Shifted his body right round in his seat until his face was 270 degrees from hers, and beckoned to the waiter for the bill.

For Jamal Benarbia, time was very much of the essence. The yacht was, in theory, under police guard, but that was a joke. He'd got on board easily enough, but no sign of the bangers. This was not good. He knew the stuff had arrived. It was there, somewhere, on the island – Ali had told him so last night. The question was, where? With or without Ali, the operation would go ahead. Without the Semtex, though . . .

without the special effects, the Jabal Tariq job would not have anything like the same impact.

He'd waited and watched while a succession of cop teams went through the motions. They sealed off the jetty, finger-searched every centimetre, let the dogs have a sniff around. Eventually, they carried him away. The Prince. He'd had that coming to him, Ali. It was sad. He'd shown great promise. But he'd only been with the Young Umayyad for just over a year. No one could go making unilateral decisions like that without facing the consequences, let alone a greenhorn. Thought through properly then, yes, maybe, the poisoned tablets could have been inspired. Symbolic, as well as practical, it could have been beautiful – the ultimate message to the decadent West. But the Unit could not stand for egos and individualists. *The Prince!* The name said it all. The boy wanted to be a legend, a star. It was no surprise at all that he'd ended up like this. Most legends are dead ones.

Trudging back down from D'Alt Vila, the proppers hit them with flyers for bars, happy hours, grand opening nights. Millie stopped dead under a weak amber street light.

'Hello, hello, hello,' she smiled. She stepped closer to a small, one-sheet poster, already beginning to curl at the corners.

'What is it?'

Very gently, she slid her fingers underneath and eased the poster off the wall. She turned to Mac, holding it up.

'Ku Club,' she grinned. 'Grand new-season opening. Tomorrow night . . . I've got a funny feeling we know who's going to be there . . .'

'Sold. We're there.'

Millie gave her hair a slight shake, tried to find McCartney's eyeline.

'Best get our beauty sleep while we can then . . .'

He averted his eyes; said nothing. They got back into the Shogun and headed out of Ibiza Town.

Mustapha saw the last of the crates into the old fishing vessel, as he always did. It was the way he'd always done it. The boys were forever going on at him. They could use Tangier; it was wide open for business now. They could pack four, five, six times as much into one of those millionaires' yachts and sail, unchallenged, wherever they wanted – Palma, Malaga, Marseilles . . . But that was them. For Mustapha, it was tradition. It was superstition. He had always used this trusty old sardine boat, the *Alharam*. Robust; undistinguished. The *Alharam* was supremely fit for purpose – his purpose: the easy loading, transportation and unloading of six tonnes of first-grade shit. That was another thing the boys liked to nag him about. The hash was only going to end up mixed with tobacco and nicotine in some degenerate Viking's spliff – why send them the best? Second grade, even third grade would pass muster for those redneck louts. But that was them, too. Mustapha was known for the best, had always sent the best and he'd always sent it from the fishing port of M'diq.

Why change a thing that worked so well? Mustapha didn't care at all for bigger, more, better; he didn't care for influence and power in Tangier. He could have that, whenever, if ever, he needed it. Mustapha already had all the power and influence he needed, just where he needed it. In Chefchaouen. In the foothills. In the mountain paths and roads into and out of the Rif. *These* were the real corridors of power. His boys had a lot to learn. He kissed Yousef on the cheek and clasped his hand.

'Safe voyage. Allah be with you.'

'God's will be done.'

Both men were silent for a moment, then Yousef's young face creased into a broad, affectionate smile.

'Four days, three nights, Father . . .'

'Bring me a fair one.'

'Blue eyes?'

Mustapha made a gesture towards the azure sea, lapping gently at the *Alharam*'s bows.

'Bluer than the ocean.'

They laughed, and hugged, and Yousef jumped aboard.

It was Roig.

'We have to meet.'

'Sure. Where?'

'Take the C-733, direction Portinatx. There are many, many signs to Club Portinatx, *sí*?'

'Sure . . .'

'On your left is the parador, how should I say this . . . a panorama, OK? Good view . . . beautiful place . . .'

'Beauty spot?'

'*Sí sí sí!* Parador Cala Xucia. OK. There is a parking place right there, at the parador. Pull over. I am with the silver Ford Mondeo.'

'We'll be there.'

'Just you.'

'Really?'

'Just you.'

Half an hour later he was there. Roig was at the furthest end of the car park leaning over a rough stone wall, staring out over the bay.

'Beautiful, no?'

'It is. *Muy bella*. What's up?'

Roig turned to face McCartney. Pulled his Foster Grant's down to the tip of his nose.

'I like this with you, McCartney. Straight to the business. No bullshit . . .'

'Sir . . .' The question was on the tip of his tongue. He swallowed it, waited for Roig to speak. Still, he gazed out over the silver-rippling sea. Mac found himself blurting it out before he realised he was going to speak. 'The girl, sir. Millie. Why won't you involve her?'

Roig batted a hand at thin air. 'The girl?' He turned towards McCartney, a sneer on his lips. 'We should keep her back. No?'

'I don't understand, sir.'

'I think it is better like this. Separate. It could be possible, maybe later, that we send the girl for this . . .' He made a grabbing movement and bared his teeth, mimed an animal ensnaring another. 'If Millie stays away, then we have the option of using her for trap. Yes?'

McCartney was struggling to understand, or perhaps did not want to comprehend. Was Roig saying he wanted to keep Millie back so he could send her in as bait, if needed?

'I'm sorry, sir, but that's just not the way we do things.'

'That is very nice to know, Billy.' He moved a step closer, frowning. 'But here? In this place? We do things *my* way . . .'

McCartney said nothing for a moment. His impulse was to walk away. As though sensing it, Roig forced a smile and placed a hand on his shoulder.

'OK, we have work to do . . .'

He pulled out a photograph. Stone-faced, dead-eyed North African male, staring directly into the lens. It was neither a passport picture nor a police-style head shot. Whoever this kid was – and he was no older than twenty, twenty-one – he was trying to project a message with this photograph. He was saying, don't mess with me; look away, if you know what's good for you. He'd seen that kind of look, that same expression, many, many times; in the Criminology textbooks, the test cases, the psychological profiles. The face looking out at McCartney was that of a cold-eyed killer.

'Who is he?'

'This is Jamal Benarbia. French Algerian, raised in Marseilles. If you are thinking you might have heard this name before, is not impossible, this. His grandfather is Abdul Benarbia. Big, big name in the Café Wars in the mid-fifties . . .'

'Right . . .'

'Now the boy is a fully nationalised Algerian – and a full-time radical, also. Benarbia travels around the universities and communities, speaking to students, looking for the . . .' He rubbed his thumb and forefinger together, international sign language for cash. 'But not just money. Benarbia is looking for support. More numbers, more young radicals, yes?'

'What kind of radical?'

Roig shrugged. 'The Young Umayyad are, how-say . . . idealists, OK? They want to change the world. But they will do this by using terror. For Roig, there is no difference between Islam or Christian, where terrorists are concerned. No difference. A threat is a threat. Yes? Danger is danger. It makes no difference to me if is ETA or Islam. Bomb is bomb.'

'You think there's a bomb threat here in Ibiza?'

Roig gave a theatrical shrug of the shoulders, his bottom lip drooping downwards in a show of disdain.

'Jamal Benarbia is here in Ibiza. That alone is sufficient for questions to be asked.'

McCartney gazed off past Roig, out to the speedboats beginning to cut their silver trail across the horizon.

'OK. What do we do? What do you want *me* to do?'

'You? Nothing. But if you see him, you call me. Yes? Straight away. Forget Hamilton. Forget these tablets, these drugs.

This is *real* danger, no? It is possible many dead if we don't find this guy.'

'I hear you, sir. But, with respect, that is hypothetical. We already *know* that Hamilton's drugs are killing –'

'Hamilton, sure. Sure. If we get him, we get him . . . but Jamal Benarbia is priority number one. OK? We want Benarbia.'

I'm sure you do, thought Mac – but E is for England, not España, here, and McCartney's priority was the pills. He tried to disguise a mounting unease with Roig, and nodded his head.

'Understood.'

'Good.'

They shook, but McCartney's mind was already back on the Ku Club. It was work, of course – it was business – and he had a feeling that tonight would bear fruit. Let Roig chase his Islamist extremists. As if! While Roig pursued his fantasy collar, he and Millie would make their mark at the Ku. Rob and Sophia. He killed the thought and climbed back in the Shogun.

The waves had almost worn themselves out by the time they lapped over the rocks outside the cafe. Hassan studied the near-black espresso, swirling around the tiny porcelain cup as he spoke.

'I thought we understood each other, John-John . . .'

'We did. We do . . .'

'So why it is, then, that my little brother lies dead?'

'I don't know. It wasn't me.'

'No?'

Hamilton leaned forward, angry now.

'Listen. The kid was out of order. Out of his depth. I doubt I'm the only person he's fucked over. But it wasn't me that whacked the lad.'

Hassan held his hand up; bowed his head in apology. 'John,

please, my most sorrowful apology. But you understand – I have to see with my own eyes? I have to hear with my own ears?'

'You really think I done it?'

Hassan put his coffee cup down; eyed Hamilton sadly, slowly shaking his head. 'I cannot say the thought did not enter my head. Our conversation . . .'

'The phone call? It was *you* saying do what has to be done!'

'I did not say kill him.'

'Hassan – listen to me, will you? I'm getting fucking angry here, right? Listen. I. Did. Not. Do. Your. Kid. In. Hear me? He sold me a fucking load of jarg pills and he deserved a fucking caning . . .' He looked away; caught his breath. 'But it was not myself that done it.'

'So *who*?!'

Hamilton jumped up, wild-eyed. 'Are you fucking deaf, lad! I don't fucking *know* who done it!' He stood there, his chest heaving in and out as he tried to calm himself.

Hassan had the flats of both hands up now, nodding his head, pleading for silence. 'OK. I'm sorry . . .'

'It should be myself kicking off, making threats . . . stunt he fucking pulled on us!'

'OK, OK! Please – I accept that the burden is with my family. We will compensate you.'

'Thank you.'

'But I hope you can help me, too . . .'

Hamilton visibly tried to calm himself. 'Help you how?'

'I need to take care of Ali's . . . situation.' He stared without blinking, right into Hamilton's eyes. 'In our culture . . . well – let me simply say that I cannot leave him here, like this.' He grasped JJ's hand. 'Please?'

JJ nodded, once. The two men shook hands. Each had given the performance of their lives; neither had the faintest idea the other was acting.

'Good, good,' smiled Hassan. 'Now the world is normal again. At –' he consulted his Rolex – 'about 1800 hours arrive Yousef with the shit. By midnight we will be celebrating, yes?'

John-John Hamilton drained his *caña* and got up. 'Let's fucking hope so, my friend. By midnight I want to be sailing on cloud nine.'

They laughed and embraced and went their separate ways. But Hamilton's smile evaporated as he rounded the corner and saw the mirthless youth sitting on the bonnet of his Lotus Esprit.

'Is that what you're wearing?'

Millie made a thing of standing back and pulling at each garment.

'Well, let's see – is this a vest top and am I wearing it? Yep. Affirmative. Am I clad in the denim shorts I feel between finger and thumb? Certainly am. Are these pristine white Superga pumps . . .'

'All right, all right . . .'

'All in all, sir – Mr Martindale – this is, indeed, what I am wearing. Problem?'

'No . . .'

'You think I look cheap?'

'*No!*'

'We're going to a *club*, sir. *Robert*. In Ibiza. We –'

'You look knockout. Really.'

'Oh . . .'

McCartney realised he was staring. Forced a smile. 'You look great. Ku Club, watch out . . .'

They got to the end of the jetty before the kid spoke again.

'Shall we sit?'

'No,' said JJ. 'I'll stand, if it's all the same to you. No offence.'

'*C'est rien*,' he shrugged. He turned, face-on, to Hamilton. 'So. We had slight problem. But for me it does not have to be problem – so long as you have the fireworks . . .'

'Fireworks? I don't know what you're talking about . . .'

Again the young Arab shrugged; dipped his head and cast a glance upwards at Hamilton.

'OK,' he said, and began walking away. Hamilton stayed where he was, looking at the yachts bobbing on the diesel-streaked water, but checking around and about for any move-ment, too. Jamal stopped. For a beat or two he stayed quite still, before turning in one movement and pacing back to Hamilton, his espadrilles clipping the wooden boardwalk. He stood a foot from JJ and looked into his eyes. 'Mr Hamilton. Now the Prince is gone, this is very easy. I give you the money the Prince has cheated from you. You give me the Semtex. Yes? Semtex. I say the name out loud to you. Now you know . . .'

Still Hamilton didn't move. His face gave nothing away. He focused on one yacht, a speck on the horizon only discernible from its emblem.

'You understand how much money we're talking about?'

'Yes.'

'It's half a million pounds. Cash. No banker's drafts. Sterling *inglés*, in cash.'

'I have dollars.'

He watched the yacht getting closer to port, and allowed the seedling thought that, perhaps, the day was turning out better than he could have dared hope.

'Do you have one million dollars?'

'Perhaps.'

For the first time the men relaxed in one another's company. JJ nodded – once, as usual.

'I'll see what I can do.'

*   *   *

'McCartney!'

'Hello, sir.'

'Meet me at Café del Mar. As soon as possible.'

'Just myself, again?'

'I think it is for the best . . .'

'Your call, sir.'

It was all just a part of the job – orders were orders – but he hated this; having to accept it. From her forced enthusiasm when he had reported back, after the parador meet, Mac suspected Millie had already worked out Roig's game. He was certain now, as she pretended not to listen, pacing around outside in her cut-offs. He went out to tell her the latest; he didn't have to.

'Rob, I've been thinking. Maybe you and I shouldn't be . . . perhaps we'll get more done if we operate individually?'

He hated it; hated himself for going along with it. Yet it gave Millie a way out; a way of continuing, without having to take Roig's shit. Mac shrugged.

'Could be. Not sure . . .'

'I mean, there's the risk factor, too. You know – if people start linking us together . . .'

Again, Mac shrugged. 'I don't know. I think the duo thing works . . .'

She winked at him. She knew all right. 'Let's give it a try. I'll go to Ku. See what I can see . . .'

'And I'll just join you there?'

'Sure, yah. Or not. You and I both know we're a team. We can hook when we hook . . .'

Mac felt himself leaning forward to peck her on the forehead; pulled back before he did so.

'You be careful, then. I'll get there soon as I can.'

'Sold.'

Millie went to crank up her moped. McCartney watched her go, a visceral dread eating away at him.

For Rodolfo Molina this was too much. The retainer was good – it was generous, compared to previous deals, ample enough to see his children through college on the mainland, never to have to return to the Vice Island. And he could square it with himself, to the extent that he only had to turn a blind eye. Ibiza had always been a place of excess. This was why people came here – had come here since the Phoenicians, since Roman times, in their droves. To relax. To forget. To party. Oh yes, Rodolfo Molina was well aware of the part drugs had to play in the island's allure. He understood the economy of Ibiza, the symbiotic relationship between the hedonism of its world-renowned clubs, the spend-spend abandon of the clubbers and holidaymakers and the narcotic high that fuelled their incautious bingeing. He could look the other way while the stuff came in; busy himself elsewhere while little platoons of foot soldiers cut it up and trotted it out into the bars and clubs; into the bloodstream. He could come to terms with all that; in its own sick way, it benefited Ibiza. But, of late, they'd been asking for more and more. He'd done as they'd asked, and it killed him. He had no choice but to carry on. This latest 'special favour' – he had no choice. But it was too much. This was going way too far.

Hamilton made a concerted effort to regulate his breathing as the Lotus ate up the San An road. On top of everything else, Davey Lane had turned bandit on him. After what had gone down with the *Bandera Verde*, he'd announced that he was abandoning ship, for now. If he was ever going to reclaim his crime-scene yacht he would need a top-notch international lawyer to argue the toss for him. Coincidence, they would postulate – a fateful incident that had nothing to do with my client. Refusing him access to his domicile is a clear infringement of his human rights blah blah – but that was all going to take time and money. Davey was asking for a hotel and exies for every additional day he was delayed on the island – like he didn't *want* to stay! With this rebate from Hassan though, and the Jamal one's dollars, he could box Davey off and ship him out. Fuck, he'd drive him to the airport himself and put him on a first-class flight back to Dublin, just to get the nutter out of his hair until this whole fucked-up situation died down. Just needed to get the explosives from him – that was the main thing . . .

Tonight was going to be mad, but it was doable. If he followed the rules and took things one step at a time, all things were achievable. In this profession, at that time of year, he was going to get days like this when it was one thing on top of another, each problem's safe husbandry critical to the next one's paying off. It was a house of cards, but it was very much there to be built. To JJ, nothing was impossible. You just had to keep on breathing through it, take things step by step. Step one was the Semtex. If he could sort Davey and get the mad gear back to this Jamal case in one round robin, that'd be a job well done. With a fair wind, he could have that one boxed by nine bells, driving into the night with a high six-figure sum in his boot – one down, two to go.

Step two was Frankie Nolan. Jesus. Sick fuck, Frankie was – one of those who are just born wrong. No light or shade with the likes of Frankie; for as long as JJ had known him – and nobody really *knew* Frankie Nolan – it had been a case of damage limitation, and with Nolan, there would always be damage. He was a beast, a sadist, a pornographer; he enjoyed pain – taking it, but even more so, dishing it out. The first thing that ever struck JJ Hamilton about Frankie Nolan was the sheer hatred he exuded. It went beyond disapproval or menace, even – the man just bristled with malice. Women, in particular – he hated them. JJ had never, ever seen Frankie Nolan smile at a girl.

Yet he was worth it. His thing – the films, the network – was good billing. Dependable. He was a sound investment. He always took a bit of man-management, but he made it worth your while. Frankie was flying in this evening – pray to God him and Davey didn't end up tearing lumps out of one another – and JJ knew he'd have to give the old psycho some time. Real time. Then, on top of all that, there was the fucking hash landing and the fun and games Hassan and Yousef would be banking on – the afters. He tried to stay focused on that side of it; the after-show, the winding down, kicking back in the Ku, recruiting the ladies, then driving up to the glass house for the mother of all celebrations.

Jesus – if Davey Lane got wind of the party there'd be no getting rid of the fucking hillbilly! He'd be up there, balls deep in ladyboys, starting fights with anyone who looked at him funny. He'd deal with that one later. For now, it was a case of lining all his little ducks up, one after the other. He let out one almighty pent-up sigh, slowly, feeling better by the second, and put his foot down to overtake a chugging campervan.

Mac would have preferred to sit out on the terrace or away from prying eyes and ears on the still-warm rocks, but Roig had nodded to a spot near the door. Mac went and sat at the little table, its surface tiled with ceramic sea horses and dolphins, watching Roig pick up the beers from the bar and start into his lopsided, slightly ungainly amble back to their seats.

Apart from one or two ageing hippies stood at the bar in

their matted dreadlocks and billowing pantaloons, there was no one to eavesdrop on their hushed conversation. A mellow piano with hypnotic snare drum oozed out of the speakers, and Mac was all but zoning out. Roig placed the frosted glasses on the table, the crunch of stray sand grains sitting McCartney up.

'*Salut*, Billy Mac!'

'Bottoms up, sir . . .'

Roig brought him up to speed. He'd been tailing Hamilton – Mac felt a brief jab of pique – and the trail led to this very cafe, just outside of San Antonio.

'So I follow him, and Hamilton meets up with this guy . . .' He threw a blown-up black and white on the table and sat back, sipping his beer while McCartney studied the mugshot. 'You want to know who this is? It is Hassan El Glaoui – brother of the dead Prince . . .'

'Ali . . .'

'Ali. Exactly. So John-John Hamilton and Hassan El Glaoui meet, but it looks to me like a not-good meeting? I could not get close enough to hear very well, but Hamilton is shouting. Very, very shouting . . .' His face broke into a huge grin. 'So, after some minutes it's all OK. They shake hands, kiss cheek, Hamilton goes this way, Hassan goes another way. I follow Hamilton . . .' He made his two index fingers walk across the table as he whistled noiselessly. 'He goes out here . . .' He nodded at the door. 'Past those shops and *apartamentos* to the car parking, walking very fast . . .' He paused to check whether McCartney was as excited as he should be. 'OK, so now for the crazy part. I try to keep John-John Hamilton in my eyesight, and it's difficult. I don't want him to see me. So I wait a moment, then, when I look again, who is there? Can you hazard? No? Then I tell you who is there – sitting on Hamilton's fast red sports car. Is

Jamal!' His entire face lit up, childlike. '*Sí!* Jamal Benarbia, sitting on the car. It is a *miraculo*, no?'

'It's dynamite!' McCartney laughed. 'What happened?'

'So, once more, it is difficult to hear very closely what they say – but Benarbia was making a very how-say . . . *animated* conversation with John-John Hamilton. After a little time, depart Hamilton's car and, by now, it is of course impossible for Roig to follow. Have you seen Hamilton's car?'

Mac nodded. 'An Esprit SE? She's a goer all right . . .'

'Same as in *Pretty Woman* film, no?' smiled Roig. 'I think Hamilton is looking for his Julia Roberts!'

The invitation was there for Mac to leer; to add his endorsement. A surge of anger prickled under his skin. He lowered his eyes, addressed his *caña*.

'Sir – I'm uncomfortable about our bypassing DS Baker. Millie is here as part of this operation.'

Roig looked wounded, briefly – then his eyes twinkled.

'*Sí sí sí*, don't worry about it, she still has a big part to play, Camilla! *Sophia*. But like I say – I think the best is that she is . . . *available*. Yes? Make the bad guys come for her . . .'

'I see that, sir. I do. And I think Millie – Sophia – will be on board with that . . .' He hesitated; began tearing at the beer mat. He looked up and met Roig's eager stare. 'But I do think she should be here, now, to have this conversation with us. We need to give her the choice.'

'The choice? Is *job*!' He forced a laugh, stood up and patted Mac on the shoulder. '*Choice!*' he laughed loudly, picked up his glass and drained it. 'One more?'

Mac shook his head; picked up the remaining shard of beer mat.

'Sir – where there's an element of danger –'

Roig held up both hands, irritated now.

'I hear you. And you are not wrong to be agitated about

the safety of Camilla. OK? It is not absurd to speculate about the danger. But we are here. We are watching – always. OK? I understand John-John Hamilton, and I understand that he and Benarbia are dangerous men . . .' He pushed his thumbs together. 'But, still – I think the best plan is that we are direct, yes? Let us not wait and hope. *Direct*. If Hamilton sees Camilla, I think we have no problem gaining entrance into, how-say . . . the lion's den . . .' He pulled down his Foster Grant's and stared at McCartney without blinking. 'Do you not think?'

Once again that remote but persistent nausea gripped McCartney. He met Roig's look head-on.

'I'll ask her.'

They stared at one another for a beat longer, then McCartney got up. He went to the door, out into the warm evening air. He felt sick.

John-John Hamilton swivelled his head left and right as he guided the Lotus down the slope, brushing back the unruly stems and branches of the flora that overhung the narrow harbour road. Roof down, there was the heady melange of the different pollens they dislodged, but JJ was preoccupied. Dara and Moz were already down there, waiting on the little wharf with the Jeep. In an ideal world he'd meet Yousef off the boat as he'd always done, then leave him and Hassan with the Rozaki kids to bring the swag back to the place. There was still Davey and the Arabian Knight to sort, not to mention Frankie Nolan rolling up to shoot his latest triple-X. And on top of that he was getting all sorts of scrapes and scratches to the car's wide chassis as he piloted it down this steep, overgrown alleyway. Hassan turned to him, his white teeth glinting.

'I don't believe I have ever seen this – the famous John-John Hamilton in fear!'

He threw his head back and guffawed. Hamilton looked straight ahead, smiling gamely.

'You any idea how much one of these costs, Hassan, lad?'

Hassan fluttered his hand at an imaginary horizon. 'Buy another!'

He roared with laughter again. JJ slowly shook his head.

'Off your cake, you! Two hundred large, these are – if you can fucking find one for sale! Buy another . . .'

They got to the end of the slip road. The Jeep was parked up on a patch of rubble. JJ pulled up next to them, asked Dara to back up so he could turn the Lotus round. If the distant speck out on the bay was Yousef, then he was bang on time – but then Yousef was never late. He had an excellent captain to see to that. He turned to Hassan.

'You going to tell him about Ali?'

Hassan's eyes misted over. He chewed on his lip and looked out across the sea.

'I must. I must tell him . . .' He turned to JJ. 'But not yet. OK?' He clasped JJ's thigh, firmly. 'You had a conversation with your man? About Ali?'

Hamilton nodded. 'I spoke to him.'

'And? Is all OK?'

'He hasn't told me it's not OK . . .'

He glanced at his watch and tried to gauge when he could make his move.

Millie veered left onto the Santa Gertrudis road and, the breeze in her face, began to succumb to the swell of well-being that had been percolating. Just being here, in Ibiza, seemed to bring all those tendrils of anticipation to a head. She couldn't help herself – she felt good. Riding through the twilight, warm gusts gently buffeting her bare legs, the sky streaked in weird shades of green and amber, the evening took on a scale to

Millie – a queer magnificence she could not tag. Every element of herself that she was conscious of seemed to thrill with anticipation – an intrinsic sense of fate or destiny. The job was a challenge. It was dangerous. It was fucking exciting!

She hadn't thought about it for years, but it came surging back. The anxiety when Jen had gone missing. Her own terror, dressing in her sister's clothes for the police re-enactment of her last known movements. Then the sheer, near-unbearable relief when the call came to say they'd found her. The kidnappers – or whoever had abducted her – had left her at an A-road cafe and, hallelujah, she came home to them. She didn't speak, for months – but she came home, and her sister Camilla was addicted. She had had a big part to play in bringing Jenny back alive, and she was smitten. She wanted more. From that point on, Millie was always joining the force.

And here she was, on a real case. A proper job. She knew she could do this – she knew she would pull it off. There'd be praise and recognition, she could show them all what she was made of, what she could do. But there was McCartney, as well. There was something about McCartney. She wanted to impress him – make him proud of her; of them, as a team. Riding through the warm amber gloaming, it felt great to be alive, doing this. She was good at it – they'd see that. She rounded the bend, hit the accelerator and gasped at the scintillating onrush of wind blasting through her.

It wasn't good; on a night where he needed everything to click into place, the Bar Costa meet was not going well at all. For all that he was a peasant, Davey, he was sharp as a tack – no doubt about it. He'd seen right through John-John's act – too smooth to be credible; so laid-back and matter-of-fact that Davey could smell the fear coming off him. The more he tried to act like a man who had all the time in the world, the more JJ found himself licking his lips, glancing at the wall clock, picking at his salad.

'Not hungry, John-John?' said Davey. His pale grey eyes followed JJ's tongue as he flicked his top lip again, smiled and waited for him to realise he'd been watching him.

'I'm fine. Lot on my plate, tonight . . .'

Davey leaned over and helped himself to a big slice of *jámon serrano*. He sat there, chewing, smiling at his partner in crime and, his mouth full, he pointed his fork at him and came out with his proposal.

'This kid that wants the other stuff. He's a nutjob, is he?'

'How d'you mean?'

'Fanatic. Stop at nothing for the cause . . .'

JJ shrugged. 'Can't say that I know the kid. I done the deal with the El Glaoui lad, didn't I?'

Davey leaned forward, a gleam in his eye. 'You're not getting me, are you, John-John? This is very simple . . .'

And he told him just how simple he wanted it to be. He'd hand over the Semtex. He'd given John-John his word and taken his deposit; he wasn't about to let him down. But he didn't like the sound of this Jamal headcase. Didn't like some Arab calling the shots. So he'd come up with an idea that suited all their needs. He wanted the Jamal one to do something for *him*. He wanted him to steal his yacht.

'See? Simple. He gets what he wants. Nice little getaway cruiser – good, fast craft, the *Bandera* –'

'Davey! For fuck's sake, lad –'

Davey put the fork down, the twinkle gone from his eye, now. 'Listen to me. Just tell him, will you? Tell him. Who the fuck's in charge here, boy?'

JJ felt like crying. This was not good. This was not what he needed at all.

'And, OK . . . supposing he says yes. Where's the loud gear?'

Davey Lane stood up, his eyes smiling once again. 'I'll bring it to your place.'

'My place?'

'I'm thinking I'll stay on a bit. Let the shite die down. Anyway . . .' He pronounced it as though there were two ns. '*Annyway*.' He nodded his head at the poster on the wall for the Ku Club's big opening. 'What's the story with this Ku thing tonight?' JJ's spirits sagged. He dropped his head, trying not to show his utter despair at this turn of events. Davey grinned his demented, leering grin. 'Island's fucking plastered with posters, John-John. Is it a bit of a hoolie, is it? Will I try my hand, do you think? Will the boy perhaps get lucky!'

Now John-John really *was* panicking. Not only would he have to tell Jamal that he didn't have the bangers, he was facing down his worst nightmare – Davey fucking Lane as a house guest! He summoned up all his reserves of character; tried to force his lips, his teeth, his cheeks into some distant approximation of a smile.

'No problem. That's cool. Meet us at the club, yeah?'

Lane laughed and dabbed his lips. He stood up and pointed at JJ, imitating his mannerisms.

'*No problem. That's cool*. Dear God, John-John. What on earth are we going to do with you?'

He threw a large-denomination note on the table and strolled out into Santa Gertrudis's picturesque square. The evening was still warm, and the artists, the jewellers, the hippies selling tie-dye were setting up their stalls. He was minded to buy a painting of some sort; perhaps a ceramic. Something to remember his stay by.

Roig had mixed feelings about this McCartney guy. He seemed soft. He was one of these intellectual types that seem to fascinate the English. Good at talking, good at the theory of crime, no doubt – but did he have the *nariz* for it? The nose. Roig didn't think so. But he liked what he knew of Shanley and, to a degree, he trusted him. Shanley raved about Billy McCartney; said he was *the* man for this case. Time would tell. Keeping his distance, he followed the Lotus, checking his rear-view mirror periodically, too, in case he was being tailed himself. The madness of Hamilton, driving a car like this – madness! It was as though these guys were saying: Fuck you! I don't need to be careful. I am the king around here. Well, John-John Hamilton had better be very, *very* careful! Roig would let him lead him to the Islamic maniac; but once he'd dealt with Benarbia and taken his bow, he'd be back for Hamilton, because one thing was for sure – that sap McCartney would not get close. Where was he now? Where? Here was Roig, hot on his main target's trail, while McCartney was off holding his dick, doing everything by the book. Well, good luck to you, Billy Mac – *this* was how you caught the bad guys. You made things happen!

Hamilton roared away in the direction of San Rafael, and Roig let him open up a distance. He had a very good idea where he was going and who he was meeting, and once he was certain, he'd call in the cavalry. He'd get Benarbia, by God – and wouldn't that be a feather in the cap of Juan Sebastien Roig? He'd get him all right – one of America's most wanted, cornered and caught by one of Spain's most able. There was no doubt about it – Jus was born to this. He was just a goddamned natural.

The queue wasn't moving. In the hour or so he'd been there, two flamboyant trannies had been waved through, along with a silver-haired sleaze with a retinue of pouting beauties. He pulled out a wallet and tried to slip the gorilla on the door some notes. The doorman eyed the cash, tempted, but held up his hand to decline before ushering the playboy inside.

Mac knew Millie was in there – the moped was parked up with dozens of other two-wheelers on rough ground in the overflow car park. He'd taken a walk around the grounds – a desert of russet rock and cactus – just to get a feel for the lie of the land, should matters come to a head. If it came to it, he could probably get in over a stretch of wall towards the back of Ku Club, where two huge turbofans were being installed – enormous, hollow eyes staring out over the scenes of abandon beneath them. Even down there in the scrubland at the back of the club – a building site, basically – Mac had witnessed a boy sucking an older guy's cock. The old man had just looked at him, expressionless, as though it was Mac who was the transgressor. He had lowered his eyeline and shuffled back round to the queue. All the heat had gone out of the day; McCartney shuddered, cold all of a sudden. As mosquitoes began to circulate in search of fresh blood, the cicadas struck up their electric plainsong, adding a dissonant but oddly complementary sub-note to the throb of the bass from inside the club.

Two young Turkish-looking guys, early twenties, properly cropped hair – scissor-cut, not shaven – sauntered up the ramp, right past him, straight to the front of the queue. The gorilla stepped forward to block them. The smaller of the two smiled and held out a hand to shake. The doorman ignored it.

'Johnny Hammo's guests. Said to ask for Stefano . . .'

Scousers. The doorman's face lit up.

'Ah, *sí, sí!*' He seized the dangling hand while it was still on offer. 'I am Stefano, yah! Friend of Hammo, *sí?* Señor John he just arrive. *Just* arrive!'

There was a terror underpinning the fanatical smile. He pulled back the cord and, damage limitation in full flow, ushered the two kids inside.

*   *   *

Declining the champagne from the smooth talker at the bar and wincing at the price of her vodka tonic, Millie stepped back into the palm trees and marvelled at the bacchanalia around her. There were beautiful creatures on stilts, gender indeterminable, parading the various dance floors and open spaces, blessing the congregation with incense sticks. There was a succession of topless dwarves carrying sliced fruit – orange, kiwi, strawberries, melon – on platters. She plucked a piece of orange, its flesh frosted over with an ice patina, and bit through, releasing the acidic juice. It was nectar. It was ecstasy.

On a catwalk straddling a sub-lit swimming pool, a string of divinities gyrated to the meaty, piano-driven Balearic beat. Guys in tight denim shorts, bare-chested, their glistening muscles sprayed with a gossamer sheen of sweat, seemed lost to their surroundings as they reached up to the heavens, heads back, eyes closed. In and among them, girls twisted their slender arms and ducked and dived, in and out of the moment. A man who looked like a wizard raised his cane above his head as the tune reached its climax and, as one, the swaying mannequins seemed to snap out of their individual revels and join in one intuitive celebration. Millie could barely resist. This was no nightclub, no discotheque – it was a cathedral, a carnival. She wanted to throw her clothes off and join the acolytes on the catwalk, in the pool, work herself into the same exultant frenzy that was, at the flick of a switch, surging through the whole club. She necked her cocktail and pushed her way into the thick of it.

Anxious, but highly excited about the next day, Roig decided to call it a night. The meeting with Benarbia – if you could *call* it a meeting – had been productive. The stupid fuck-you machine had pulled in to a car park near the marina. Roig

66

parked up where he was and waited. Jamal Benarbia stepped out of the shadows at the far end of the car park and waved, once. Hamilton's Lotus prowled towards him. Roig got out and jumped over the little perimeter wall, crouching down alongside a locked-up public lavatory. He peered round the wall, into the car park. They were right there! The ludicrous doors of Hamilton's ridiculous car opened upwards and outwards, like wings. He got out sideways, ankles together, using his momentum to push himself up. They shook hands and got down to it, making earnest conversation accompanied by various shrugs and gesticulations. Benarbia appeared cool. He stood back, listened, folded his arms. Hamilton spoke some more and, this time, Benarbia started laughing. He paused and shook his head and, as clear as anything, said: 'Really?' then laughed again and clapped his hands. Eventually, he settled himself down, though his mirth made his voice carry.

'OK, OK. *La Bandera Verde.*' He looked John-John Hamilton in the eye and shrugged. 'Sure. Why not?'

They spoke some more and began pacing away from Roig's hide. Hamilton got back in the Lotus and sent its wheels spinning. Benarbia stayed where he was, watching the sports car zoom into the greenish twilight. He turned and left the car park via a path on the opposite side. Still Roig waited, barely moving. He heard a moped's engine and satisfied himself this could only feasibly be Benarbia. He gave him five minutes before making his own exit.

So – *La Bandera Verde*. Thank you for that, gentlemen. He started up his engine and began to envisage how he'd go about this not-uncomplicated bust.

He'd seen Stefano turn down cash, so that was out. Shame. There was no shortage of wealth in the Ku from what

McCartney had witnessed so far, but he knew how these things worked. It was the same in casinos, same at the races, same everywhere; you splash the cash and the word goes round. He fingered the tattered permit in his pocket. Should he? No. That was a bona fide get-out-of-jail card; he'd save it for when – and if – he really had no other option.

A taxi pulled up and, as its passenger was getting out, one of the young Scousers appeared at the entrance to the club. Stefano ducked to listen as the kid whispered in his ear. This was Mac's chance. He had to seize it.

'Hey! Boys!'

Rob Martindale stepped out of the line, arms spread wide, a huge smile driving his eyes back to slits. The taxi guy, white hair, bent nose, just looked right through him with piercing, killer-blue eyes. The young lad stopped long enough for Mac to embrace him.

'It's Rob, Robbie Marto, remember?' He was busking, busking badly; acutely aware that he had less than ten seconds to make his play. All Scousers shortened their names with an 'o' on the end. All Scousers went to Quadrant Park. 'John-John's mate from Quad, remember? Mind you, if you can remember, you probably weren't there . . .'

He laughed at his own cheesy truism. Breakthrough. A smile. Close it, now. Close the deal. This kid isn't bottom rung, but he's seeing the money without really feeling it, yet. Let him see the money. The money . . .

'Listen . . .'

Out came the wallet; the fat, crammed wallet of the filthy rich. A wallet so tightly packed with high-end notes its clasp could barely keep it closed. There was thousands, there. The kid could see it. He could taste it. Close, McCartney. Martindale. Close the deal, now.

'. . . you got any, er . . .'

Mac opened his eyes wide. The kid turned to the old hard-case.

'Go on through, Frankie. Stefano'll take you to John-John. I'll be two minutes, tell him.'

He jerked his head at Mac. 'Stef. This lad's with me.'

The wild flash of anger Millie thought she'd trained out of her psyche ripped right through her as she saw him, bold as anything, strutting into the club like he was some kind of celebrity. Frankie Nolan – the rapist. The strangler. Three women he'd beaten and suffocated – and those were the ones they'd been able to prove. She knew it innately – with men like Nolan, it was never a one-off. When had they let the monster out? He was supposed to be doing life. It was things like this – bad, bad men who walked free after serving a fraction of their sentence – that made her seriously question the job. It depressed her. It reawoke her livid anger.

With his boxer's nose and his gangster's face he stood out horribly as he pushed his way through the gay menagerie. She crossed the little footbridge and followed him to Coco Loco, a roped-off club within the club. Below it, a raised stage comprising a shamrock cluster of three podiums – small, medium, large – and suddenly she saw him, too. Hamilton. It wasn't so much that she saw him, she became aware of his eyes, lit up with desire, devouring the array of writhing nymphs on the stage.

She felt uneasy, horribly compromised all of a sudden – yet these were the men she was here for. If she was going to get them, they'd have to get her. She climbed up among the gyrating dais dancers, worked her way to the edge nearest Coco Loco and let herself go. McCartney had been urging them to go method with their legends. OK then, Billy Mac

– here's hoping you're right. Deep breath. Forget who you're performing to – here comes Sophia Yorke.

McCartney was transfixed. The fiesta had gradually slowed to a standstill as people became aware of the willowy Rasta guy in their midst. A mesmeric instrumental began to throb through the dance floor as the lithe dread lifted his arms and his face to the clear black sky. His eyes blank and his soul seemingly transported to another place, he began to disrobe, slowly, his limbs liquid as he acted out a ritualistic ballet, removing his blouse, casting it aside. Mac wanted to get closer; yet movement of any sort, now, would have gone against the natural order. He watched with a horrified thrill as the guy stepped out of his leather jeans and, as he turned into the mellow spotlight, displayed his thick and arching penis.

'You wish, eh?'

Millie tugged him away to a cluster of palms, jerking her head back to ensure all was clear.

'So listen. Got to be very, very quick here. I think I'm in. Hamilton's a fucking sex case, but I'll be OK –'

'Whoa, what d'you mean, Mill? Slow down . . .'

'I can't. He doesn't relax. I need to get back there –'

'You said sex case. I'm not having you put yourself –'

Her eyes were darting left and right. 'Listen to me. It's fine. I'm fine. He watches *everything* but I'm fine . . .'

'You *sure*?'

She nodded, once. Certain. 'He's got this gang of thugs and dealers. Couple of Arab guys. Talking about a party up in the hills –'

'Hills? *Which* hills?'

She shrugged. 'Presumably the beetle house Abi described.' She glanced back towards Hamilton's table. 'Oh – and Frankie Nolan's there.'

'*Nolan?* What the fuck . . .'

'My thoughts exactly. I thought he was still banged up.'

'Jesus. Right. No way are you going in there alone, hear me?'

She took a step back; appraised him, hands on her slight hips. 'Mac. Boss. Either we're doing this, or we're wasting our time. You *know* how this works . . .'

McCartney eyed her; held her stare. 'But *Nolan*, though . . .'

'I know.' She forced a smile. 'But he doesn't know I know . . .' She craned her head back round to where they were all sitting. 'I'd better get back. Try and worm your way in, if you can. If not, like I say – I'll be fine . . .'

He waited for the Scouse kid to head down to the toilets and followed at a casual distance. The urinals had dividers, but he loitered by the washbasins, nonetheless. The kid finished pissing, buttoned up his jeans.

'*Hola!* Some place, eh?'

He could see the kid wanted to blank him, but the lure of Rob's dinari was fresh in his mind.

'It's all right, isn't it?'

He talked in Mac's direction without once looking at him. He was going to have to work fast, here.

'Any more of that . . .?'

'That was it, lad. Where are you tomorrow?'

Shit! Tomorrow was useless. He had to get closer; keep tabs on Millie.

'I mean, what about if I join you guys? I –'

'I dunno, lad. Not really up to me, like . . .'

He was looking Mac up and down. Mac caught sight of himself in the mirror, slightly red-faced, his T-shirt stuck to him. He tugged at the sweaty cotton fabric, eased it away from his skin.

'Have you seen those dirty big bottles of bubbly? Bigger than a fucking bungalow!'

'I don't drink.'

'Oh. OK. Well . . .' He felt pathetic. Years of training and he was drawing down a big zero. Was this the best he could do? It was going down the pan, anyway, so he pulled out the only card he had left. He slotted the lad a sleek, silver-grey 10,000-peseta note. 'Get the big fella a drink from me, anyway . . .' He knew, absolutely, that the note would go directly into the kid's pocket, and stay there. 'Robbie Marto. Nice chatting with you . . .?'

He held out his hand, and left the question dangling with it. The kid shook.

'Moz. Nice one . . .'

But he didn't smile.

He'd almost lost them on the interminable crawl along the track leading down from the club to the San Rafael road. Hordes of spaced-out revellers trooped down the middle of the track, banging on the sides of passing vehicles as much in camaraderie as in any hope of hitching a lift. McCartney heard the deep-throated growl of the Lotus as it hit the main drag and rocketed off into the night. Millie was in that car. He'd had to sit back and watch as Hamilton's retinue was waved into a flotilla of cars and taxis, while the funnel of vehicles edging out of the car park was held back. Millie had tried to get in a cab with two girls, but Hamilton had near coerced her into his passenger seat. Mac caught sight of the taxi carrying Moz and Frankie Nolan, five or six cars ahead of him; breathed a sigh of relief that Nolan hadn't latched onto Millie. He lurched out into the road, the blare of an onrushing minibus making not the slightest impact as he accelerated to catch up with the cavalcade.

* * *

John-John Hamilton was beginning to realise he'd read this one wrong. He'd received every sign, every encouragement that this Sloane was into the kinky game. The way she'd targeted him; tossing that blonde mane to the music, running her fingers through her hair, all that looking over at him, from the podium; making sure he'd clocked her. He'd clocked her all right, right from the start. Hot, sexy dancer; long legs; tight little arse. Beautiful. She knew the score and all. Came right over and put it right there; *right* there. Reaching for the beak when it came out, no second bidding. All that eye contact; letting her fingers stray against his wrist. She knew what she was doing. If ever a girl was up for Frankie's game then this Sophia – *Soff-Eye-Ah* – was up for it, lock, stock and barrel. Yet, when it had come down to lights, camera, action, she'd made a show of him. Started off trying to joke her way out of it – this an audition? This your casting couch? All the usual crap, as though he'd never heard it before. Frankie fucking Nolan stroking his hard-on in front of all kinds, telling them time was money.

No dice. Fair enough. On to plan B, then. This fucking Sophia didn't want to play nice, they'd just have to play dirty. And after the day he'd just had, John-John Hamilton was ready to cut loose.

Mac felt like driving his fist into the car's roof. It was a road-block – a routine breath test for inebriated or drug-high drivers and, in the oh-so-predictable nature of these things, the Shogun was one of those they pulled over. Of course it was. He was a solo, tourist driver of a certain age, driving a certain type of car down this particular autoroute and this time of the pre-dawn hours. He could have showed them Molina's permit and made them let him through. He could have – but that old gut instinct that had seen him through, and seen him right, held him back. He wound down his window, processed the world-weary expression on the young cop's face and recognised this for what it was. He was going to have to let it run, take its time. He got out and asked if it was OK to smoke. The cop shrugged and glanced over Mac's papers.

'Señor Martindale?'

He nodded. Another officer approached, barely restraining a frisky Alsatian on a short chain leash. The dog lurched forward, its two front legs scrabbling at the upholstery of the driver's seat. Mac wanted to tell them to cool it; teach the dog some manners. But he knew it would only make things worse. The Alsatian began sniffing furiously at the car seat, pulling harder at the leash. Fuck. The cocaine. If the dog smelt something on the car seat, he was going to have a field day with Mac. He backed a little further away, fingering the little wrap in his hip pocket. How the hell was he going to explain *that* away? For crying out loud, he was a trained professional – a master, supposedly, of his own craft. This was basic stuff. Yes, he could explain himself, if needs be, to the police. But come on, McCartney – come on! He should be on top of this, and he knew all too well why he was misfiring. He was absolutely preoccupied with Millie Baker's well-being. He couldn't think straight at all.

The younger policeman was beckoning him back to the car. This was it, then. Bugger! He'd have to come clean with them; throw off the legend. He was reaching for Molina's police permit when it dawned on him that the sniffer dog and handler had moved on to another car.

'OK,' said the young cop and stepped back to let him into the Shogun. 'Goodnight.'

McCartney wanted to slump across the wheel and breathe a huge sigh of relief, but he was grateful just to get out of there. He didn't overdo it. He started up the engine and gave the *guardia* the slightest nod as he eased past the roadblock. He gave it two or three hundred yards before accelerating and, hopeless yet with no other plan, driving hard into the night in the same direction the party convoy had been heading. He came to a four-way crossroads and was smitten with the crashing futility of his quest. He'd head back to the villa, snatch an hour or two's sleep then see what was what come the morning.

Millie didn't so much wake up as find herself conscious again. A deep-lying anguish came first, preceding any physical sensation. She knew instinctively, immediately that this – whatever, wherever this was – was bad. Her eyeballs ached. She could barely move her limbs. Her throat felt raw, stripped of any membrane; arid.

She managed to sit up. A tumult of nausea flooded her from her cranium to her guts; yet the agony of throwing up nearly killed her. She tried to keep it down. She had to hold it in. Gag, gag, gag, gag, gag . . . the venomous kill of the bile strangling her solar plexus; poisoning her bowels, her innards.

She could picture Nolan now; those deadly, deathly eyes penetrating her, pitiless, unblinking, as he leaned closer and closer to her.

'Do it . . .'

He just spoke it. Said it. It made it worse.

Then the high-pitched cry. The young Arab guy who'd flung himself in front of him. The look on Nolan's face. Hatred. Vicious, unadulterated hatred.

'Maybe we should come back again later . . .'

Just said it. Spoke it. She screwed her eyes tight shut and fell back down, willing a blackness, a void of some kind, any kind of an ending upon herself. An end to this.

*　*　*

He didn't sleep. Dawn was breaking in spectacular streaks of pink and tangerine, way out over the bay. Another time and he'd have been vulnerable to the purity of the moment – but McCartney's guts were in knots. A leaden dread dragged, deep down – a fearsome foreboding that Millie was in danger.

No comparable crisis had descended on McCartney since Chinatown; since Hattie. The sensory short circuit; the inability to think clearly – to make the right, the *only* decision. If he were to alert Molina, that was them finished, on day three. He went into his bedroom; pulled out the kit. Found a vein and hit it. Waited for the rush. Waited for a clue.

He paced around the villa, up and down the stairs, unable to settle, unable to think. Should he tell Roig? No. *No.* Not yet. He'd made it clear what he thought of Millie. To Jus Roig, she was the bait, the honeytrap; and McCartney was determined to do anything, everything to prove him wrong. Camilla Baker had done her training. She was a clever kid. She was smart, and she was cool. If there was trouble, she'd find a way out of it. She would. There was no need to involve Roig. No need for him to know, so soon into the operation, that the pair of them had made fundamental errors; that they'd brought this upon themselves.

He threw off last night's clothes and forced himself to stand under the stunning cold crush of the shower, strafing his scalp under the icy jet until he could stand it no more. He was awake, now; ideas and plans of action ricocheting around his tingling brain. He dressed – a *No Alla Violenza* T-shirt, Lee needle cords and a pair of vintage Korsika – and went outside onto the terrace for one final lap, right around the villa; their sleek, whitewashed, designer villa. He checked himself out in the mirror and laughed bitterly at another near error. If he were to locate what was left of the party at Hamilton's villa, his story would be that he'd been invited up there last night, at the Ku.

He went back indoors and undressed again and, reeling from the clammy dank stench, forced yesterday's clobber back on. He steadied himself in front of the mirror, confident, now, that he could pull this off. He grabbed a litre bottle of water from the fridge and jumped into the Shogun.

Palate dry, head banging, eyes stinging, Hamilton stepped over the comatose bodies and let himself out. There was still the odd splash from the pool, the occasional squeal from some bint or other. He got in the Lotus, enjoyed its roar as it fired off down the gravel track. He was doing this for the money, yes. But he was doing this for his name. John-John Hamilton did not welsh on a deal. If he wanted respect – real respect, international renown – then he had to see the tricky deals through. Obviously the Jamal kid had tried to chisel him on the dosh side when he told him about Davey's boat, but it had been fine. He was half laughing about it. The Arab had wanted this whole thing done and dusted just as much as JJ did.

He looked right and left, pulled out onto the main drag. It had been near enough dawn before he'd got the gear from Davey. The nutter had it on him the whole time, in his pocket – just like he was carrying two packets of chewing gum. He'd still had to sort him, mind you; had to find him what he liked. That whole party last night was full of sick heads, whole gang of them, wanting their own funny little thing. Frankie Nolan with his skin flicks. The Moroccans and the perks they always wanted. Fuck, that was another headache – getting things sorted so they could up and leave as per fucking usual. Load of weirdos and perverts, the lot of them – and they all came to him. When it came to the next stage – kicking on, finding new markets, bigger deals – he'd have to choose his partners more carefully.

He started to relax as he hit the open road. He'd get this

bit of business done. Nice little breakfast in the City Café or somewhere, then back up to the house to see who was left, who was worth a look. He thought about that Sophia. Disappointing. Him and her might have been good together. Maybe they still could be. But no – too late. It was all coming back to him. He'd already told Hassan.

Mac found the taxi place easily enough. The guy on duty was proving trickier, though. He gave him the cursory glance, the bottom lip, the uninterested shrug as Mac told his tale. He told the guy he'd left his camera at a party he'd been at last night. He gave the operator the licence plate of the cab that picked him up from the Ku Club around 4 a.m. Could he please check the address the taxi took him to?

'I don't know this. Many cab –'

'No. *No* many cab. *This* cab!' He slid the scrap of paper across the counter again, jabbing his forefinger at the registration number. Switching to Spanish, he asked the operator to check his log. He looked up at McCartney, scratched his stubbly chin.

'Is no possible, this. Is no easy . . .'

McCartney twigged. He pulled out a thousand-peseta note. 'Try . . .'

The guy sighed and shrugged and went out back. He returned with a big, faux-leather album and began flicking through, shaking his head.

'No, I think no . . . many, many, many car . . .'

Mac locked the fingers of either hand together and leaned forward over the counter.

'Please try . . .' The guy didn't move. McCartney straightened, reached once more for his wallet. The operator's eyes flickered for a moment, then glazed over again. Mac pulled out the permit. Laid it, face up, on the taxi-office counter.

The taxi boss blanched, desperate eyes boring into Mac, still seeking a way out. McCartney shook his head and wearily sighed: 'OK. We have tried it *this* way . . .' He laid another thousand next to the permit. 'Perhaps we have to try *this*, instead. May I use your telephone please, señor, ah . . .?'

The guy picked up the thousand-peseta note and scrawled down the address of the house on the hill. McCartney thanked him. He looked scared.

He drove past, twice in each direction, before he spotted the dirt road. It was easy to miss. There was a slight drop down from the main road, a cattle grid, then the track narrowed away until it was not much wider than a goat path. There was no way he'd get the Shogun down there – and no chance he'd want to, anyway. By Mac's reckoning, they'd all be crashed out, stupefied, sleeping off the excesses of whatever had taken place only hours ago. The last thing he wanted was to squander his advantage with a noisy all-terrain vehicle. He drove on past Saint Agnes, parked up at the parador and looked across at the all-glass villa, sparkling in the early sunshine. Abi Macmillan was wrong about the villa; the way the glinting edifice squatted on top of the hill, it looked more like a giant spider than a beetle, waiting upon its prey. From its turquoise pool, which seemed to end abruptly at a little cliff, he traced a path back round the headland, scoping out his route as best he could with the naked eye. He put the water in his rucksack, pulled his shades down from his forehead and set off across the rocky path.

Sometimes, the more dangerous deals were the most straight-forward. For all yesterday's high tension, the pay-off was simple to the point of being banal. Jamal was already in there, eating eggs Benedict and perusing the *International Herald*

Tribune. He didn't look up from the newspaper when JJ sat down, just nodded and said: 'All good?'

John-John smiled to himself. Shame it was a one-off. He was getting to like this kid.

'We live in hope, lad. We live in hope . . .'

He slid the little package across the table. Jamal just left it there.

'You want some breakfast? Juice, coffee?'

Again JJ smiled. 'Some other time, I hope. For now, I've got all the juice I can handle, back at the ranch.'

Now Jamal looked up. He trained his eyes on JJ for a moment then he, too, gave way to a radiant smile.

'As you wish . . .' He slid some keys to Hamilton. 'The blue Peugeot. In the trunk . . .'

JJ nodded. 'You sure you know where the boat is?'

'I know where it is.'

'Sweet. That's us then, I think . . .'

'I think so, too. Go in peace.'

JJ stood up, shook hands with him. Jamal cleared his throat.

'Oh. There is a cop parked up outside. He has been following us since yesterday. I don't know his name yet . . .'

'I'll keep an eye out. Thanks.'

He shook his head in amusement as he exited the cafe and made his way across the car park to the blue 205.

The villa had, for the past hour, seemed just over the next brow, almost within touching distance. Yet, every time he thought he was there it remained aloof, another valley away or one more summit to climb. It came as a shock to hear voices and splashing from a pool, as though they were right in front of him. He stepped back and craned his head upwards to see the glass house directly above him. Getting his bearings, Mac worked out that the pool he'd seen from the parador was overhanging the place where he now stood; not a cliff, but a line of reinforced-concrete stanchions. He'd have to continue another hundred metres or so then double-back and penetrate the compound through the pines above and to his right.

He ditched the rucksack and scooped up handfuls of sticky pine needles to cover it up. From the sparse forest, McCartney stood back to take stock of the villa's layout. He took in the upper floors, committing to memory those with balconies, should he need to escape. He worked out where the main staircase would be, and how to find his way to it if, as was his plan, he entered through the patio doors. He made his way down towards the sun terrace, intending to keep out of view from the pool. He was wholly unprepared for the sight that greeted him.

The entire terrace was strewn with bodies. At first, McCartney thought he'd stumbled upon a massacre, so lifeless was the scene – but there was no blood, no sign of any kind of struggle. It was as though he'd found the lotus-eaters, a tangle of drug-numb sybarites at their feet. There were naked and semi-naked bodies, nubile, copper-toned blondes, stocky middle-aged men, some coupled up together, others splayed out where they lay. One slender redhead, her skin as white as milk, was laid back by the pool with her feet together, her arms stretched out wide in her own serene Station of the Cross.

'Coming in?'

McCartney started. He turned to see a gap-toothed teenage girl, her face spattered with freckles, a picture of innocent, unquestioning, *joie de vivre*. What was a kid like her doing here, in this sleaze den? What had she seen? McCartney grinned, shook his head and put his middle finger to his lip, like they were both in on a secret. He winked and slipped through the open patio door.

81

Inside, the villa was much the same; whey-faced party victims crashed out on every sofa, every surface. He tiptoed around them, dismissing the men for the face-down blondes, certain that none was Millie but checking nonetheless. He could hear distant, muffled voices and took his chances they were coming from upstairs.

The splashing from outside, the whoops of unbridled delight seeped into Millie's lurid dreams. She could hear disembodied laughter; voices; or perhaps it was all just one voice.

'Coming in?'

She felt her leaden eyelids keeling over once more and started to give way, once more, to this dark and deadly slumber. There was footfall on the staircase, a muted stumble so faint she knew it wasn't there. Yet she rolled herself over; tried to get to the door, just in case.

'Millie?'

Her mind lurched, alive again for that one pulse as she made out her name. Then the exertion – the very process of trying to think how to get to her feet – ate through her from within, ate her will, her faculty; drained her battery. She slumped, deadened to everything.

Mac cursed himself for tripping, but there was no reaction; no one seemed to hear. He hesitated at the top of the landing. There were snores of varying timbre coming from everywhere, or so it seemed. He stood back and listened hard. He could hear the distant growl of an engine, getting louder; getting closer. If the vehicle was heading here, he couldn't risk getting caught. He'd have to get back down there, and quickly. He planted his foot on the first step. A muffled thud from the room directly behind him. He stopped dead; craned his head sideways back towards the door on the landing. Listened out; listened hard.

'Millie?'

No reply. Not a sound. Nothing. There were voices from below now. Fuck. He tried to plan it out; three steps to the half-landing below him, then another six leading directly onto the big, open-plan room. Nowhere to hide himself in between. The voices were audible, yet difficult to locate. Was there another floor, underground? Another thud from the room at the top of the stairs, like someone had fallen out of bed. No time to check it out; and no chance, either. The voices – definitely subterranean – were getting closer and closer. Mac might just about get himself downstairs and back out onto the terrace before he was seen.

Just. He picked his way through the bodies, tripped as a sleeping beauty stretched out her leg, and managed to half crawl, half bunny-hop out onto the patio on one foot and two flat palms. Out of the frying pan . . . footsteps now, right in his ear. In that queer way that the senses transmit micro-messages to the brain at superspeed, the processor in his ear warned him someone was coming a splintered moment before they appeared round the corner. Mac was able to fling himself face down on a sunlounger and play dead until they'd passed.

But they didn't pass. *These* voices he recognised. It was John-John Hamilton and Frankie Nolan, standing right there, right above him. They carried on talking as though they were completely alone in a company's boardroom.

'I'll take 'em off your hands, son. How much d'you want?'

Mac was desperate to peep, but he knew what he'd see – Frankie Nolan and John-John Hamilton perched side by side on the edge of the next recliner.

'Frankie – are you not hearing me, fella? The pills are no good. That's what I've been telling you. Whoever's cooked them has fucked the whole fucking batch up. It's cyanide.'

'All of them?'

'No! Not all. I don't know — a few . . .'

'Well, there we go, then! How many's a few?'

'A *few*! I don't fucking know.' He could hear Hamilton get up and pad around. 'Even a few's too many. I'm dumping them.'

'Don't be fucking stupid!'

'I'm dumping them, Frankie!'

'I'll give you 50k for them.'

'Behave! What if another kid takes the knock?'

A snort from Nolan. 'Shouldn't be taking drugs, should they?' Another sneering snort. 'Collateral damage, isn't it?'

'Know what, Frankie? You're a horrible old bastard, you are.'

'Fifty thousand?'

Silence.

'Go 'ead, then. Fifty large . . .'

Rasping, hateful, gravelly laughter from Frankie Nolan. 'I told you! What did I tell you?' More dirty laughter. 'What did Frankie say? Eh?'

There was some sort of grappling between them, then JJ spoke.

'Come on. The brothers are on the move today. Got to get these fucking arseholes out of here, soon as . . .' He raised his voice. 'Moz! Bring us out some champers, will you, lad?'

'Will do, boss.'

Moz. The young Scouse kid was there. Fuck. He'd half arranged to buy coke off him, hadn't he? He was going to have to lie flat out, dead still, until they moved back indoors, then see what opportunities arose. More than anything, Mac just wanted to stand back, blend in and work out as clearly as possible the layout of the villa here. Once he'd pieced things together, he'd have a much better sense of where Millie might be right now. A bony finger poked him in the side.

'Wakey-wakey, rise and shine!' He let out a desolate groan and peeked out through one eye. JJ Hamilton was on his feet now, clapping his hands and addressing one and all. 'Champagne breakfast on its way, people! Party, PAR-TAY!!'

Music blared out from poolside speakers and, one by one, the living dead began to drag themselves up. People were in fun mode immediately – peeling off their clothes and hurling themselves in the pool, whooping and screeching. And, just like that, the solution hit him. Before Moz came back out with the drinks – and whatever else he'd been bidden to lay on – Mac could ditch his jeans and Gazelles, and lose himself in the tumult of the pool party.

The ballyhoo from outside stirred her. Millie dragged her eyelids open. The same instantaneous dread – she was still there; leaden. Yet there was something, some chip of hope. Yes! Before – McCartney had been there. She had to alert him; let him know where to find her.

She could not coordinate her legs, her limbs; nothing would compute. She wanted to lift her left arm up, grab the table and haul herself to her feet, but it just wouldn't move for her. She couldn't feel a thing. Arms and legs just lay there, splayed out; numb, dead. The only part of her she could control was her head. She lay on her back, staring up at the window, listening to the gaiety outside. And now, the intuitive expectation that help, or some solution, was just round the corner was suffocated by a more fearsome inner dread. How long would this nightmare last?

Treading water in the least frenzied corner of the pool, McCartney rested a forearm in the overflow sluice to keep himself upright and scanned the entire scene; villa, sun terrace, grounds, people, sun terrace, villa again. Every time, his focus took him back to the upstairs room to the right of the house. There was no science to it; Mac just knew it. That was the room. Whatever was going on here at Bates Motel, that room was its heart of darkness – the storeroom, the counting house – and that was where he needed to be. He shielded his eyes with his hand and tried to squint to get a better look, but all he got was the dazzle of the glass as the sun pounded down.

He ran his eye over the sun terrace once more, all round the villa's grounds where stragglers stood in knots, some dancing, some in their underwear, swaying and chatting as though it were an everyday thing to cavort in one's smalls. There was no sign of Millie. He hadn't known the girl long but he was sure he had her pegged. No way would she have put herself in danger. The likely, the *logical* scenario was that she'd taken advantage of the bacchanalia to slip away, unnoticed. Yet the foreboding that sucked his guts strangled all hope of a simple, happy solution. He feared for Millie. He had to find her.

Away on the terrace, the dead-eyed youngster, Moz, was making stilted conversation with Frankie Nolan. Both men stared straight ahead. Neither was laughing, neither betraying any emotion at all. Moz glanced down at the sunlounger next to him. McCartney squinted against the sun – yes, no, fuck . . . that was *his* sunbed! Where had he left his jeans? He'd kept his T-shirt and boxers on and folded his jeans over, twice. But had he stashed them away, underneath, or left them out flat, on top? He was sure he would have laid them on top of his Gazelles, under the sunlounger. Yet, from here, it looked like Moz's attention had been snagged by something at his feet. Mac's mind vaulted away from him. His money was sticking out of his pocket. Moz wouldn't be able to resist, would he? He'd slide his thieving fingers inside and find the car keys, the wallet, Martindale's ID. Fine. He'd find the wrap of coke he'd sold Robbie Marto last night. And he'd also find Molina's police permit. Mac was dead.

A fluffy, fantasy cumulus drifted in front of the sun, blotting it out for a second. Something caught his eye now. The window; *that* window. There was movement. He could see a figure, then another, both looking out over the terrace, gesticulating. The older, more affable Scouse lad came out and said something to his brother and Nolan. All three of them went back inside. If McCartney was ever going to get out of there and call in the troops, that time was right here, right now. Forget how daft he and Millie would look for blowing their own cover so spectacularly, forget his blessed reputation – if he was going to raise the alarm to Roig, or Molina or Shanley, whoever, then this was the moment. The evidence they were after was up there, in that room. He knew it! And he knew he'd have to make a break for it. Now.

He rotated on his tiptoes, taking in a 360-degree view of the surroundings one last time. There were dishevelled people dotted all around the grounds. The pine woods were his best bet. There was a little cluster of older, Eurotrash types gossiping and smoking in the shade, but no one would take a blind bit of notice if he were to just amble past them, into the trees. He hauled himself out of the pool, dripping rivulets from his sodden shorts and T-shirt as he began to navigate his way across the spiky grass. He did a little jog on the spot and shook off some excess water, then started weaving his way past knots of people – girls in bikinis, most of them, smiling, laughing, dancing minimally to the languid breakbeat tripping from the poolside speakers. As his ears popped he realised, in a shock of recognition, that the track was built around a phrase from an Erik Satie Gymnopédie that Rebecca used to play.

He snapped himself out of the reverie and kept his eyes on the pines, gently pushing his way through the poolside throng. He nodded as he passed smiling faces, patted backs, returned jokes about sunburn from matey blokes. He stubbed his toe on a submerged water sprinkler, cursed, gritted his teeth and carried on back to the sunlounger. He wiped himself down, lay back and wriggled into his jeans. He squeezed his still-damp feet into his trainers and began scanning the terrain for his exit spot. A distorted feedback sound preceded the sight of JJ Hamilton at the patio doors with a megaphone.

'Hear ye, hear ye! Kop on the move! Much as we would love to entertain you beautiful people all over again, one thing we cannot do, sadly, is feed you. Not in the everyday sense, ha!' There was a chorus of chuckles and light-hearted boos. Hamilton held up his hand. 'We're all out of bread and fish, brothers and sisters – and I doubt that even I can turn that swimming pool into wine!' He waited, laughing silently until the catcalls died down. 'OK, you crazy motherfuckers, the good news is that the party *does* go on! Our friends at Pike's will be lighting their barbecues round about . . .' He consulted his watch. Slim. Elegant. Mac's money was on Cartier. Hamilton looked up again, smiling brightly. 'Right now! Let's get this show on the road . . .'

There was a buzz of conversation and people began drifting towards the sun terrace. Mac used the cover of the congregation to duck off in the opposite direction.

'That's the way, ladies and gentlemen. Right round to the front of the house, thank you. Plenty of transport; plenty of space . . .'

Mac carried on towards the trees. Ones and twos started walking past him the other way, their faces aglow, not wanting to miss the next instalment. Mac felt that surge, the inner charge that precedes your major action moments. It was the diving-in moment, that crisis point that tells you this is it, now, the point of no return. Do it. He felt the balls of his feet tingle. He rocked backwards on his heels and began to envisage it; himself rolling into a gentle jog, further and further away from the glass-beetle house, deeper into the trees and beyond. He took a deep breath. It was easy, this. He was halfway across the crunchy grass. The woods were right there . . .

'Yo! Fella!' He didn't turn round. He might have been shouting to someone else. 'Not bailing on us, are you?' He was talking to him. He was right there, now – Mac could feel his proximity – a yard, a foot behind him. He was going to have to come up with something good, and he'd have to do it quickly. Thinking fast, McCartney prised the wrap of coke from his hip pocket and gently flicked it onto the spiky lawn. He turned round to JJ and winked.

'Does a bear shit in the woods?'

Hamilton laughed. 'Not in my woods, I hope!'

Although both men made a show of being tickled, McCartney was well aware he was on a time trial here. His next line would have to be good.

'No, being honest with you, mate, I was with this girl last night. Well . . .' He pulled the requisite leery face. '. . . this morning . . .' He jerked his head towards the pine woods. 'Over there we were . . .' He gave a silent laugh and shook his head as though recalling moments of tender depravity. 'Anyway, I'm in the pool just now and it all starts coming back to me. I'm seeing an image of this daft cunt with his arm around a beauty queen, fucking Bianca Jagger she looks like, and he's pleading with her: please steal my drugs!' If Hamilton had any misgivings they seemed to melt away right then. He relaxed, visibly, his smile transforming itself from tense to playful amusement. McCartney held his arms out wide. 'I

89

mean, yes – I was punching well above my weight with young Bianca, but come on – there are certain standards one has to uphold . . .'

Hamilton laughed and clicked his fingers. 'Fucking coke-whores, eh? Fucking ruthless, aren't they?'

Mac pulled his most reasonable, reconciliatory face, arms out wide, palms up.

'Didn't even leave me a fucking bump . . .' Hamilton's eyes crinkled as he clapped his hands. 'Anyways – just thought I'd check the scene of the crime, like. Make sure I didn't just fucking drop it somewhere . . .' Mac winked at JJ. 'Before I call the police.'

JJ burst out laughing again, clicking his fingers in approval. Mac turned and gave the scene one last hopeful look – the method actor in him envisaging JJ Hamilton finding the coke one day and recalling the chummy Southampton club fool; then banishing the image, just as quickly. Hamilton would never get the chance to stumble upon that cocaine. He'd be in jail. The club fool would put him there.

'Anyway. Should you happen upon Miss Nicaragua, please advise her she owes me a gram – or a nosh . . .'

It was a delayed reaction. One second Hamilton was staring at McCartney, the next he had his arm around his shoulders, chuckling to himself, guiding him back towards the villa. Feeling the wet T-shirt, he gave a little hop sideways.

'Either you're minging, lad, or we best keep you out of the sun!' Both men over-laughed. 'Come on. Better get you a nice dry shirt if you're joining us at Mr Pike's . . .' And with that, some dishonourable kinship was sealed between the two. Hamilton, once he'd stopped giggling – and his laugh was childlike, generous, energetic – put his arm around McCartney again and steered him back towards the sun terrace.

'Just remind me who the fuck you are again?'

Mac stopped and did the silent-laugh face. Us boys, eh? What are we like! 'I'm still Rob, señor . . .' And then the moment of inspiration hit him. 'The Saint, to my friends. So you can call me Robbie!'

They laughed and laughed, their faces going red. Twenty minutes later the Saint was being bounced around a minibus full of whooping clubbers as they sped down the hill road towards San Antonio.

Millie was slumped against the wall underneath the window. She felt nauseous now. The door opened again and the Arab guy was back; the one with the long chin. He stood over her, smiling.

'And how feels my beautiful canary, today?'

He knelt down, the love shining out of his eyes. From behind his back, he produced the syringe. She remembered, all over again. She felt sick; felt like sobbing her heart to broken pieces. And then she blacked out.

Roig was palpitating as he reached the gangplank; not out of any fear or doubt, but from the rare, racing extremity of the situation. The sheer satisfaction that, any minute now, he would, personally, single-handedly – as fate would have it – be bringing down and bringing in a bona fide Muslim fanatic; one of the Most Wanted villains in the world. In an already illustrious career, this would, by some stretch, be his greatest moment yet. He'd taken some risks; kept some key informa-tion to himself. Any moment now, it would all pay off.

He stopped and mapped out the path he would take. *La Bandera Verde* was about three hundred metres away; third jetty on the right. Should he call for backup, at this point? Was it clear enough that this coup had all been Roig's and only Roig's doing? Perhaps, perhaps not – but he wasn't going to risk his moment of triumph. How could it possibly go wrong? It was himself, armed, with a lifetime's experience and the powerful element of surprise, versus a kid who was not expecting him. Even if he were to run, where could he run to? Nowhere. He couldn't. He smiled to himself. He'd do this solo, and take him in like a sheriff in the Westerns, running down a fugitive and bringing the bastard back to justice.

He padded along the walkway, calm inside, excited but oh-so calm, then took a right onto the third jetty. Up ahead, the crime-scene tape had blown away – or been pulled down. The local yokels had done their sweep. The armed guard had been stood down; the last of the rubberneckers had melted away. To all intents and purposes, *La Bandera Verde* was, once more, just another luxury cruiser in a marina full of similar opulence. It was an irony too delicious for Roig that Benarbia, this warrior against decadence, should be about to take flight on such a craft. He stood at the top of the little walkway and, for some reason, counted the ridges between himself and the boat. There were seven; lucky for some. Shame that Hamilton had been in such a hurry, this morning. Roig would have liked to have got both of them at once. Still, he had his main target in his sights, now. All that remained was the climax.

Silently, he observed Jamal on his knees, rubbing at the outboard with a rag, ready for departure. He'd get the shock of his life when he turned round.

'So. We have a choice here. *You* have a choice . . .'

It wasn't Roig doing the talking. It wasn't Jamal who was in shock. Driving home his advantage, Jamal jumped to his feet, with what looked very much like a mousetrap raised above his head.

'We are both intelligent men, Señor Roig . . .'

He paused for a second, allowing Roig to digest the fact that he knew his name; had obviously known he was coming.

How, though? Who was the weak link? Was there a snitch? Jamal waited for Roig's full attention.

'I know that you know what this is. I know that you know I can blow us both to pieces – and that I shall do so, without fear. Such an explosion as they will never find our teeth – let alone our heads . . .' He smiled at Roig – a smile of strange innocence, laced with regret. 'So I give you a choice, Señor Roig. I give you a simple, simple choice. Do we both live?' Again, the childlike smile. 'Or do we die?'

Roig stayed stock-still, eyeing Jamal. He looked at his face, looked into his sad, smiling eyes. 'He is mad,' he thought. 'He is fucking insane.' And, as though reading his thoughts, Jamal stooped to pick up a roll of thick tape, his eyes never leaving Roig. He took a step closer.

'You never know, do you? You never know with these fanatics. What do they call us? Mad mullahs? Crazy funda-mentalists?' The smile. A strand of saliva on his two front teeth; one slightly misaligned, Roig noticed – its edge tucked just behind the other. 'Who knows if this crazy Islamic fanatic will blow us both sky-high . . .?' He took another step towards Roig. 'Is that a fuse I see? Is that the detonator? Will he do it . . .?'

Roig cleared his throat. 'I won't insult your intelligence. There is no armed unit on its way to back me up. I am here alone. But make no mistake, Benarbia. We have you. We have you . . .' Jamal laughed, but dropped his head in irritation. 'We have your DNA all over the El Glaoui kid. We can trace the gun and the bullets all the way back to you . . .'

Jamal Benarbia took another step up the gangway, smiling.

'Really? This flatters me. I would like very much to take the credit for this . . . but the fall of the Prince is not my work.'

'No? Yet you know he's dead . . .'

'We are well aware of his demise, yes – though, again, I regret to inform you it was not of our doing. Even if he deserves his termination, I would not kill a brother this way.' His eyes, once more, went dead. 'You realise, of course, that under Declaration III of The Hague Convention of 1899, the use of expanding bullets violates the conventions of war?'

'War?'

Roig could hear the pathetic squeak in his voice. Letting things turn out like this – pathetic. Benarbia walked towards him, businesslike.

'Now then. Enough talk . . .'

He stopped halfway up the gangplank, between the third and fourth; the fourth and third ridges. 'Kneel down please. I assure you I do not pretend . . .'

Roig looked into his eyes one last time; deduced that, insane or not, there was a very high chance he would kill them both, outright, and knelt, as asked. Jamal Benarbia was astride him in a second, tugging his arms behind him and binding his wrists together, tightly, with the tape. Before Roig had a chance to react, Benarbia whipped the tape around his eyes, stinging his eyelids horribly, then wound it around his head, yanking his ears back and snagging his hair.

'OK. Stand up now, please . . .' Roig stood. 'You notice I leave your mouth. This is so you can shout for help . . .' He laughed a dry, staccato laugh. 'OK. Listen.' There was a click. 'I have pulled the detonator . . .' Roig felt Benarbia's hand drive something deep down inside his pocket. 'I have now placed the device inside your jacket, OK?' There was something final, something fatal in his soothing tone of voice. It took Roig back to the mountain farmers of his Andorran youth who would speak lovingly to a calf before slitting its throat. In spite of himself, in spite of all that training, Roig could not contain himself. He began to tremble uncontrollably, and the urine leaked freely down his inner thigh, soaking his jeans. Jamal Benarbia shook his head slowly and tutted. 'No, no, no . . . this is no good, señor. You shake too much. The explosive . . . bang!' Roig could hear him, could sense him, circling him. 'You must stand perfectly still please, Señor Roig. Too much movement, I don't know . . .' His voice became distant. 'Maybe somebody will see you, soon. It is important you tell them to call the, I don't know the name in España. The explosions police. OK?'

He turned and walked away. It was bad enough for Roig to stand there, emasculated, humiliated, drenched in his own piss. It was worse that Benarbia had witnessed it. Had engineered it. Had humiliated him from start to finish. But the worst of all was listening to the Arab's cackles as he sauntered away. Roig had to stand there and listen to the jittering outboard engine crank into action. It started third go, puttering away until he could hear it no more. He could only imagine now; imagine the yacht slipping out of the harbour, out to sea. At least he knew its name.

Molina caught sight of himself in the wing mirror as he sat, dead still, in the Jeep that Hamilton had supplied. He stared at the haunted face looking back at him. How had it come to this? No more, Rodolfo. No more. The English were waiting for him down at Pike's, waiting to glad-hand him. To raise a glass, toast the new season; the bounty it was sure to bring. Hamilton would subtly steer him to the shade of the olive grove and check it had all been done. And it had. It had all been done, just as he had asked. Had ordered. But no more, Rodolfo. This had been the last time. He started up the Jeep and exited the hospital's service road.

Mac took a good look around Pike's grounds. He could slip away easily enough. But the lane leading up there had gone on forever. In this heat, it could take him half an hour to make it back down to the San An road – and what would he do once he got there? Hitch? No. He'd have to think on his feet here. Two of the girls from the ride down were sitting at the pool's edge, dangling their feet in the water. He sat down next to them, tucked his knees under his chin.

'Hi,' he smiled.

'*Hola!*' grinned the nearer of the two. The other just carried on swishing the water with her big toe. Mac turned so he was facing them now.

'Hey, do you girls remember the lady I was with last night?'

Both shook their heads. 'Sorry . . .'

'No bother. Just . . . haven't seen her since the party. Probably made her own way back . . .'

The nearest girl bit her bottom lip. 'Sorry, mate. What does she look like?'

Mac nodded at her friend. 'Bit like you. Blonde. Tall. Denim cut-offs. Not being very helpful, really, am I?'

'Lot of girls like that at Hammo's parties . . .'

'You know him?'

'Who doesn't!'

'What's he like? I mean . . .'

They both pulled identical 'so-so' kind of faces.

'He's OK, you know . . .'

Her friend butted in. 'But you definitely want to keep your distance.'

Mac nodded, hoping they'd continue.

'Listen to her! She fancies the arse off him!'

'Do not!'

That was it. The blonde girl pushed her friend into the pool and dived in after her. The pair of them splashed McCartney.

'Come on in!'

He winced and stood up. 'Maybe later . . .' He winked at the wet faces smiling up at him. '*Adios, señoritas.*'

He spied Moz, sitting alone in a loose-stone shelter. Mac was getting nowhere, and a growing sense of grief about Millie – a simple recognition that this entire situation was of his own making – was beginning to make him desperate. Wherever Millie was now, Hamilton was the key to finding her. Mac was certain of it. He had to get in there – right to the very heart of whatever was going on. He idled over.

'*Hola.* How goes it?'

The lad didn't look up. He shrugged. 'Sound.'

'Good.' Mac paused, made a big thing of checking behind himself, making sure they weren't being overheard. 'Listen . . .' He took a step closer. 'Can I, er . . .?' He gestured to the slate plinth the kid was perched on. Moz slid six inches to his right. Mac sat next to him, arms folded. Moz still stared straight ahead. 'So . . . I just wondered . . .' Mac stifled a laugh and dropped his head down so it was almost touching his forearms. 'I mean this . . . all this . . . there's nothing like this where I come from . . .'

He took his time, but eventually Moz spoke. 'Where's that, like?'

'Southampton. Hence the name . . .'

Blank expression from Moz. A minimal shrug. 'Never been there.'

'You wouldn't want to.' Mac shook his head again. 'Boring. Don't get me wrong, great place to live, bring up kids, what have you . . . there's none of this, though.' He sat back, let out a silent whistle, slowly and deliberately shook his head one last time before turning to face Moz. 'I mean . . . you guys . . . shoot me down if I'm out of order here . . .'

'Go 'ead . . .'

'You know . . .' Not a tic from Moz. 'What we were talking about last night? In the club . . .'

The slightest shrug. 'What was we talking about?'

Mac let out a nervous chuckle, to let Moz know he appreciated his discretion.

'OK. Here it is. I mean . . . could you boys, like, sell me some stuff?'

'*Stuff*? Not with you, lad.'

'Just enough to get me started . . .'

'I don't know what you're talking about.'

'Fair enough.' His instinct was to walk away, but to where? To what? He had *nothing*! He left it a second. 'Look. I've got money. I can front this.' Moz stared straight ahead. 'I mean, I wouldn't waste your time . . .'

A flicker of animation tugged at the corners of Moz's eyes. 'You want to get in the game?'

'Yeah. I think so. Look . . .' He did his checking-around routine again. No one was taking any notice whatsoever. People were sitting by the pool, sipping beers, cocktails; one or two nodding their heads to the ambient sound system. 'Depending on price . . .' He started pulling out his wallet. '. . . I can pay up front –'

'Whoa, whoa, whoa, lad . . . easy!' Moz stood up. 'One small step for mankind and that.' His eyes raked over McCartney, cynically appraising, as though he were considering purchasing him. 'Wait there,' he spat. And off he went.

Roig heard footsteps approaching – a woman upbraiding a child. Could he risk them? If there was a God at all, how would He look upon a man who, knowingly, jeopardised the lives of others to save his own skin? He could not do it. He would let them pass by.

Laughter. The galloping, hiccuping laughter of a child.

'Nicola! Shh!'

It sounded as though the mother was trying to pull the child past.

'Look! Look at the funny man!'

'Nicola!'

The child had broken free. Little footsteps clattering towards him.

'Please! No . . .' Roig whimpered.

'Why has the man got a funny face?'

Any second now the device would explode. They would all be blown to damnation.

'Señora . . .'

'Is everything OK, señor?'

Slowly, barely moving, he shook his head. Once again his tears leaked out, silting up his eyelids, nowhere to run free.

'Should I call the police?'

His moan of dismay lowed from his guts before Roig could prevent it.

'Noooo! No police . . .'

The little girl stopped laughing now. 'Mama. I don't like the man . . .'

'Shh! I am helping him . . .' Her voice became louder; nearer. 'What can I do to help?'

Save yourself, thought Roig. Step away. Go. Any second now . . . how would it happen? How would it feel? What would be the first he knew of it – and the last? He bit down hard on his lip, tried to stem the bilious fear.

'Here . . .' The woman began tugging at the tape behind his neck.

'Please! No . . .'

She stepped away. 'Then what?'

'I am a bomb,' he whispered. He heard her stifled gasp. 'Walk away. Very slowly. It will be fine.'

There was no sound. The woman and her daughter had not moved. Roig tried again.

'Please go. This is my fault – not yours.'

'I cannot just leave you here.'

Roig thought on it. 'Do you have a nail file?'

She must have rummaged in her bag.

'I have scissors. Only small . . .'

He turned, one centimetre at a time, minimising his movements to the merest insinuation. Now he had his back to her; his bound hands, fingers wiggling.

'Can you cut the tape – here?' She stepped closer. 'Just the first incision, then you must go. I can take care of the rest.'

He took a deep breath and held it down, forever. She snipped. No explosion. He let his breath gust out and, once again, the urine flowed freely. By the time he'd ripped off his bonds and torn the tape from his eyes, his rescuer and her girl were well away, Nicola still tugging at her mother and looking back round at the man in the mask.

Moz was back. He jerked his head for Mac to follow him. They took a circuitous route past the tennis courts and over a threadbare stretch of grass to the back of the main hotel, entering the old casa through a shady courtyard. Moz led McCartney down a short passageway and indicated an ancient leather armchair. 'Wait.'

Moz knocked once, then twice, then once again, stood back and listened.

'Yiss?'

He went inside. Mac waited, looked around. He could hear a young woman's voice just down the corridor, Australian, possibly, taking a reservation over the telephone. He could just amble down there, order a taxi straight back to the spider house and no one would be any the wiser. What if he was wrong, though? What if DS Camilla Baker was sunning herself back at the villa, awaiting her further instructions? Here was a one-off opportunity for Mac to plug himself directly into the nerve centre of John-John Hamilton's operation, and the thought both exhilarated and terrified him. He had no idea what to expect, in there – just that he'd have to play the role he'd been preparing, the eager Rob Martindale, and he'd have to play him brilliantly. He got up out of the armchair, tiptoed to the door, put his ear to the big, decorative keyhole. Raised voices. The cockney guy, Frankie, upset about something. JJ smoothing and soothing, telling him that things would run like clockwork tonight. Then there was another voice, right there, right by the door – clipped. Impatient.

'Your friend the Irishman. He is still there?'

Foreign. Then came John-John again, muffled, but again the soothing, sing-song tone. 'Davey won't get in your way . . .' His voice got nearer – louder. 'The thing you want is in a black Jeep at the furthest end of the car park. OK? These are the keys, brother. Dara's back at the house to help you. Get yourselves busy.'

The foreign voice snapped back, cold and crystal clear. 'I apologise for my atmosphere, John-John. My brother . . . he has lost his heart. Lost his head. Next time . . .' His voice faded out, like he'd turned his face in a different direction. 'Next time things will be more calm. As they used to be.'

JJ must have come across the room to give him the personal treatment. Suddenly his voice was coming right through the keyhole, right in Mac's ear.

'They will be, Hassan. You take Hammo's word for it. They will be . . .'

Footsteps. McCartney tiptoed back to the leather chair,

lowered himself noiselessly back down. Sat, looking at the mosaic-tiled floor.

Roig, having dry-spewed a string of bile into a myrtle bush, pulled himself together and switched his disdain from himself back to his target number one. That Arab shit who had just laughed in his face; who had played him, completely; knowing, absolutely, how he would react; who was sailing away, unchallenged, unmolested, to begin his bombing campaign, no doubt, on Spanish soil – he had better enjoy that bracing sea air. If Juan Sebastien Roig had started into this thing quite certain that the Prince and Davey Lane were his route to glory, then his priorities and his focus had shifted suddenly, and radically. Wherever Jamal Benarbia was heading, he was going to nail him. He was going to see that bastard suffer if it was the last thing he did. He wiped his mouth and checked himself out in a Kawasaki's wing mirror. His entire forehead was pink and raw where he'd ripped off the adhesive tape. One of his eyebrows was missing altogether, the other decimated. That piece of shit! Roig solemnly swore to himself, there and then, that he was going to catch that bastard Benarbia and flay him within an inch of his life. He increased his pace, hoping for their sakes that Molina and the Guardia Civil were ready to play ball. Play ballistics.

The door opened and a young Arab pushed past, scowling. Mac tried not to stare at Hassan El Glaoui, up close and smaller than he'd pictured him. Moz just stood there, holding the door, until Mac cottoned on, got up and went inside. 'Here we go,' gulped McCartney and his face lit up with one radiant, innocent, life's-great smile.
　　'Hi, guys, thanks for –'
　　'Sit down.'
　　John-John Hamilton did not look up at first. He was wearing

spectacles, studying a map – or an architect's blueprint. Mac sat, fighting back an onrush of bile in his throat. Frankie Nolan just stared at him, as though trying to decide whether to hit him, or worse. Eventually JJ looked up. All the matey familiarity of a few hours ago was gone, for now. This was business. Hamilton noted the fear in Mac's eyes, the painted smile – and smiled back.

'So. Saint. How can we help?'

'Well, I . . .'

'My associate here tells me you're looking at a small start-up?'

'Well. Not so small, maybe . . .'

'Always best to start small, we find. Don't we, Francis?'

'Tell him my fucking name, why don't you?'

JJ laughed and clicked his fingers. 'Everyone knows your fucking name, you leg-end . . .'

The pair of them laughed, loudly, for ages. Moz stayed silent. Mac sat there with a fixed, somewhat puzzled smile on his face. Suddenly, JJ snapped to attention.

'I take it it's the Gary Abletts you're wanting?'

'Yes. I reckon . . .'

'Just tablets, or?'

'Well. Yeah. I think so . . .'

Hamilton looked at Nolan. Nolan didn't blink.

'I think we just might be able to accommodate you. Francis?'

Nolan twitched and clenched his fists, then, slowly, eventually began to nod. 'Maybe,' he murmured. 'Maybe we can.'

'What do you mean, out of contact? We are *never* out of contact in this force. *Never!* Call whoever is with him.'

The blinking desk sergeant cleared his throat. 'This is what I am telling you, sir. Captain Molina is working solo in this . . . *operation*.'

Raw ire crackled through Jus Roig's bloodstream, sending his jugular throbbing and his temples pulsating out of all control. He felt a passionate desire to smash his fists down on the solid wooden counter, scream, kick, vent his fury – but he swallowed it. He held his breath down, let it out slowly, slowly, slowly . . . then tried once more with the hopeless pen-pusher.

'OK. Look. This is a matter of national security . . .' Calmly, now, he placed his ID face up on the counter. There was a culture of mutual suspicion between Roig's unit, seen as robocops, near paramilitaries who only went for the glamour collars, and the boys-on-the-beat of the Guardia. He steeled himself for the usual resistance; the hiding behind procedure and invisible, incontestable 'bosses'.

'What do you need, sir?'

Incredible. The halfwit was going to assist. Roig leaned across the counter so the guy was in no doubt.

'I need to see the body of one Ali El Glaoui, assassinated at approximately 2200 hours yesterday evening. I need to see the bullet or bullets or fragments thereof, recovered from the crime scene. I need to see all photographic and video evidence to date. And I need the fullest and most up-to-date statements and files relating to this case. Shall we start with the body? Where is it currently located?'

Thirty minutes later he was being accompanied by a silently disapproving clerk along the echoing, highly polished floor of a modern hospital on the outskirts of San Antonio. He'd been fully appraised by Ballistics as to the method and means of execution. The Prince had been slain by the 9 x 19mm Parabellum bullet of the longslide Glock 17L, currently the pistol of preference of the Spanish Guardia Civil. The clerk opened up the mortuary and stepped back to let Roig inside. At first he thought it was an optical illusion, and squinted up to make sure that all the strip lighting had winked into action. He looked back at the vacant trolley, and checked all around the stark and naked room. He turned to the immaculate clerk.

'Where is the body?'

A look of puzzlement, more than concern, passed over the clerk's face. He fished a pair of spectacles out of the breast pocket of his salmon-pink shirt and, with great care, sidled past Roig. He ran his eyes over all four corners, all four walls. There was no doubt about it. The morgue was empty. Ali El Glaoui had vanished.

McCartney could not relax; could not tear his mind away from Millie, the realisation that every minute he spent here was time he should devote to finding his colleague. He was starting to torment himself; was Mac the sort of cop who gambled with his comrades' safety? Yet he'd started something here. He had to do things properly, for the sake of *all* their futures. Rob Martindale had new friends to meet, champagne to quaff, glasses to clink. JJ led him out to the pool bar, his new special guest, and introduced him to the Bad, the Evil and the Worse. Rob smiled and laughed at their jokes, especially the ones about his wealth source.

'Just a bog-standard business then, lad?'

Braying, cacophonous laughter.

'I heard you was on your arse when you first started out.'

Convulsions of merriment. Rampant high-fiving.

'Typical rags to riches story, eh, kidda? You must've made a pile!'

Near-hysterical giggling – led by Rob Martindale himself. And if Mac hadn't physically needed to double over to get his breath, Rodolfo Molina might have caught sight of the courteous English cop McCartney, getting pally with the Liverpool

Firm as he approached the swimming pool from the car park. By the time McCartney straightened himself, Molina was at the bar on the far side of the terrace, blind to the world as he made earnest conversation with John-John Hamilton.

McCartney took one raking, 360-degree glance around the party scene and disentangled himself from the pipe-cleaner arms of the girl in the bikini who was, somehow, now entwined around him, swaying to the music. Keeping his back to Molina, he picked his way across the crazy paving to the far side of the pool and sat back in the cool of a rough-stone gazebo. A voice from nowhere made him start.

'So. You're single-handedly dragging Southampton into the modern age, are you?'

Saah-fampton. Frankie Nolan. Just his voice terrified Mac. He found himself striving for Rob Martindale's jaunty banter.

'Well, yeah. I suppose. It'd be rude not to, wouldn't it?'

Nolan leaned forward, visible now Mac's eyes had adjusted to the shadows.

'What else you into, Saint? Apart from bog roll?'

Mac forced a laugh. 'How d'you mean?'

'I mean, is it all just Es and raves and that? Or is there more to you than meets the eye?'

And suddenly McCartney sensed blood. Frankie Nolan, he was already well aware, intended to sell the adulterated Ecstasy to him. He was fine with that. He was happy. They'd be taking the poison off the streets, and Shanley would have all the evidence he wanted, seal-wrapped and delivered right into his lap. But Mac's antennae were twitching now. There was more. This could be the breakthrough.

'You talking coke, mate? I could definitely go some coke . . .'

Nolan shuffled along the stone bench. 'Fucking hot, isn't it?' He was chilling. He was right next to McCartney now, his supernaturally blue eyes diving and darting all over Mac's face – wise; mercurial; deadly. He carried on staring, then cast his eyes over the poolside party. 'What gets into 'em, eh?' He shook his head slowly, deliberately. 'Coke we can get you, hash we can get you, fucking smack we can get, if that's what floats your dinghy, Saint. Being honest with you though, that ain't my thing. You're best speaking to JJ about all that. He's the boy, where gear's concerned. Nothing he can't sort . . .'

Mac nodded, as though he were giving Nolan's every word his serious consideration.

'I hear you. Thanks. So . . .'

'You wanna know what I have in mind for you?' He rested his head right back against the rough stone wall, let out a deep, calculating sigh. 'I may be way, way off beam here, Rob – but I'm thinking you're a man after my own heart.' He jerked forward and dropped his head down, clasping his hands between his legs. After a beat, he glanced sideways at Mac. 'You're a risk-taker, ain't you, Rob?' He winked – horrifyingly frightening, so close up. 'You like money, sure – who don't? But you like the thrill of it . . .' *Frill.* 'So what I'm thinking I can do for you . . .' He shifted right round now so he was facing Mac, and gave him a smile so chilling it made his heart stop. 'I reckon you're, let's say . . . one hundred master tapes, for starters. Hardcore. Schoolies or grannies, mega-tits or no tits, anal, shaved, spanking, golden showers . . . dogs, horses, fucking *tapirs*, I kid you not!' His eyes went as wide as they were physically able to as he tried to emote just how serious he was; how trustworthy. 'Whatever you want, Rob. Whatever the fuck you want.' He saw Mac's face and started laughing. 'What? Not your thing?' The bright blue eyes started sparkling, betraying, for the first time, a hint of mirth. 'Oh, shit, oh my fuck-ing-*word*! Of course! Southampton! Well, I've got plenty of that gear, too. Black boys, dicks down to their knees, Arabs, pre-pubes, Boy Scouts in tiny, skintight shorts, ask and you shall receive . . .'

Mac snapped out of it. OK – think, McCartney. Think, think, think. He could get them all here, the whole fucking circus – but his mind kept vaulting back to Millie. The racing certainty, the rational probability was that the able DS Baker would be out there, now, looking for *him*. She'd be desperate to debrief him, delighted with the info she'd gleaned. That was the likelihood – but Mac just wasn't feeling it. His gut kept taking him back to the big glass house; the closed door – but that was as far as it would take him. Every time he tried to think beyond the door, inside the room itself, his psyche refused to process it. He couldn't, or wouldn't, visualise it; had no clear notion how to get back there; how to bring this to a head. Yet here, now, was a direct way in. Instead of forcing the issue, these monsters were going to lead him right to the heart of it, right by the nose. If he set this up right he could reel in Nolan – easy. But he could tie in Hamilton as well, and, with the luck that had eluded him thus far, Davey Lane too – tie them together at the ankles and watch them trip each other up as they tried to run away. And he knew what to do. You're at your greatest advantage when someone under-estimates you; better still, when they're blinded by greed.

'The films – I presume we're talking films, Frank?'

'That we are, boss. That's exactly what we're talking . . .'

'And in terms of viewing them . . .' He cleared his throat. 'Taking delivery and so on. Where might I, ah . . .?'

'Back home, mate. All back home . . .'

The grand plan he had just inflated with hope's raw spirit leaked flat.

'I could do with, you know . . . just a little butcher's, make sure it's . . . I mean, no offence, but . . . Nothing I can see right now?'

'Nah. We shot some shit last night but . . .' Mac barely heard the rest. His guts were strangling him; an acrid fear squeezing his throat. He tried to pull himself back; get back in the game. 'Might have to shoot it all again tonight, fucking uptight fucking mare . . .'

McCartney cleared his throat and concentrated, minutely, on every syllable. 'Who was she?'

Nolan flapped his hand at thin air. 'Ah, some toff. Didn't wanna play . . . Hammo was all for drugging her and goosing her, but that don't make for the best viewing, if you catch my drift . . .'

McCartney felt dizzy with dread. Even if the old bastard wasn't talking about Millie, he'd presided over unthinkable abuse, up at that monstrosity in the mountains. Suddenly, he couldn't care less about the drug bust. The likes of Millie, Abi, any of these feckless blondes by the pool – Nolan and Hamilton were coercing them into sex slavery. He tried to suppress the hatred, the will to maim him. He lowered his voice.

'I mean . . . did you get anything at all? Anything I can see?'

Nolan shook his head slowly. 'Nah, not yet kid. We don't process 'em out here. Anyways . . .' He clapped his hands together and beamed across at Mac. 'Southampton ain't so far from Essex. I'll come to you. That way I knows where you live . . .' He creased up laughing that deadly laugh, then came back straight-faced. 'Just need a small deposit now, as it goes. Just to show we're in business. Know what I'm saying to you?'

Mac nodded, still numb, still trying to drag himself back into role. 'And the pills?'

'The pills you can have now, mate. Save me fucking about with transport and suchlike.'

'So – will I meet you back up at the glass house, or . . .?'

Nolan's calculating eyes sparkled as yet another opportunity, another scam occurred.

'Know what, son? We should break the golden rule. We should mix business with pleasure. How about a little night of it *ce soir*, eh?'

'You not filming, then?'

Frankie Nolan squeezed McCartney's leg just above the knee, making him squirm. 'I can do whatever I want, my son.' He winked. 'The joy and beauty of being one's own boss, what-what?' He grinned again – demonic. Insane. 'So what say you? A little outing to celebrate our little arrangement?'

'Sure. Definitely. I mean . . . can I come to your place, first? Have a little look-see?'

With that, just like that, all the joy bled from Nolan's eyes. His lips looked mean as he looked McCartney up and down.

'Robert. In business, nothing is impossible. It's all a case of showing a bit of willing. So . . .' He leaned forward, tapped him, once, on the knee. 'Can you show a bit of willing?'

'Sure. What's the –'

Nolan threw his arms out wide, looking right and left. 'A drink. A gesture. Show me you ain't some tart.' He shifted right round in his seat now. 'Say fifty large, just so we both know where we are . . .'

'Pounds?'

'What do *you* think?'

He thought he was going to be sick. He swallowed back the fear, fought to keep the tremor out of his voice.

'Fifty thou. That's for the pills, or . . .?'

'It's a ton for the pills, same again for the Frankie Vaughan. That's for the masters, yeah? You can run off fucking tens of thousands off of them fuckers. You'll be in fucking clover.'

'So two hundred thousand, yeah?'

'Correct. Fifty tonight.'

'I can do it. But I need to sort a transfer.'

And Nolan was transformed. His face was childlike as he reached across to squeeze Mac's biceps.

'I'd be highly indignant if you didn't, Robert. And a stout holdall to carry it in!' He stood up, almost banging his head on the low roof, laughing to himself. 'You're only a good 'un, son. All the lads is going to this foam party tonight. Es Paradis. You know the gaff?'

'I'll find it.'

'Very good. Let there be business . . .' He smiled. Mac felt violated. '. . . and pleasure. In equal . . .'

Mac realised Nolan was waiting for him to complete the rhyme. He forced a cheeky wink.

'Measure . . .'

Nolan ruffled Mac's shiny crop.

'Love it. Midnight. Thereabouts. Bring your doings and I'll take you for a drive, show you some things . . .'

McCartney shuddered. Nolan was beaming at him – the smile of death. He was stone-cold certain he knew what 'showing him some things' would entail.

He was going to have to get moving here. Think this plan through, access the cash, then strike. Bang, bang, bang.

Above all else, he had to get Detective Sergeant Camilla Baker back to safety. When these arrests were made – and they would be made, that night – he wanted Millie to be there to enjoy the moment. Then, perhaps, Mac would be able to look Shanley in the eye; let him know he was right to give him this gig. Give *them* the gig. He got up and shook hands with Frankie Nolan.

'Pukka. I'll get on to the bank right now. Make my apologies to JJ, yeah? Tell the boys the Saint'll catch them all tonight . . .'

Nolan winked and ambled away, cupping a young girl's

bottom as he passed. McCartney watched, steeling himself. These men thought they had it made; they thought they could do what the fuck they wanted. Well, they had another think coming to them. Catch them all tonight? Damn right! He hung back and made sure Molina was nowhere to be seen then slipped through a gap in the hedging and made his way back round to the front desk to call a taxi.

Back in the Shogun, away from the parador, McCartney tried to think like a cop instead of a friend, a loved one. He reasoned that he could do more, quicker, get more answers, better set things in motion if he returned to base. The telecoms were there; he could speak to Shanley. Get some advice. And besides, she'd be there. She'd be there, waiting for him. As he passed through Sant Miguel and turned off down the approach road to their villa, Mac's heart was in his mouth, hoping against hope. The huge blue fan palm occluded the villa until he rounded the final bend, taking him directly onto the property. The blinds were down; the shutters locked. The parking area was vacant. No moped. No Millie.

He delayed going inside; went round to the front, still believing he'd see her long limbs stretched out by the poolside; a cocktail to hand, an ironic smile as she squinted up and shielded her lovely face from the sun and said: 'Better late than never . . .'

But she wasn't there. The pool was perfectly still. Way down on the bay, the distant thrum of speedboats. Other than that – nothing. The intermittent chirrups of two yellow-breasted serin. McCartney slumped on a recliner and caved in to the crashing grief that surged up and swamped him, keening and sobbing till the birds flew away. What had he done here? What had he allowed to happen?

He got up and wiped his eyes and blew his nose on

Hamilton's shirt; dragged his disparate thoughts together. This had been folly. Ego. He'd wanted the prize, the praise, the plaudits – and he'd abandoned his junior colleague in pursuit of all that. He could have called Roig; could have called Shanley. Now he was going to have to account for a missing person. If he could fix it, now – if he could trade a dressing-down and an immediate recall for the safe return of Camilla, he'd grab it with both hands. But how to bring that about? What best to do?

He went indoors and pulled out the transmitter. Put it back down. He should inform Shanley. He really should put the boss in the picture, at this point. What if the worst were to happen, or had already come to pass? He'd have to contact her family, make arrangements for them; probably start the formalities of bringing Millie's body back home. It didn't bear thinking about, but Mac was already long past the minutiae of protocol. This was his mess and he had to own up to it. He picked up the transmitter again, laid it out on the rough pine table. He cleared his throat, composed himself and mentally prepared the call to Shanley.

Ten minutes later, Roig was on his way.

The plan was simple – as good plans should be – but potentially very dangerous, too – which they should not. McCartney – Robert Martindale – was going to simply walk right in there, grinning like an idiot. His private prayer was that Hamilton and co. were still down at Pike's, halfway to oblivion. If the coast was clear, excellent; he'd try every single door and check every single room until he found Millie. Then, and in any event, he'd call Roig in and the pair of them would search the place centimetre by centimetre, piecing together the evidence they needed to secure the convictions they craved.

But if, on arrival, the cars were back at HQ, they would still go ahead. Martindale would wander in there, wide-eyed, jejune, acting like he'd been made – he was one of the boys. He would be overeager; excited at this, his first big deal. He would tell them he couldn't remember the name of the club they'd said they'd meet at; he was keen to prove himself, show them all he meant business; he had not wanted to let Nolan down. And it'd work. They wouldn't quiz him – they'd humour him. They would think he was stupid. He would have them where he wanted them.

There was always the risk that Mac might incur serious personal harm. He felt OK about that. Without Molina or the Guardia Civil to call upon, Roig was going to be Mac's sole backup for now – for better or for worse. He'd swap his slacks and slip-ons for overalls, and potter around the woods, keeping an eye out. If anyone should challenge him, he was the game-keeper, the gardener, the handyman. But their hope – their gamble – was that they'd get in there, unhindered. They'd find Millie and they'd find drugs and money and guns and the para-phernalia of pornography – all the evidence they needed. They'd wait for Hamilton's entourage to return to their den of iniquity and then – and only then – would Roig dial his special number and the storm troopers would descend. Nonetheless, though, the thought of fronting this, solo, gave McCartney stomach cramps.

'Are we sure we don't want to just break the doors down and steam in there mob-handed?' asked Mac.

'We can do this . . . but what if there is nothing? What is our story?'

McCartney thought it through; swallowed hard. It was as it should be; it was down to him and him alone. He'd started this bloody mess; he'd have to see it through.

* * *

Hassan could hear his brother up there, trying to soothe her. He checked his watch. They were going to be late. He hadn't even brought the Jeep up yet, there was Ali to take care of . . . He marched up the stairs, into the room the old guy had been using – Nolan. Yousef was kneeling over the frigid one, stroking her hair.

'Come, my beautiful. Is all OK . . .'

She was looking up at him with frightened, sleepy eyes.

'I'm not going anywhere with you.'

'Yes, yes . . .'

He leaned back and tugged at her wrists, but the blonde jerked backwards.

'Leave me alone!'

'Yousef!' Hassan strode over, shoved his brother to one side. He jabbed a finger into the girl's face. 'Listen, bitch! You do what he says –'

He didn't finish his threat. She spat in his face and tried to run. He dragged her back by the hair, striking her hard with the back of his hand.

'No!' Yousef leapt between them. 'Don't hurt her!'

'I'll do more than hurt her . . .'

Hassan drew back his fist. Yousef punched him, hard, in the stomach. He doubled over, coughing. Yousef bent over the girl, dabbing at her cut mouth.

'Let me see . . .' Blood was running freely through her fingers. He held his shirt to her mouth. 'Oh, poor angel . . .' There was a small, bloody hole where Hassan had knocked a tooth out. 'My brother did not mean to harm you.'

Hassan straightened himself. 'Listen to me. If you do not get that bitch down those stairs and ready to go, the two of you can stay right here. I mean it.'

He glared from Yousef to Millie, then marched out.

Letting out a hiss of pique, Yousef went next door to get the syringe.

With persistence and a business card, Mac was able to spring the rudimentary lock on the double-glazed patio door without too much trouble. He placed his gloved palms flat against its surface and slid it open, a little at a time. Noiselessly, he stole inside, checking all around, listening hard. There was a brief, distant sound, just a muted bump, but so muffled, so far off that he couldn't be sure it had even come from the villa. Walking on the balls of his feet, he crossed the main living room's floor and stood and listened at the bottom of the stairs. Knowing that Roig was in the woods outside, patrolling the property, watching his back, he steeled himself, ready, now. Breathing in and out in shallow, staccato gulps, he took one final big deep breath, held it down a moment and eyed the steps ahead; tried to visualise his ascent.

He started up the staircase. Keeping to the hessian runner down the middle of the cool, polished marble, he took a step, then stopped; a step, then stopped. Holding his breath. Listening out. Was there someone there? He could sense it. He was not alone. He got to the half-landing and crouched, let his neck fall loose and his head drop down as he listened, above and below. There were voices, some way off; conversational. No conflict, no menace – just two people, working something out. He strained to hear. They were not speaking English, nor Spanish, either. The timbre, the cadence – even though Mac could not make words out distinctly, the speech pattern was unfamiliar. Still on his haunches, balanced on the balls of his feet, he glanced up at that bedroom door and felt the same surge of anxious nausea as he'd had earlier, returning to their villa. Let her be there, he prayed to himself. Let her be safe. Yet he knew. He knew . . .

He took the last four steps two at a time, angry now, focused, determined. He put his ear to the door. Nothing. He gripped the round, brass-plated handle, serrated key slot in its centre, expecting it to be locked tight. It opened. Slowly, he pushed the door wide open, still remaining outside. He shut his eyes. What was he about to see? Would Millie be tied up? Beaten? Would she be dead? He couldn't picture it, at all – good or bad. He bit down on his lower lip and went inside.

There was no one there – but the room was far from empty. In three of the corners stood miniature scaffolding towers with arc lights, sealed off with plastic collars. There were cables running into a multi-socket adapter. McCartney spotted three indentations in the thick, white wool carpet, spaced out in a near perfect triangle. He crouched, ran his forefinger over the first dint, got back up. There was no camera, but Mac surmised that the pockmarks had come from a tripod bearing a hefty weight. This room had been used as a mini-studio, a film set. He swallowed hard; fought the rising nausea in his guts. He was about to exit when something caught his eye by the window. He stepped across to make sure. It was – it was blood, spattered across the whitewashed wall. In the corner below, two more bloodstains, each roughly hand-sized – one shaped like a map of Australia. He knelt down and touched it lightly. It was still moist. And lodged in a small gap just beneath the window was a small, perfectly white tooth, strands of bloody gum still strung from its crown. This time he couldn't keep the bile down.

Had not the Brazilian transvestite swallowed his entire, diminutive cock at that precise moment, Davey Lane would have gone out onto the landing and given the Arab a hiding. Today had already been messy enough as it was; Hassan and Yousef kicking off on each other, arguing like tarts. The younger one, Yousef, had taken a massive shine to one of the bitches, so it seemed. Davey heard the whole thing – proper girlie shrieking match – but he didn't understand a fucking word. He had to get the gist of it from Dara – good lad, that one. He'd make the grade. He said that Yousef kept sloping in there, trying to give this bird a length, telling his big brother he loved her, but Hassan was having none of it. Just fucking told him no, end of story. So there's all sorts of drama and John-John just basically fucks off and leaves them to it; gets everyone out of the house. Ha! Not Davey Lane, by the way! He knew he couldn't budge the man himself. Just left him there – left him to it. It was the least he could do, all things considered . . .

He'd heard the Yousef one creeping around, sneaking upstairs. Typical of your North Africans. They were into all that – sneaking up and watching you. Fucking perverts. At least he'd had the last laugh with that Jamal cowboy. Semtex my arse! How John-John could give those plastic revolution-aries the time of day . . . Davey clutched the Brazilian's head tight and resisted his natural tendency to yelp like a puppy dog as he came in his mouth. He lay back and caught his breath. The Brazilian got up, shot him a sly smile. Davey reached across to the bedside table; opened the drawer; threw him a pack of cigarettes. The Brazilian lit up, held out the packet to Davey. He shook his head. Leaned back into the drawer and pulled out the Glock. Spent, now, his natural pique and ire was restored again. If those Arabs were hanging around, smirking and nudging one another when he went downstairs, Davey Lane reckoned he'd shoot them. Both of them.

Mac headed for the stairs. No more delays – Roig had to call in the specials immediately. He got to the half-landing when a door opened outwards at the bottom of the stairs. McCartney stepped back, just in time. An Arab kid staggered out, bent double, hauling a rolled-up rug. Mac's second sense kicked in;

he knew that was a body. He was followed out by the older Scouse lad, Dara, carrying the other end. The absolute certainty of it took his breath away. That was Millie, wrapped up in the carpet there. Jesus fucking Christ! What had they done to her? What had *he* done?! Mac flung himself down the final few stairs.

'Police! Lie down! Lie fucking down!'

Yousef dropped his end of the rug and ran out of the open door. Dara turned round, ran his eyes up and down McCartney's slender frame and, with barely any backlift, knocked him down with one punch. He ran over and kicked him once, twice, three times in the ribs, the chest, the back of his head. Mac saw him walk calmly to the door and stoop to drag the rolled-up rug out of the house.

'Yousef! Get back here, you tit!'

Mac passed out.

They took Roig completely by surprise. Circling the property from the woods, Roig was just about to take up his hide once more, up on the elevated woody slope that overlooked the front of the house, waiting for a signal from McCartney. He had emerged from the side path and was getting ready to cross the parking bay into the trees when the glint of a reflection caught his eye, immediately followed by the deranged revving of an engine. A black Jeep was reversing up the track towards the house at high speed. Roig froze, then tried to sidle off back round the side. Suddenly, the front door opened and a guy backed out, carrying his end of a rolled-up rug. Seconds later another guy emerged, bringing up the rear. The Jeep screeched to a halt, the engine left in neutral. The driver jumped out and ran to help the other two. All three men were dark – Arabs or Turks. All three stopped dead when they spied the startled Roig. He smiled and walked towards them.

'No problem, gentlemans. I am pool man. If is no good time this, I return . . .'

The driver turned to the young guy holding the back end of the rug. 'You know this guy, Dara?'

Dara shrugged, pulled a face; the face that says 'never clapped eyes on him before'. The driver went to the rear of the Jeep, leaned inside the storage well and unplugged a latch either side of the tail panel. He let the flap down and beckoned to the other two. They shuffled forward with the rug, the first guy dropping his end down on the tail flap, Dara following suit. The rug was bound with a ring of thick adhesive tape at either end, another securing the middle. They dug their hands underneath and rolled it over until it came to rest in the centre of the storage well.

Roig went to take a step closer, the idiotic grin fixed firm on his face. The driver turned sharply; held up the palm of one hand as though stopping traffic. He turned back to the kid.

'Is that right? He's the pool guy?'

'Telling you, Hassan, lad – I don't know him . . .'

A minimal nod of comprehension from Hassan. He jumped back inside the Jeep and revved the engine wildly, sending the wheels spinning into a frenetic three-point turn as he whipped the Jeep round and drove directly at Roig. He didn't have a chance to run.

Mac was brought round by a passionate screaming from outside. He forced his aching head up. The door was still wide open. He laid his head back down on the cool, terracotta tile. A slap. The engine outside, revving. More voices, then footsteps running towards the house, more shouting, a fight on the doorstep. He saw feet and knees, grappling for position; Hassan fighting with the other Arab, his hands squeezing his wrists, trying to turn the gun on him. The other Arab kid was being forced backwards, desperately struggling to point the gun away. He lost his balance and fell into the lobby. He turned, and stared directly into McCartney's eyes. The gun was in the kid's hand. For the first time in a long time, Mac was scared witless; he was petrified. He closed his eyes and began to anticipate the bullet. What would he feel? Anything? How long would it take to die? This was no more than McCartney deserved; for Millie, for everything, he had this coming to him.

There was shrieking, demented crying. Moments later, a thunderous blast – so loud that its crazed reverb was still, now, echoing in his ears. McCartney didn't black out. He didn't feel the evil sear of a bullet crashing through his skull. He heard a desolate wailing; shouting from outside the house; the skid of frantic footsteps and the wrench of the gears and the Jeep's engine, the crunchy skid of the tyres on gravel. More shouting, footsteps running, fast – then the engine faded off into the distance until there was nothing.

He left it another minute or two before he dragged himself up. Lying face down in the sticky-dark pool of blood that leaked steadily from beneath him was the younger Arab. Most of his long chin was missing. The instrument of his death lay beside him. A Glock pistol with an elongated barrel. There was a faint moaning from outside. He felt the pain in his ribs, in his chest, as he limped outside. Roig was wincing in agony, his dark face drained as he tried to sit up. Mac hobbled over to him, tried to lie him back down.

'No. I am OK. No fracture . . .'

McCartney checked him over, felt his pulse, looked into his eyes. Roig grinned. 'I made a good play of the dead.'

'Me too.'

Mac locked his arms around his chest, bit down on his own pain and gripped him under the armpits, helping him up. They stumbled to the front door, into the house, skirting the body in the hall. Roig pointed at the pistol and began to speak, but his words were slurred.

Mac laid him down and took his pulse again. He went to the kitchen, poured a glass of water, made Roig take small sips. He was badly shaken, but not badly hurt. He tried to sit up. Mac got some cushions behind his head. He began to tell Mac what had happened. The Jeep had just appeared out of nowhere. The driver rammed him, sent him flying. Roig had played dead. Felt the guy's shadow standing over him – then another voice started shouting at him in Arabic. There was this huge, screaming argument. He couldn't understand, couldn't see much of it, but the two brothers were right in each other's faces, shrieking at each other. The older one punched the one with the chin and tried to drag him into the Jeep.

'They were arguing over Millie. Hassan killed Millie . . .'

Roig nodded, as though everything now made sense. 'One brother, he ran back to house. But I only see this far. Very soon after this, there comes the noise. The gun. Then drive away the Jeep truck . . .'

Once Roig was able to hold the glass, McCartney left him propped up. He checked, although he already knew, that the kid was dead, and stood over his strangely serene body, hunched in a tragic foetus position. Much of his face and skull had gone – he'd been shot, he was certain, at close range – with the same kind of expanding bullet that had done for the Prince. He looked around for the shell, tried to estimate the trajectory. There was a small crater in the wall behind. He didn't want to tread in the mess of blood, brain and bone, but he could see shrapnel, and a good piece of the bullet. A 9mm, it looked like – the longer, Parabellum bullet with a groove right down the middle. Serious ballistics. Someone meant business. He shouted through to Roig.

'Soon as you're ready, sir, you're going to have to call in the Guardia. Get them up here. Set up some roadblocks. Put the ferries and airports on special alert. Those bastards have got Millie's body there.'

Roig appeared in the doorway. 'I will speak to them now.'

He went to the phone. McCartney stood by the door they'd emerged from, at the bottom of the stairs. No wonder he'd thought he'd heard noises and voices from behind that wall – there was a secret, spring-action portal leading down to a spacious basement. He clenched his fists and took the first stair, hesitated, then descended into the floodlit cellar. The first thing he saw, leaning against the wall, was a movie-style camera – bigger and bulkier than McCartney had envisaged. Below it were cans of film. He shuddered and, his eyes now better accustomed to the light, went over to a stack of wooden fishing crates. He grappled the top crate down to the floor and got its lid off. It was packed with pressed, shrink-wrapped, bars of waxy grey hash. Mac cast his eyes all around the room. Away in the corner there were other crates, plastic storage boxes with air-seal lids. He made his way over there, prised the first lid off with ease; bars of a different constituency, different hue. He took out a puck, crumbled a corner, dabbed it on his tongue. Cocaine. Reasonable purity. He opened up more and more storage crates. There was amphetamine, there were mixing agents, there was one crate that held only bags – thousands and thousands of tiny, plastic snap bags. And there, under the stairwell, were the tablets; the same tablets he'd be taking delivery of later this evening; the tablets that had, already, killed four kids. He scooped up a handful and let them sprinkle back down through his fingers like hundreds and thousands until there was just one pill left in his palm. He felt like crying. The things men did . . .

He rested his forehead on the cold plaster wall; composed

himself. Mac had blundered here. Almost from the moment they'd arrived on the island, McCartney had played this badly. He could afford no more gambles; no risks. He climbed back up from the basement to get Roig.

The souped-up military vehicle came out of the side road so fast, Molina had to swerve to avoid being shunted into the ditch. Hassan was driving, a wild, scared look in his eye. He didn't even see Molina, just veered onto the main road, tyres screeching, and, once he'd regained control of the Jeep, tore off down the hill.

Molina had to make his mind up – quickly. He'd gone as far as he was ever going to go with these animals – he'd already gone way further than was ever, *ever* mentioned in their original conversations. He knew it was the end, for him. All he wanted, now, was to claw some pride back; try and put right some of the many things he'd done wrong. He wanted the El Glaoui brothers. He wanted John-John Hamilton. He wanted them all off the island, locked up, left to rot in their own rotten countries. But he wanted the drugs, too; he wanted the guns. He wanted the cash and the watches and the rest of their ill-gotten gains. He wanted to call up his bosses, call up the media and tell them all, tell them proudly: 'Come and see this. I know I am finished but, please – come up here and see what I've got for you . . .'

He turned the car round and followed the Jeep at a distance. Without indicating, it screeched to a halt next to a row of overflowing bins. Hassan El Glaoui stepped out and began shouting into the back of the vehicle. Molina pulled over to observe. Clearly unhappy at the turn of events, Hamilton's young foot soldier, the Turk, got out, pointing and shouting at Hassan. Molina radioed in. He gave a description of the young Rozaki kid – they had his records there, anyway. It looked as though they were going to fight, then the Arab jumped back into the driver's seat and drove off at speed, sending a huge cloud of white dust all over Rozaki, all over the bins. Molina told the patrol car where to pick the kid up and went after El Glaoui's Jeep.

Roig surveyed the still life in the cellar before returning his gaze to McCartney. His coal-black eyes appraised him, as though trying to ascertain how much more he could take.

'We don't have a choice, now . . .'

'No.'

'Molina is out of the question. For sure?'

'Yes. He's theirs. I saw him . . .'

Roig closed his eyes and began gently shaking his head. 'The best, I think, is that you continue with the plan. Yes? Go to the club. Meet with Nolan, and go ahead as you agreed, everything nice and normal –'

'Nolan? *Normal?!* Sir, the kid will have already tipped them off! Normal . . .'

Roig smiled with his eyes. 'The Policia Local, they have the kid . . .'

McCartney's heart lurched. 'They do? What about the Arabs! Have they got the body?'

Roig had been shaking his head, eyes closed, even before Mac asked the question.

'Only the boy. They picked him up on a country road. We will question him, but I think the best is that we continue with the plan, no? There is Hamilton, there is Nolan, there is Davey Lane, all there under one roof . . .'

'There is about 100 million pesetas' worth of drugs right there, now! How much more evidence do you need?'

'Mac. Have the evidence, yes – but don't have the persons . . .'

'They're down at Pike's, *right now*! All of them . . .'

'Maybe. Maybe not. But why take a risk? Why alert Hamilton? Mmm? I am not, how-say . . .' He tilted his head back and looked at the ceiling. 'Roig is not new in this job. Is not *verde*. I have put much thought into this plan, and the best is to get *all* criminal in one place. Yes?'

McCartney turned away from him and sat down on the bottom step, trying to stem the tears. He realised he didn't care what happened. He was responsible for Millie; nothing else mattered. Let Roig have his moment of glory. He spoke in deathly monotone.

'I suppose you're right. We really don't have any choice . . .' He left it a beat, then lifted his face to Roig. 'I'll meet them as planned, then.'

Very, very quietly, Davey Lane returned to his room. He held his finger to his lip and waited for the front door to close downstairs. He listened for their footsteps on the gravel. Cops. So? He paid the Brazilian and began packing. That docile old thug Nolan could swing for it as far as he was concerned; he was better off dead. John-John Hamilton, though – he was a different beast entirely. There were years and years of business left in JJ. Somehow he'd have to warn him.

They sat in the little anteroom, Roig showing him how to bundle and wrap each pack of cash; little stacks of high-denomination banknotes providing the bread in each sandwich, fat pats of toy money making up the filling. Each wad was poly-wrapped in stacks of 100,000 pesetas, made up of 50 x 2,000-peseta notes. This was a gamble. As Mac intuited and Roig confirmed, most banks would dispense a cash transaction of that magnitude in either 10,000- or 5,000-peseta notes. But the silver-grey 10,000 and the copper-brown 5,000 were distinctive, difficult to forge, and even making up 8.5 million pesetas, as they were now, would have required less than one hundred of the sleek 10,000-peseta banknotes; far too easy and way too tempting for Nolan to count the lot. If they went the other way and did the whole lot in 1,000-peseta notes it would piss him off no end and, no doubt, invite his suspicion and further scrutiny. The 2,000-peseta notes were a gamble but they looked good, no doubt about it; good enough to pass a cursory flick-through in a nightclub or a car park, even an emptying out of the bag. The trick was to leave out one or two perfectly legitimate wads which Mac could break open for Nolan's inspection. The gamble was that he was so greedy, so lazy and so grossly underestimated Martindale that he'd take the whole bagful on trust, without too much fuss. So long as Martindale rolled his eyes and blamed the bank for all the notes; sold Nolan a story about how long they'd kept him waiting, the implication being that he was victimised as a Brit, then there was a good chance that Nolan would buy it. It was risky, nonetheless. From now on in, it was all a risk.

The kid wasn't happy at being thrown out on the San An road; swore that his boss would do this to them, do that. But John-John Hamilton was a businessman. He would understand.

There was no way of contacting either boat now – he'd have to maintain absolute radio silence – but Hassan knew the Guardia Civil would be out soon, looking for him. He'd killed a cop back there. Yousef, too, lay dead – the fool. And Ali – with Ali there was no choice. Father would comprehend – he was, after all, following his own precious principles.

He would have ditched the vehicle, but one thing his father would *not* comprehend would be his arriving back in the Rif without a prize for him. At his time of life, it was the thing that gave him greatest pleasure – Yousef should have understood this better than anyone. He detoured towards Ibiza Town just in case, then doubled back through the lanes and side tracks, across country and down to Cap Martinet. As he rounded the spur, he could see the boat below. Nabil had brought it in as close to the little wharf as possible, but they'd still have their work cut out. He'd trust Nabil with his life. He knew he wouldn't pry. They'd get the *Alharam* loaded then he'd head up the coast, prep the cruiser and make sure the canary was nice and relaxed for the crossing. Given any choice in the matter, he would always sail with Nabil. Ever since he'd taken over the transportation side from his father, though, Hassan had always travelled independent of their cargo. It cost a little more, but you could never be too careful. This time, his insurance policy would pay out. The Jeep bounced down the rocky track sending clouds of dirt and dust in its trail. Up on the cliff above, the little Seat pulled over. Molina decided he'd do the rest of this on foot.

For John-John Hamilton, it felt like the end of the world. He hadn't even had a chance to go back for his suits, let alone the cash, the drugs, the trappings. He'd had to apologise to Davey – he nearly punched him. There he was, stood at the poolside bar at Pike's, trying to decide which of these Dutch girls he'd lie down with first. There was Sylvie, the actress – so she said – elegant in heels and sarong, and her friend Marta, quiet, dark-haired, intense green eyes that never left him. JJ knew the score. They'd chat. He was a good-looking guy and he'd stand a chance, whatever; but once they knew he had beak, once they twigged at how everyone deferred to him, once they saw he was the real deal, there'd be nothing they wouldn't do for him. He was running the possibilities through his mind when the Irish loon came striding over the terrace, grabbed him by the arm and said: 'Say fuck all. I mean it. It's over. Walk with me. Now.'

He'd pulled himself clear, laughing it off, apologising to the ladies but thinking he'd have to chin Davey if he did it again. He grinned at him.

'It's over?! What's over? Fuck you on about, lad?!'

Davey stood back, his lip quivering. 'It's up to you. I have a small Cessna arriving in precisely thirty minutes.'

Something in his eye got to JJ, this time. This wasn't just Davey being Davey. He was frightened here – and he had never, ever seen Davey Lane scared. Whatever he was trying to tell him, it was all too real. He looked Hamilton in the eye for a beat longer, then turned on his heel like a Gestapo captain and strode away. John-John Hamilton turned to Marta and Sylvie, still not entirely sure he could tear himself away from them.

'Will you excuse me for a moment, ladies?'

Sylvie's eyes sparkled with mischief and amusement. 'Don't take too long, sweetie,' she said in her deep, American-inflected voice. 'Maybe bring your boyfriend back,' she teased. 'You know how we are on holiday, darling. Anything goes . . .'

Hamilton straightened his back, only now accepting that this was an offer he'd have to refuse. He followed Davey, intuitively resigned, already, to a deep misgiving that it would be some time before he lived like this again.

Mac had got there too early. There was no sign of Frankie Nolan or any of the others. Apart from a little knot of British kids already E'd up, dancing to 808 State, the club was pretty empty. There was a huge sunken dance floor surrounded by balconies, podiums and viewing decks, the whole place seemingly held up by vast white Doric columns. More clubbers arrived; happy, jumpy, ready for good times. The music seemed to get louder. The Shamen, 'Move Any Mountain'. The dance floor began to fill. He took a gentle stroll, hands behind his back, swaying lightly as he walked, nodding his head to the beat. Still no sign of Nolan.

The Boca Juniors track came on and the crowd lit up. The dancing was unhinged now – clubbers able to abandon themselves as the numbers swelled and the pills kicked in. Mac went to get a drink but the bars were packed, too. He toured the ground floor, sussed out the emergency exits, checked which one led back to the car park where the Shogun – and the money – was waiting. He felt conspicuous, circling the dance floor, trying to look relaxed. He could queue up, get a drink and while the time away on the balcony, but he just couldn't settle. This didn't feel right. The track segued into the Orb's 'Little Fluffy Clouds', sending the Brits into raptures. Mac went up to a bay on the far side of the club and watched, and waited.

Nolan spotted the Southampton mug straight away. Shitting himself, trying to look cool, wringing his hands and licking his lips as he leaned over the railings up there. He amused himself for a while, watching the aspiring gangster take surreptitious glances around and about, heart thumping, no doubt, hope beginning to drain away as he waited for the Man. Ha! Frankie Nolan was not the Man, but Hamilton had thrown him a double earner here, if he but knew it. He didn't need JJ's permission, but he knew what he was like. No way would he have gone with this if he knew what Frankie had planned. He'd get the mug outside. Make sure he'd brought the readies. Drive him down to where the pills weren't, and away we go. Boom-boom-boom, thank you and goodnight.

Just as the foam started oozing onto the dance floor, Mac spotted Frankie Nolan in a bright green shirt down below.

What was the natural thing to do here? Should he wave? Nod? What would the Saint do? Today's turn of events had battered his confidence. He'd struggle to carry off Martindale's blithe super-cheeriness – except Martindale would probably be tense here, too. He headed down the nearest flight of steps. The foam was already up to clubbers' waists, gushing down from the sides and up above. The kids were loving it, squeals of merriment clashing with the sinuous build of the Grid's 'Flotation'. A little knot of long-haired boys in white Levi's dominated the middle of the dance floor, scooping up the foam and gyrating their upper bodies, feet rooted to the spot. Mac could barely see a yard ahead now. Trying to keep Nolan's shirt in sight, he set about skirting the dance floor. Girls in sequins were being lowered from the roof, pirouetting in a mannered yet theatrical mime routine as the wires brought them down. Dancers held their hands out wide as though celebrating a descending goddess, and Mac could not help stopping and watching for a second. When he looked back again, Nolan had gone.

A girl tugged McCartney by the wrist, tried to ingratiate him into a foam-fight with a group of revellers. He resisted, tried to smile his way out of it. He got free, but her arms were around the back of his neck now, her tongue in his mouth. He wrenched his head away, caught sight of Nolan's hideous lime shirt heading for the exit. The absurdity of it – Mac realised that he didn't want to appear rude by shrugging the girl off too brusquely – then, suddenly, none of it mattered. A shot rang out. The scene seemed to freeze – a video on pause – then Nolan came running back inside the club. Screaming, people running for cover. Another shot. Frankie Nolan running through the foam, his face in shock – running right towards McCartney. He processed it in a microsecond.

'Frankie. Quick . . .'

All Frankie Nolan knew was that this Southampton no-mark was leading him out of a side exit, and he was his only hope. Moz, the Scouse kid, had walked in there, hyper but still fully alert, businesslike. He'd told him, quickly, coldly, what he needed to know. They'd been busted. The Guardia Civil were swarming all over the glass house, all over the island. They had to get out, lie low, then plan their flight. They had to move fast. Now. He was a good kid, that Moz. He'd go all the way. It was stupid, but Frankie Nolan, a veteran, felt safe with this kid. He didn't think twice – he followed him out of the club. But the robocops already had the club surrounded. Searchlights in their eyes, guns pointed at them, some nonce with a loudhailer screaming at them to get on the floor. Some fucking chance! The moment they ran, the bullets started flying.

'Here . . .'

Martindale threw open a car door, pushed him into the back seat, ran round to the driver's side. He sat there, undecided. His eyes were flashing, frightened. He seemed to take a few deep breaths, then make his mind up and start the engine. He edged the car out round the front. There was a roadblock; police cars with flashing lights. Checkpoints policed by armed guards.

'Fuck do we do now then, Saint?'

Martindale craned his neck back over the headrest. 'Get right down on the floor. Face down. And lie there, dead still, until we're out of here.'

'They ain't gonna let us just fucking well drive out!'

'Lie still.'

Martindale took the car out front; but it was McCartney who spotted Juan Sebastien Roig. Flashed the headlights at him once, twice, three times. Allowed himself and Frankie

Nolan to be pulled over and searched. Roig found a serrated dagger concealed in the sheath sewn into Nolan's jeans. Triumphantly, he hauled Martindale out of the car and allowed Nolan to see the holdall, stuffed with cash. Martindale shrugged at Nolan as they were both arrested and driven away.

Shit! He was on his way back. Where was the cavalry? Molina had called for backup immediately El Glaoui sent his signal. He'd parked up, flashed his torch once, twice, three, four, five times – then action. The little dinghy came chugging ashore. Molina had watched Hassan and the old boy struggling to haul the rolled-up rug into the dinghy, then they'd set off back to the old fishing boat, moored out in the bay. He couldn't see too clearly as they dragged the rug from the wobbling dinghy, up onto the deck. But he'd been in the job long enough – it was dead weight. He knew a body when he saw one. Where were they? The coast patrol and the Guardia Civil should be here by now, making arrests – but El Glaoui jumped back in the dinghy and began speeding back towards the wharf.

Molina crept away from his hide and began to scramble up the scree. His hands and feet dislodged loose rocks, sending them tumbling down the slope. Fuck! Hassan would be back ashore in no time, into that Jeep and away into the night. Molina's Seat was parked on the headland above. He began to jog back up the steep track, but realised he would never make it. The bastard was going to get away.

Jamal Benarbia knew these waters well. Many a time had he made the crossing from Tangier, Oran, Algiers. They'd crossed to Tarifa and Cadiz; to Cartagena and Almeria. They'd entered Spain and France from all sides, through all ports, depending on circumstances – and circumstances, always, dictated every-thing. But he knew this stretch of the southern Mediterranean best and, this time, Jamal would come in through Algeciras. A rest, some time to think, to pray, then, with a fair wind and the love of Allah, he would hit their rock with all the might of his Umayyad forefathers. The Rock of Gibraltar would, once more, be the holy Jabal Tariq.

Frankie Nolan started laughing, and before he stopped, he was crying with mirth. He'd steadfastly sat there, face set in an insouciant smile as the cop who looked like the older Noodles tried to break him down.

He hadn't said a word. The cop tried to tell him the Scousers had set him up; lured him out of Es Paradis so they could hit him and shut him up. Shut him up for what? Bringing the Guardia down on the gaff? Behave! John-John knew Frankie; he'd die before he ever breathed a word to the Old Bill about anything. Ever. All the same, though, it was getting to him; the idea that that younger firm, those oh-so-quiet Rozaki boys, might have tried to have him off. They were New School, those lads – that generation that come here from war zones or revolutions; kids who'd seen it all before their voices broke. Kurds, Kosovans, Somalis, you could see it in their eyes – they'd stop at nothing. And, as De Niro pointed out, where *was* he? The rat had got away.

'Where is Benarbia based?'

Frankie shrugged. They could ask him that one all day. He genuinely did not have a clue.

'Never heard of him.'

'We keep you here. When bomb goes off, when hundreds, thousands they die . . . we charge *you*, yes? Accessory to murder . . .'

He shrugged again.

There was a knock at the door. De Niro sighed.

'*Sí!*' he barked.

Moments later, the Saint strolled in – the Southampton drug monster, bold as brass – and Frankie Nolan laughed and laughed with all his heart, until the tears flowed.

'Oh my days! You cunts really are worse than the villains, ain't you?'

McCartney bowed and smiled, and turned to Roig. He beckoned him outside. Roig followed.

'A certain Señor Molina requests our company.'

Seeing them as they descended the staircase, Molina stood up, head bowed. Roig marched straight across and, gritting his teeth, jabbed his finger into Molina's chest.

'Arrest this fucking bastard!'

Molina took a step back. 'OK. Arrest me. I accept. But there is El Glaoui with the boat . . .'

McCartney stepped between them. 'What boat? Where?'

'Come. I will take us there –'

Roig gave him a sharp, backhanded slap. 'Murderers don't tell us what to do!'

Molina held his hand to his face, stung, confused. '*Murder? Me?*'

'Do you deny that you shot Ali El Glaoui?'

'Ali? No. I deny! Of course I deny!'

'What about his brother, Yousef? Were you there?'

'NO! It was me who called this in –'

'Really? So you deny any involvement, even though the bullet that killed both brothers comes from the very *specific* gun –'

'That *all* police can use! You, with respect, *jefe* – *you* can take this gun . . .' Molina dropped his head and took a step back. 'My boss tells me that Yousef killed himself –'

'Suicide?'

McCartney thought back to the struggle on the step. He

135

was groggy; he hadn't seen clearly – but this made sense. Hassan could plausibly have been trying to wrest the gun out of Yousef's hands.

'*Sí*. Suicide.'

He mimed a kneeling stance, put an imaginary gun to his mouth. Mac tried to blot the image out of his mind. Roig gave Molina's shoulder a conciliatory squeeze.

'I'm sorry, Rodolfo . . .'

Molina bowed his head.

'What about John-John Hamilton?' asked Mac. Molina shook his head and made the *pffft!* vanishing sound. 'No sign of him?' More grave head-shaking.

'He is gone. Nothing . . .'

'Didn't they manage to pick up *anyone?*' McCartney could hear the desperation in his own voice. Molina shrugged and shook his head again.

'Only the Maroc. The dead. I see Hassan El Glaoui driving very crazy. OK, is necessary pursue. I call for car, apprehend the Turk. Rozaki, yes?' Mac and Roig both nodded. 'OK. Then telephone my boss, speak of Hamilton . . .'

'What else did he tell you?'

'Everything. He tell me who is Billy McCartney. Why arrive in Ibiza . . . He tell me the most important now is Hassan El Glaoui . . .' He made the *et voilà* gesture. 'But is necessary be quick. Let us hope . . .'

On the short drive from Port Ibiza, Molina explained as much as he could. How he'd started to take small bribes to look the other way for the English gangs. How Ibiza had always had a culture of hedonism, and how he squared things off with himself. It was part of the equilibrium on the island; it was almost expected. And it worked; they'd never had deaths on his watch. There had never been murders. The Brits had always been wild and, since Ecstasy, since acid house, they'd been harder to control, but still he felt the balance of power worked. The gangsters and the club owners knew how far they could go. But this latest lot – John-John Hamilton and friends – they were indiscriminate. They asked for more and more; more favours. More compromise. They were making life difficult for everybody.

The other day, Hamilton had asked him to arrest Ali El Glaoui; just lock him up for twenty-four hours, wave a gun at him but tell him nothing, put the frighteners on him. Hamilton had said the kid had tried to cheat him; he owed him big money. Molina didn't like JJ Hamilton, but he could say for sure that he wasn't a liar. He would always pay – sometimes more than they'd agreed. Molina admitted that he'd been only too happy to comply with the gun request. He liked guns – perhaps a little too much. He'd had his own licence revoked for using Guardia firearms on weekend hunting trips to the mountains.

But by the time Molina had got down to the boat Hamilton had directed him to, the kid had had his head blown off. It was sickening. He'd sworn to himself, on his way back, that that would be the last time. But Hamilton had blackmailed him over the gun. He'd coerced Molina to seize the kid's corpse, and this time it really had been too much. He had done it. He had delivered the body to Pike's car park. And, after that, he'd told himself he would rather rot in jail than carry on as the dogsbody for an English criminal. He knew he was going to lose his job, but he was desperate to help bring Hamilton down. The police car inched down the *passeo* and pulled up next to Cap Martinet's little landing stage. There was nothing to be seen. The bay was deserted.

'It was right there . . .' Molina began to stutter. Roig held up a hand for quiet as his walkie-talkie crackled. He tuned in and listened and made three curt remarks; questions. He nodded, disconnected and turned to the others.

'The vessel, it is not so far ahead. We can gain . . .'

He strode briskly to a tall, thin officer and conversed in quick, animated bursts. The tall guy nodded and sprinted off towards a military-looking vehicle.

'What now?' hissed McCartney.

'We wait,' whispered Molina.

The auxiliary team signalled to let them know the dinghies were in place. They filed down to the rough concrete tide-breaker and joined the coastguard and the team of arresting officers. Last on board were four figures in diving outfits. Mac went dizzy. What exactly were they expecting here?

'OK?' asked Roig.

McCartney nodded, his face drained of colour; his oesophagus constricted.

'OK,' he said. But it came out in his old voice, a timid squeak.

The inflatables skidded out across the surface of the silver sea, bouncing up, time seemingly suspended before they would crash down again. In spite of his nauseous dread, Mac was exhilarated by the sleek pursuit. On the far horizon, the silhouette of the *Alharam* chugged for the high seas, ignorant, for now, of the chasing posse. At this rate, they'd catch them up within the hour – but there could be no element of surprise now. The wildly revving outboard motors would alert Hassan and his crew, perhaps giving them a chance to hurl evidence overboard. Now he understood the need for divers . . .

As they closed in, seemingly without any order or signal, the engines went off, one at a time, and officers took up oars and rowed the fleet of dinghies right up to the *Alharam*'s weathered hull. Roig was first to stand up, steadying and readying himself. He hesitated; caught McCartney's eye.

'You sure you are OK, Mr Mac?'

McCartney was far from being OK. He was dreading this; finding Millie, whatever remained of her. He knew it was his fault. He ran over it all, again and again and again . . . the night she hadn't come back to the villa. He should have acted then; immediately his guts told him something wasn't right. Roig, too, should have forced him to act – but they both knew better, didn't they? Roig was standing back now, instinctively aware that McCartney would want to get up there and get this done. Mac winced and nodded his thanks. He secured his standing foot on a thick rope buffer, stretched up to grab the handrail and hauled himself up. Roig, Molina and the elite arresting team did likewise. Mac steeled himself. His guts were in turmoil here. He retched, held it back. Retched again, pictured Millie, violated. Dead. He couldn't do it. He stood aside; waved Roig past. Roig nodded his understanding; signalled for silence – then kicked in the cabin door.

'POLICE!! POLICE!! POLICE!! DOWN! DOWN! DOWN!'

He dived inside the cabin with his pistol out, supporting his right wrist with his left hand, turning left, right, left, right, expecting Hassan El Glaoui to burst out, all guns blazing. There was no one there. He instructed one of his men to cut the engine. Three steps led down to a little galley. He stood on the first step.

'UP HERE! NOW! THROW YOUR WEAPONS OUT FIRST!'

There was silence; then a snuffling, whimpering sound.

'COME OUT!'

A terrified face appeared at the bottom of the steps. An old man with a silver-white crew cut slowly came into view, his hands held up above his head. Tears ran down his leathery, unshaven face. Roig leaned down, grabbed him by the scruff of the neck and dragged him up into the cabin. He lay on the floor, arms stretched out, too frightened to speak.

'WHERE IS HASSAN? WHERE IS EL GLAOUI?'

He let out one long, dismal whimper. Roig kicked him in the side. McCartney held his breath and went down the three steps, poked his head inside the little galley. It was deserted. Mac crouched down next to the old man; supported his head.

'Are you alone?'

The man looked at him, his eyes wild with fear, and began shaking his head. He stuttered some words, still shaking his head.

'Anyone speak, what? Moroccan?'

Molina nodded. 'The boat is from Morocco . . .'

One of the frogmen pulled down his mask and raised his hand. 'I can speak. Sure.'

McCartney waved him over. 'Ask him what he has on board. Thanks.'

The frogman asked him. The fisherman began to stand up, his hands clasped tight in pleading. He grabbed onto McCartney's arm, buried his head in his sleeve and began gesticulating and jabbering and crying all at once. Roig stepped over, drew back his hand to slap him. McCartney stood in his way.

'Please, sir. No. The man is terrified . . .'

Roig turned away, irate. 'Don't be fooled . . .'

Mac smiled at the old fisherman, addressing the interpreter. 'Can he take us below, please? Show us his cargo . . .'

The man digested the message, bowed his head and bid them follow him. He fished some keys off a nail, flipped and jiggled them, one at a time, rotating them around a rust-brown iron ring until he isolated one small, modern key. He walked them to the stern of the fishing vessel, slotted the key into a new brass padlock and opened a stout wooden door. There were steps – more of a wide ladder with slats – leading down into the hold. McCartney picked up a flashlight and turned so he was facing Roig as he backed into the alcove and began his climb down the ladder. Roig covered him with his Glock. McCartney eyed the handgun's long barrel.

The old fisherman struck up another ceaseless monologue, tugging at the frogman. This time Roig slapped him, hard, with the back of his hand.

'Tell him to shut up!'

'It might be important, sir. Something about the brothers . . .'

Roig scowled; made a beckoning signal with his three middle fingers to tell the old captain to speak up. He was calmer now. He looked up at the frogman and spoke directly to him.

'What is he saying?'

'He's saying that Hassan came some hours ago in a black military vehicle, like you see in the war films. *Desert Rat*. He came ashore to help him. Brought the tapestry on board; stowed it down below. Then he said it was bad luck for him to travel with this cargo. He ordered the captain to set sail . . .'

Mac saw the rolled-up rug straight away, three deep magenta stains soaking through like horrific stigmata. He knelt down and pressed his thumbs along the rug's bulk, every six inches or so, feeling out its contents. There was no room for any kind of doubt. There was a body wrapped up inside. Sickened, forlorn, utterly without any escape now, McCartney got up and staggered to the bottom of the ladder.

'Going to need lights down here, Molina,' he shouted up. 'And you're going to need your scene-of-crime team . . .' He paused, tried to conquer his grief. 'Sir. Inspector Roig. You should probably come down, too . . .'

Roig appeared immediately, followed by Molina. The team rigged jump leads to the boat's battery and ran a cable down into the bowels of the boat, flooding it with pristine white light. There were various crates; one or two zip-up bags. And right in the centre of the hold was the rug. Millie. McCartney could feel his lip starting to tremble out of control. He pressed both hands to his eyeballs, his temples. He forced down big hard gulps of stagnant air. Roig stepped forward; produced a Swiss army knife; knelt. He began to gently cut at the adhesive tape, the blade slicing through it with ease. The first binding was cut; the rug peeled partially open. He went down the other end, prolonging the agony; cut the tape. The other end unfurled. There was just the middle section to cut through, then Roig could roll the rug open. At that point, this stage of McCartney's life would be over, and a new phase – Post Millie – would commence.

Roig looked puzzled. He glanced at McCartney. Mac was too far gone to follow his eyeline to the shoes now sticking out from the bottom of the rug. He quickly knelt back to his task, methodically cutting through the last hoop of tape, flicking the blade back and slipping the knife into his pocket. Ceremonially, he spat on his fingertips and set about rolling the rug open; rolling the body out. McCartney looked down at the corpse and choked on his uprising vomit. Staring up at him with one wild eye, with half his head missing, was Ali El Glaoui.

Millie woke to find the dark guy smiling down on her, stroking her hair. Whatever he was saying to her, it was soothing – like an incantation. Seeing her open her eyes, his face broke into a besotted smile.

'See? You are beautiful! All this trouble . . . for me it is worth every pain.'

She didn't want to ask him what trouble; what pain. She neither wanted to engage nor provoke him. If she were merely polite, pleasant, it might buy time enough for her to make a plan. She smiled back.

'Thank you,' she croaked. 'Water?'

He nodded, padded away and returned with a plastic beaker. He watched intently as she sipped at it.

'Ah, peace, finally . . .' he sighed. He gazed up at the clouds in the sky and spoke dreamily. 'Two brothers, now in heaven . . .' His eyes glistened. 'One, he loves you very much. You remember my brother, Yousef? He cries for you, but I tell him he cannot have . . .'

'Thank you.'

He looked puzzled for a moment, but continued in his sleepy voice, smiling as he spoke as though about to tell her, any second, that this was all a big joke. But then his eyes went deadly.

'The other brother . . .' He was staring at her now, suddenly angered. 'Very stupid boy, Ali! My father and I, we give him everything. Give Ali all the whole world, but he doesn't want any of this. Only want to bring trouble for the family. So I have to think business, yes?' She nodded. 'I have to think family . . .' He was smiling again now. The drifting lilt returned to his voice. 'I am the oldest son. Of course – I have to take care of business . . .'

'Yes. Business is business . . .' Mille whispered. It worked. His face rippled with something akin to a release; or relief.

'Yes!' The spark was back in his eyes. 'Business is business. Always . . .'

143

She smiled back. 'May I have some more water?'

'Yes. Of course. Hello. I am Hassan. Apologies for my . . . my *talk*. It is not usual for me, this. But I am sad. Three days ago I had to go to a place, a boat, where was waiting my baby brother, Ali. I called his name. He turned to me, and smiled . . .'

Hassan, too, smiled now – a sad, melting smile. He knelt down and kissed her on the forehead; took her beaker from her and went to refill it. She got to her feet, unsteady, her legs feeling numb, disconnected. Seeing a railing ahead, she allowed herself to fall forward, grabbing it as she fell. She pulled herself upright and stared out at a flat and never-ending nothingness. There was the void she had willed upon herself. She was at sea. All around her was water; no land in sight. And with that desolate realisation, all hope leaked away. For the second time in two days, she thought of the search for her poor sister. How eaten up with jealousy she had been! Even when she wasn't there, Jenny was getting all the attention. Not now. Now they'd all be talking about Millie.

'Is beautiful, no?'

She turned round and Hassan was back, drink in hand. None of this felt real. She stared into Hassan's innocent brown eyes and burst into tears.

Shanley sat right back, his shoulders hunched tight, and slowly let out one prolonged, disconsolate sigh; relieved it was over as much as he was horrified – no, heartbroken – by its contents. He sat like that for a moment, still shocked, appalled but, gradually, realising that he had been holding himself tense, barely breathing. He was one of those hoary old coppers who liked to think he was unshockable. He'd seen it all, over the years; mutilation; molestation; depravity and evil in its basest incarnations. This, however – this mercifully short, hatefully stark and clinical film they'd seized – had left Ken Shanley reeling. Not just because its subject – its object – was someone he knew, had known, had encouraged and nagged and pushed to fulfil her potential. And it wasn't the bald fact of a line of faceless males quietly waiting their turn to abuse her supine form in ways too sick to comprehend. The thing that sucked the air from Shanley's lungs, popped his eyes and stopped him breathing when he saw it, was the casual way that Nolan had stabbed her as she lay there – simply drew his hand back and jabbed her while the camera ran and his fellow rapists chatted quietly, none of them even pausing to acknowledge her death. She simply passed away, right in front of them.

A chink of light, just as quickly snuffed as the operator entered the screening room.

'Do you need me to run that again, sir?'

He could hear it in his voice; please, no. No. Not again.

Shanley dwelt on it. He could not let McCartney witness this. The operation had near cleaned him out as things stood. He'd come back broken; defeated. In many ways he'd done well. He'd got a result. But in the way they both held dear – the bottom line – McCartney knew he had failed. The bottom line was that Shanley had given him seniority. He'd told him he was ready. He'd entrusted Millie Baker's well-being to McCartney, her senior. Mac was already all too well aware he had failed that trust. What good would it do, now, to let him see how badly? The girl was dead. He didn't need to know the gruesome details. Shanley half turned towards the tape op.

'No. Thank you. That's all for today . . .'

He nodded, hesitated for a beat, then left. Shanley pushed himself up out of the low-slung seat and padded towards the door. He'd better call McCartney as soon as viable and get his report in so they could shut the lid on this sorry case and move on. Not that they would ever be able to leave this tragedy behind.

As was his custom when meeting Kenneth Shanley at his place of work, McCartney swerved left at the latest possible moment, lest he were being followed. Not that he'd notice, or care, if he were being followed. He parked the XR2 and stood for a moment in the cool of the shadows. It had been the briefest of calls from Bunty Soames, asking Mac to come in; he knew what was coming. He knew that only bad things lay ahead.

Shanley had had his report for ten days now. It didn't make for very good reading: Hamilton – escaped. Lane – escaped. Jamal Benarbia had been picked up off the coast of Gibraltar – Jabal Tariq, in Arabic – but all Special Branch had found on him was some guar gum. They hadn't even been able to get him for the theft of the boat – the owner, one David Patrick Lane, known to police, was not pressing charges.

There were plus points, though it seemed to count for little as he wrote them up. The poisoned Ecstasy tablets manufactured by Ali El Glaoui in his one-man strike against Western hedonism had all been seized and destroyed. His victim, Abi Macmillan, recovered in time to attend her brother's funeral.

And they'd got Francis Nolan – the pornographer, the maker of snuff movies, the sickest of the sick. He'd spent three-quarters of his sixty-one years in institutions, and he was back inside, again – forever. Without a body they'd been unable to make a murder rap stick, but CPS went to town on Nolan, regardless. Neither he nor his hideous skin-flicks would ever be in circulation again.

It was all there for Shanley — all in the report. They had also, on top of the death tablets, taken an enormous quantity of narcotics out of circulation. No doubt, given the Hydra tendencies of the international drug trade, there were already new gangs, new suppliers, new victims — but John-John Hamilton had not, as yet, resurfaced, and the crateloads of shit he had earmarked for Liverpool would never, now, find its way there.

In many ways, he'd done well — but it mattered not one iota to Billy McCartney. Everything paled into nothingness next to the beast he awoke to, every single morning — if he ever slept. Millie, turning to him and smiling at his question. 'The lady thing? Can't harm us, can it . . .?' It was a month since her death; a month since she'd swallowed her hurt and gone off, solo. Fucking Roig. 'Sold,' she'd said — and then she rode off into the evening. Mac could not bring himself to digest the full, awful horror of this.

The body of DS Camilla Baker had still not been found. Nolan, of course, would say nothing. He just looked at McCartney from behind that Perspex divide, goading him with those killer's eyes. So fierce was the repulsion he invoked in Mac that he felt a ravenous, alien rage tear through him, urging him to smash his fist right through the plastic barrier and grab the monster by his scrawny throat and strangle the fetid life out of it, staring right into his eyes as he did so. But he couldn't do that; he wouldn't. He'd drive away from Belmarsh, tears stinging his eyes, the rage still branding him. Guilty.

Since returning from Ibiza Mac had jumped up screaming from nightmares, soaked in his own sweat, images of sharks circling Millie's decomposed body; her eye sockets trained on him, beseeching him: help me. But he could not. He'd failed her in the most basic way. Whatever Shanley were to throw at him up there, he could take it. He deserved it. He entered the code he'd been given. That lift only went to one floor.

Part Two

The Red Fort

2013

She came on the day of the big thaw. It was still viciously cold, but the snowdrifts were gone and the ice caps on the roads and pavements had started to melt. The first tap at the door was so faint that Mac took no notice; thought it was another great slab of snow-pack sliding down from the roof. The second knock was barely any louder, but it was accompanied by a hoarse and desolate voice.

'Please . . .'

He went to the door. His senses were overloaded at first sight of her. Fear, confusion, curiosity, but, more than anything, familiarity – an absolute certainty that he knew this waif who stood hunched on his doorstep, dressed in an ill-fitting track-suit, shivering violently. He couldn't say for certain where, but he'd met her before.

'Mr McCartney?' stuttered the girl.

Even after all this time, it sometimes took him a second to recognise his own name.

'I'm McCartney, yes. Come on in before you freeze to death.'

Four months into his sabbatical and with no overwhelming desire to return, the cop in McCartney still saw him check outside and around before shutting the front door.

He led the girl through to the sitting room. She was

extraordinary. With her green eyes and light brown skin he guessed she could be Turkish, maybe Maltese. Yet the closely cropped, wiry, cotton-white hair made her other-worldly; a brown albino. She was beautiful, but, staring up at him with those never-moving eyes, she was spectral, too. For a moment she didn't move or speak, just sat with her shoulders hunched against the cold, shuddering every few seconds. McCartney, too, sat and stared. He knew this girl, he was sure of it. He *knew* her! He became aware that her teeth were chattering.

'Here – let me pull that sofa nearer the fire. I'll get a brew on, then you can tell me who you are and how you found me . . .'

The latter was of particular interest to Mac. He'd sold the eyrie, imagining a bold new start at this definitive time of life, yet here he was, unable, quite, to drag himself away from the dirty old town. Still, Woolton was virtually in the countryside and he was only renting – for now. He gestured for her to stand, then wiggled the sofa left and right, until it was right up close to the hearth. Mac rested his arm against the mantelpiece.

'Tea or coffee?'

Still she didn't move. She stared at the fireplace, the amber glow of the coals reflecting in her astonishing jade-green eyes. Eventually she looked up at him. Haunted. Desperate. She spoke with a strange, dissonant cadence, up and down and up in a jarring iambic rhythm.

'Please, Mr McCartney. You have to help my mum.'

He very nearly buckled at the knees. Her mother. Of course! *That* was where he knew her . . . but surely not? He dared not even hope it, let alone say it.

'Your mother?'

'You know her.' A beat. An eternity. 'Her name is . . . she was called Camilla Baker . . .'

McCartney felt himself falling. He gripped the carved oak ledge.

'Millie?' he stammered. The girl nodded, tears in her eyes now. McCartney could feel his heart thumping. 'She's . . . she's *alive?*'

'If you can call it that . . .'

McCartney had to sit back down next to the girl before he fainted. An onrush of powerful euphoria was quickly smothered by fear, and questions; a hundred different questions.

'What, I mean where . . . where is she?'

The girl looked at him, her eyes sad and fearful, slowly shaking her head.

'She is in Maroc.'

James Rae knew he'd fucked up badly. He only came up to the Red Fort every few years, now, but he'd seen Yasmina grow from being a gangly, cheeky kid into a reluctant but strikingly beautiful gamine. He'd always had a soft spot for her; felt somewhat responsible for her. And she knew that, Yasmina. She played to it. Whenever Uncle James came to visit, he always brought her presents – things she'd asked for, things her father would not allow and must never hear of. The iPad, the books, the Wii – all gifts from James, all carefully, ingeniously secreted away up in the South Tower, where only herself and her mother would ever have access to them.

Ah, her mother, her mother . . . she was another source of regret for James Rae in his late-middle age. He could never tell her of course – why would he? Yet, even he, a man known for callous and calculated self-interest, felt a pang of conscience about Fatima up there in the tower like a princess, imprisoned, forlorn.

When he'd arrived for the funeral, Yasmina had been – not flirtatious, if he was being honest about it, but, yes – *suggestive.*

There was no doubting this minimal yet discernible vibe from her that, perhaps now, perhaps in time, their familiar, affectionate relationship might develop into something more promising. Was that wishful thinking? Probably, but fucking hell! Who would not wish for that, with her? She was still a gangly kid, but she was eighteen now. Yasmina was growing into a uniquely beautiful young woman. She'd wrapped him around her little finger, hadn't she? She knew he was never going to check her story with her dad. And the stupid thing was, he'd half known she was playing him. He'd done it with his eyes wide open and his brain in neutral. She told him she needed the bank account so she could start ordering tunes for the iPad he'd brought her. Maybe he'd known, on some subconscious level, that she was planning to do a runner. Maybe he'd wanted her to succeed.

Whatever, he didn't have the first idea how he was going to find Yasmina – but find her he must. The Red Fort hash was, by common consent, the best in all of Europe. Quality over quantity was the motto and James Rae had become the concierge-dealer to a select but big-spending client base because of his dedication to quality. He could wave farewell to all that, though, if he didn't find the El Glaoui girl and bring her back. Clever, Yasmina – how long had she been planning the scam? How long had she been playing him for the sucker he was? He shook his head in pained admiration – she was good.

He was starting to wish he hadn't gone out there for the funeral, but that would have been bad in a different way. Since pot had gone mega again, Mustapha and Hassan were probably the two most important people in his life. But they hardly ever did business at the Red Fort any more. Hassan would fly out to Palma, or the Dam, and they'd broker the next chunk out there, while Hassan had himself a ball in the casinos, the clubs, the brothels.

But there was no way he would have contemplated missing Muzzy's funeral. Mustapha El Glaoui was a living legend in the Rif – had been a living legend. In every practical sense he'd remained a tribesman – an old-style village elder, with the significant difference that he and his son presided over a long-established hash business worth upwards of a hundred million dollars a year, these days. He'd been old-fashioned like that, Mustapha. Always dollars. James Rae had long since given up trying to talk him through the advantages of playing the currency market.

'I like greenbacks,' he'd smile. 'Uncle Sam always good to me. What difference it can make, a million here, a million there? Why change a thing so good?'

But Mustapha was no more. He'd led a charmed life high up there in the Rif, producing and exporting hashish of uncommon finesse and potency, but now he was gone and it was up to his son Hassan to continue the dynasty. And James Rae knew for an absolute fact that Hassan El Glaoui would be very well attuned to the difference it could make, an extra million here, a million there. Hassan was a guy who could never have enough money. He loved dealing; he was addicted to it. He lived for the next one, and the one after that.

The day after the funeral, on the first night of feasting, James had taken him to one side and shown him the numbers; and Hassan seemed to like the numbers – a lot. But on the final night, the night of the grand banquet when the white-clad women joined the men for the climax of the festivities, there was one notable absentee; Mustapha's favourite granddaughter, the exquisite Yasmina. Hassan didn't know it yet, but it was Rae's fault she was gone. If he didn't find her, quickly, and bring her back to the Red Fort, James Rae could forget about the next deal, and start looking for a new identity.

*　　*　　*

The train raced through Watford, and he began to plan ahead. Shanley was retired these days but Mac knew he could still pull strings – would be desperate to. He could have gone through Hodge, could even have gone straight to the SIS – but with such a personal stake in the Camilla Baker case, Kenneth Shanley would move mountains to make this happen. No obstacle would prevent her safe return home.

He smiled at Yasmina; got the same tense, somewhat untrusting smile back, then the fear returned to her eyes. When he'd tried to press her to find out how she'd tracked him down she merely tapped her iPad's screen and muttered: 'Everyone leaves a trail . . .'

She'd spent most of the journey bent over the tablet, emailing, tweeting and messaging people. Mac had managed to glean very little more from her, other than that she was very much a fugitive, in fear of being caught. He nodded at the tablet.

'So, what about you? If you found me so easily, are you not concerned that they can trace you?'

'Who?'

'Whoever you're running away from.'

Anger flashed in her eyes. 'My father still counts on his fingers.'

But there was doubt there. She chewed her lip and closed the iPad down.

McCartney didn't like taxi drivers – London cabbies least of all – but Shanley lived out in Dulwich and, after everything the girl had been through, Mac didn't want to drag her halfway round London on public transport. As they queued down the steps at Euston and it eventually came to their turn, he steeled himself for a ride's worth of opinions from a portly skinhead. He was mildly gratified, then, when

Euston's taxi roulette delivered them a cherry-red cab piloted by an obliging driver no older than thirty. She, too, was portly and without much hair, but she greeted them cheerily and got them on their way.

Yasmina cheered up, too. For a while she kept stealing glances at the driver. She leaned into Mac and whispered: 'But, it's a woman, no?'

'For sure . . .'

'And this is possible, here? Really?'

'What?'

'A woman with a job like this?'

'Of course!'

She caught the cabby looking at her through the rear-view mirror. They stared at one another for a beat, then Yasmina looked away, a faint blush to her cheeks.

'That's good,' she whispered, then, snapping out of the reverie, turned so she was facing McCartney. 'In Maroc, no. Not even the bravest.'

Mac thought he might insinuate the cabby into the conversation, but instinct overrode him. He followed his gut.

'Does that interest you then, Yasmina? Politics?'

She shrugged. 'I wouldn't call it politics . . .'

Her English was near perfect, if slightly accented. There were occasional Spanish-tinged inflections and something of an American twang – but her mother's tongue was hers as well. Mac laughed.

'I assure you, Yasmina – when you're a woman, *everything* is politics!'

She gave him an odd, almost surprised look, then – for the first time – she laughed, properly, tilting her head back to show two rows of tiny white teeth. Her eyes glittered as she giggled – a girl again, for the moment.

'I know what you mean,' she said. 'Many intelligent women

in my country . . .' Then the eyes clouded over again. 'In Maroc, many still choose to wear the veil.'

'Even after the Arab Spring?' She nodded, staring out of the taxi's window as they rolled through south London. He'd lost her again. 'That's a shame,' he added, almost to himself.

They pulled up right outside Gail's bakery. Yasmina took a picture of her first London cab while Mac paid, told the driver to keep the change. He spotted Shanley through the window, just as he looked out and caught sight of them. He stood up to wave them inside to his table. He looked good. He must have been around seventy-five, now, but he looked healthier and more spry than the stooped and careworn figure who had signed Mac off on compassionate leave after Millie's death, all those years ago. Even now, it was hard to compute that DS Baker was very much alive, if none too well.

Shanley greeted Yasmina first, thanked her for coming, then gave Mac a firm handshake.

'It's been . . . how long?' he smiled.

'*Too* long . . .' said Mac. 'Happy New Years!'

They both laughed.

'You missing the job?'

'I should ask you the same question, Billy! All those baddies, making hay while you're away . . .'

'It's knowing who the baddies really are though, isn't it, sir?'

'*Sir!* For goodness' sake, Mac . . .' Shanley laughed again and gestured for them to sit. 'I bagged this one for us,' he said, tapping the bleached-pine tabletop. *Forrrus.* The rolling *r* took Mac back. Shanley jerked his head over his shoulder at a large, communal table. 'Never can be too careful – even in Dulwich Village!'

Mac sat down and, very slowly, Yasmina followed suit. She was wary all of a sudden, reluctant – now the time had come – to open up to these two strange old men. McCartney seemed *simpatico*, but was it wise to put so much faith in a complete stranger? She'd come this far on her own raw wits. Cops were all the same. She'd have to box clever.

Shanley turned to her and, his eyes seeking hers, said: 'Now then, Yasmina. We'd very much like to help reunite you with your mother. If that's what *she* wants?' Yasmina nodded slowly, her eyes probing Shanley's for any sign of compromise. He stared right back at her – clear; determined. 'Good. Then we're going to do everything in our power to help bring Mum home. Please take your time, and if there's anything that is in any way difficult for you to address, please just say. We want to make this as easy as possible for you . . .'

Yasmina was hesitant to start with but found that, as she got into her story, there was a release – a relief – in telling it. She spoke faster and faster, the burden easing as she weaved little patterns with her fingers, gesticulating and cursing. And what she had to tell them sank McCartney's heart like a plumb. Millie lived – as she had done herself – in virtual slavery, in a remote compound, high above a ravine in the Rif Mountains. She was known as Fatima, one of Hassan El Glaoui's wives. To Yasmina, though, she was not even Mum; she'd always asked her to call her Millie.

So, in the privacy of the tower where they spent much of their time, Mum was Millie. Only on those occasions when the men were up at the plant, the women had gone down to the market and the compound was absolutely deserted – only then did Millie come alive. Telling Yasmina stories, sometimes sad ones, about who she was and how she came to be here; who she used to be. But they'd laugh and joke, too; dance around to music; compete like maniacs at tennis on the Wii, crying with frustration then with laughter, by the end. But Millie was sad. She was desperately lonely and sick with longing for home; for her sister, her parents – for everything. And, over time, Yasmina and Millie had hatched a plan to do something about that. It was madcap. It was doomed. But it was a plan – and that had given Millie hope. McCartney became aware that he was smiling, inside.

Of the safe-house options, they went for the place in Maze Hill, so Shanley could keep popping in on her, as required. Mac had mixed feelings; part of him hoped that the welcome, welcoming sight of Una Farlowe might open the door to them. But most of him was perfectly relieved when the handler was not cherubic and jolly, but elfin and businesslike. She introduced herself as Lydia. Mac left them to it while she and Yasmina went through all the initial health checks, declarations, statements and paperwork. What Yasmina had told them was almost certainly going to be acted upon. If her story checked out, it would mean an Operation – and, if offered it, there was no doubt in his mind McCartney would accept the job. The knowledge that Millie was out there, perfectly well though living a half-life as a virtual slave, tore him up, and drove him on.

He cut through Greenwich Park and headed across and down the hill towards the house, trying to visualise what scant detail Yasmina had been able to give to him and Shanley. They could hardly criticise the girl – her flight from Morocco had been well planned and audacious – but she'd managed to bring little that would be of much use to them. No maps, no photographs and, for someone who had lived her entire eighteen years up in the Rif, no great local knowledge.

Still, there was enough to work on. There were several families – cousins, important co-workers, servants – who lived together in a kind of compound way up in the hills beyond Chefchaouen. It was known to all in the locale as the Red Fort.

Yasmina said you could see it for miles around, high up in the Rif – not least for the enormous satellite dish on top of one of the outbuildings. It was not a fort, as such – from her sketches it was more of a heavily guarded mountain lighthouse, though bigger, wider, more squat – and neither was it red. She told them this was a local nickname, bestowed because of the way the setting sun would backlight the building in dramatic, glowing scarlet. But as for routes in and out, weak points, secret tunnels, anything of specific insider detail – she had drawn a blank.

Her father, Hassan, was a drug dealer. Higher up in the mountains was what she understood to be the processing plant, but she had no idea what exactly went on up there – she had never been. All she could really tell them was that the nearest town was Chefchaouen, and the mountain pass up to the fortress was guarded and patrolled by police. She herself was rarely allowed outside the compound and only then when she was chaperoned – while her mum was often physically locked up. And yet, in spite of what Mac now recognised as Yasmina's burgeoning feminism, she had found it hard to bear witness against her father. She hated the lives he was enforcing upon her and Millie, yet – or so it seemed – she didn't quite hate him.

He reached the cloisters of Queen's House and turned back. He couldn't see it. Mac just could not envisage himself being able to breach that compound and get Millie out of there, and back down and away to safety. He didn't have the foggiest idea how they'd go about it. But he was going to try – by God he would die trying to bring Detective Sergeant Camilla Baker back here, safe and sound.

'You just want the serial number?'

James Rae chewed on his mounting ire and swallowed it down.

'Yes. That's all I'm asking for.'

'Can't you just look on the iPad itself?'

'This is the problem. That's why I need it. As I explained, I lost the iPad, or it was stolen, but now it's turned up, the police have it, and I have to be able to demonstrate to them that it is, in fact, my property.'

'And they need the serial number?'

'They need the serial number . . .'

'Where did you buy it from again, Mr Rae?'

'John Lewis.'

'So it's under warranty?'

'Yes! I don't *know*! It doesn't need repairing.'

'But it came with their standard two-year guarantee.'

'Yes. I assume so . . .'

'Do you have the guarantee?'

He didn't. He'd popped all the relevant paperwork in with the package, just in case Yasmina should ever need it. Hadn't really thought beyond that.

'Yes. Somewhere.'

'Excellent.'

'Why? Why is that excellent?'

'Because the serial number will be there on your guarantee.'

'What if I can't find it?'

'Then I can only suggest you take this up with John Lewis, sir.'

He waited for Bunty to leave the room.

'Bunty's the best,' he sighed. 'I think she realises it could so easily have been her . . .' He glanced up at McCartney. 'Anyway. Anything you need . . .' Mac could feel it coming. 'You *sure* you want to run this solo?'

Mac straightened his back, ready for a more strenuous

rebuttal, but Shanley was there first, both palms out flat as though pushing away Mac's objections.

'OK, OK, I'll leave it with you, Billy, but I want it on record that I sincerely recommend you touch base with Roig.'

McCartney shook his head in bemused admiration.

'With respect, sir – let it go! You're supposed to be retired. God help Mrs Shanley!'

'As you wish, McCartney – as you wish. I'll leave it with you.'

If he'd said it once he'd said it a dozen times, 'I'll leave it with you . . .' – then he'd gone at it all over again. The El Glaouis had a base in Palma de Mallorca these days that was the subject of great interest from Roig's UDYCO – the Unidad de Drogas y Crimen Organizado – as well as the specialist Customs squad, the SVA. Roig had an up-to-date file on all Hassan's activities and assets.

'You heard about the jet-ski gang, last summer?'

'I think I might have had my mind on other things, last summer, sir . . .' Shanley blinked at him. 'HMS *Rozaki?*' Mac grinned. 'Heroin Mainline Ship, all the way from the Bosporus . . .'

Shanley nodded both his comprehension and his apology.

'Well, this was a Moroccan gang. Hauled the hash across the Straits in fishing boats – sound familiar? Then they brought it ashore on a fleet of jet skis . . .'

'That was the El Glaoui mob?'

'No. But it was Roig's unit that nicked them. Brilliant.'

It wasn't simply that Mac didn't want to meet with Roig – and, in spite of Shanley's persistence, he really did *not* want to involve the Andorran agent. Billy McCartney had, over decades, perfected his own craft in a way and to a routine that best served his skills. When it came to donning and successfully implementing a legend, Mac believed absolutely in method. It was Shanley himself, back when he'd first been selected for aptitude training, who had delivered a definitive masterclass.

'It's never too early to step into your persona,' he'd told them. 'Start living their life as far as possible in advance of the op. You must become that person. You must *be* them. Right from your first few moves, act and speak as though your every tic is being monitored. Assume they know where you are and what you are doing. Live your role and live *up* to your role. It will, ultimately, take you to them . . .'

He believed that. He had come to know that it was true. He'd worked in Amsterdam, Marbella, Bangkok, Veracruz, everywhere; different gangs and methods, different types of criminals; yet with each operation, his skills grew sharper; he himself was more credible with each new case. And, with what he knew of Morocco, he expected those skills and that believability to be given a severe workout. With the magnitude of the fortune the El Glaouis were creating up there in the Rif, it was an absolute given that their wealth would trickle down exponentially, greasing palms, buying favour, paving the way and softening any rare blow. He knew he would be up against it, right from the start.

A trip to see Roig, as well as being painful emotionally, would necessitate a detour to Madrid and everything told him that would work against character. He'd elected to play this op as a Mr Nice-type pot connoisseur – a slightly eccentric dope idealist of independent means, who was serious about importing the best shit in big quantities. For Mac, the naming of his legend was paramount. It wasn't simply a matter of the name's mechanical aptness, it was his entire way in to the new persona. He tried on and abandoned several capes and hats before settling upon Philip Davies, the louche and slightly disappointing only son of James, who'd been something in the City. He needed to be sufficiently maverick for the Moroccans to drop their guard while still making it clear he had the substance to front a major transaction. Mac *knew* Davies's character intuitively, and he knew for sure that his Mr Davies would make this trip to Morocco by sea. Moreover, on the assumption that his every move would be tagged – if not now, then subsequently, in retrospect, for sure – it made sense to lay his bait early, with an electronic trail starting in Amsterdam. He'd spend an evening there, fly down to Malaga and cross to Morocco from Tarifa, Algeciras, maybe even Gibraltar, for superstition's sake . . . He hadn't quite decided which port Mr Davies would sail from – but, sorry, Señor Roig, he was adamant it would not involve a detour to Madrid.

'Here we go then,' the cabby laughed as they pulled over at the address in Elephant & Castle.

Yasmina hunched forward, tense now. Lydia would already have found her room empty. She'd have to move quickly, and cover her tracks. She pushed a £20 note through the gap. The driver waved away the fare.

'Nah. You look like you need it more than I do.' She looked up at the building. 'You sure this is where you want to be?'

Yasmina nodded. 'This is the place.'

'Date?'

She gave a short, nervous laugh. 'Not in the way you mean.' She smiled and tried to steel herself. 'Though hopefully. One day . . .'

The taxi driver winked. 'Well. Good luck. I'm Carrie, yeah? Carrie the Cabby – you've got my number now. If it all goes pear-shaped . . .'

Yasmina let herself out. 'Thanks. I may well be taking you up on that.'

They held one another's gaze for a beat. Yasmina cleared her throat.

'Listen. Carrie. It's really, *really* important that nobody knows you brought me here . . .'

Again, the hoarse chuckle; the playful eyes. 'If I had a nicker for every time some runaway tells me that,' she winked. 'Seriously, though. You look after yourself, yeah?' The burly skinhead looked anxious now. 'Be lucky, beautiful.'

She pulled off into the Waterloo rain. Yasmina took a deep breath and stepped to the door for her meeting with the ILGIG.

McCartney had not thought to imagine how Algeciras might look, but he wasn't expecting Middlesbrough. As the cab passed by stretch after stretch of hulking great salmon-pink tower blocks, the cranes and crates of the vast port came into view ahead. Infinite colonies of container tanks and their rusting husks spread out over the horizon, stacked high, as far as the eye could see. He thought back to Misha hiding out in the abandoned containers at Garston Dock – they never would have found her here. The port was a never-ending cargo town.

He passed an enjoyable half-hour in the waiting lounge, trying to guess which passengers were for Tangier and who was heading for 'Morocco Lite' by way of the Spanish-controlled port of Ceuta. Ceuta was geographically closer to Chefchaouen, but it was Spain's version of Gibraltar – a much-resented exclave within Morocco that wasn't worth the hassle. Besides, a man as *simpatico* as Davies would show his solidarity by sailing into Morocco proper. He'd booked a wide, reclining seat in the Neptuno lounge on a Balear crossing. Sliding low in his berth, Mac twisted his headphones in and selected *If You Leave*, track 10 – an ever-present for him, for months. He slipped the iPod back in his pocket, barely registering the Rock to his port side as the ship cut outwards and onwards, through the deep, choppy sea. He sat back and succumbed to

'Shallows', haunted by its spectral delicacy – again; conjuring images of Hattie and Virginia, drowning.

If first sight of Algeciras was an anticlimax, the port of Tangier was a crushing let-down. Just as Hercules had rested up in Tangier before tackling the first of his labours, McCartney fancied Davies might acclimatise himself here, too. It would be good for the story, anyway, when it came to interacting with the folk who would, ultimately, lead him to the doors of the Red Fort. If he could present himself as a rake, something of a boulevardier rich with tales of his travels, then an anecdote or two about high times in Tangier could only aid his credibility. He'd been imagining a smooth glide right into the belly of the city, docking on a bustling quayside, ducking the beggars and vendors and finding his way via souk, bazaar and kasbah to an atmospheric pension where he'd lay his head. All that came into sight was a distant hilltop town looking down upon a huge new container port, itself dominated by a concrete spur and a sprawling oil terminal. A tugboat came out to meet them, pulled the ferry round 180 degrees and helped them shuffle backwards in to dock.

He let the foot passengers flood off the boat, trying to cast around for a sign, a clue – anything that meant he wouldn't have to ask. A young traveller in an old Oasis T-shirt was waiting to embark.

'You lost, mate? Looking to get into town?'

Five minutes later he was queuing for a *petit taxi*, graciously repeating to a bamboozled Japanese couple what the young Kiwi had told him – that they'd docked at the brand-new Tangier Med. Only the Tarifa ferry, now, would take you right into Tangier Old Port. A scintillating sun seared right through his hat to pulverise his scalp and, though McCartney custom militated against it, he accepted the couple's offer of a shared cab into Tangier.

In his crumpled linen jacket, baggy T-shirt, shorts and Birkenstocks – and with his smiling companions in their cannabis-leaf T-shirts – the aristo-hippie with the rucksack was a magnet for *faux guides* and hustlers. Once he'd said his farewells to the Japanese couple, though, Mac slowly got into sync with the bustle of the old town. Climbing up the time-worn steps, passing by the open windows of cafes and *riads*, his senses were blitzed by the smells and sounds of the souk. The plangent, ever-present lament of the Berber flute drifted above the chatter of bird call, the bark and barter of the marketplace, until he could no longer distinguish the intimate notes in the melange. He passed huge hessian sacks piled high with fresh-ground, brightly coloured spices – cardamom, pepper, ginger, turmeric, paprika, saffron, cumin, cinnamon, nutmeg, anise – making his mouth and his eyes water. It was midday and he was glad of the cool passageways and the shadow of the alleyways as he forged through the kasbah in search of a likely *riad*. He passed through a small souk, shaded by an island of tall palms, and was about to investigate the white-washed *riad* in the furthest corner when his eye was taken by a flurry of gaudy colour. To his left, along with the rugs and vases and leather goods, was a wooden frame caged with bird wire. Inside fluttered a frenzy of saffron yellow as hundreds of tiny canaries flitted back and forth.

'*Monsieur?*' smiled the vendor, and Mac realised he was standing right up to the cage, staring. '*Très belle. Très belle prix . . .*'

He realised, too, that he would not be staying the night in Tangier after all. His story could stand or fall. There was no time to lose.

*   *   *

She'd had no other preconceptions when she'd set up the appointment, but Yasmina had assumed a certain basic sympathy as a given. It wasn't that the interviewer she'd been allocated was unfriendly, as such – she was just a little remote, and ultra-professional. Aasiya – Somali, she guessed – looked mid-twenties and she was a volunteer at the centre. She explained that she was a psychology graduate who assisted the lawyers with all the background to each case history, and stressed the importance of detailed and accurate information. She gave Yasmina an earnest look and asked if it was OK to record the interview.

'Of course . . .' she muttered, still unsure about all this. 'Please do.'

'Excellent. OK. It's now 2 . . . 13 p.m. on Wednesday 12th February 2013. Present at this meeting are Aasiya Abdikarim for the Islamic Lesbian and Gay Immigration Group, and Yasmina El Glaoui representing herself. I want to start with some very general background, Yasmina, and even if some of this sounds rudimentary or even trivial, I must make it clear that it's vital in preparing your case for asylum that we are in possession of all the salient facts. Is that clear? Your account has to be watertight – and it has to be the truth . . .' Yasmina nodded. She could feel the tears coming already. Aasiya managed a smile. 'OK. Shall we start? Give me as detailed a picture as possible of your upbringing in Morocco . . .' She fixed her eyes upon her. '. . . and your recollections as to when you first knew you were gay.' Silence. Yasmina swallowed. Aasiya tuned into her anguish and, this time, smiled with her eyes as well as her lips. 'There's no hurry. Just . . . whenever you're ready.'

Yasmina collected herself, and started into it. She spoke for three hours, requiring Aasiya to stop twice and open a new sound file. She spoke about her mother – kidnapped, held against her will for nearly a quarter of a century; half her life. She repeated the tales Millie had told her; how, for the first few years, Hassan had not worked out that she had a contraceptive coil. He never beat her, but he cursed her for failing to provide him with a son. He had other wives and mistresses, some of whom lived with them, in their compound, a fortress, high in the Rif Mountains. One of them bore him a son, Rachid, and he was happy for a while. But one of the other girls, Krista, disappeared one day. She'd been brought there to live with Hassan's father, and Millie and she had become friends. Krista, from Stockholm, had a similar tale to tell. A party. Rich guys. Plenty of drugs, lots of fun – then oblivion. This Krista, too, had a coil. Krista vanished without trace, and the word from the peasant girls who loved to plait Millie's golden hair was that Mustapha had tired of her failure to conceive. After nearly five years in the compound, Millie faced up to her future. She told her daughter, many years later, that this was the moment she finally gave up hope. When she pulled out her coil with tweezers, she also pulled out her heart. Yasmina looked up and reached for her hot water – already she hated English tea and coffee. Aasiya's face was stricken. She had heard many a harrowing tale, but Yasmina's shocked her to the core.

'Shall I stop?' she whispered.

'No. Please. If you can, please go on . . .'

She went on. She told of her earliest memories of the compound – a brown girl with cotton-white hair. She told of the gradual stirrings of her sexuality; how she'd become infatuated with Salma, one of the older girls, unusually tall and beautiful with flawless light brown skin and long, raven-black hair. Aasiya smiled as Yasmina spoke – a shared experience. She went on. She told of her mother's feminist teachings – how tough it had been for her, at first, in her job with the police. How she'd had to become one of the boys, simply to get along, and do the basics she was paid to carry out. She told of secret parties with her mother and some of the other girls – frantic, sometimes frenzied dancing during which she felt a transcendental lift-off, as though connecting with another self. She told of her first dalliances with Google and the World Wide Web – for her, literally, a portal into another world; a glimpse of a different life. She read up on everything. She followed events in Libya almost round the clock, charging up her iPad from her father's flatbed truck, sometimes running his battery flat. She followed blogs like Global Post, Kickass and Most Cake, and came to know that she was not alone – far from it. She felt alive, at last. She was engaged, aroused, inspired – and angry. Above all, she was angry.

And she decided to do something about it. She quizzed her mother on everything, with no stone left unturned. She made her go over everything about Ibiza. McCartney. The glass house up in the hills. She entered information, looked for links and, little by little, she built up a picture. McCartney, in particular, became her focus and, in spite of all her misgivings, Yasmina sensed he could be the key to their liberation.

She began to blog herself, under an alias, of course. Tainted Love – her tales of life behind lock and key and a love that dared not declare itself – began to garner a loyal and growing readership. Followers began to speculate as to who and where she was – a Saudi royal, a Mormon daughter, a Persian prisoner; and both her mother and herself *were* prisoners –Yasmina a prisoner of passion, too. Arab Spring or no, a love like hers had no place in Morocco, no matter how progressive the new wave purported to be. The guessing varied wildly as Tainted Love's following grew, but everyone urged her to come out, wherever she was; whoever she was. Come and join us, was the message – and that was her plan. With the patience of a fanatic and a dogged attention to detail she formulated a long game. Sitting there, now, in ILGIG's London office, was merely the next big step. When the alarm buzzed to tell Aasiya that the third sound file was full, she got up, walked round the table and held Yasmina close. Both women sobbed freely, now.

'Sister,' she whispered. 'You are not alone.'

Fifty dirham secured him a seat on the air-conditioned Volvo CTM bus that now poked its way out of Tangier past clumps of ancient cedars, their trunks daubed with a belt of white preservative unction. They hit the N2, the tatty chic of Tangier receding as the terrain grew rougher. Passing through dry and rutted countryside, Mac delighted at the sight of shaggy goats perched high in the branches of barren olive trees, gnawing at the bark. Towering ahead and above he could now see the peaks and cloud of the Rif. The bus ducked south on the outskirts of Tetouan and began its steady climb. Over to the left was the ancient route to Dar Ben Karrich, a white fortress marking the way. The smooth pull of the bus insulated the climb but, as the mountain route narrowed, the drop below became ever more acute.

A barely discernible drilling noise whined in his eardrums. He took a sip from his water bottle and swallowed hard, flushing the congestion for a moment before it started up again. It was painful, now. Looking out of his window, Mac was shocked to see a sheer drop below as the bus veered around hairpin bends without slowing. He pulled the slatted curtains and closed his eyes, trying to shut out the vertiginous gorge immediately to his right. Never the superstitious sort, Mac was nevertheless relieved when the coach, finally, began its descent. It felt like a breeze was whirring through his brain. His ears popped and, though he hadn't been aware of any restriction, he could hear clearly again, as if waking from his slumbers – and what he heard was their driver, asking them to have their papers ready for inspection.

The big bus weaved inelegantly through a slalom of spiked security barriers, set up in such a way that only one vehicle could pass at a time, one direction at a time. At the end of the run of barriers, two armed guards waited, guns pointing down, while a sprightly old captain bounded aboard the CMT and went about his routine. He spent a little time quizzing two young Moroccans at the front of the bus, barely checked Mac at all and seemed to run out of vim halfway down the aisle. He hopped off, shook hands with the driver who finished his cigarette and climbed back on board.

The engine grumbled back to life, the air conditioning blasted out and, though Mac could see the kasbah of Old Chefchaouen up above them now, the bus continued its slow rumble downhill, past newer, whitewashed housing developments. Ten minutes later they pulled into a teeming bus station, the Volvo easing its way to its allocated bay, its giant engine shuddering to a standstill. Mac immediately heard the horns of a dozen taxis vying for business. Smiling boys yanked hard on ropes to restrain donkeys that had no intention of moving anywhere, anyway. There were steps and paths and signs, all leading up to the medina, but Mac sat back and watched the kinetic buzz of touts and taxis outside his window, waiting for fresh meat to land. Once again, he let the majority off first, while he worked out his strategy.

He made up his mind it would do no harm to be touted, for once. Essentially, he was here to start up a chain mail that would, he hoped, reach the Red Fort itself – and sooner rather than later. In a smallish town renowned as a trafficking centre, word of Philip Davies would spread quickly if he laid his ground bait well. He watched as the sharks and the fly boys moved in, gabbling twenty to the dozen as they fastened upon handles and luggage and shooed their cattle into taxis. Hanging back watching, a glass not much bigger than a thimble clamped between his thumb and his forefinger, was a dapper little man of indeterminate age, his intelligent eyes raking left and right. He was light-skinned, with black, side-parted hair and a well-tended moustache. Dominating his face was a nose of near-pyramid proportions, so prominent that it could have been fashioned from papier mâché. His excellent paunch was girdled by a tight turquoise Lacoste T-shirt, worn with white golfing slacks and navy-blue deck shoes. A vagabond, for sure, but Mac rather liked him on sight.

He got off the bus and made sure Lacoste man noticed him squinting at the various signposts. He shielded his eyes from the sun and craned his neck for a better idea of how far away the old town was, then, seemingly satisfied he could make it, shifted his rucksack around until it felt comfortable and started up the steps. He got as far as the fourth.

'Excuse me! Sir! No, no, no! This way lies certain death!' Mac turned to see the little tout approaching him, his arms spread out in supplication. 'English? American?' Mac said nothing. The fellow was on the bottom step now, a foot below him. 'No matter. Just a friendly word. Dehydration leads to expiration! Take a cab!'

His face, which Mac could now see was lightly pockmarked, dissolved into a rapturous smile.

'I am Ahmed. I know – so is everyone else! But I am Honest Ahmed. No rip-off here. I know – everyone says the same. But check out my perfect English. All I require of you is one short ride up one very taxing hill . . .'

Mac smiled, and nodded to accept. Ahmed gave a shrill whistle and an off-white Mercedes cab appeared. 'Home from home,' thought Mac, as he steeled himself and got inside.

* * *

James Rae got off at Turnpike Lane and walked back down Green Lanes to the little cafe Mehmet had suggested.

'Quieter up that end,' he'd laughed. For Mehmet, nothing was ever too serious. Even when he was talking about blood-shed between rival heroin gangs, he said it with a trill in his voice. 'Those Tottenham Boys – crazy. Never stop! *Never* stop . . .' Coming from one of the leaders – though he denied it – of the Tottenham firm's deadliest foes, this was praise indeed. 'I don't know, James, the kids today . . . they don't want to do business. Tottenham Boys, Bombaciler, now we've got the fucking Kurds on top, too! None of them wants the good life!' He laughed again, bemused at the folly of youth. 'Only want to be top dog . . .' James knew all too well about some of those Kurds wanting to be top dog.

Mehmet had given him the name of a cafe towards the Turnpike end of the Harringay Ladder which was mainly frequented by old boys and students, he said. Even at that time of morning, Green Lanes was alive with noise and bustle. James walked the stretch between Frobisher and Fairfax twice, looking out for the usual signs of cafe life. It was only when he spotted a stooped old chap shuffling into a dingy-looking shop that he twigged that this must be the place.

Inside it was an oasis of early-morning serenity. Old men – everyone in there, bar James himself, was white-haired, no-haired and male – sat in groups around the bigger tables, some playing *dama*, some in earnest debate, all sipping rich maroon tea. At the back of the room, a handsome, white-haired man sat alone with his *çay*, browsing the sports pages of *Olay Gazetesi*. He looked up as James came towards him, his face creasing into a smile as he stood up.

'Ay! My friend!' he beamed, his arms out wide. The two men hugged closely, like long-lost brothers. 'Where you been, man?'

Rae winked at the old Turk. 'You wouldn't believe me if I told you . . .'

Mehmet laughed out loud, making a sign to the guy behind the counter as he gestured for James to sit.

'See? Always the diplomat! Why can't you teach my boys?'

'Still on the warpath?'

He rolled his eyes. 'I do not understand them! We are all Turks . . .' Rae smiled to himself. Mehmet had risen to the top of his trade by ruthlessly and systematically eliminating his rivals – sometimes only months after making strategic alliances with them. 'There are enough dogs to fight without killing one another.' He shook his head slowly, staring into his tea. 'You ever go to see those Rozaki bastards?'

The guy from the counter brought over a double-spouted pewter teapot and another glass and, on receiving the nod from Mehmet, took a step back and poured, solemn, one hand behind his back. He went to take the pot away but Mehmet placed one hand on his wrist and smiled. The guy backed away, face pinched with fear.

'Not for a long time,' sighed Rae. 'Besides – I try not to enter such establishments on a voluntary basis . . .'

Mehmet slapped the table. 'I shouldn't laugh! That was our gear they lost, the stupid pair of pricks. More fool me, giving them terms, eh?'

He shook his head and both men raised their glasses, nodded and took a sip of their tea.

'Best *çay* in London,' smiled Mehmet. 'Now – how may I help?'

James thought about it, as he'd been thinking about it all the way there. He'd known Mehmet a long, long time now – long enough to know he could never trust him. If he told him about the hash angle – the El Glaoui connection – he'd be all over him, trying to muscle in or trying to palm him off with inferior

Afghani or Lebanese hash. It had taken years of patience for James to reposition himself in the marketplace, and his market was very much the high-quality, highest-price niche. He couldn't let Mehmet Surin anywhere near that. On the other hand, he did happen to have in his number the very best tech-head in town. If you wanted to trace a mobile, a laptop, a credit-card transaction, anything with an electronic trail then Zafer the Gaffer was your man. He didn't come cheap – indeed he didn't come at all, unless it was on the say-so of his 'manager'. Rae looked Zafer's manager in the eye.

'I need to track down the whereabouts of a certain iPad, Mehmet . . .'

This taxi driver was not so agreeable as Carrie. He stared straight ahead, his lips pursed, cursing every now and then if another driver interfered with his progress. They passed a post office, a shop selling bridal wear; she was starting to see the same shops, repeatedly – Specsavers, Carphone Warehouse, Starbucks. How could people in one area need so many pairs of spectacles? She was intoxicated by the verve of the street, though. So many people milling about, up and down, so many different shades of skin and types of dress. There was a tree-lined parade with a few interesting-looking stores, recessed from the main road; a second-hand bookshop, a little clothing store and an Internet cafe. Yasmina craned her neck as they passed, trying to get a better look at the fashions in the shop window.

'Sturgeon Road?' the driver barked, without moving his head.

Aasiya was equally curt with her reply. 'Yes.'

He veered his taxi into a right-hand turn, Yasmina keeling over for a second. After another minute or two's bumping along another busy side street, they pulled up outside a big old house. There was a park just down the road. She thought she might like it here.

He pulled back the cyan shutters and looked out into the mellow plaza below. In the corner, weather-twisted and hanging down across the square, an unruly juniper sprouted from a drystone rotunda. In the distance he could hear the gurgle of spring water gushing down from the mountains. There were two bottles of it on his bedside table when he'd come up to his room – blue glass, of course, with a stout rubber stopper. He'd gulped down three thirsty glasses full already, the chalky bite of the minerals slaking his dry throat.

He stood there and watched and listened, and he realised he was in love with Chefchaouen. He'd known a little of what to expect from his research, yet still, now, just as on the taxi ride up, he found himself becalmed by the friendly spirit of the town and intoxicated by its contrasting shades of blue. Every wall, every door, every window frame was painted in different yet complementary blues; an alleyway daubed a delicate shade of cornflower with its archways and brickwork highlighted in strident indigo. It was mesmerising – the free-ranging clash and meld of Andalusian and Moorish architecture, the clamour and clatter of the souk, the clear and immediate sense of something special – McCartney was seduced. His job had taken him all over the globe, everywhere – yet he'd seldom fallen in love with a place like this. He'd never *been* to a place like this. Whatever happened here, with the mission, he'd be back. He was certain of that.

He hung up his small but versatile selection of clothes – tees and cotton shirts, jeans, a change of shorts and one pair of chinos to make up a 'suit', should the occasion demand. He showered, and got ready to meet Ahmed.

He decided he'd stick with him for two reasons. Firstly, he

hadn't tried to put him off his choice of *riad* on the ride up to Old Chefchaouen. Much as Mac would have loved to have stayed in the Lina and pamper himself with hot-stone massages, seaweed wraps and deep-tissue facials, he had to admit that the Dalia was much more the place for a travelling head. He'd got a decent rate and booked it from Amsterdam and, as the old diesel engine nudged its way on through curious crowds, he was looking forward to just flopping out on the bed for half an hour. He'd been bracing himself for Ahmed to warn him of the Dalia's notorious cockroaches or other such nefarious booby traps, but no such imprecations came forth. Neither was there any glowing recommendation of a rival hotel, no last-minute hard sell for tours, day trips or all-you-can-eat tagines. His only vice was to keep up a non-stop commentary all the way to the medina, pointing out notable buildings. The taxi eased into a central plaza and turned off into a narrow, cobbled side street. Ahmed asked the driver to pull over. He pointed through a ceramic-tiled arch to a smaller, shady square. In the corner was a small, ice-blue pension, shaded by a gnarled juniper.

'There is your hotel, Mr . . .'

'Mr Davies.' He held out his hand. 'Phil . . .'

Ahmed shook, once, and smiled. 'I shall alight here, if I may, Mr Davies. I'll be taking a small libation just there . . .' He nodded at a cosy-looking, powder-blue, hole-in-the-wall bar. 'Bar El Zhar. Should you desire company later on, that is where you will find me. It's been a pleasure. Thank you for the ride.'

He got out, touched his forehead and ducked inside the little bar, leaving Mac to heave open a heavy, studded, cast-iron door. What lay beyond it took his breath away; an oasis of palms and almond trees, and the shrill yet calming chorus of birdsong. There was a small, intricately tiled mosaic square with stone benches set back behind the cool shade of over-hanging vines. Only once he had passed this secret paradise did McCartney locate the *riad*'s small, carved reception desk. There, an envelope awaited him, with room keys and a welcoming note. The owners would return after prayer.

Unpacked, and unburdened, for the time being, Mac decided he'd take Ahmed up on the offer of a drink. He knew how these things worked; each step led to another one, and Ahmed was his entry-level move. Who could say where it might lead? If he was a crook, he was an honest one. Ahmed would, he felt sure, be able to give him at least a basic mug's guide to the dope scene in this blue-washed citadel. And, besides that, he had a second reason for meeting him. He liked him.

Long after James Rae had departed, Mehmet remained at the table, flicking his iPhone round in anticlockwise circles. He liked James — *James*! What a name for a gangster . . . One of the main reasons he liked him was that James understood, absolutely, the core value of their trade — a value that hadn't altered in decades, maybe centuries. The simple homily that business is business was the hub round which they rotated. Mehmet understood that. James Rae understood it. Both of them swore by its simple and intrinsic truth, both of them lived by it. Mehmet often thought he would die by it, too.

He picked up the scrap of paper with the information that James had, finally, been able to elicit from the helpline. Make, model, serial number. He hadn't been so stupid as to tell him the user's identity — simply insisted the device had been bought in his name. They both knew he was lying, though. Mehmet chuckled to himself at the futility of the fib. He did it himself, all the time — mainly to his wife. It came as naturally as telling the time but, being so practised a liar, he could recognise the trait in others at a blink. Besides, he had Zafer. If the iPad in question had been reconfigured, recalibrated or simply reassigned to anyone at all, near or far, he'd be in possession of those facts in two shakes of a lamb's tail. Two shakes – that was one of James Rae's, too. *James!*

He sat back from the table, undecided. Should he just do as his old partner in crime requested and trace the cursed thing for him? *Could* he do something so straightforward when, whichever way you came at it, it smelt so appetising? He tilted his chair sideways, still flicking absent-mindedly at his phone. Zafer was a grand-a-fix communications whizz-kid. Rae would not be calling upon his services if this weren't worth serious money to him. Whatever the secrets locked up in this iPad, he was certain it was information worth knowing. Perhaps he *should* just get a little more detail from Zafer – assess the real value of this proposition. The likelihood was that the answers would be worth a lot more than £1,000 to James Rae. Depending on who had the iPad now, that knowledge might be worth a lot more to Mehmet himself. There was only one way to find out. Muttering the appropriate apologies to God, and James Rae, Mehmet reached for his mobile and scrolled down to Z.

Apart from one old guy with a nut-brown face and snow-white stubble, Bar El Zhar was deserted. A young man was drying glasses behind the counter. He smiled, revealing two prominent, rather long front teeth.

'Welcome to my country! You look for Sam?' Puzzled look from McCartney. 'Ahmed? You are his good friend Davey?'

Mac chuckled. So Ahmed had two names already – he wondered how many more.

'Davies. That's me.'

'I am Jawaad. Jo . . .'

He held out his hand. Mac leaned over and shook, admiring Jo's impressive teeth at close quarters.

'Good to meet you, Jo. Is he around? Ahmed?'

He nodded at a glazed door, its glass occluded by numerous faded stickers – Sprite, Pepsi, Orangina. Mac smiled his thanks and ducked his head as he passed through the door. Outside was a little garden shaded by olive and lemon trees, yet when the breeze rustled the leaves, the dominant aroma was mint. For all the heat and dust of the town, it somehow smelt *green* in the garden. Ahmed stood up and held his arms out in greeting.

'Mr Davies! A pleasure!'

Mac padded across a little mosaic patio. Ahmed half bowed, went to kiss him on the cheek then laughed and held his hand out to shake. He gestured to a weathered cedar table in the shade of an ancient olive tree.

'Please. I am taking a small pastis, but do not feel obliged. Whatever you want . . .'

Mac gave it a little thought. What his senses had been primed for – what he *really* wanted – was a chunky fresh-mint tea, its vapours steaming up his nostrils and winding him down from the journey. But he was Philip Davies, the eccentric, monied pothead – so he reckoned he'd better dive in.

'I mean, what I'd really love is a nice cold beer. For now . . .'

'Of course! Jo sells our excellent home brew, Flag Speciale. It's OK?'

'Bring it on!'

Ahmed clapped his hands twice, sharply, and Jo appeared, smiling, at the garden door. He took the order and ducked back inside. Mac sat down and eyed his new friend.

'So. Do I call you Ahmed? Or Sam . . .?'

Ahmed fished inside his shirt pocket and pulled out a slightly bent, pre-rolled cigarette. He lit up, and spoke as he exhaled. 'Either will suffice. I am Ahmed El Samir.' He held out his hand once more. 'My old friends call me Sam.'

Once more, Mac shook his hand. 'Which do you prefer?'

Ahmed sucked on his reefer and leaned his head back, blowing smoke at the sky. 'I prefer Ahmed, if you don't mind.' A sweet and spicy aroma drifted out and upwards.

'Ahmed it is, then.' McCartney hesitated, then added, 'That smells good.'

Ahmed sat up, alert all of a sudden. 'I'm so sorry. How rude of me . . .' He passed the skinny spliff to Mac. 'Please . . .'

Mac didn't hesitate. Sometimes in these situations he would think back to Hattie Vine, holed up in Thommo's shooting gallery all those years ago; the deep-seated dread of someone offering the needle. At times like that he'd have to steel himself and throw himself into the fray. Not today. Since giving up the cigars, Mac quite fancied the gentle head-buzz of a joint or two, and what better way to enjoy it than out here, with the fridge-cold beer that the ever-smiling Jo was now placing in front of him.

He took a long draw on the spliff and handed it back to Ahmed. He held the smoke down and the crackle of a low-level euphoria was steadily invaded by the tentacles of a subtle fear. He tried to ignore it. There was no way he could allow the experienced Euro-Head Philip Davies to suffer a white-out on his first evening, after his first toke. Yet his subconscious would not leave it alone; the misty Flag Speciale bottle, its brown glass dewy from the chiller, dragged him inexorably back to that first evening by the poolside, in Ibiza. Him and Millie. San Miguel. Crooks to catch under a blood-red sky . . .

'It's OK? The smoke? Only third grade, just for my own pleasure – or so I thought . . .'

Mac swallowed and bent his brain back to buoyancy. 'No, no, no – it's excellent! Thanks so much. No, just been a very long trip, that's all.'

'You fly from London?'

'Oh. No. I had business in Amsterdam . . .'

A look, very nearly a twitch, flickered across Ahmed's face. Then he passed Mac the joint again.

'Please. Finish it.'

'It's your last?'

'I have more at home. And besides . . .' He held up his wrist laboriously, as though his watch were made of lead. '. . . I should return to the bosom of my ever-loving wife before too long.'

Mac took a draw, held it down, stubbed the roach out and exhaled. 'Bloody hell! If that's your third grade I'd love to try the good stuff!'

Ahmed smiled and his eyes sparkled. 'Maybe we can . . .' He got up and smoothed his polo shirt down over his tight round belly. Mac got up, too. 'Maybe we will.' His face cracked open into a broad and generous grin. He threw his arms around McCartney and hugged him, holding him close for a moment or two. 'Perhaps we shall meet again tomorrow, Mr Davies.'

Mac gave him a semi-bow and smiled back. 'Phil. We live in hope. May the road rise with you.'

Ahmed laughed hard, his guffaws turning into a coughing fit. 'Oh dear me! I like this. I like this very much indeed! May the road rise equally high for you, too, Mr Davies.'

He stumbled his way back through the bar. Mac sat down to finish his beer and straighten his mind. If the weed was going to form a part of his diet out here, he was going to have to find ways of steeling himself.

Aasiya hesitated in the doorway.

'I will have to put it in my report . . .' She cleared her throat; gripped the door jamb for fortitude. '. . . that you have discharged yourself from Maze Hill.' A look of panic flashed across Yasmina's face. Aasiya held her palms up and made a gentle calming motion. She smiled kindly. 'But I don't have to tell them where you are.'

'Thank you.'

'It's not a problem. But . . .' She twisted the bottom of her headscarf. '. . . you can only keep running for so long.' She looked at Yasmina with earnest brown eyes. 'You have to think clearly and decide what you want to do.'

Aasiya bit her lip, eyed the waif a moment longer and turned to leave.

'I will,' murmured Yasmina – but Aasiya was already halfway down the narrow stairs. She dipped into her bag and pulled out the iPad. She went to switch it on, but thought twice about it. Placing her things firmly under the bed, she gathered up her keys and purse and set out towards the Internet cafe they'd passed on the way there. She could send her latest instalment of Tainted Love from there. That would set the cat among the pigeons.

'You're going to need to box clever,' said Bunty. 'He is who he says he is – but he's a bit of a rum sort . . .'

'Go on,' said Mac, resting his back against the headboard. Bunty's aristocratic tones purred down the line. He closed his eyes.

'Well, you'd hardly describe Ahmed El Samir as a dealer. But from what we've been able to dig up on him, he's certainly no stranger to the boys in blue – or is it white over there? He's done, let's see – one, two, three, *four* stretches inside, ranging from three to ten months. Mostly possession. One for trying to sell a small quantity of dope to an undercover *flic*.'

'So, if he's not a dealer, what is he?'

'He's more of a fixer, pretty common in the Rif, it seems. There's loads of them – a step up from the old *faux guides*, if you will. They'll spend days, weeks, waiting around for a likely mark, get their hooks into them, try to gently suss out whether they're buying and, if so, what sort of quantities and, based on that, they may or may not act as a kind of local agent.'

'I'm with you. A broker, sort of thing?'

'Exactly. He'll act as negotiator for you, probably take a commission fee either end.'

'The wily little sod.'

'I know. Clever, too. University in Rabat, spent a year in Oxford as well, it seems.'

'Really? Reading what?'

'Listening, mainly, I'd imagine. He was at the language school . . .' Mac laughed. Bunty's tone changed. 'I know. So, like I say . . . you look after yourself, Billy. Be careful.'

'I will be.'

'Stout fellow.' She hesitated, wondering whether to tell him that the girl had flown. What good would that serve, though? None. She gave a resigned smile into the mouthpiece. 'Ciao.'

She hung up. Mac sat there, flipping his BlackBerry over and over in his hand, forewarned but not, as yet, forearmed. He lay his head back and listened to the plaintive yearning of the call to prayer drifting in, sad yet sublime. With none of his usual gradual slide into slumber, Mac fell immediately into a deep and heavy sleep.

He woke, still in his linen shirt and shorts, knowing immediately and intuitively that he'd slept well. Background noise had started seeping into his dreams – a persistent, scraping, scratching noise; the soothing gush of the mountain stream; the lugubrious clip-clop-clip of slovenly hoof. And, now he sat up, there was laughter, too – a distant, distinctly female merriment. He padded across the cool, tiled floor and flung open the shutters, only to find himself shrieking and jumping back in shock. A small, inquisitive monkey sat on the window ledge, staring directly at him. It showed its teeth and held out a hand. Mac, still shuddering, backed away to the bed, picked up a pillow and shooed it.

Moments later he was chuckling to himself, sitting on the ledge with a glass of crisp, clean mountain water, watching a laden donkey making slow progress up the steep stone steps below his window.

Having showered and dressed, Mac reckoned he'd take a gentle stroll. With no hard-and-fast plan, he began his amble up the stone steps, following the sound of the water. The further he climbed, though, the more the aquamarine wash of the old town began to give way to tatty alleyways patrolled by packs of ravenous cats. He cut across a narrow footbridge and, once more, the sound of female gaiety clashed with the surge of the waterfall. He followed the path and he could see them now, a group of women, some older, but many of them still girls, gathered around a Roman-style outdoor bathhouse, washing and thrashing their clothes dry. He nodded and smiled *salaam* but nobody responded. The women stayed quiet until he'd passed.

He was aware that his stomach was starting to rumble. His assumption was that this downhill path would, if he didn't overshoot it, take him back to the main plaza. If so, he could delve into one of the cobbled side streets and see about a light breakfast, some reviving juice and a socking good cup of coffee. He passed through the archway into the souk and, setting his face in a permanent smile and his eyes on a mid-distant spot, he manoeuvred his way past hopeful stallholders, their luxuriant rugs bending their display ropes low under their weight. He passed rows of spice displayed in sacks dyed in vibrant blues, magenta, brilliant shades of yellow, green and orange;

trestle tables near buckling under abundant piles of handbags and leather goods. He walked on by, ignoring ranks of beady traders, unready, as yet, for commercial combat – his ambitions stretching no further than a thick, freshly pulped orange juice.

He found a cafe in the shade of an alleyway and sat himself down at the sole outdoor table, perusing the menu. A middle-aged man came out, nodded and stood almost to attention.

'Welcome to my country.' Mac was scarcely feeling the love, but he nodded his thanks and returned to the menu. The owner continued with his spiel – his name was Yesil; he hoped to make McCartney happy – then headed back into the cafe.

Mac was enjoying trying to work out what was what. He'd thought most Moroccans spoke French, but the menu was written in Arabic and Spanish. He was subconsciously aware of approaching footsteps and felt the presence of an onlooker but, his controls still set to contact avoidance, did not look up.

'Nice leather belt, sir? Very good price! Two hundred dirham . . .'

Mac readied a polite rejection but burst out laughing with relief and pleasure when he looked up to see Ahmed El Samir standing over him, clad in a more generously cut Hugo Boss T-shirt and charcoal-grey jeans. Mac gestured to the other chair.

'You'll join me for coffee? Have you eaten?'

Ahmed sat, his eyes playful. 'I shall gladly share some *bagrihr* with you,' he grinned. 'Perhaps some *yoaurt*, also? But please, Mr Davies –'

'For the last time! Call me Phil.'

'Philip, sir . . . *coffee*? No. Please, no. We shall drink tea. Fresh, reviving mint tea . . .'

Mac bowed his head in acceptance, and Ahmed went inside

to order. A moment later he reappeared, pulled out a chair and sat. Mac smiled.

'So? Just passing?'

'Yes indeed, sir. Though it is no real coincidence. I pass this way every day, on my way to work.'

'And what is your line of work, Ahmed? If I'm not prying . . .'

'Prying? No! What is this? *Prying!* Purely a European construct. No, no, no, no, no . . .' He leaned the chair back onto two legs and looked McCartney over. 'I feel I know you, Philip, sir. I feel I trust you. I *know* I like you!' He gave a hearty guffaw.

Yesil came out with a jug full of thick, bright vermilion orange juice, two glasses, two teacups and a glass pot of green-brown tea. He set them down, turned on his heel and went back inside. Ahmed let his chair plop back onto all four legs. He leaned forward, picked up the jug.

'Let me ask you something, Philip, sir. And please – you must tell *me* if I am prying . . .' He poured the orange juice, so fresh and full of pulp that it slid from the jug in chunks. He placed the jug carefully in the centre of the little table and looked directly at Mac. 'Are you a policeman?'

Mac's face must have expressed the precise opposite of the vicious stroke of panic that ripped through him. Ahmed started laughing again.

'OK, OK, OK. Sorry, I had to ask! By all the heavens, I would so love to show you a picture!' He clapped his hands together, laughing hard.

Yesil returned carrying a plateful of semolina pancakes in one hand, sand-brown and puckered with crispy dark surface bubbles. From his other hand, he laid down a bowl of syrup. He nodded and returned to the cafe. Ahmed leaned forward again, his eyes twinkling.

'So. Philip. Let's dispense with Sir and Mister, now we are friends . . .' He held out his hand. Mac shook it. Ahmed eyed him. 'May I ask, then – are you a drug dealer?'

It was Mac's turn to laugh, but he understood that this, now, was critical. How he replied would dictate the manner and the speed at which things moved forward. He looked Ahmed right in the eye, playful but deadly serious too.

'A drug dealer? I don't know. I've certainly never seen myself that way . . .'

'But?'

'But what?'

Ahmed laughed again, his eyes encouraging Mac to relax; to trust him. 'I definitely sense a "but" . . .'

Mac sat back and, his eyes never leaving Ahmed's, took a glug of his orange juice. He'd trained repeatedly for moments such as this, with regular refresher courses, new techniques and counter-surveillance developments to be aware of. But he'd been away from the front line since the Rozaki case and, if not self-conscious, he was aware he was rusty. He needed to close this, yet he was hideously self-aware of his every tic.

'Ha! Yes. Well, here's the thing . . .' And as he spoke, the assurance came flooding back. He was believable. He believed in himself. 'I like pot. I think pot is A Good Thing. I'm here to smoke some – obviously. And it has certainly crossed my mind that I might send a little something home, too . . .'

'Just a little?'

'Depends how good the smoke is.'

'It is the best.'

'Well, then . . .'

Ahmed's face broke into one of his enraptured smiles. 'Well, then, Philip. I think we gentlemen understand one another, no?'

Mac gave it the full eye contact, lowered his voice to a hush. 'We understand one another. Yes.'

Both men reached across the table to shake.

Zafer Ertegun shaved, as he always did, with his eyes closed. He soaped his blighted face with carbolic, whipped it to a rich, creamy lather, and feeling out the stubble with his fingers, stretching his loathsome skin tight with his chunky big thumb, methodically, rigorously, he sliced away his beard. He would shave himself, then repeat the operation, soaping his face, running the razor over every last resistant clump until his face was glowing. Only then would he open his eyes. Still the same. It was still there. He sighed and dried his face and lumbered through to the office to start Mehmet's job for him.

Mac surmised that the 'friend' they were en route to meet would be another intermediary, one more link in the chain of command that might, if he played this right, take him inside the Red Fort. The taxi bumped its way over potholes and splits in the rough mountain road.

'You ever been busted, Philip?'

'Of course!' He racked his brain for places he'd worked, places he'd read up on, places Ahmed might not know. 'I've been banged up in Thailand for a month, done a week in Buenos Aires, just for smoking *chala* in a public square. More often than not, though –' he rubbed his fingertips across the top of his thumb to signify cash – 'the local cops are ready to listen to reason. If they bang us up, it's a cross we have to bear, isn't it? You?'

Ahmed shook his head slowly, his face clouding over. 'To be honest, I've done a little time. Like you say, it's an occupational hazard. A bit of time isn't so difficult. It's the flying that kills me.'

'Flying?'

'They don't do that in Thailand? I thought they did. You're lucky . . .' He winced and shook his head again. 'It's not so bad at the moment, but every so often, the secret police here will have a purge. They pose as a buyer . . .' He winked at Mac, who tried to stifle the rush of an adolescent blush. 'If you're unlucky and you try to sell to one of these bastards, that's when the nightmare starts. They throw you in a cell, strip you, make you lie like this.' He hunched himself like a kid at a swimming pool, about to attempt a bomb, then jerked his head back. 'They put a sack over you, cuff your wrists together under your knees.' Tears were beginning to form in his eyes. 'Then they slide a steel bar under your knees and hoist you up like this.' He wrestled with himself on the back seat. The driver gave a nervous glance in the rear-view mirror and continued, unabashed. Ahmed gazed wistfully out towards the encroaching white cloud of the Rif Mountains. 'Strung up for days, like a trapeze. Seriously. Man cannot endure a pain worse than this . . .'

Mac didn't know what to say. He searched for the right facial response – understanding, fraternal, outraged – but Ahmed was back again, pointing up to the mountains.

'Not so far now . . .'

Mac was dying to ask – *where are we going?* – but he knew he'd just have to sit, and wait, and hope. The taxi's tyres skidded in the grit as they hurtled round another dizzying bend. He glanced out of the window and winced. The drop was sheer and terrifying – unrelieved cliff and rock with a 300-foot plunge to the ravine below. The driver accelerated into a short, straight stretch then slammed on his brakes as they hit the next bend. Ahmed pointed to a little roadside hut with a peeling, faded sign, a few hundred yards ahead. He said something to the driver, who hauled the Mercedes off the road, a physical drop down of a foot or two that sent the chassis crashing, then crunched over a stone-strewn parking area before coming to a halt. Ahmed scanned the car park and slapped Mac on the thigh.

'My friend is not here yet. Come. See . . .'

He shouted at the driver, who scurried round to open the door for him, avoiding eye contact as Ahmed heaved himself out. Mac got out his own side and followed Ahmed to a low stone wall. Beyond it was a drop of a thousand feet, easily, then the distant domes and minarets of Chefchaouen way down below and, beyond that again, the valley stretching out back towards the coast in swathes of clay and rust.

'Look . . .' Mac followed his pointing finger to two huge rocks astride a peak below them. It looked as though the rocks had, on a count of three, fallen sideways towards each other, their peaks colliding head-on so that they held each other up, forehead to forehead, for time ever more. 'See? The Bridge of Heaven!' And it was. They were. It was supernatural.

Ahmed's hand darted into his pocket and whipped out his vibrating phone. He paced away to the far side of the car park and then, after a terse conversation in Arabic or Berber, shuffled back to McCartney, smiling.

'So. Philip . . .' He gestured towards the shack. 'Some lunch?'

Ten minutes later they were sitting at an outdoor table, enjoying spit-roast lamb smothered in fresh mint with a fruity couscous on the side. The place looked decrepit and, even at this altitude, no stranger to fleas and other such pestilent crawlies but, in spite of his misgivings, Mac was smacking his lips in delight.

'Bloody hell!' He held up a forkful of lamb as he chewed, nodding his head in approval.

'What did I tell you?' beamed Ahmed. 'Fresh mountain

lamb. There is no comparable taste in the world, anywhere. None.'

'Not even the goat?'

'The goat is good. The lamb, though . . .' He kissed the tips of his fingers. '*Parfait!*'

A black, open-back pickup truck bounced off the mountain road, into the stony car park. Mac, still a stickler for trucks and wagons, made it straight away – the Isuzu i2o8 from a few years back. This one was battered, scratched and scraped from its working life, but it still made McCartney's heart sing.

The driver stepped out and stretched. He was taller than Ahmed, lean, with a look of the young Omar Sharif about him. He was dressed in a khaki shirt, buttoned right up to the collar, and cotton slacks in a slightly darker khaki. In contrast to Ahmed's cheerful demeanour, this guy was giving nothing away. He was also, quite clearly, the boss. He cupped his hand and beckoned Ahmed towards him, keeping his eyes on Mac all the time. Ahmed trotted over. The two men had a brief discussion then Ahmed went across to the taxi, leaned inside the passenger window, muttered a few words and handed the driver some notes. The cabby reversed the Merc towards the cafe shack and, tyres crunching in the scree, turned his car round and headed off back down the mountain pass. McCartney felt a lurching stab of apprehension as he watched the sun glint off the roof of the receding taxi. He was vulnerable all of a sudden, isolated and wholly at the mercy of two men he barely knew.

Ahmed cupped his hands around his mouth. 'Phil! Please. Here, if you will . . .'

His tone was false and jaunty, over-friendly. Omar Sharif leaned against the side of the truck, eyeing Mac carefully. If the idea was to intimidate him, it was working. He put his best foot forward and strode towards them, eyes on Omar, trying to give back some attitude.

'Philip. I'm pleased to introduce my good friend Rachid.' So *this* was Rachid! Hassan's son by his mistress. He nodded, still reluctant to embrace the newcomer. 'Rachid has very kindly agreed to let you observe some of our . . . sorry, what I mean to say is he's happy for you to see the ethical procedures and organic process that goes into the production of the excellent, first-grade hash that bears not just the name of the Rif but its particular and distinctly wonderful flavour, too . . .'

And you're not a dope salesman, smiled Mac to himself. He waited for Ahmed to finish his spiel and offered Rachid his hand, and his most businesslike face.

'Tell Rachid thank you. I am grateful, and very honoured. I hope to make this visit worth his while.'

Ahmed gabbled his translation and the three of them jumped aboard the Isuzu. Rachid revved the engine to its maximum and turned to Mac.

'Welcome to my country,' he said.

A fleeting smile then he was solemn again. He released the handbrake and commenced their journey up the mountain with a crunching wheelspin.

'Morning, Kenneth . . .'

It was Bunty.

'Have they found her?'

'Not as yet. But we *have* had an interesting call . . .'

'Go on . . .'

'Absent friend flies in. Customs flagged him as iffy, but couldn't hold him on anything. They've been running it since Tuesday. Guess who?'

She told him. Shanley was, briefly, lost for words.

'Fuck me,' he said. 'That *cannot* be a coincidence . . .'

After climbing the Ketama road even higher into the mountains they turned right just before the clouds and began a bumpy descent along a narrow track. Once or twice the big truck's wheels skidded over the edge, only to right themselves and continue the journey. Mac held his guts in and tried to keep his face in neutral. Ahmed leaned into him and whispered in his ear.

'He doesn't usually do this. Maybe three, four meetings first. I have assured him you are cool.' He winked at Mac. 'So be cool . . .'

Rachid eventually took a left turn towards what looked like an abandoned mountain goat farm. He pulled up in a partially enclosed yard. Through a wide, crumbling stucco arch was a verdant slope where donkeys grazed. Rachid jumped out, clapped his hands and walked briskly towards the main farmhouse, jerking his head for Mac and Ahmed to follow.

On a big, rough-hewn table in the centre of the frugal kitchen was a small pile of tendril-type leaves of a sort Mac would have recognised anywhere: the distinctive, faint mauve trichomes of the organically grown cannabis plant. He smiled, picked up a stem and smelt it, and nodded his head, relieved at the chance to prove he was cool.

'Nice,' he said.

Rachid retrieved the bud, and muttered something to Ahmed.

'First grade,' said Ahmed, making a little ring with thumb and forefinger. 'The best.'

Rachid ushered them through a whistle-stop tour of the farm. The outbuildings, dairy and abattoir had all been reconfigured for purpose – that purpose being the harvesting, stripping, thrashing, pressing, wrapping and transportation of potent Rif Mountain hash. Various workers bowed their heads as Rachid came into their part of the production line, their faces taut with fear. As they walked from workhouse to workhouse, teams of young men hunched over long tables or sheets of muslin gauze, immersed in their own part of the process. Ahmed explained that the main harvest was reaped throughout summer, with bales and bales of *branche* brought down from the mountains, where it grew in abundance, for drying and separating. Some of the kids seemed to be just rolling the trichomes gently across the surface of the gauze. Ahmed didn't comment, so Mac tried his best not to stare.

They went outside, Rachid hauling open stable door after stable door, gesticulating towards gigantic bales of dried-out *branche*, as though an enormous cannabis tumbleweed had blown down the mountain, gathering up more and more bud as it rolled on and on, until it crashed in through the barn doors and holed up there, the size of a hot-air balloon. Ahmed nudged Mac. He looked concerned.

'I don't think he likes you . . .'

'What have I done?'

'I'm not sure. But try to, I don't know . . . try to be more interested!'

'I *am* interested!' he hissed. Jesus, if Ahmed only knew – he was fucking fascinated!

He sidled closer to Rachid and turned to Ahmed. 'If it's not impertinent, can you ask Rachid about prices?'

Ahmed's face broke out in a radiant smile. He clapped his hands together and muttered in Rachid's ear. Rachid turned to face Mac, looked thoughtful and, eyes never leaving McCartney, barked a few words at Ahmed.

'Where does your interest lie, Philip?'

Mac kept up the eye contact with Rachid. 'In what sense do you mean, Ahmed?'

'Do you want the third grade, which is, I assure you, good

enough for most casual smokers in Mother England. It's excellent. Very cheap. We hardly smoke it at all here, unless it's rolled with black tobacco.' He took a step closer towards Mac. 'Or there's the second-grade stuff, which is very nice, soft and malleable, very good hash indeed . . .'

'I'd like to know about the really good stuff. What's the story there?'

Ahmed turned to Rachid to relate all this and, for the first time, the taller man visibly relaxed. He smiled without anger, gave one curt but conclusive nod of the head and, palms outward, swinging both arms to herd them back to the farmhouse, he walked behind them, whistling.

Back at the table, he twisted his head round towards a side door and shouted out instructions. Moments later a young man, facially quite similar to Rachid but wiry and much smaller, brought in a small puck of resin the size of a chocolate bar. Rachid pointed to the table in front of him and dismissed the kid. He smiled and unwrapped the bar, chattering gaily to Ahmed, now. Ahmed turned to Mac.

'Philip. Rachid asks if you would be so good as to remove your ring.'

Mac's heart lurched. The ring! Would they compute the Masonic symbolism of its crest – a standard geometric set square and compass framing the letter G? If they recognised the symbols then they'd understand that the G stood for any God, regardless of faith. His big concern was the Masonic iconography, though – hardly in keeping with an international free spirit like Davies and more usually associated with the police, the judiciary or the armed forces. He was less worried about the words engraved on the back of the band but, even there, there was cause for minor concern. The signet ring had been his father's. The engraving was highly personal – a message about their nature, and the nature of their work – yet he had no choice but to take it off. Two eager hash dealers were smiling expectantly, waiting for him to play his part. He smiled back, wiggled the ring free and passed it to Ahmed. Rachid glanced at the ring, hesitated for a moment. Mac felt the first stabs of a fear-sweat prickle his top lip. He gave a little cough and covered his mouth, wiping his lip at the same time. Rachid held his hand out, and Ahmed passed him the ring. He held it up, as though assessing its worth but, although he seemed to watch him carefully as though expecting a reaction, there wasn't the faintest flicker of a question in his eye. Rachid sparked up a Zippo lighter and whacked the flame up to its highest setting.

'A man of good taste,' said Mac in an attempt to work through his anxiety. He'd given up the carlotas for New Year, but still presided over an extensive collection of Zippos. Rachid seemed to understand, looked at the lighter, nodded, and began gently heating the seal on McCartney's ring. Ahmed observed Mac's face, amused at his growing consternation.

'Don't worry, Phil. Watch . . .'

Rachid held up the ring, seemed satisfied and, holding down the bar of hash with his left hand, gently pressed Mac's ring into the surface of the dope. A mild but woozy aroma rose up from the table, prompting laughter from Ahmed and Rachid. Rachid beckoned McCartney closer. He pointed at the bar of hash. A circular pool of almost-clear cannabis oil had risen to the surface where he'd pushed the ring into the puck. Ahmed clapped his hands together.

'See? The very highest quality . . .'

Mac smiled and nodded. 'Wonderful . . .'

Enjoying himself, seemingly, Rachid lifted the ring to reveal a perfect, patterned Masonic seal, imprinted on the face of the hash. Again, Ahmed chuckled and clapped his hands.

'You can create your own Mr Davies seal of excellence!'

Mac beamed back at him, for all the world the besotted pothead who has just this second had a glimpse of his bountiful future. The kid came back in, whispered in Rachid's ear. A quick flash of consternation shot across his face but it was gone in an instant, as though he'd merely willed it away. Ahmed clocked it though, and bit his lower lip. He stood up and clapped his hands again, less ebullient, more businesslike this time.

'So? Gentlemen. Philip – would you like to talk quantities?'

Rachid sat back in his chair, his gaze flitting from Mac, to Ahmed, back to Mac. He stayed on him, his eyes narrowing until they were like two sharp gimlets probing into him. McCartney tried to conjure a number that would get him off the hook and – maybe – get him an audience with The Man. He mugged up an expression, shrewd and calculating, suddenly, aiming for the insouciance of a man of the world who played for high stakes.

'Let's go a ton, for starters.' He flicked at his fingernails with his thumb. 'If the price is right . . .'

Ahmed smiled and shook his head and shared the joke with Rachid. His coal-black eyes bore into Mac and, for an eternity, he just stared at him. Every spore and instinct told Mac this was judgement hour. He didn't flinch. Seemingly satisfied, Rachid beckoned Ahmed over and spoke into his ear. Ahmed nodded.

'We do not offer the first-grade in tons, Philip. But a bar such as that in front of you is two thousand dirham. As a new and – please, do not take offence – *untried* customer . . .' Mac was already closing his eyes and nodding his 'no problem' back at Ahmed and Rachid. Rachid just looked at him. No expression. '. . . Rachid could, once consent has been given by his people, consider selling you one thousand bars . . .'

Mac popped his bottom lip out as though mildly disappointed but, generally, satisfied. He shrugged again.

'Tell him that's fine. Two million dirham? I'm in.'

Ahmed relayed it to Rachid. In spite of the order, he still didn't seem overjoyed. He snapped back at him.

'Rachid wishes to learn how you propose to pay such a sum.'

From somewhere deep within, Mac found a calm and confident voice, and a face to match it. He was terrified. They weren't talking fortunes – it was about £150,000 – but he had to get this right.

'However he wants, really. Obviously I don't carry that amount of cash . . .' He forced a laugh. Ahmed joined him. Rachid stayed silent. 'But I can arrange a banker's draft, a cash transfer to a named account or, if this is what Rachid prefers, given twenty-four hours I can arrange a cash payment in any of the major currencies . . .'

Ahmed nodded and translated the gist of the message to Rachid. He gave McCartney his killer's eyes once more then, after a short eternity, seemed to relent. Ahmed waited for Rachid to get up from the table. He winked at Mac as Rachid dictated his terms. Ahmed nodded.

'It has to be dollars. He says he'll do that weight for a discount price of two hundred thousand US dollars – in cash. Can you do that?'

Rachid circled the table and lingered behind Mac. McCartney got out his phone, brought up the calculator and went through the motions of working out sums.

'I reckon so. I'll need to send an email to my bank. OK?'

Ahmed reported the latest to Rachid. He nodded, eyed McCartney again, said a few more words to Ahmed, then left. Mac rattled off an email to a bot they'd created, and named Stephen Robinson at the RBS. Stephen's email account would be monitored by one Bunty Soames at the SIS, who would, with great discretion, forward key correspondence to her former boss at MI6, Kenneth Shanley, MBE. He pressed Send and waited an age for it to fly.

'There!' he smiled. 'Job done.' Only then did he get up. He held his hands out to Ahmed. 'So? What now?'

The Isuzu's engine fired up and, with the same theatrics, Rachid revved and raced away.

'He's gone to speak to his boss,' said Ahmed.

'Right,' Mac nodded. He waited, and fixed his eyes on the fixer.

'Who's his boss?'

Ahmed didn't blink. 'His name is Hassan El Glaoui.'

The sound of the helicopter approaching had long announced a dreaded return to her living hell for Millie. Even as a child her fairy tales had given her nightmares, and here she was, locked up in a tower with no one to let down her hair to. Today her bleak mood was tinged with fear, too, as she spied the black hornet in the sky, whirring ever closer. He'd be back shortly, and then it really would be game on.

She and Yasmina had laid this plan with patience and forethought. The breakthrough was getting the iPad but, even there, they'd had to resist an overwhelming urge to simply and very loudly shout 'HELP!' They knew they only had one shot at this – one life – and they had to get it right. If Yas had, as they'd considered, announced to her growing band of followers that they were being held captive in the Rif, what then? Her father had a mega-powerful security, surveillance and Wi-Fi system, all channelled through the enormous satellite dish on top of the storehouse that was now as much a part of the landscape as the Red Fort itself. If the men weren't watching the Spanish or EPL football, they were surfing the Net, downloading pornography, eavesdropping on celebrities' Twitter accounts. It was one thing posting accounts of their privations in the hills under an assumed name. That could fly peacefully under the radar. But if Yasmina named herself? If she began to describe the Fort itself? They'd be onto it and onto them in no time at all, and that would be their life used up.

Besides, suppose she went for it and blew the whistle, loud and long. What if no one took her seriously? What if they *did*? Hassan had everyone from politicians to army officers in his pocket. He owned every other policeman, every checkpoint on that mountain road. And Morocco had its independent sovereignty, too; there were no extradition treaties, no way the SAS could parachute in to their rescue, bayonets in mouth . . . if she and Yas were going to do this, they'd have to go solo. Tainted Love would play its part when the time came.

It was the third day now, and she had to keep believing Yas had made it there. She was a resourceful kid. She'd find McCartney. The big task for Millie since she'd gone had been postponing the discovery of Yasmina's flight. It could, all too literally, become a case of every extra hour they bought being critical. She'd laid the ground bait with the girls, telling them poor Yasmina was unwell. Next she developed the story, playing to their preconceptions by telling them it was a rare, contagious Western illness, chickenpox – she must have picked it up from one of the European guests at the funeral. As a European, she herself might be susceptible, too – so it was best that everyone kept as far away from the tower as possible.

She knew for an absolute fact that Dr Azabal would not risk his own health coming up there to treat a contagious disease – not for a woman; not unless Hassan ordered it. The main thing now was to ensure that Hassan did not order it. The helicopter, hovering like a giant black cockchafer, was slowly beginning its descent to the landing pad. He would always come to her first thing on his return, Hassan – but this time she was ready for him.

Shanley stared at the RBS email. It sounded as though McCartney was making progress. Reflexively, he started analysing the email for any hidden code, before catching himself out and chortling at his own obsession. He keyed in a non-committal but hugely credible reply, assuring Davies his request ought to pose no problem, but politely asking that he pop into one of their partner banks – listed – with photographic ID to confirm such a large cash transaction. He pressed Send and, although the mail went instantaneously, habit made him wait there to satisfy himself it had gone.

Fear and anticipation flooded Mac as he tried to think on his feet. So it was definite; it was the El Glaouis they were dealing with here. Within the hour, they'd be off into the heart of darkness. How to do this? If Millie was there, if he *saw* her – how best to pull this off? The thing he knew for certain was that, if he fucked this one up, they would both be dead.

'Please. Five minutes,' said Ahmed. Mac nodded mutely, barely registering the portly go-between as he slipped outside. Checking he wasn't being followed, Ahmed climbed a rough scree slope and kept climbing until the cannabis farm was way below him. He pulled out his phone and deftly removed its SIM card, slotting in another straight away. He put the battery back in, cursed how long it took to reboot then, after an eternity, checked for reception and dialled. Three long, almost continual ringtones, then the recipient picked up.

'Roig.'

'*Hola . . .*'

Ahmed spoke to him quickly, in Spanish. 'I'm worried. Rachid isn't stupid. I think he suspects –'

'Suspects? Suspects what?'

'I don't know. Maybe not. He didn't confiscate my phone, so maybe it's OK.'

'So? What makes you think he's on to you?'

'It's just instinct. I saw it. That kid, his brother –'

'Rifat?'

'Him. He told him something. It was important . . . I felt it.' He turned 180 degrees, looking for a landmark. He spotted a sole, football-sized rock, daubed red by the goatherds – a path stone that had come detached and, over time, toppled down the slope. 'Listen. Make a note of this. I'm a few hundred metres above the factory. It's mainly scree – but there are two little bushes springing out. As you look up from the factory, a few metres past the bush to the right, there's a shepherd's stone, painted red. OK?'

'Yep, hang on . . . just getting that down . . .' Ahmed waited. 'OK. So . . .'

'So I'm going to stick what I've got under that stone. OK? Just in case . . .'

'Sure. But you'll be fine.' A pause. 'Aren't they going to miss you?'

A mile below, there was the Isuzu, thundering down the mountain pass. 'I'm going back down now. Did you run the Brit?'

'Yes. Not much on him. Seems legit, though . . .'

'Has he got money? I don't want to get in there and –'

'He's loaded. Inherited wealth. Look – don't start wobbling now, Askri. This is it. We've got Hassan this end, wire-tapped, photos, audio, everything, right here on Spanish soil, setting up a big shipment with the Ukrainian lunatic. Fucker left Palma heliport ninety minutes ago. He'll be back there any time now. You know how to play it with El Glaoui – he's greedy. The Brit bangs in a big order. The money changes hands. The shit is there on site . . .' A pause. Ahmed could hear Roig's laboured breath rasping as he got more excited. 'Just hang on in there, Younes. We're on our way. You line them all up, kid – money, drugs, guns – line them all up in a row and we've got these fuckers at last!'

UDYCO Special Officer Younes Askri – Ahmed – nodded and tried to picture the endgame. 'Don't worry about it. I'm not going anywhere. You sort the paperwork?'

Roig had not sorted the paperwork. It would take the pen-pushers months to debate the ins and outs, if they ever got around to it at all. They could enter Morocco on a surveillance-only brief. Arrests and any subsequent charges would have to wait until Hassan El Glaoui strayed back onto Spanish soil. But if he were to cut up rough with their agents out there, if force were to be their only option and, God forbid, Hassan El Glaoui were to be injured in any rearguard action, then nobody would be crying themselves to sleep over him. No one could say El Glauoi hadn't had it coming to him for years, the bastard.

'All sorted. Where's he staying, anyway? Davies?'

'He's at the Dalia. Why?'

'Might just check in there myself, you know? Give it the once-over, while you guys are up there bonding in the peaks.'

'Just . . . be wary, boss. These guys are sharp as knives. Keep me posted.'

Roig rogered that and hung up. The call over, Ahmed slid the dedicated SIM card out, removed the media card with all the photos, the videos, the conversations – including the last twenty-four hours – and replaced them with his regular-use substitutes. If Rachid and co. *did* turn him over, all they'd find were texts and calls to non-existent contacts, referring to deals that would never take place. He sighed and tried to get an accurate sense of things, but all he knew for sure was that something wasn't right. He started back down the slope towards the farmhouse, stopping at the red-daubed rolling stone. Holding the SIM and the media cards on the flat of his palm, he dug down into his pockets for a note. Their entire case against Hassan El Glaoui and associates was there on those two small chips. A gust of wind, a sudden stumble and all their work would be as nothing. His fingers located a fifty-dirham note, wiggled it loose and laid it flat. Gently, deftly, he placed the SIM then the media card on the note and wrapped them tightly in the crown currency of Morocco. He moved the rock to one side, cleared some stones and dug out a hollow with his index and middle fingers. He slotted the evidence away and rolled the rock back over the shallow grave, making sure the red-painted surface was facing up. He stood there for a moment, surveying the silent, perfectly still landscape. Who would ever guess what took place, up here? Hundreds of feet above, an eagle soared; beyond it, the distant but unmistakable chop of a helicopter. Ahmed bent his knees low to the scree, and scrambled back to the cannabis farm.

Hassan was willing the helicopter down so he could get on with this. The meeting with Martinez had been worth the cop's weight in grade-one hash — which was, no doubt, what he'd end up paying his man in Palma, once he'd shored up this latest threat. The young officer's revelations had shocked him at first, but he was calm now. He and his father had seen off worse before — his father had told him to shoot his own brother, for God's sake! This was his first big challenge since taking over the business, and it was one he would rise to. He'd called Rachid straight away and told him to be there when he landed. He glanced up at the tower, but today the girls would have to wait.

Rachid was already waiting by the storehouse. The two men went inside. He could see from his eyes that Rachid had news, but he knew better than to speak before his father. His boss.

'So. You want to say "I told you so", don't you?' He smiled and clasped Rachid's shoulder. 'Well, you were right . . .'

Rachid acknowledged the half-apology with a nod.

'What about the Englishman? Did your guy know anything about him?'

'He ran him on their system. He's real. But let's have one of the boys take a look in his room.'

Rachid smiled his slow, pantomime villain's smile. 'Already done.'

'And?'

'And it's not just our stuff he's into . . .' Again the smile, accompanied by an injecting motion into his right forearm. 'Seems like he's fond of wild horses . . .'

Hassan clapped his hands together. 'Excellent! A degenerate. This could be very good for us.'

'Good? How so?'

'Perhaps this . . .'

'Davies.'

Hassan winked. 'Perhaps Davies is less . . . *disciplined* than the others. Don't you think?' He grinned again. 'I think we should put our Mr Davies to the test.'

'How? Give him smack?'

Hassan placed his hands on Rachid's shoulders and looked into his eyes. 'No. We don't need horse to see how far he'll go. Have Rifat bring them down here.'

'Both of them?'

'Yes. For now.'

Rachid shrugged and plucked his phone from his pocket.

Ahmed was not himself. Ever since he'd returned to the farm-house he'd been preoccupied and as the old wagon bumped along the track and edged out onto the mountain road, his face was etched with fear. All of a sudden, Mac worked out why. On a deal this size, he stood to earn a decent commission – enough to keep him in shirts and chinos of every conceivable hue, for quite some months. Mac patted him on the leg.

'Ahmed, before we get to wherever we're going, you and I need to discuss terms. Does Rachid – or his boss – pay you? Or do I?'

Ahmed forced a rueful smile and a laugh. 'To be honest, I like to try for both. If people are happy with my work, I don't believe it's immoral to expect some token of their appreciation . . .'

The kid gave them a languorous glance then returned his eyes to the road.

'So – there's no set commission, as such?'

The playfulness returned to Ahmed's eyes. 'Indeed not. It is a matter for your own immaculate discretion. Please do not feel restrained. The sky is the limit!' He threw his head back and roared with laughter, but there was no mirth in his eyes.

Stretched out on the bed in the sparse flat, Yasmina found herself flitting between fear and excitement, anticipation and dread, rampant hope and asphyxiating despair. She understood the sense in lying low. She knew this was never going to be a quick, one-stop fix. Yet, after the terrifying and ceaseless thrill of the last few days, she felt flat and vulnerable. She'd waited in the Internet cafe to see how the latest Tainted Love went down. The usual supporters had rallied around; the same encouragement, positivity, sisterhood and love. It was great, but somehow she'd expected more. She'd expected a saviour to emerge. It wasn't just that, though. Right from the start, this had been a joint effort between herself and her mum – and that, it now hit her, was what ailed her. It was simple. It was primal. It was biological. She was missing her mum. She took out the iPad, thinking she would watch their videos. She booted it up and, straight away, saw the Wi-Fi connection. She'd be five minutes, no more; have a little look at the blog. See what was happening in the world. What harm could five minutes online do? She tapped in her code.

McCartney tried not to react or give anything away as the old cattle wagon juddered round the bend and the Red Fort loomed into view. It was squat and foreboding, teetering at the very edge of the ravine. It had none of the maudlin grace he'd anticipated, yet Mac had no doubt that this was it; this was the place and now was the time. Somewhere down there, Detective Sergeant Millie Baker was alive and none too well. He was going to find her. He was going to free her. Poor Ahmed, the dupe, knew none of this and would no doubt pay the price at some point. No matter. Whatever Hassan might do to him, it was as nothing compared to what he had taken from Millie. With a crashing sadness, Mac realised his mind's eye was picturing Millie as he'd last seen her – half a lifetime ago. How would she look, now? How great a toll would her ordeal have taken on her?

They veered off the mountain road and bumped along a rocky dirt track, Mac feeling every jolt in his hip bones and backside. With an awful finality, the Red Fort rose up out of the dusty earth ahead of them, more of its spectral silhouette coming into view the closer they got, until the entire compound was right there, dwarfing them. McCartney could see its huge wooden gates being dragged open, like a scene in a Western. This mission was different, though. This time, he would not be riding in on a fast mustang, his lasso spinning above his head, ready for the catch. This time, it felt very much as though he *was* the catch. There, legs apart, standing a yard or two outside the Red Fort's gate, was Rachid. He walked towards them, raising one hand for Rifat to stop. He came to the passenger side, put his head through the window – and smiled.

'May I have your telephones please, gentlemen?'

Ahmed swallowed hard before translating for Mac. 'Do not worry,' he said. 'It is perfectly standard procedure.'

But his face told another story.

Hello, hello, hello, smiled Zafer. What have we here, then? Kennington, hey? Ho ho ho, let's home in on that, shall we? Iffy signal, darling. What's wrong with you birds and broadband? Always the bare fucking minimum! Hang on, hang on, hang on, don't bail on me now, baby – let's see who you are. *Hoooold* it! Oh. Now then. Nice. *Very* nice.

He reached for his phone to call Mehmet, then changed his mind. Her face was looking at him, pleading with him; so beautiful. Such a fucking waste! He popped his flies open, fished it out and flicked back to her blog page, reading the whore's fantasies, ardently working his cock. Mehmet could go to hell. This one belonged to Zafer.

At Jo's suggestion, Roig stood out back in Bar El Zhar's pretty garden, but it wasn't a simple matter of mobile reception. Younes Askri's – Ahmed's – phone was dead. He went back through to the bar and rolled his eyes at his colleague from Customs. Jawaad Callas – Jo – had been the Servicio de Vigilancia Aduanera's first ever agent up in Chef when they'd started the op two years ago and it irked Roig he couldn't pull rank on him.

'Nothing?' asked Jo. Roig shook his head. 'What now?'

'He's in trouble. I can feel it . . .' said Roig. 'He's up there, Jo. He's on his own up there, behind enemy lines . . .' He paced up and down, his forefingers pressed to his temples. 'The drugs are there, the Englishman's there . . .'

'What you thinking, Roig?'

He turned sharply.

'It's now or never. We've got to go up there and get them.'

'When?'

'First thing.'

'With respect, Jus – how the hell do you suppose we're going to do that? *How?*'

'I haven't quite worked that out yet . . .'

'Do you not think we've spent our every waking hour out here, trying to work up a credible way of doing exactly that?'

'I know. I'm sorry, Jo. But Younes is my man. He's UDYCO's responsibility.'

Jo held up a bottle of brandy. Roig nodded. Jo examined and wiped two little tumblers and poured two good measures. The officers sat down in silence, sipping at their liquor. Roig pulled out a tattered map and spread it out on the table, pondering how to make his move on Hassan El Glaoui.

McCartney could not quite pinpoint what was making him so apprehensive. It wasn't that they'd asked Ahmed to go with Rachid and Rifat so abruptly. Rachid returned some time ago, and there'd been no further reference to Ahmed – yet he'd seemed fine about going with them. The implication was that Hassan just needed time alone with the Englishman. Talk business. Straighten out any loose ends. That was normal.

It wasn't the fact that Rachid had stood silently in the doorway, since his return. He was like some deadly sentry, guarding against possible invasion – or rescue. Mac now realised that the thing making him jumpy was almost indiscernible. It was Hassan's attitude, his demeanour. He was forcibly cheerful, his conversation skittering trivially from one vague topic to another. Has Mr Davies been to Moro in London? Delicious! Best food in town! And he had it on good authority they might be opening a restaurant in Palma, too. What about the football team, though?! Hodgson! Was he really the best England could do? Was the nation that gave the world its favourite sport reduced to this eccentric old guy to deliver them from evil? He laughed dementedly at his own quip, looking and sounding like a cokehead. He caught his breath – Mac had had to throw himself into minor convulsions, too – then changed the subject again, never once threatening to get down to business. McCartney observed him, thinking back to Ibiza, all those years ago. This man had callously and with malice aforethought gone to the White Island and kidnapped his adored colleague Camilla. And he could kill him, for that – with ease. He could reach across now, before Rachid had time to react, and slash Hassan's scrawny windpipe with that stoning knife next to the dates on the tabletop.

Maybe *that* was why he was nervous, too. It had taken him until now to recognise it, but the fact was that he was sitting there harbouring murderous intentions. He'd have to regain control, pull back – sit tight. Without method, there'd be madness. If he had any realistic intentions of getting Millie Baker out of captivity and safely reunited with her daughter, he was going to have to get back into role. And, as though reading his mind, Hassan leaned forward.

'What a poor host I am! You must think me very rude, Mr Davies –'

'Philip. Phil . . .'

'Phil . . .' Hassan smiled and stroked his moustache as he

cast his eye over him. 'My friend – would you like something to smoke?'

It was absolutely the last thing in the world he wanted. He shifted in his seat and smiled back.

'I thought you'd never ask, Hassan.'

Both men guffawed and clapped their hands.

Yasmina had flirted before, but never with the option of actually meeting her correspondents. She was frightened now. She was aglow. She'd followed Jessika Flannagan's blog, on and off, since she'd first got the iPad. Kickass had a cult following, with J-Flan writing about her life as a kick-boxer who liked girls in a straight-ahead, almost macho style. She split opinion right down the middle. Her detractors accused her of a latent misogyny, and it was true – she described her sex life in uncompromising detail, if not objectifying her lovers then coming within a stiff nipple or a cute backside of doing so. With Jessika, everything from bottoms and Vespa scooters to the roof garden on a Dalston loft were 'cute'. Yet Yasmina couldn't help it; she loved her tales in all their dirty bravado, especially reading them from the austere confines of the Red Fort. Only two weeks ago, J-Flan's world had read like fantasy to Yasmina; a world she would never, *could* never know. Now Jessika Flannagan was messaging her, telling her she 'ruled' and asking her if she fancied meeting up. There was nothing Yasmina fancied more, but God – she was petrified. She made the arrangements and called up her guardian angel.

'Yes, I'm not kidding. The Macbeth. It's a pub –'

'I know it's a pub. I know it very well, as it goes . . .' Carrie chuckled. 'I knew you wouldn't let us down. Pick you up in ten.'

Yasmina rifled the wardrobe in despair. It was great of Aasiya to find her this place, but it was spartan beyond belief. And it

was *so* lovely of her to bring round those clothes, but for this –
a sort-of date with Jessika Flannagan? Even in this weather, she
would rather wear her vest top and shorts than any of the
assorted figure-denying jibabs that her friend had donated.

Eavesdropping on virtual sex was one of his very favourite
kicks, but the lezzers hadn't got it on. Were they toying with
him? They knew he was out there, watching them. Everyone
fucking knew! Well, if they wanted to mess with him, he'd
mess with them. Simples! He looked up the pub, huffed and
puffed a bit at the distance, but decided they were probably
worth the cab fare. He stared at his phone for a moment, as
though the very act of looking at it would magnetically draw
it towards him. Accepting that he'd have to move, he heaved
himself up from the sofa and lunged for the mobile as he
plummeted back down again. He caught his breath for a
moment and dialled.

'Mehmet. Got an address for you . . .' He sat back and
listened to the praise. 'Well, that's why you come to me, right?
If you want to track her, talk to Zafer the Gaffer!' They
indulged one another with laughter before Zafer was able to
speak again. 'So. Obviously I can't be precise as to flat number
et cetera, but I'd lay very good odds the bitch is in this place
in Kennington . . . no, *Kennington*. Yes. Oval. You got a pen?
Here we go, then . . .'

Mehmet diverted, it was now his sole and pleasant duty to
decide what he was going to do to them. To a degree, that
was up to the lezzers themselves and how they decided to
play it. Whatever, this Young Turk was going to have some fun.
He dialled up a taxi and lumbered to the door to wait.

Mac hoped they'd just leave him there playing dead. They were
pretty done in themselves – the hash was absolutely

mind-blowing – and McCartney had made a wonderful job of his deceit. For a start, they'd got along well, the three of them. Rachid slowly began to relax – presumably after they'd rifled his BlackBerry and read the email to Stephen Robinson at the Royal Bank of Scotland. Whatever it was, both of them had a different attitude to Mac – Hassan was less jumpy, Rachid much more personable. One sat either side of Mac who was given pole position at the head of the table. After a couple of apple brandies, Hassan slid his arms across the table, craning his head towards McCartney.

'Philip. So. Our mutual friend Ahmed has asked some questions and gained some answers, which leads us to questions anew . . .' He laughed self-consciously and continued. 'Earlier, purely as precaution, we mentioned to you a level – an entry level, if you will – at which we would be prepared to fashion a deal. But now . . .' His eyes were gleaming. '. . . A situation arises whereby we find ourselves holding excess stock which we're keen to dispose of. As a gesture of goodwill to a new partner, we'd like to invite you to be among the first to benefit from this . . .'

Mac summoned up every ounce of pop-eyed enthusiasm he could muster. 'Wow! I mean, *yes* . . . like, how?' he spluttered. Hassan leaned right into his face.

'How would it sound to you if we were to multiply that offer by ten?'

He did his best to look both flattered and dismayed simultaneously, slowly shaking his head from side to side and letting out a long, quiet whistle. 'Twenty million dirham? I just don't know if –'

A quick glance between Hassan and Rachid, then Hassan cut in.

'That's where this gets better and better. It's almost too good to be true. I shan't go into details – discretion is longevity in this business. Suffice to say there are certain economies of scale, Philip. We can do you a deal, so long as you can move decisively and immediately.'

'What sort of deal?'

'A crate this size would usually attract a price of around two point five million dollars. We can do business at a million . . .'

'Such a discount being for cash, I take it?'

'Correct.'

'For ten thousand bars?'

'Yes. It's a one-off, half-price, cash deal, that we're able to offer because of exceptional circumstances . . .' The leery smile was back. Mac tried to repress a shudder. 'And because it's you.'

'And in terms of delivery?'

Hassan, for the first time, looked irritated. 'We're an international operation, Philip.'

'You can deliver to the UK?'

'Depending on where in the UK, there is a small additional charge. Alternatively, we have situations in Mallorca, in mainland Spain and in Amsterdam where you are at liberty to collect, at your convenience . . .'

Mac couldn't resist. 'Where in Spain?'

Hassan held his stare for a beat, his face betraying nothing. 'We have a smallholding within driving distance of Tarifa and Algeciras,' he smiled. 'Is that convenient?'

Mac tried to pitch his response as though used to fielding such propositions on a regular basis. It was a combination of the accommodating shrug, the jut of the lower lip, a fleeting, calculating expression and an acceptance – perhaps just a shade too hasty – that, all things being equal, this was a proposition he could sustain.

'Fifty per cent now, balance on collection?'

'We can live with that.'

'I'll have to finesse things with the bank, obviously . . .' He smiled at Hassan. 'To which end, I could do with having my phone back.'

'Of course.'

Hassan nodded to Rachid who, with some reluctance, placed the device back on the table. Face benign and smiling, Mac retrieved his phone and held out his hand to shake. First Hassan and then, curtly but not impolitely, Rachid shook hands, at which point Mac's expression gave way to childlike euphoria.

'*Fantástico!* Gentlemen – we have ourselves a deal!'

And so the party started. From nowhere, a troupe of musicians filed into the room. The little band set up, and in no time they were playing a hypnotic hybrid of Berber folk and mizmar-infused Levantine jazz as McCartney tapped his feet and slapped his thigh. A succession of women brought in plate after plate of Moroccan mezze – lamb meatballs spiked with paprika and fresh mint that McCartney could have devoured all by himself; tiny chops, seared almost black on the wood-fired grill, yet pink and tender to the knife. There were skewers stuffed tight with fat langoustines and fleshy cubes of moist white fish, grilled to flaky perfection. There were bowls of couscous and crunchy romaine salad sprinkled with orange blossom – ambrosia to Mac as he nibbled then gorged on the delicate petals. And there was drink – lots and lots of drink. Leather flasks of sweet, brown shepherd's wine, sprayed directly into the gullet from an arm's length, head tilted right back; there were flagons of cloudy aniseed liqueur; there was beer and champagne, cold from the refrigerator; there was brandy of differing hues, flavours and textures – apple, nectarine and an earthy oak-aged cherry brandy as slick and punchy as anything Mac had ever tasted.

He could hold his drink, McCartney – in this job, it was

obligatory – but he was light-headed well before the tasting menu of cannabis treats came out. He tried a good-natured refusal, palms held up as he pleaded with his hosts.

'Gentlemen! Hassan, my friend . . .' He rasped out a throaty cackle, trying to seem more wasted than he was. 'Picture the scene please, as I enter the bank . . .' He wobbled his head and rolled his eyes. Hassan laughed and clapped his hands. Mac continued, his face contorted for comic effect. 'Excuse, Mr Bank Manager. I am a man of substantial means. Please hand me two hundred thousand dollars –'

Hassan held his hand up. '*Five* hundred thousand of your finest American dollars!'

Mac acknowledged the mistake, begged Hassan's pardon with a nod but quickly found his comic tone again.

'Please arrange for me to collect, in cash, half a million of Uncle Sam's excellent dollar bills as soon as you can rustle them up! I am an international businessman of substance. Please take me seriously . . .' He was again planting the seed of an idea that the local banks might not have such enormous stocks of dollars to hand. If he could legitimately buy some time and get away to Tangier or Rabat, he'd be able to orchestrate the rescue more effectively. 'Seriously. This is big, gents. I think I'd like to do it, you know . . . straight.'

Hassan grinned back at him. 'What? And miss all the fun? Don't worry! We have already spoken to the North Star Bank in Chefchaouen. They will have sufficient stocks of dollars by tomorrow afternoon.'

'Tomorrow? That's . . . fast!'

'Like I say – we are an international operation, accustomed to dealing at the highest level. Consider it done. Meanwhile . . .' He clapped his hands and a troupe of servers in ornate costumes brought out trays carrying a variety of long-stem, intricately carved sebsi pipes with their stone skuffs, and one huge, ornamental silver hookah with several crimson smoke pipes leading in and out of its swollen glass belly. 'Tonight we get fucked up! Yes?' He grinned deliriously. Mac felt queasy. 'Tomorrow is a new day. A new life. Rifat will drive you wherever you need to go. So? A little light kif to start?'

It was futile demurring. The scene was set. He had to make the best of it. Mac reached deep within to dredge up his most enraptured smile.

'Absolutely!'

Hassan clapped his hands in delight. Here was a man who loved the prospect of business and loved it when things went his way. Mac got up to survey the pipes.

Though by no means a Furry Freak Brother, he was well versed in the rituals. Every six months or so for the past twenty-odd years he'd attended various seminars and tutorials on what the job knowingly called Best Practice. He could do this stuff in his sleep, but he was aware that, behind him, Rachid was still analysing his every move. With an expert's eye, he ran his fingers over the sebsi murmuring his appreciation at the detail, the finish, before settling upon an elegant walnut stem with a carved-bone crucible. He reached into one of the raffia bowls, took a pinch of bud and rolled it gently in his palm, sprinkling in a bit of black tobacco. He plied the mix, tamped it down into the skuff and, before he got a chance to ask the question, found Rachid leaning over him with the Zippo. Mac craned his head back over his shoulder and smiled.

'Thank you, my friend. Come! Sit down! I have a story to tell you . . .'

And, for the next few hours, that is precisely how McCartney entertained his hosts. He regaled them with tales of derring-do in the drug trade; all true, of course, with the essential detail of the goodies' and baddies' roles being reversed. Rachid in particular loved Hassan's translation of the tale about Dougie Doughnuts in Fuengirola, a legendary fugitive and dealer they'd heard tell of, but never encountered.

The musicians took the mood down a notch, playing a soothing and beguiling Sufi blues while Mac spieled the Moroccans, and they smoked and drank and listened, enthralled. After a while they stopped offering him the pipe. Both Hassan and Rachid were past the point of no return. Mac rested his head on the table and feigned sleep, the plaintive clarinet soothing his buzzing mind. A harsh voice brought the music to an end – Rachid. Footsteps approached, then rough hands dug under his armpits and pulled him up. A younger voice, laughing – Rifat enjoying the spectacle of the far-gone Brit. A shrill stab of panic. What to do if they began to undress him? Simple. He wouldn't let them. He'd wake up. Mac let himself go floppy, mildly enjoying the sensation of the night zephyrs as they carried him out across the courtyard. It felt like he was flying.

Ahmed's spine was breaking. Trussed in a foetus position, suspended from the roof in the time-served style for snides and snitches, he'd long since stopped crying out for mercy. It only made the agony more intense – and no one could hear him down there, anyway. Rachid and the young driver had escorted him away as soon as they'd entered the compound. At first they'd marched him straight ahead as though they were going to hurl him off the edge of the cliff – then they'd veered right and opened up the white storeroom with the huge satellite dish on its roof. That was the last he saw of daylight. They'd bound him up and flown him from the ceiling. He had no idea, now, how long he'd been hanging there, upside down. If he tried to move or spread his weight out, shift the pain elsewhere, his throat seemed to tighten; yet, from this position, he couldn't get a clear look down at his neck. The mere thought that they might have hoisted him in a self-strangling garrotte was as horrific as the reality that they probably had.

Yasmina recognised her straight away. Leaning back against the bar, her elbows tucked in behind her, Jessika Flannagan was spectacular. She was rangy, wiry – taller than her pictures betrayed. She was wearing ripped, faded denims – jeans and a sawn-off Levi jacket – and Yas could not help but stare at her. Her arms, though slender, were tough and sinewy, slim muscles packed under ultra-white skin that was dappled with bruises of varying prominence. She seemed to sense she was being watched. She turned, initially angry and ready for a row, then softened when she saw the fudge-brown girl with the white crop. Her face split slowly as she smiled, as though separating into two. Her eyes narrowed as her big mouth pulled back, and Yasmina found the collision of opposites in her features – the beautiful and the ugly – all the more mesmerising. She stood there for a moment, agape, as Jessika approached her. She found her breathtakingly beautiful, imme-diately – yet everything was out of proportion. Her eyes were pushed right to the sides of her face. She had no breasts, but large hands, and, so languid was her gait, it seemed like she was walking in slow motion.

'Are you Yas? I'm so made up to meet you at long last,' she shouted before she'd even reached the petite Yasmina. There was an accent there; in some way reminiscent of James, back in the days when he first began coming up to the fort. He spoke differently, now – slower, much more deliberate and conscious of himself.

'It's great to meet you, too. I feel like we –'

She couldn't finish the sentence. Jessika threw her arms around her, pulling her face into her chest and holding her close. Yasmina inhaled her musky aroma, and she could imagine the effect it had on her was just like the men who lay around the compound, stoned on kif. Jessika released her from her embrace and stood back, taking her hands in her own big fighter's mitts.

'Just *look* at you, all cute and shy . . .'

Yasmina smiled and looked down at the floor. Her groin was pulsating and she felt her attraction was transmitting itself right through her limbs to her cheeks, her fingertips. If she didn't let go, she'd be getting an electric shock! She just wanted Jessika to smother her again or kiss her with those big, generous lips, but she stood back instead, still holding her hands. Just the one tattoo, she noticed – a wasp or a hornet, hovering above a vaccination mark. Jessika tugged her towards the bar.

'Come on. What you having to drink?'

'I don't, er . . . I don't know. Orange juice?'

'I said what are you having to *drink*?' Her mouth was exceptionally attractive, Yasmina thought. The way her lips curved upwards as she spoke – it was like her voice had a smile of its own. She liked her. She liked her a lot. She shot a sly smile back.

'I've never actually been in a bar before.'

'OK! Now you're *talking*! You do know there's a first time for everything, yeah?' She bent her knees and dropped down so they were face to face. 'And I do mean *everything*!' She pecked Yasmina on the forehead.

'Well, yeah. One thing at a time. I'll have a pineapple juice.'

'Jesus! I thought you'd sacked all that submissive shit off?'

'I have. I just don't like alcohol . . .' Her voice tailed off. There was a man watching them.

'How d'you know if you've never tried it?'

The man stood out for three reasons. Firstly, because he was one of only four males in the pub. The others were camp locals, performing a loud and gleeful character assassination on an absent friend. Secondly, because he was, physically, enormous – approaching seven feet tall but gigantically overweight, maybe thirty or thirty-five stone. The third reason he would stand out anywhere, let alone an eclectic Hoxton scene pub, was the livid red welt that clung to one side of his face. It was neither birth-mark nor burn, more like a growth, moulded to his face like a huge mark of Cain. It was hideous. She couldn't look away.

'Do you know that guy?'

'Which guy? I don't know *any* guys!'

'That big man with the, the . . . thing on his face. He keeps looking over . . .'

Jessika turned sharply, spotted Zafer and marched right over.

'Excuse me, fatso. You got a problem?'

'No. Why?'

'Cos you're freaking my friend out . . .' She looked him up and down. 'What you doing in here, anyway?'

'Free country, ain't it?'

'Is it? You could have fucking fooled me!' Zafer looked at the floor. She softened her voice. 'Look, no offence, mate – but fuck off, will you?'

He finished his drink and left. Jessika loped back over to Yas. She walked like she was skipping, without a rope. Yasmina found her face creasing into a delighted smile, all of its own volition.

'That was cool . . .'

'Anything for you, gorgeous!'

A girl with a platinum bob waved over from the elevated DJ booth. Jessika grinned and waved back excitedly with both hands. A shocking ire singed through Yasmina, the like of which she had never experienced before – her first stinging stab of jealousy. Jessika ran over to the booth, extended herself up on tiptoes and kissed the girl on the lips. She came straight back to Yasmina.

'Who's that?' she murmured.

'Who, Kat? Ah, she's just an old mate. She's the DJ here on Tuesdays.' She grabbed Yasmina's hand. 'You want to come and say hello?'

'No thanks.'

Jealousy was a wholly alien concept to Jessika Flannagan. She didn't notice a thing.

'Hey! Let's pick a record for you! What's your bag, sweetie? Let me guess – Pussy Riot?' Yas shrugged. 'No? Chvrches? Too obvious for a chick like you, eh? I know who you're into . . . Bleached. You fancy fucking Jennifer, don't you, you slag! I know it's not Jessica . . .' She pulled a clown-style sad face, then broke off into a throaty, dirty chuckle, coming up for air after a minor coughing fit. 'Come on, put me out of my misery. Name that tune!'

Yasmina couldn't help smiling. Her clit was still throbbing but her heart was pounding louder. She was in love. She pulled Jessika down and nibbled her earlobe as she whispered in her ear.

'My mum and I used to bop about to "Papa Don't Preach". It was her favourite, when she was –'

'Really?! Yesss!! Fucking *cute* or what!!'

She ran over to Kat, whose face lit up. On went Madonna, and the little dance floor was overrun. Even the three queens were up, Vogueing up and down then turning to each other to make 'keeping the baby' mannerisms. Yasmina bumped up to Jessika, lost in the moment. She never thought this time would come, for her – and it was heaven. Then, out of nothing, Jessika stopped dancing and leaned down and kissed her, slowly and fully, sliding her tongue into her mouth, scratching her nape with one broken fingernail. Yasmina was gone. She wished the song would never end.

Though he'd heard the crunch of the key in the lock downstairs – it sounded big, and final, somehow; the fatal thud of a deadlock – and the tip-tap of their footsteps ricocheting back across the courtyard, Mac lay there for several minutes longer until he was sure there was no one else there. The room was in absolute darkness. He couldn't risk putting a light on, not even the small bedside lamp he could feel but not see. He couldn't recall a blackness so dense; even now, his eyes had not adjusted to it. Movement would have to be painstakingly slow, quiet and instinctive. He stood there and listened out, then took his first step forward, his arms fully extended in front of him. He stopped, then took another step, stopped; then one more step. His knee crashed into something hard that moved slightly. A dressing table or chair, most likely. He'd been heading in the wrong direction. He turned and now, on the other side of the room, he could just about make out the faint outline of a door. He stopped, gripped by a sudden fear that, obviously, they would have locked him in. Yet he had no recollection of that – perhaps they thought he was so out of it, he'd sleep till noon. He shuffled across the floor and tried the handle. The door opened with a deafening creak.

Mac winced, waited, digging his nails into the palms of his hands then inched his way out to the staircase. Mercifully, it was lighter out there. Looking up, there was a central skylight where the old opening had been glazed to keep out the elements. There was a central stairwell with sturdy wooden doors leading off. Beyond one of those doors, he was certain, lay Camilla Baker – awake, asleep or, more likely, in some endless limbo in between. Well, not for long. That was what he was here for. Billy McCartney was going to find Millie and bring that limbo to its end.

Keeping his shoulder to the wall – the steps had no rail – Mac began a languid bend-and-push motion, crouching on a step and, leaning into the wall, straightening himself and taking a step up before repeating the routine, so he made slow but very steady progress upwards. He got to the first door, stopped and listened. He couldn't hear a thing anyway, but instinct told him the room was empty. He carried on, upwards. Would they really have her at the top of the tower, imprisoned like some forlorn folklore damsel? He was starting to think they had, when his elbow came into contact with a smaller, iron-studded door. It moved slightly. He pushed it ajar and peered around it into the blackness beyond. It was difficult to see, but the door seemed to open onto a narrow passage. He took the single step upwards to his right and felt his way inside. The passageway was cool and musty, the brickwork slightly moist. The corridor came to an abrupt end when Mac hit his hand on a jutting wall of rough stone. He turned, minutely panicked and claustrophobic. If this was a trap, if they locked him in there . . . he breathed his way through it and out of it and now, looking back the way he'd come, he could see another little door set into a recess in the passageway. And, just as he'd known for sure that Millie was not in the first room, Mac felt a shiver of absolute certainty that this, in front of him, was her cell. He put his lips to the keyhole and hissed: 'Millie!' Nothing. He tried again. 'Millie! It's me. McCartney!' He waited. 'Mac!' he hissed. Still no noise; no response. It did not deter him. Nothing could shake his conviction that she was in there. He glanced around and behind himself and shut the little door leading back out onto the stairwell. He knocked, too gently at first. Inaudible. He gritted his teeth and clenched his fist and knocked, harder, with the knuckle of his middle finger. He stood back. Waited. Listened. And it came – something. A sigh, or a groan, some mewling, off-key howl, but it carried that same plaintive note and the same timeless, unilateral meaning that accompanies ruptured slumber the world over:

'What? What *now*?!'

Mac felt an almighty, quivering shudder of relief and elation, up and down his backbone. He clenched his fists and tilted his head backwards as if that would tip the tears back inside his eyeballs. He bit his lip to suppress a joyous yelp and lurched back to the keyhole.

'Millie! Come to the door!'

There came the faint pad of sleepy footsteps. A grumpy, unfamiliar voice.

'Who's there?' She sounded alien. 'Who *is* this?'

Another shiver of fearful anticipation. What was he going to *do*? If this was Millie – and it was – if she were able to open the door – and she might – what, then, would they do? Could they just flee down the mountainside? They would have no choice, but their chances of survival, let alone success, were abysmal.

'Millie? Can you hear me? It's Mac . . .'

'Mac?'

'McCartney . . .' He swallowed. 'From Ibiza . . .' Nothing from Millie. Silence. 'Millie?'

'I'm here . . .'

'I've come to find you. To take you back . . .' No answer. 'Can you open the door?'

'It's locked . . .'

From outside the tower, voices drifted on the wind, changing in volume and direction.

'Don't worry. What's your routine?'

'Routine?'

'When do they bring meals? Do they let you out, at all?'

'Is this you, sir?'

The onrush of emotion – not sorrow, not guilt, not shame, but something of all three, a deep and sudden and painfully felt understanding of her tragedy – made him dizzy for a moment. He had to strangle it tight, but he felt like crying.

'Yes, Millie. It's me . . .' The voices were, suddenly, coming from directly below. That same, thudding clunk of the deadlock. Shit! Why? What were they doing back here? He hissed through the keyhole: 'Millie. I'm so sorry. About all this. Everything. But I swear to you – I will get you out. Please believe me. I will get you out of here –'

'Don't leave me!'

He rapped out the necessary info with none of the necessary feeling, lest he were heard. 'I have to. Yasmina came to us. She's safe. We will come back for you!'

A disconsolate howl from behind the door as McCartney backed away. He could hear Rifat's voice below. Mac peered down. Still in the stairwell, talking to somebody out of shot. His back pressed tight against the wall, Mac edged down again, sideways, one step at a time. Rifat laughed loudly, then one slap, two, like he was giving his colleague a high five. Then, out of nothing, a light splintered on and Mac was caught in the white glare, trapped on the staircase. It flickered off again, but there was a low buzz from above. Mac jerked his head upwards to see what, and where – strip lights high up above, set into the double-glazed panel. Swift, nimble footsteps. Rifat was bounding up the stairs and Mac was feeling his way back down. The door was in sight now, just a few steps down. The strip lights winked on again, and Mac could see the top of Rifat's head bobbing up the stairs below, almost close enough to touch. He fell into his room and pushed the door tight shut just as the light from the stairwell flooded in under his door. He lay on his bed, facing away from the glow. The footsteps skipped past. Rifat didn't even hesitate outside. Mac listened and, a moment later, things were clear. He could hear Rifat click the smaller door tightly shut; the jiggle of the key, finding its way in; the crunch of the lock. He must have remembered, or had misgivings that he'd left the door unlocked. Shit. Five more minutes and Mac would have been spending the night in a damp corridor. And tomorrow, when they went to wake Philip Davies and drive him down to town . . . It didn't bear thinking about. He screwed his eyes tight shut and tried to will himself to sleep. Tomorrow, he could feel it, was going to be a big day.

James Rae found the place easily enough; a residential road off Pasley Park, and there was only the one building that had been divided into flats. Getting inside there was trickier. He did the usual thing, rang every buzzer, to no avail. Either there was nobody home – which would be bad – or they were a particularly wary bunch of residents, which would be even worse for an uninvited guest. He stood back by the wheelie bins and observed the building close up, his fingers entwined by the handkerchief in his pocket. Chloroform would get him – and Yasmina – a certain distance along the way. He still hadn't quite worked out how he'd get her back to Morocco. Same way he'd got her mum there, he mused, as a woman with dyed-red hair arrived at the main door and let herself in. Careless. She didn't wait for the door to click shut before scurrying off to her own bedsit. James caught the door before it closed and waited silently in the hall until the red-haired resident announced which flat she'd gone into. Within moments music blared out and he could hear her shouting down the phone. Satisfied, he crept up to the top floor and set about finding Yasmina's hidey-hole.

* * *

Yasmina woke to the buzz and blare of traffic. Even semi-awake, she felt the thrill in her guts. She propped herself up in the big old bed and, once again, succumbed to a powerful surge of liberation; of being reborn. She'd felt it last night, speeding through the slick night streets of London, clinging to Jessika as she piloted the Vespa through the rain. Yasmina had held her face up to the sky and let the rain fall down on her, in love with the moment; the night. The big casement window was open an inch or two, and the sounds of the city wafted up from the street. She could hear Jessika clattering around in the little kitchen where they'd made toast and Horlicks last night. There was another crash, another shout of 'Shit!' Yas smiled to herself and snuggled back down under the thick duvet. Then she thought of her mother. She would have to tell Jessika about her mum. She would know what to do. She'd probably fly over there herself and fight them all, one at a time.

Jessika came in carrying a laden tray. She laid it down on the bottom of the bed and gave Yas an indulgent smile.

'Here you go, girl. Get this down you . . .'

She stretched across to pass her a glass of pale orange juice and set about pouring coffee from a big stainless-steel pot. Yas took a sip of the orange juice and tried not to wince. She pointed at the egg cups.

'What are those?'

A look of pure adoration backlit Jessika's eyes.

'My God, you are fucking gorgeous . . .' she whispered. 'Come here.'

She took the glass from Yas's hand and kissed her tenderly. Suddenly she jumped out of bed and ran to the little desk by the window. She flicked her laptop's lid up, sat down and began typing at feverish speed, her tongue sticking out to one side.

'What are you doing?' laughed Yas. 'Sudden inspiration?'

'Spot on,' grinned Jessika. 'I'm making a humble announcement to my people that, for the first time in her miserable, hateful life, Lady Jessika has been hit by Cupid's arrow!'

Yasmina hesitated, then came out with it.

'If I told you her story . . . would you write something about my mother for Kickass?'

Jessica turned round.

'Fucking right, kiddo. Fire away.'

A gentle tap on his door.

'Yes?'

'Philip. No rush, but breakfast is laid out in the main house whenever you are ready,' Hassan cooed. 'And Rifat is at your disposal, once you receive word from your bankers . . .'

Mac padded over to the door. He was going to enquire about Ahmed – surely *he* should accompany him – but decided to bide his time.

'OK, Hassan. Thanks,' he shouted back, trying to sound bright and breezy – up and about and raring to go.

He thought his best policy was to act as gung-ho as possible, just as though he were among friends. They were already beginning to underestimate him nicely – all he had to do was keep up the idiot-savant act. They'd had a terrific time last night; they were going to formalise arrangements today. This was just the start of a profitable ongoing relationship. Why *wouldn't* he take a stroll around the compound? So long as he wasn't furtive; he should whistle, greet people, let his goodwill be felt all around.

He dressed quickly and splashed cold water on his face. There was a new toothbrush, toothpaste, shaving gear, soap and towel in the little en suite. He gave his teeth a scrub and neatened up his stubble. He stood up on the bed to try and snatch a view through the glazed loophole and get his bearings, but all he could see was the sky. He had an idea. Stepping down onto the bedroom floor, he rolled up the towel, got back on the bed and craned his arm up towards the arrow slit. Straining and stretching up as far as his sinews would let him, Mac managed to suspend the towel from the window latch.

He let himself out of his room. Standing out on the stone staircase, he had to suffocate the compulsion to nip back upstairs, slip a note of reassurance under Millie's door, make sure she understood that the countdown to freedom had commenced. It was all too close, now. Any slip-up, any false move, and the likelihood was they would both end up dead. He went down the worn-hollow steps and out into the courtyard.

He looked up at the tower, and could see the towel, just, dangling pitifully halfway up. He tried to make a mental trace of where the door would be, which direction the steps took him and how far up the little recessed door had been. He walked back round the tower and over to the low wall. Below and beyond it, a sheer drop. Just peering over and down made him giddy. He stepped back and went round to the other side of the tower. Here there was a little promontory, just a short spur of rock and scrub overhanging the ravine to its left, but its right side gave onto a gently sloping headland, scarred down the middle by a rocky goat path. Deadly dangerous but, next to the cliff face, not impossible.

'It's beautiful, no?'

Mac didn't turn round. 'Unbelievable . . .'

He could hear the relaxed smile in Hassan's voice.

'Our visitors never want to leave!'

'I'll bet!'

Hassan came and stood alongside him. He was wearing a pristine white linen shirt, jeans and pearl leather deck shoes, with shades perched on his forehead. The two men stared out in silence over the gorge, right down to the plains below. Mac prayed Hassan would not look up and see the towel in the window. His host turned and squeezed his shoulders.

'Some breakfast?'

Mac knew he'd have to get back up to his room first; put everything exactly how he'd found it.

'Sure. Thanks . . .' His best bet was, as always, to play on his opponent's greed. 'Just let me go grab my phone. Make sure the transfer's all fine.'

'Good move.' Hassan patted him on the back. Mac could feel his tension. 'I'll see you in a minute, then.'

He strolled across the courtyard to the big house. Mac gave it a moment then headed back into the tower.

'Sir, I've got to tell you . . . I think this is only going to end up one way,' said Jo.

Roig laughed and clapped him on the back. 'You're right, Jawaad. The way this ends is glory all the way!' His face lit up as he leered at his junior. 'It ends with another promotion for you, salvation for Younes and incarceration for El Glaoui and company. *That's* how this ends!'

'I just don't think . . .'

'Good! Excellent . . . because strategy is what UDYCO does best. No offence, Jo, but you Customs boys never did have much guts.'

'Sir, with respect . . . this is not a lack of courage, I promise you. It is the reluctant acknowledgement of reality. Younes and I have been up to the fort on surveillance how many times in the last twelve months? You've seen the photographs and the video footage we shot. That place is just . . . *impenetrable!*'

'That's why we need the chopper!'

'Sir, Younes is your guy. But he's my friend as well as my

colleague. I do appreciate the gravity of the situation. I understand that we need to act, and we need to do something fast,
but the *helicopter?* They'll hear it coming almost as soon as you
take off –'

'Nonsense! Filipe has assured me we can follow the coast
and cut inland at the very last minute.'

'*No offence*, sir, but Filipe has seldom left Ceuta in the short
time he's been stationed there.'

'Fine!' Roig was livid. It wasn't simply Callas questioning
his leadership, his strategy, his audacious rescue mission. It
was his overall manner. Ever since Roig had come up with
the idea, Jo had been talking to him as though he were insane.
But this was the direct opposite of risk. It was deliciously
simple. The little enclave of Ceuta was Spanish territory,
under Spanish control – a bit like the English and their
alleged acquisition of Gibraltar. There was a small but patri-
otic Spanish community in Ceuta, along with a naval and
military presence and a token police force. Half a bottle of
brandy into the night, Roig had jumped out of his seat, his
eyes wild with excitement, slapping his hands together in
triumph.

'Got it! The bastards! They won't know what's hit them!'

He'd bolted off to his hotel, made the calls he had to make,
sought the permissions and understood the caveats and condi-
tions before racing back to inculcate Jo.

'First light, Jo! First thing – they won't know a fucking
thing about it!'

Roig walked slowly and purposefully to the bar's doorway,
his every move exuding a barely suppressed ire. His back to
Callas, he stared out onto the street, tapping the door jamb
with his fingers. He turned suddenly, fixed his eyes upon the
SVA agent.

'You think this is madness, don't you?'

Jo thought exactly that. Any attempt to take the Red Fortress by surprise would require more thought and much more detailed planning than this. It was madness.

'No, Jus – sir . . . I'm in awe of your positivity. But –'

Roig held his hand up.

'It's fine. Stay here. Wash glasses.'

He walked out, turned right and didn't look back.

Rifat drove with one hand on the wheel, one arm dangling out the window, whistling gaily all the way down from the mountains. Mac tried to enjoy the scenery – the goats perched up in the highest branches, nibbling on the last remaining leaves still made him look twice, and then again – but his brain was crashing through the gears, eagerly trying to drill some cogent plan of action through the manic clash of ideas and contradictions. Mac gazed out across the valley to the domes and minorets of Chefchaouen. He filled his lungs with fresh mountain air as they descended, aware that his cool appraisal of the situation – or otherwise – would affect more than just his own well-being.

Juan Sebastien Roig looked down at the glittering sea below and clenched his fists tight to drive away the tears. To his right, the peaks of the Rif were cloaked in cloud. The moment was upon him. He looked round at his men – young, determined, ready – and he smiled to himself. A few minutes from now, it would all come together. He had enjoyed some exciting times since UDYCO was formed, yet the big-profile, international bust had somehow managed to elude him. In the early days, all those hateful Brits on the Costa, it had been the likes of Shanley, even McCartney who got the recognition. The Spanish put the hours in, and the men; they did the square-bashing, the intelligence and the backup; but they seldom got the plaudits. On the contrary, he himself had garnered something of a reputation as a cavalier. He touched the hardware gently with his forefinger, as though reminding himself of his own potency, his invincibility. They had tear gas, pistols and sub-machine guns, and, furthermore, they had right on their side. They had the ultimate weapon of surprise. And they had him. He touched Filipe on the shoulder to wish him the best and turned to his fine young officers.

'Three minutes, boys. Be ready.'

The helicopter began its descent.

Karim called Rachid from the control room – the Crow's Nest, as the student insisted on calling their observation deck. Rachid alerted Hassan, and the two men hastened up the short flight of stone steps above the storeroom. Karim would usually stand up when the boss came in, but this time he barely turned round. He pointed at the intermittent dot on the screen.

'How far away?' asked Hassan.

'Less than a mile.'

'What is it?'

Karim shrugged. 'Small aircraft or large helicopter. Almost certainly the latter, but neither represents good news . . .'

Hassan smiled and squeezed the kid's shoulder. They'd spent a long time looking for a prodigy like Karim, and now they'd found him, he was relentless. Since they'd brought him up here from Ibnou Zohr, Karim had not missed one single attempt – though he'd also scrambled them for an eagle (twice) and a paraglider (once). The paraglider's accident had been regrettable, indeed. He stepped back, eyes still on the screen.

'Tell them to get the bad boy ready.'

Karim grinned. '*Con mucho gusto!*'

As casually as though he were writing a letter or typing out

237

an invoice, Karim entered the code into his keyboard. He lassoed and highlighted the area surrounding the pulsating dot on the screen, then honed in with a crossbow sighting.

Rachid, his face tense, whispered to Hassan: 'What about Rifat?'

'Tell him to come back.'

Rachid nodded. 'The Englishman?'

For a split second, Hassan took his eyes from the radar screen. 'Abort.'

Rachid stepped away to make the phone call. Karim, lining up the target, isolated it on-screen.

'In range,' he said.

Hassan went outside to deliver the message.

Ahmed – Younes – picked out the distant whirr of the chopper's blades. At that point, he knew it was the end – and he willed it. He had almost stopped feeling the pain. All that was left of him were his thoughts and memories.

He could feel the impulse in their footsteps as they raced up the steps to the little cabin. The helicopter's approach grew louder. He could admire the audacity, but this was doomed. Why had Callas allowed it? Surely Jo knew as well as he did that they stood no chance. He heard one set of footsteps pacing around on the roof above. He knew who it was. He waited to hear his voice give the order – then that would be it.

Roig could see the layout clearly now. The El Glaouis had been considerate – there was an excellent landing space, right by their own black helicopter. Directly beneath them, a matter of a few hundred feet away, he saw the door to the little hut open up. A man came out and stood there on the roof, next to the enormous satellite dish, looking up at them. They continued their descent. The man was shielding his eyes from the sun. He looked as though he was smiling and, as they dropped closer, Jus Roig recognised the man. Yes – it was El Glaoui himself! Roig smiled too. This was perfect! It was going to be leader-to-leader. One of Europe's most ingenious and prolific hashish smugglers, Hassan El Glaoui, was accepting his fate and paying his great foe the ultimate compliment. He had stepped out to personally greet the indomitable force of law and order, Juan Sebastien Roig himself, ready to be taken down.

With slight dismay, he reflected that the hardware might not be needed after all. Then Hassan El Glaoui turned to his right and gave a signal. Roig was close enough, now, to follow Hassan's eyeline. Two men in camouflage emerged, and took up positions on a hillside platform. One was kneeling, a large, sleek, ground-to-air missile cradled in his arms like a baby. The other was pointing a rocket launcher right at them. Hassan El Glaoui dropped his arm. Fire! He'd never been a missile target before. Somehow he expected it to be louder, more raucous – yet it was almost serene. With an awed fascination, Roig watched the missile rip inexorably towards him, barely rippling the sky before it smashed into the side of the helicopter. He was already dead by the time the stricken aircraft burst into flame on the rocks below, so he did not see Hassan El Glaoui give the sign for his ground team to put out the fires.

For the second time in as many days, James Rae found himself exiting Turnpike Lane Tube station and heading down Green Lanes, head bowed against the bleak drizzle. He entered the cafe, but this time Mehmet wasn't there. Although his table was free – James suspected that table would remain free all day, every day, on the off chance Mehmet would come in – he sat down at the smaller, adjacent table. The same guy, recognising him as a man of some significance, scurried across with smiles and a menu, but James told him he'd wait. He turned to the inside back page of the *i* and commenced the basic crossword, barely registering their arrival when they came in.

'Now then!' laughed Mehmet, all smiles. A big, simple-looking lad traipsed behind him. 'What you do, sitting here?' He cast a perplexed look at the owner, simultaneously gesturing for James to rise and follow him to his regular table. 'This is Zafer,' he said, jerking his head at the kid behind him. He had a birthmark on his face so extreme that it looked like Spider-Man's mask. 'He'll be the one looking at the thing for you . . .' He sat down, heavily, bidding James to join him. Only when the two men were seated did Zafer sit down, pushing his chair right back so his legs could fit under the table. Mehmet beamed at the pair of them. 'First, however, breakfast is an absolute must!' He signalled to the owner for his usual. 'Then we talk business . . .'

James Rae didn't like the sound of that.

When McCartney came out of the bank with the bag full of dollars, Rifat – and the truck – had gone. The entire transaction had taken over an hour, so he wasn't surprised the kid had gone for a walk – a coffee, a mint tea or what-ever. There'd been a stringent security process which saw him, at one point, standing in a constricted alcove with reinforced-glass panel doors ahead of and behind him. For twenty minutes, nobody even acknowledged him. He remained there, trying to banish paranoid thoughts, focusing solely on the day ahead. Standing inside the cool, musty-smelling bank, another flashback to the flat in the Triangle where they probed the inner sanctum of Lance Campion's cocaine empire. He was thinking of old Shakespeare – how they'd sent him in there with the device buried deep inside a wad of notes; how the Granby boys had tricked them, and tricked them good. He was wondering whether Shanley's team would have the wherewithal, or take the risk, to plant a device in this batch, when a smart young clerk finally appeared on the banking-room side of the glass barrier. He smiled professionally and pressed a button.

'Mr Davies. Welcome to my country.'

The barrier slid back and Mac was welcomed inside. Half an hour later he was leaving with half a million dollars in cash – but Rifat had gone. McCartney walked up and down the street where he'd left him, fielding many more welcomes and several offers of tea, rugs, ceramics and drugs. He was baffled. There was simply no sign of the boy. His phone rang. Shanley.

'Mac. Thank God . . .'

'What?'

'I'll tell you in full when I see you – but you've got to get out of there.'

'*What?*'

'Flag the first cab. Get yourself to Ceuta and take the hydrofoil to Gib. Someone will meet you there. I'm on my way.'

'Boss! Sir! *Whoah!* Reverse . . .' McCartney found himself pacing up and down under a pulverising sun, the sweat trickling off him in torrents. 'What's happened?'

Shanley repeated, quickly and emphatically, what Jo had told him. Mac digested the news and, belatedly, stepped under the shade of a thickset palm. He took a deep breath and came out with it. 'Sir, I can't leave now. I won't. Camilla Baker is up there –'

'McCartney, listen to me. El Glaoui will have an assassination squad hunting you down already.'

'I don't care about that. And anyway, sir – I very much

doubt that is the case. I doubt that Hassan El Glaoui is thinking about anything other than getting away from the Red Fort for a while and lying low until the situation dies down.'

'Really?'

'I'm certain of it. He's a wily bastard. He may well have half of Morocco sewn up, but the guy's not stupid. He's just blown a Spanish military aircraft out of the sky. That's not something he can cover up with a few backhanders and an all-expenses-paid trip to Mallorca.'

'I hear you!' Shanley snapped. Then, relenting, murmured the words again. 'I hear you.' He paused. 'What do you suggest?'

'I suggest that, as we speak, El Glaoui will be packing up for a long stay in one of his mountain bolt-holes. And I'm very, very afraid that . . .' Mac hesitated, trying to drive the image from his mind. '. . . if she's still alive at all, sir – he won't be taking Millie with him.'

'Right.'

'I'd say we've got what remains of today to get her out of there.'

Shanley said nothing for a moment, then came back, his voice drained of emotion. 'Go and see Jo Callas. He'll be able to help.'

Zafer was at the little table James had occupied, his brow knit as he bent over the iPad. He sat back and waited, drumming his fingers on the tabletop, his eyes never leaving the tablet's screen. Something made him sit up. He picked up the iPad and began reading.

'What is it?' asked James.

Zafer said something to Mehmet in Turkish. His eyes smiled first, the rest of his face quickly catching up. He turned to James, beaming.

242

'Now I understand why you are so interested in this lady . . .'

James felt an alien jolt of anger and tried to suppress it, searching instead for the right balance of humility and business practicality.

'Indeed. So, now you know . . .'

'Now I know you are desirous of contact with the only daughter of the notorious Hassan El Glaoui, needless to say my curiosity is pricked . . .' he grinned. He slapped his hands together and sat up straight. 'But no matter! Ignore me and my vulgar ways. You know precisely what I am going to say to you, don't you, my friend?'

James did. James knew very well what Mehmet was going to say to him. He was going to tell him not to be offended; that business, as always, was one thing – friendship another thing altogether. He would express the wish that James was able to distinguish between the two, without emotion, without hurt – particularly without hurt, as the next thing Mehmet was guaranteed to tell him was that he'd be needing money in exchange for the information his man had prised from Yasmina's device. He didn't know how much money Mehmet would try to extort from him, but it would be more than £1,000 for sure. He twitched and contorted his face until he was smiling back gamely at Mehmet.

'I know *exactly* what you're going to say to me, my friend!' he chuckled. 'So the only question is how much?'

Mehmet looked him up and down, as though he wasn't quite sure how far to push it.

'Shall we say fifty thousand pounds?'

James Rae felt the stirrings of an almighty rage start to quiver. He bit down on his lip; tried to keep his eyes smiling.

'That's a lot of money.'

'It's a lot of information also, my dear friend James. Worth a *lot* of money . . .'

James made a pretence of giving the matter due consideration. He sighed and nodded. 'Very well, then. Fifty large.' He shook his head in acknowledgement of the Turk's cheek, his charm, his absolute ruthlessness in matters of business. He decided, there and then, that Mehmet would die for this. 'It'll have to be tomorrow, though, you heartless rogue. OK?'

Mehmet smiled. He was about to make the fatal mistake of underestimating his old acquaintance's own ruthless streak.

'For you?' His face dissolved into an enormous, affectionate grin. 'No problem. I split the difference, OK? You bring a bag to me here. Come this evening, late on, once the regulars have gone. Nice and quiet, nice mezze dinner, yes? Nice and civilised . . .'

James nodded once more and looked him in the eye.

'Yes. Sold. Tonight, then. So . . .' He turned his attention to Zafer. 'Where is she? Where in the world is Yasmina El Glaoui?'

Mehmet nodded to Zafer, who pulled out a pen.

'There are five locations in London where the girl spends significant amounts of time. One you have already visited and eliminated. I shall write down the other four addresses but, clearly, I cannot identify from historical usage which of these places, if any, she is likely to be at . . .'

Mehmet held out his hand as Zafer scribbled down the hot-spots she'd logged on from. What he omitted to tell him was that Jessika Flannagan had, in the last hour, updated Kickass to make a plea for Yasmina's mother's release from captivity and safe reunion with her daughter. And the hot-spot he did *not* note down was the name and address of the club where they'd be holding a fund-raiser that very evening. He was saving that particular reunion for himself.

Hassan pressed his lips to the keyhole.

'You are my wife. She is my daughter. We do not leave without you.'

Millie bit down on her lip to keep the tremble out of her voice. She inhaled, held it down, breathed out slowly, rocking backwards and forwards, then repeated it – once, twice and a third time. She came to the door.

'My darling. We cannot risk the journey. Not yet . . .'

'Then when?'

'Speak to Dr Azabal . . . he will better explain the complexity. There is a risk of infection to yourself and the others . . .'

There was a prolonged silence from the other side of the door. She could feel the kinetic energy of his ever-plotting, overheating mind. Just as she was beginning to wonder whether he had slipped away, Hassan spoke again – less impassioned, now; staccato.

'I shall send them on ahead with Rachid. Karim and I shall wait here. We do not leave without you and Yasmina.'

She choked on her grief; tried to swallow it. 'Very well, my dear. Thank you.'

She heard him stomp away down the corridor, heard the little door slam, then bounce back open against the wall. She waited, and listened. He didn't come back up to lock the door behind him.

Jo spread the map out – the same map Roig had stared at and obsessed over just the night before – and pointed out the landmarks to Mac.

'So it's . . . what you say? Easy sailing?'

245

'Plain sailing . . .'

'*Sí!* OK. Plain sailing, sure enough, until here . . .' He stabbed at a point marked out by the typical grey cartography shading that signifies mountainous regions. 'But here, yes? Bab Taza? After this, is no Morocco. Is El Glaoui. *Sí?*'

'I understand. Yes.' He looked up from the map and took a sip on his tea. 'How many men?'

'Is not just men, OK? Is time. Many, many, *many* check, yes? Many barrier in road . . .'

'Roadblocks?'

'Yes. Security check, see papers, see identification . . . I think is very difficult, this.'

McCartney heaved out a sigh of despair and, subconsciously, reached across for one of Jo's Camel Lights. He sparked up, sucked the smoke deep down and spoke as he exhaled.

'OK. So what are our options? How do we get up there? Now?'

Jo Callas sat back, eyed the English detective up and down and decided it was this, or nothing. So he told him how they'd get up to the Red Fort – and back down again – before daybreak. Just as Hassan's father and Mustapha's own father had done when they set up the trafficking route all those decades ago, they would take the goatherd's route up the western ridge of the mountains. But whereas Hassan's forebears had made the arduous journey by the painful and painstaking means of donkey transport, Jo was suggesting they rode up the mountain path on horseback.

'You can ride this, yes?' McCartney nodded. He could ride this very well indeed, as it happened. Jo smiled and nodded. 'Good. *Muy bien.* Is no just horse, this. Is Barb stallion, *sí*? Very fast, very good for the *hard*, yes? Very *valiente!*'

McCartney smiled back. 'I get you. Like mustangs, yes?'

'Berber mustang, *sí. Brava.*'

Mac nodded haltingly, unsure. 'Wild. Right. We don't have to *catch* these wild horses, do we?'

Jo looked at him as though he were the crazy wild horse. 'Of course! Must catch – then tame . . .' He winked and started laughing. Mac joined in, acknowledging his gullibility – a rare and blessed release of tension. He finished his tea and returned to the map. 'Is OK. I know where can get.'

'OK – and assuming we make it up there and get inside the compound in one piece, how do we get back down again? More to the point – how do we get Millie down in one piece? And how are we going to get her *out* of here!'

Jo got up from his chair and paced the little garden. 'Is no easy, this. First, I have question. You have the contact in Gibraltar?'

'Gibraltar? I think so. Why?'

'Is very important establish the, I don't know . . . is necessary all OK for you, for me, for the lady in the Gibraltar. Is possible?'

McCartney shrugged. 'Only one way to find out . . .'

Jo stopped at the far end of the little garden, smiling. He was starting to enjoy himself. 'OK. If is possible Gibraltar, then is possible this idea. OK?' He came back to the table and looked Mac in the eye. 'I have idea very, very strong . . .'

He sat back down again and told McCartney his idea.

The ranch was in the foothills just north of Amrah. A stick-thin woman with cropped hair and anthracite-black eyes greeted Jo like a brother.

'Manu, this is my friend Billy McCartney.'

Manu was already striding over to Mac though, hands on her hips, eyeing him up and down. She knew straight away – she saw right through him. She gave him one last look then turned sharply to Jo, speaking to him – speaking *at* him – in rapid-fire Spanish. She led them across to a pen, fenced on three sides by five-bar wooden panels and, on the fourth, by a low-roofed stable compound. Over by the stable were three muscular grey horses, prowling a sandy enclosure. With their short backs and powerful, slightly crouching flanks, all three steeds looked primed and ready for rampage – and McCartney had doubts he could master such a beast. As though reading his fears, Manu started laughing.

'Mean machines, hey?' she said, in English. She started looking him up and down again, legs astride and hands on her hips, smiling with her eyes. 'Not too much for a tough guy like you. Come on. Try . . .'

She leaned over the fence and slid the latch out, swinging a long, low gate back. She turned to Mac and beckoned him towards her with her three middle fingers.

'Come.'

She put her arm around him and walked him over to the horses, stooping slightly to whisper in his ear.

'This one, nearest, is Alvaro. He is a pretty crazy beast. Thinks only of himself, this horse . . . always looking for adventure.' She turned and eyed him intently. 'Do you like adventure, Mr McCartney?' He said nothing; looked at the hoof marks in the sand. She smiled and gently tugged him on. 'Perhaps Alvaro is not for you. Perhaps is best for Jawaad, Alvaro . . .' She pointed to a sleek, graceful horse that had, by now, stopped still. It stared at them as they got closer. 'This horse we call El Alemano – the German. Very good animal. Efficient. Obedient . . .' Her gaze carried on past Alemano to the third horse, bucking now, seeming to understand he was under discussion. 'But this little beauty . . .' Manu winked at Mac. 'Let me tell you. When it comes to the big things in life, I judge everything – *everyone* – by the Abba Test. Yes?' Mac chuckled at the absurdity of the situation – yet he understood, immediately. 'So – where do you stand, Mr McCartney, on life's most profound question? Agnetha or Frida?'

Mac twinkled back at Manu. 'Myself, I could never understand the big deal about Frida. Don't get me wrong, nice voice, couldn't imagine Abba without her, but this whole thing about her being the real beauty, the soul of Abba, no . . .' He shook his head slowly and decidedly. 'No question in my mind, Manu – gentlemen prefer blondes . . .'

She smiled sagely, slowly shaking her head. 'I knew it! I just knew it . . .' She took McCartney by the hand and led him across the enclosure. 'Come and say hello to Frida.'

The horse turned away from them and looked out and upwards to the hills. She ceased snorting and bridling and simply stood there, perfectly still, as though already mentally prepared for the task ahead. McCartney ran his hand along the mustang's sleek back, its pungent horse-sweat taking him back to childhood days. Virginia, the consummate equestrian. They were friends, back then.

They dismounted and tied the horses up by the abandoned shepherd's hut. Mac stood back in wonder at the silent magnificence of the Gates of Heaven, stupendous and ancient, the distant foothills and valleys shimmering in the heat. Jo laid down a tin bowl and filled it with water for the horses, then, dribbling a drop or two into his scalp and massaging the water through to his temples, he passed the bottle to McCartney and sat down. He patted the flat rock for Mac to join him, and pointed at the map.

'OK, so if I no make it, this is important, *sí*? This is life and death. When you get back to this place, here –' he jerked his thumb at the loose-stone hovel – 'is where arrive the . . .' He made an accelerating gesture with his wrists, turning both hands in on themselves.

'Scramblers,' nodded McCartney.

'The moto-scrambler, yes. OK . . .' He began tracing a line down the map. 'See? We are here. OK, now look – very important, this . . .' Mac got as close to the map as he was able. They were looking at a broken line that snaked all the way from the Rif foothills to the coast near Oued Laou. 'This is the old Via Contrabandista, yes? Very, how-say . . .'

'Dangerous?'

'OK, yes, is dangerous, but no for *attack*, yes? Is . . .' He picked up a handful of loose shingle and let it sprinkle out through his fingers. 'Is very difficult for the stability.' He straightened the back of his hand and made a steady forward motion. 'On *caballo*, yes, is no problem. But the moto . . . best to ride quick, but no crazy. Yes? If drive too speedy . . .' His hand came out again, this time signifying a crash.

'Cool. Can I see this?' Jo passed the map across, keeping his finger planted at their current location. Mac wrinkled his brow as he followed the smugglers' track down to Oued Laou. 'And what happens here?'

Jo grinned. 'Here is the best – if we get here!' He started laughing. 'But I think is very big *if*, Mr Mac.' He shook his head and visibly swallowed his misgivings. 'OK, here . . .' He pointed at a spot just north of the port. 'Here will be Djimi. Djimi is a *very* good guy – the best. Arrive Djimi in a speed-boat very fast . . .'

McCartney felt an inner thrill of excitement as the penny dropped. 'That's why I had to clear Gibraltar?'

Jo nodded, pleased with himself. 'This is the shortest crossing. For Djimi – no problem. But is necessary the conversation with Gibraltar, *sí*?'

'Fucking right . . .'

They shook hands, then, after a second, hugged warmly and

clapped one another on the back. They untied the steeds and mounted once more, squinting against the sun at the steep route past the gorge and up to the Red Fort.

Davey gave one minimal shake of the head and gazed out onto Kilburn High Road.

'You're sure this is what you want to do, Jay?'

James smirked into his pint, peering at his old comrade over its rim.

'Not like you to turn a job down, David . . .'

Davey laughed and jerked his attention away from the street life outside. Stirring his tea ceremoniously, he ran his eye around the Lion's ornate interior, his home from home when he was in town on business. Deep in thought, his attention eventually returned to his old collaborator. Now his full beams were focused on him and, again, he shook his head.

'It's not the job, my friend. It's the consequences. Think on it . . .'

'I've thought on it. I've no choice.'

Davey Lane took a sip of his tea, his eyes still trained on his colleague's twitching face.

'There's always a choice, Jay. Always . . .' He took another short sip. 'It's not as though these are nobodies we're talking about. Kill Mehmet Surin and we bring the whole of the fucking Bombaciler down on us – and not just the London end. Is that what you want, John-John? You want to go back on the run?'

James Rae – as he'd been for the last twenty-odd years – gave a resigned smile.

'I was going to have to do that anyway, Davey Boy.'

'How come?'

'I've fucked up with Hassan. Proper. I need the girl now for different reasons . . .'

'I don't follow you, boy.'

'Oh, it's simple enough, Davey. I had to find her and get her back just to keep the business alive. Now I need her to keep myself alive . . .'

Davey nodded his comprehension. 'And – suppose we do this – you've somewhere to lie low?'

James started laughing as he sang. 'Whoa! Back to the island!'

Davey Lane let out a loud, long sigh. 'Ay-ay-ay! Anything for a peaceful life. OK, Ned Kelly – what time, and where?'

The last of the convoy left the compound for the safe place, and Hassan signalled to Karim to come down from the observation deck. He understood intuitively that a storm was coming, but he felt sure he would ride this one out, as he and his father had survived all the other lamentable attempts on their livelihood – their way of life. Instructing Karim to secure the gates, guard the fort – and the skies – and keep an eye on the women, Hassan jumped in his truck and skidded off out of the fort's impressive portals. Karim heaved the door closed behind him, as Hassan headed up the mountain pass. Had he looked down – way, way down – as he rounded the first hairpin bend, he might have seen two microscopic figures on horseback, picking their way carefully but steadily up the eastern slopes. He did not look, however; Hassan El Glaoui seldom looked back, lest the past catch him up and bite him. He dropped down to second gear and revved as he hit the second hairpin, a delicious rush of well-being blasting through him with the wind that parted his hair.

The last great flight had been six years ago, and they'd survived that one just fine. Word came up from Tangier that the new inspector was keen for a trophy scalp, keen to make his mark. They'd do now as they did then – strike down the factories, burn out the storage barns, destroy all product in stock. Poor Philip Davies – the Englishman would go home empty-handed. Hassan smiled to himself. There would be others, dozens of them – there always were. He and his entourage could survive months, years in the caves; tourists would pay thousands to live in such lodgings, back to nature but with all the comforts a simple man might desire. He'd slip away after a week or two; spend some time in Spain, perhaps. Marbella. Mallorca. Ibiza. He had money – lots of it. He'd be treated like royalty.

He turned off the mountain road and bounced his way down to the farm. It was a chore, all this, but it was right that he attend to it personally. He'd roll all the bales out, like a sacrifice. He began to imagine the sight as the flames turned the sky red – the heavenly smell as the *branche* burnt to vapour. He'd sit back and watch, close to his land, his mountains, and he'd let his mind free itself of care. Afterwards, he would go for his wife and daughter; they'd have to come now, whether they liked it or not. Had Rachid taken care of Ahmed? He forgot to ask. No matter – he'd get the student to see to it. Then he'd have to kill him, too.

They reached the steep embankment to the west of the gorge and pulled up in a shallow dip. Calming the mustangs, gradually and eventually coaxing them to lie in the shade of the sole tree growing almost horizontally from the slope, Mac and Jo tethered the horses and began their ascent. From the dip – the size and shape of a grand piano – it was a sheer climb, with doughty bushes to cling onto as they hauled themselves up the gradient. Even through his canvas hat, the sun drilled a white-hot laser onto McCartney's scalp. Perspiration ran in rivulets down his nape, dispersing across his shoulder blades and down his spine, soaking his shirt so thoroughly that arm movements became restricted. He pushed on and up, driving hard through his calves and thighs, and with the small of his back. To his left, Jo seemed to be floundering but every time Mac looked across he bared his elongated teeth to demonstrate that all was well. Looking directly up at it now, with the sky above a vast cerulean, the fort seemed to be leaning over the incline – pink, unreal and perfectly, eternally still. She was up there. Millie. He hoped to God in those endless heavens that she was up there. A grey-green wispy strand drifted past. Following its trail back and up to the distant peaks, a column of smoke plumed upwards in a belching, near-straight gust before toppling west, thinning out and dispersing on the thermals. A forest fire – yet there were no trees up here.

Having trained himself to mistrust the illusions of proximity that heat and altitude could conjure, Mac was taken by surprise. They pushed themselves up and over a jutting kop and the Red Fort was right there, in front of them, rather than looming up from the distance above. This was it; they were there. The squat and solid wall – rendered, he now saw, with a coral-coloured stucco – was cool to the touch as they slumped back and gulped the last of the water. Enzo, the scrambler guy, would ensure there was food and drink in their packs down below but, for now, they were draining the last drops.

'OK,' gasped Mac, wiping his mouth with the back of his hand. 'What now?'

Jo shrugged. 'I said I could get us up here . . .' He pointed to the hazy ochre plains. 'And back down there . . .'

Mac gave him a sarcastic smile and took two steps back. He looked up at the wall and began measuring his paces, muttering to himself. Jo slid down and sat on his haunches, waiting. Very slowly, Mac crept round the corner and, straight away, saw his entry point. There was a small rocky outcrop – jutting out towards, and almost overhanging a bevelled watch tower. There were five or six steps leading up to the cubic, whitewashed outhouse he'd seen the day before. Millie's tower was directly opposite it. To the right of the little box house were more steps leading down, presumably, to the courtyard. It was a risk – everything was a risk; he'd have to take a running jump and hope he cleared the drop and landed on the floor of the watch tower. He'd have to hope he landed quietly. Could he take his shoes off? No – he'd break a bone in his foot. He tiptoed back round to appraise Jo of the plan.

Hassan rolled out the last of the big bales and stopped to wipe his brow. He was about to call Karim, tell him to prepare a packed meal for the road, when a distant glint caught his eye. He stepped closer to the drop and squinted down towards the fort, shielding his eyes. Again, the jagged glint. A stirrup. Someone was making their way up there on horseback. It wasn't uncommon, these days – the green tourists loved their Real Morocco; their backs to the land, eco-friendly day trips where they'd eat with the goatherds and contract responsibly sourced gut rot. Nevertheless . . . He ran to the truck for his binoculars, climbed up onto the bonnet for a better look and trained his viewfinder on the gorge, but whoever it was had disappeared behind the mound. He jumped down, bending his knees to break his fall, and sprang into a jog back to the farmhouse. He fished out his iPhone and dialled Karim.

Headphones on and Pampers – it had to be Pampers – baby wipes to hand, Karim wriggled his Levi's down to his knees and sat back in his leatherette swivel chair, trying not to rush it as the busty cougar entertained two well-endowed builders. His Samsung Galaxy rattled and rotated next to the control desk as the student self-pleasured in splendid isolation.

Mac made a small heap with his hat, shirt and socks to soften Jo's landing.

'Come on!' he hissed. 'You can do this . . .'

Jo looked down at the drop. He'd aborted three jumps already, shaking his head, unable to overcome the mental block.

'I am sorry, Mac. I cannot . . .'

'You *can*! Don't look down.'

He stood at the lip of the watch tower's ledge and urged him on, pointing to where he should aim his feet. Jo took a run and, this time, almost launched himself into a leap of faith, only pulling up at the point of lift-off, his momentum almost taking him over the edge of the rocky overhang. Mac held a finger over his lips to silence him.

'OK. Go to the gates. I'll try and get them open.'

Mac bounded down the short flight of steps and made his way across the courtyard, his thorax tightening with every gravel-spitting step that seemed to ring out and reverberate across the quadrangle. He got to the gate, stood back and tried to work out the system for the gigantic latch. Up in the mountains above, the smoke was billowing wildly now. He wiped his top lip and applied both hands to the sleeper-sized metal bar that bridged the two huge doors, but he couldn't move it.

'Fuck!'

He looked around for a stick, a pickaxe – anything that might help him lever the crossbar up and out of its slots. He turned a full circle, and it was only then that he noticed the door to Millie's tower. Open. There was no decision to be made. He'd get her, now, find a brick or something to slam that bar up and get the gates open, then Jo – the better horseman of the two of them – could take her on the back of Alvaro, down and away to the scrambler bikes. His heart was pummelling his ribcage so violently he could barely breathe, let alone think this whole plan through. No matter. No time for caution now. He'd allowed Millie to go out into the badlands, alone; now it was up to him to bring her back. He checked left and right and, head shrunk down into his shoulders, ran across the courtyard on the balls of his feet.

It was only as he was wiping himself down that Karim spotted the red light flashing on his phone. Expecting nothing more taxing than a Google Alert he continued the clean-up, deposited the wet wipes in the little wicker waste basket and, wiping his hands on the sides of his jeans, picked up the Galaxy to see what was what. Missed calls. And a new message. He pressed the keypad and held the phone to his ear. Three messages. Hassan, irate. Check for intruders – *intruders*, ha! As if! And open the gate. He sounded mad . . . Karim stretched and deleted his browsing history before heading outside into the searing afternoon sun.

As was always the way when he was in a hurry, the job in hand slowed Hassan down. The final bale of *branche* was still green and fragrant – and it doggedly refused to light. He hastened to the tool store and, hurling aside stacks of spades and choppers, ransacked the shelves for paraffin. There was nothing. He ran across to the old farmhouse and there, in the pantry, was a tin of kerosene and a cooking tray, full of wicks. He scooped up a handful, just in case he needed them, then, on second thoughts, took both the kerosene and the tray itself back outside. He sprinkled kerosene all over the bale of hemp, then filled the tray to its brim, too. He laid a trail of wicks, stood back and lit the first. The tray of kerosene went up with a theatrical whoosh! A pause, then the *branche* just lit up, all at once, towering above him like a pagan pyre. He called Karim again to open the gates and sprinted to his truck.

Jo's only other option – he could slither back down the kop and flee – was unthinkable. The Englishman had not opened the gates. He must have been attacked or apprehended. This left Jo with but one possibility; he'd have to make that jump. Every second he delayed might be critical for McCartney. He backed up to the thick end of the spur and closed his eyes tight, trying to envisage a safe, successful jump.

Millie buried her head in McCartney's shoulder and wept. At first Mac just held her. There was danger, for sure, and a hazardous journey ahead but, for now, all that could wait. She had aged, of course – but she was beautiful; sad and serene and, somehow, wise-looking, but with such an aura. Such grace and presence. How old would she be, now? Nearly fifty? She didn't look it. Somehow, McCartney had been expecting her to be tanned, her face lined, leathery – her hair dried out and frosty white. But she was Millie – older but still golden-haired, her eyes full of that sparkling vitality. Whatever traumas Millie's captivity had visited upon her, it did not look as though she'd suffered physically.

'Millie – we have forever to talk. Are you able to walk OK?'

She looked up at him and, for the first time, she smiled. 'Yes. What do you take me for?'

Mac smiled back, still unable to quell his thumping heartbeat. 'I don't know, yet . . .'

He helped her to her feet and, one arm around her, led her past the smashed-down door, out of the room that had been her sometime cell all these years, and guided her hand to the inner wall.

'Nice and easy . . .'

They began their edgy descent.

Karim was halfway across the courtyard with the wrench they used for opening the gate latch when a slight movement caught his eye. The door to the south tower was ajar – creaking gently, open and shut. The south tower was kept locked, always. He couldn't imagine there'd be anything out of the ordinary but, with Hassan's words about intruders still fresh in his mind, he gripped the wrench tighter and approached the open door.

Voices! Then, faltering but unmistakable footsteps on the stone staircase. Someone was coming! Karim jumped into the gap between the two big bins, jolted by fear. What if this were the police? Worse, it could be the Rebels, the up-and-coming young gang he was hearing more and more about. Maybe they'd been behind the helicopter attack. Maybe that was why they were evacuating . . .

He bobbed his head out and snatched a quick look across the forecourt. It was Hassan's wife, blinking and straining against the sunlight! Then, moments later, the old English guy appeared – the one who'd been there yesterday. They had their backs to him, and were walking towards the kitchen. Karim gulped and gave the wrench a gentle swing, letting its momentum take his forearm with it. He hadn't quite bargained on assault being part of his job description when he'd left the Superior Technology School at Ibnou Zohr with the best results the college had ever known. But this was no ordinary job. With little to spend his salary on he'd already salted away close to thirty thousand dollars in just over a year, and he wasn't ready to walk away from that sort of package yet. He crept across the courtyard, getting closer and closer to the Englishman. He raised the wrench above his head and picked out a spot just below his skull; he'd stun him, without killing him, and ask questions later. As Karim brought the cast-iron wrench down, a series of noises flooded his brain in fast succession. As brilliant as his mind was, he was out cold before he had a chance to process the warning sounds.

Mac turned sharply, to see Karim slumped on the ground and Jo standing over him with a brick in his hand. He knelt down, took his pulse. Mac dragged him away.

'Come on! Have you seen that?' He pointed up at the smoke fanning out from the Rif. 'The El Glaouis are covering their tracks – they'll be back down here in no time.'

He was about to enter the kitchen and get them each a cup of water, but Jo pulled him back.

'Wait,' he said, face grave. 'You'd better see this . . .'

He took him back over to the far corner, where they'd vaulted the wall – but instead of going back up the steps to the viewing deck, he beckoned McCartney towards the little storeroom underneath.

'Here,' he said, ducking as he stepped down into the dark. He stood back to allow Mac's eyes to get accustomed to the room. At the far end, a figure hung, upside down, from a series of pulleys, seemingly sniffing the ground with his stout, pyramid-shaped nose. 'I'm sorry,' said Jo, averting his eyes.

Mac stood back. It was Ahmed, his eyes wide and pleading.

'You were up at the hash farm?' Mac nodded.

'Younes told Roig he had left something important . . .' Jo was looking at him desperately. 'He did not, by chance, pass anything to you?'

Mac shook his head sadly. 'No, nothing.'

Jo squeezed his shoulder. 'OK. Don't worry. We'll get our boys up there first thing.'

Mac looked down at the lifeless, wild-eyed Ahmed. Younes. 'It's the flying that kills you,' he murmured.

'What?'

Mac turned away. 'Nothing.' He put his arm around Jo. 'Let's get out of here . . .'

Angry that he hadn't been able to get through to Karim, and enraged that the gates remained shut, Hassan El Glaoui let out a war cry – one long, demented wail, as he hit the accelerator and drove the truck at full speed, straight into the impermeable, solid-timber gates. The truck bounced back, a shrill and immediate hiss steaming out from underneath. Hassan slapped the dashboard with the palms of both hands and punched a crack in the windscreen. He reversed, the engine grinding and spluttering, and backed away far enough to take another run at it.

Millie was pointing at the gates.

'It's him,' she stuttered, a glint of terror flashing across her eyeballs as she tried to tear herself away from the buckling gate. 'It's Hassan. I know it is . . .'

McCartney stepped between her and Jo, his hands up.

'OK. We're going to have to be really calm here, and ultra-decisive. Every move we make from now on has to be the right one. We can't hesitate. We can't back up and try another plan. OK?' Jo and Millie nodded. 'There is no plan B. Follow me.' He flashed them a smile. 'And please don't worry. I've done this many, many times before . . .'

He winked at Millie and took the steps up to the observation post three at a time. Millie followed, with Jo bringing up the rear. They got up to the flat ledge they'd landed on. Mac looked down. It was a straight thirty- or forty-foot plummet – ankle-breaking height. The rocky precipice they'd jumped off was up above them, and eight or ten feet away – impossible to reverse the gravitational pull that had dropped them there.

'Jo – don't speak. Give me your jeans and your shirt.'

Jo began to disrobe. Across the quadrangle, the gates buckled again. Next time they would shatter. Mac lay on his front, looking down, trying to calculate. 'OK,' he said to himself, sprung up and vaulted back down the steps. He sprinted hard across the forecourt, ducked right into the rear courtyard and launched himself up the spiral steps. He flung the little side door open and dived into Millie's room, dragging the sheets off the bed and swooping for a dress draped over the back of her chair. He took the steps down as quickly as he was able, careful not to trip over the trailing sheets, and jogged back towards the others, exhausted.

'Tie these up. Quick. Jo, give me your jeans.'

Jo passed them over. Mac wound one leg through the door-loop of the little box room. He tied a firm knot and leaned backwards, heaving on it, testing its tensile strength to the maximum. He turned round to Jo, flipping his middle three fingers.

'Shirt.' Jo threw it over. 'How you doing with those sheets?'

'Good . . .'

'Excellent. Try and poke one *tiny* hole as close to the seam as you can, yeah?'

Jo nodded. Millie came over, pulling a pin from her hair.

'Here,' she said. Jo smiled and took the pin, jabbing it into the bed sheet.

'What now?' he said.

Mac finished tying Jo's shirt to his jeans, took another quick peep over the edge, nodded to himself and held one hand out for the bed sheets. He put the hem of Millie's dress in his mouth and, taking it out again, twisted the moistened linen round and round until he'd made a pointed tip. He narrowed one eye and threaded the tip of the linen dress through the hole Jo had made in the sheet, then tied the other end of the dress to Jo's jeans. He pulled hard on each join and turned to the others.

'Right. Jo had better go first. He knows the way down best of all . . . and if anyone's going to fall, I'd rather it was him . . .'

They both over-laughed and, without another word, Jo saluted them, shuffled down backwards so his feet were dangling over the edge and, quickly and efficiently, took hold of the fabric-rope and let himself slide down to the ground.

A sudden smash and the gates flew open. The caved-in bonnet of the pickup truck kangaroo-jumped into the court-yard. Mac ducked and whispered to Millie.

'He can't see us from there. Keep your head down . . . Go. Quick . . .'

Millie flung her arms around him and kissed him on the cheek. She got down on her front, her eyes never leaving him, then suddenly jumped up and ran back, kissing him hard on the lips.

'Quick!' hissed Mac – but his voice was singing. He was in shock; he was terrified; but, above all, he was joyous. She was back. Camilla Baker was back in his life again. She let herself down slowly at first, then, losing her grip, slipped the rest of the way, trying to hold tight to the sheets but friction-burning her hands. As soon as she was in Jo's arms the pair of them ducked away, and Mac followed on down swiftly and with goat-like agility. He ran to catch the other two, all three of them stooped and heading for the bulge of the kop. They stopped to catch their breath. Up on the watch tower, Hassan was looking down at them.

'Now for the real fun,' muttered Millie. 'He keeps his guns in there . . .'

He watched the highly polished chrome Vespa cruise down Kingsland High Street and turn left into Sandringham Road. Head down, Zafer ambled past, trying to clock where they'd parked. The Yasmina one was standing there, laughing, holding a chain up as high as she could lift it, while the angry one drove the scooter underneath, and pulled up in the little scrap of rough ground that doubled as a solicitors' car park. He crossed over at the lights and shocked himself, for the fun of it, at the price of the properties in Douglas Allen's window. Four hundred grand for an ex-council flat in Clapton!

He could hear the two lesbos laughing over the road and saw their reflection, briefly, arm in arm as they walked up to the club. He wouldn't be making the same mistake again. He was too conspicuous, for starters – plus these queer bars made him sick, anyway. This time he'd do things differently. Satisfied they were gone and would not be back for some time, Zafer crossed back over the road, made his way up to the little car park and, checking around and about, quickly slid the tracking device under the Vespa's rear mudguard. Checking once more for passers-by, he shook the scooter from side to side, but the tracker stayed in place. He crouched down to make sure the tyres would not dislodge it once the wheels were in motion. All good – nice, sturdy connection. It was now just a question of sitting and waiting. They could stay in there till dawn, for all Zafer cared. They could come home at five or six in the morning. Whatever time they rolled in, he'd be awake. And whenever they went to bed, so would he. With them – whether they liked it or not. Hood up and head down, he plodded back to the overground station and waited for a Gospel Oak train.

Yasmina laid her cheek against Jessika's back and held her round the waist, deep in thought. This thing she was feeling – had been feeling since she'd walked into the Macbeth and J-Flan had turned round and smiled at her – it was overpowering her. Jessika was all she could think about from the moment she woke, enraptured at the realisation that the woman next to her was hers, was *there*, right through till she closed her eyes and slept, fully, in a deep peace like she'd never known – Jessika dominated every mote of her consciousness. She adored her. She couldn't stand being apart from her, even those minutes when she went to the toilet or the bar. She'd do anything for Jessika; anything at all.

It was lovely that Aasiya had turned up at the benefit, but she'd left Yasmina in no doubt at all that, as of yesterday, she'd been reclassified as a fugitive. She'd sat with them for half an hour laying out various options, but each of them involved Yasmina giving herself up, returning to Lydia's safe house and trusting the auspices of due process to work in her favour.

'Fuck that,' winked J-Flan when Aasiya finally left. 'Punks like us were born to run, baby!'

She kissed Yasmina long and hard, and she could still feel the love in it as she laid her head – and her trust – on Jessika as she piloted the Vespa through the night streets of Hackney. They were going to pack a few things – Yasmina barely had a few things to take – and hit the road. J-Flan had some eccentric auntie up north who would put them up, no questions asked, for as long as they wanted. No one would look twice up there, Jessika reckoned – and she believed her. She believed, absolutely, in the love of her life. She could only pray now, that McCartney would bring her mum back to share it with them. They slowed into Defoe Road and parked in the tatty front garden. The plan was to get in, shower, pack and be out of London and halfway up the M1 before the early-morning rush hour kicked in.

They tiptoed up to the first-floor flat. Yasmina stood back to let J-Flan open up, then stepped inside behind her. Jessika clicked the light on and turned to look at her waiflike love.

'Oh dear me,' she smiled. 'You are just fucking divine . . .' She licked her clavicle and began kissing her, tenderly at first, up and down her long neck. Yasmina groaned and bit her lip and slumped back against the wall. She didn't care if the police, or whoever, caught up with them. She'd done nothing wrong. She only cared about now. Jessika stepped back and looked right into her eyes.

'God, I fucking love you,' she whispered. She took Yasmina by the wrist and led her to the bedroom.

They'd had to ride the steeds harder and faster than it was safe to do, but with bullets ripping into the rocks and ringing out all around them, there was little choice in the matter. They urged them on, galloping down an acute gradient as the gunfire ricocheted out and reverberated around the ravine.

Enzo was waiting at the goatherd's hut with an accomplice. Jo dismounted, handing Enzo's friend the reins, and gabbled out instructions to the others.

'Quickly quickly, please! I think the El Glaoui he will arrive very speedy. My friend Abdul he will return the horses now . . .' Abdul held up a hand to help Millie down, Mac sliding down alongside her. Jo slung a rucksack over Millie's shoulders and threw one across to McCartney.

'So, Mrs Baker, you will go with Enzo – very excellent moto-rider, Enzo!' He grinned his funny, long-tooth smile and patted the pillion. 'Come, my friend. Please . . . I promise I will get you to the boat very good indeed!'

Millie didn't question it; if she'd spoken she may well have been sick. Declining Abdul's help, she got on the back of Enzo's bike and adjusted the rucksack until it sat squarely and comfortably on her back. The two Eurocops got astride their scramblers, revved the accelerators and, checking one last time to ensure their passengers were holding tight, took off down the dirt path, clouds of gritty russet dust fanning out behind them.

Zafer didn't have to check any buzzers or hunt for clues, he could hear them at it from outside. The kinky bitches were putting on a show for him. Women like these might act tough and make out they weren't interested, but he knew how it worked. They liked to be forced. Sluts like these got a kick out of it. They'd left the window open a notch so he could play his part – all he had to do was get up on the ledge above the ground-floor flat without anyone seeing him and jumping to the wrong conclusions.

He gripped onto the drainpipe and, with slow, steady progress, he managed to wriggle far enough up to lean across and get some purchase on the ledge.

He could see her, bouncing minimally with every bump and skid, clinging to Enzo as his scrambler cut down through the terrace almost sideways, his knees virtually touching the scorched earth. McCartney was relieved the gunshot had ceased, surprised that El Glaoui hadn't come after them – but his overriding emotion was envy. Naked, bitter jealousy, every time he looked down at the motorbike ahead, slaloming through this arduous

267

terrain. He had to keep strangling it, swallowing it, reminding himself of the fucking severity of their situation, but it was hopeless. Billy McCartney was in love.

'OK, Mr Mac – hold me *real* tight!' Jo twisted his head round, grinning. 'This is where starts the fun . . .'

There was an arid, overgrown and long-abandoned terrace cut into the side of the mountain, an ancient olive or fig plantation with dozens of stepped, yard-deep furrows leading right down to the coast. In its day, in full culture, it must have been a sight to behold. Right now, it was an obstacle course, and Enzo was already halfway down, manoeuvring his scrambler through a series of jumps and skids, Millie hugging his back, tight.

'Ready?'

Mac nodded, mutely resigned to whatever fate might bring. Even if they made it down there, even if they got back to London, to Liverpool . . . what were the chances? Zero. Not a flicker. She'd see him as a rescuer, a saviour, at best. She would never come to look upon him the way he saw her – the way he was. Mac took a long, deep breath and held it down and accepted that things were simply how things were – and that was that. He could never allow himself to hope, not McCartney. No, worse than that – there was none.

Jo dragged the bike into the first corniche, banking so low he must have scraped the flesh from his elbows and knees. Just when it felt like he'd lost equilibrium, he'd right the scrambler and accelerate hard into the next bend. Where there were gaps in the terrace walls he'd dart straight through and, for a suspended second, they'd be in mid-air, crashing into the burnt-hard ground and bouncing on to the next level. Down below, the late-evening sea shimmered, a flat and glinting silver, close enough to touch now. But up above, a distant, chopping whirr got louder, closer. Craning his neck and twisting his head back, Mac could glimpse a speck in the sky. It could have been anything, anyone going anywhere; but he knew. He tapped Jo on the side and rolled his wrist, urging him onwards, faster.

James Rae looked at himself in the mirror – unrecognisable from the dapper, designer-dressed ladykiller of yore. The hair was long gone, of course – how he'd mourned his thick, black hair – and, just as with the best of them, he was packing a neat little globe of a paunch. He was still fit, though – fit enough to take care of Mehmet; fit enough to see this through. He was calm about the whole thing. This would work well, in the long run. Since the rise of the Rozakis he'd barely been back to Liverpool; a chris-tening, a funeral, a couple of other things where he'd asked for a walkover. They were both in jail now, but their reach was phenomenal. Anyone who thought that Moz and Dara Rozaki didn't still run smack in this country was deluded. Mehmet, for one, despised them. They'd be thankful once he was gone, that was for sure. They'd thank him. And perhaps, once again, he could walk the streets as John-John Hamilton.

Hassan would go wild over the thing with his daughter but, above all, Hassan was a businessman. If he could get her back to him . . . It would take a while. He'd have to sit tight. But maybe, just maybe, if he was able to plug some of the gaps for the Rozaki firm, start to rebuild his reputation . . . it could work out very nicely, all this. He had all the time in the world and more than enough money to tuck himself away for six months, a year, however long the process took; but JJ knew that he'd be back. He *had* to get back. He loved it! The game was in his blood, and without the cut and thrust and the sheer fucking buzz of a big run going to plan – not to mention the bounty – life was just not worth living.

Mehmet was a scoundrel. He'd made a bad call the day he decided to stiff James Rae. He'd regret that at his leisure, in hell, or limbo, or wherever else the Turks paid the ultimate price. He stashed the balaclava in his pocket and went off to meet Davey.

Yasmina, writhing with pleasure as Jessika's tongue flicked and probed, opened her eyes and let out one long, bellowing scream. She sat up, shrank back towards the headboard, covering her breasts. The man-monster with the red welt was standing over them, undoing his belt.

'Don't stop on my behalf, ladies,' he smiled. Jessika sprang out of bed and backed to the wall. She reached out and grabbed her hoodie, slung over the back of the chair. The ogre walked towards her, a strangely childlike pleading in his eyes, both hands held out. 'Come on. You won't be needing that . . .' She stood there, unsure where to land her first blows; certain she had to hit him hard now. He was a yard away, still smiling at her. 'You looked so much nicer with no clothes on . . .'

That was it — a raucous rage oscillated wildly from her synapses to her fists and feet. She clenched her teeth, looked the monster in the eye and jumped upwards and sideways, planting both feet in his ribcage. Winded, he staggered backwards, the innocence in his eyes replaced by fear; by hatred.

'Fucking bitch!'

She bounced in front of him once, twice, fists up, chin tucked in as she eyed him. Bang! She punched him on the nose. Yasmina winced at the crack; looked away as a thin dribble of blood ran down his mouth and chin. The giant was disorientated now.

'Say that again, you cunt!' hissed Jessika, her accent harder, her eyes wild. He lunged at her.

'Sick bitch!'

She stepped aside, dropping low and hacking his legs from under him with a dynamic sweep. He crashed to the floor and she was all over him, smashing his ribs with vicious kicks then peppering his face with a ricochet of thunderous punches. A low wailing emanated from his hunched-up husk – a huge, defeated foetus, howling in fear and pain. She stepped back, gave Yasmina the briefest glance but kept her eyes on the fallen ogre.

'Call the police, babe.'

Yasmina sat there, stunned. The thoughts came slowly to her, but lurid as the reality bit down. She didn't know how to call the police anyway – but weren't the police her enemy? Hadn't Aasiya told them she'd be on some kind of wanted list now?

'What about me?'

'What d'you mean, darling? What you saying?'

'Please!' the giant howled. 'I didn't mean –'

She ran into him and kicked him in the guts. 'You!' She dropped to her knees and jabbed her forefinger under his jowels. 'Shut the fuck up! Yeah? You say fuck all!'

She got up and turned to her wild-eyed, shivering lover. The penny dropped. Yasmina was terrified – by all of this. She jumped onto the bed and held her close.

'It's going to be OK, baby. I mean it. It's all going to be fine . . .'

The giant got to his knees, a strand of snotty blood dangling down from his nose. Jessika let go of Yasmina and levered herself off the bed. She went to the door, opened it, stood back, arms folded.

'Go on, you fucking beast – fuck off.' She just said it, quietly, eyes locked into the quivering man-monster. He got up, eyes averted, head hung low.

'I . . .'

J-Flan stepped forward. 'Don't . . .'

He shied away, shrinking back from the next punch. Jessika shook her head.

'Just fucking don't, right? Just fuck off – now.'

He lumbered off down the stairs. She went to the window and watched him slope away towards Church Street, then turned back to her shocked and bewildered waif.

'OK, honey. Time you and me got lost for a bit . . .'

Yasmina nodded. They dressed quickly, in absolute silence.

The Irish lad dropped them at the corner of Carlingford Road, just opposite Ducketts Common. Him and Davey had argued all the way. Davey had told him to come in a white van, for obvious reasons; the kid had turned up in an Audi Quattro.

'Let us out here, you prick!' Davey pointed into the kid's face. 'You fucking *be* here, right? You get pulled and you're fucking dead. Hear?' The lad nodded. He didn't seem too scared. 'Be. Right. Here,' said Davey, and wrenched the Audi's door open.

They cut across the park past the pond and exited onto Frobisher and, from there, onto Green Lanes. They'd talked it through repeatedly. Mehmet would know; he'd know immediately he saw that James Rae was not alone. He'd have men in there. No matter how secure Mehmet might feel in his own locale, he was a guy who always had backup. They had a choice. JJ could go on in, relax him, sit him down – then Davey would just walk in there and blast him before he had a chance to move. Or they could storm the place together and surprise whoever was in there, guns out, get them on the floor and take it from there.

'Last chance, kid. You sure this is what you want?'

'Fella has to go, mate.'

Davey screwed in his silencer. 'Your call, maestro.'

John-John smiled at his old accomplice. 'A simple matter of honour, David. Nothing more, nothing less.'

They walked past once and glanced inside. Satisfied the cafe was as empty as it was ever going to be, they ducked into an alleyway and crewed up. Back on the high street they made their way briskly to the cafe. They looked at one another through the slat-holes in their balaclavas, nodded once and burst inside, pistols primed.

'Down! Down! Down! FLOOR!' Davey screamed.

The cafe owner reached for something. Davey shot him. JJ was already next to Mehmet, his gun a foot from his forehead. Mehmet sat there, smiling, as though this were some foolish prank. A burly Turk sat to his right, his eyes screwed tight shut, tears rolling freely down his face. Davey Lane stood over his victim, awaiting word or some other sign from JJ. Mehmet leaned back slightly and gave James Rae a questioning look. He stood there, his wrist shaking slightly as he pointed the gun down on the portly Turk.

'So,' said Mehmet. 'I'm guessing you haven't brought the money . . .'

James Rae looked into his eyes and took a breath; held it down. He supported his unsteady wrist with his left hand. He bit his lip and tensed his fingers.

'Come!' Mehmet soothed. 'Look at you!' he said sadly. 'You don't want to do this . . .'

He took a step closer, so the muzzle of the gun was now touching the bridge of Mehmet's nose. He smiled and reached to lift up his teacup. Then, in less than a second, in order; a restrained yet powerful ripping zip from behind them. The cup fell to the floor and smashed. The bodyguard screamed and threw himself to the ground. Mehmet's head flopped back. Blood throbbed in pulses from his temple. Hamilton took one step away from the table. Another shot from behind him; Davey finishing off the cafe owner. He stepped over him and patted JJ on the back.

'Thought we'd be here all night . . .'

'Thanks. Appreciate it . . .'

He went round the table, careful not to tread in any blood. He put his gun to the cowering bodyguard's head.

'I'll count to three, you useless fat prick. Where's Zafer? Where does he fucking live?'

He told them. Two minutes later the Audi was speeding along West Green Road.

Zafer Ertegun had had better evenings. No sooner had he got himself up and inside the flat, and out of his clothes to assess his wounds, than the buzzer was going, madly, every five or ten seconds. He tried to ignore it, but there were stones landing on the roof now, one, then another and another whacking against the window. The next one would probably smash it. He limped across to the intercom.

'Yes?'

'Open the fucking door!'

'No. Who are you?'

'We are the people who are going to shoot you in the balls when we get up there. You've got three seconds. Open the fucking door or we'll blast the mortice to bits.'

Zafer started to shake violently. He took fast, shallow breaths to try and stifle the tears in his voice.

'I promise you – I didn't harm them.'

'Harm who?'

Shit! Who were these people? If the girl hadn't sent them, what did they want with him? He took a deep breath.

'The girl sent you, right?'

A pause.

'Where is she?'

'Do you promise you'll leave me alone if I tell you?'

Another pause.

'I promise . . .'

Zafer hit the release button and told them to come up to the top floor.

Enzo threw the scrambler into a brake-turn, bringing it to a standstill with his feet, just short of the shore. Djimi ducked out of the bushes, clasped his SVA colleague in the traditional, Roman-style handshake and led Millie down to the dinghy. Jo and McCartney followed moments later, Mac glancing fearfully up to the sky. It was definitely a helicopter; it was definitely Hassan. Jo caught up with Enzo and Djimi.

'What's this?' he hissed, pointing at the Air V dinghy. 'Where's the Rodman?'

Djimi laughed and squeezed his arm. 'Don't panic!' he smiled. 'The beast is out there . . . only so close I could bring her . . .' He began wading into the shallows, hauling the galvanised-rubber craft behind him. 'Wait till you see the speed of this little cracker. Come on!'

'Will we all fit in there?' muttered Jo. He held out his hand for Millie but Mac pushed his way between them, belting her waist and guiding her steadily to the now-buoyant motor dinghy.

'Up we go!'

Millie rolled herself over the side and Djimi pulled her fully on board. Her momentum pushed the inflatable on a few feet. Mac and Jo tried to lengthen their strides, but the sea slowed them down and the dinghy started bobbing away from them as the water got deeper.

'Swim!' shouted Djimi. 'Quick!'

The sea surface began to whip into squiggling ripples as, out of nowhere, the helicopter plummeted down and swooped above them, a powerful searchlight illuminating the shore. A shot cracked out, then another – Enzo, stationed behind a big rock, trying to draw Hassan's attention.

'You go, Mac,' winced Jo. 'Enzo and I will try to give you cover. If you make it onto the patrol boat, you'll be fine . . . only a lunatic would attack the SVA.'

Machine-gun fire dappled the water grey and black and silver, but he was firing at random. Crazed and enraged as he was, there was no way Hassan was coming into range. He hovered above, the chopper veering dramatically as he leaned out and down, trying to get a clear sight. He was on his own. They had a chance.

McCartney turned to Jo and looked him in the eye. 'Thank you, Jo. I mean it . . .'

Jo winked and began to back away. 'I didn't agree with him all times,' he smiled. 'But I do this for Younes –'

They shook.

'Thank you, Mr Mac. I hope I will see you again. Good luck . . .'

Bullets drilled the surface immediately behind them now.

'You too, Jo. Now *go!*'

McCartney swallow-dived down and swam, powerfully, just underneath the surface, covering the distance to the dinghy in seconds. Djimi already had the engine running and, the moment Mac heaved himself on board, he roared off into the ink-black straits. The chopper came after them at speed, swooping low so they could clearly see Hassan, leaning out with the machine gun propped on his elbow. A concerted burst of fire strafed the waves as the powerful dinghy cut quickly through the sea. Mac put his arm around Millie and pulled her close. Djimi turned to them and pointed ahead.

'See? Is España!' The Rodman 55, the favoured high-speed patrol boat of the Servicio de Vigilancia Aduenera, was anchored a few hundred metres ahead. Djimi gave them the thumbs up. 'When in España, *nobody* touch!'

The bullet slammed into his cranium and he fell to the deck, the dinghy rearing up and spinning round. Mac dived across to him and grabbed for his wrist, put three fingers to his neck. He was dead.

'No!'

Grinding his teeth in a desperate rage, McCartney lunged for the wheel and the control stick simultaneously, righting the dinghy and craning upwards to try and work out where Hassan would hit them next. He was a hundred feet behind them, coming at them at a fearsome speed, low to the surface of the sea. He seemingly had no thoughts for his own survival now – only the prevention of his precious canary's flight. The helicopter's metal landing skids came at them like harpoons – Hassan was going to ram them.

Mac glanced to his left – a walkie-talkie. With one eye on the Rodman, he jerked his head round to Millie.

'Millie!' He kicked at the walkie-talkie. 'Do you think you remember how to use one of these?'

She got up, but the buffeting of the dinghy on the waves knocked her back down. She crawled across, picked up the transceiver.

'Looks pretty similar . . .'

He couldn't turn round. The Rodman was only seconds away now. The whip and cut of the copter's blades was loud enough, close enough to chop them both into pieces. She found the communication channel and spoke in Spanish, before coming back to McCartney. 'What do you want me to say?'

Mac's shoulders heaved. *I want you to say something to me*, he thought. *Anything – so long as it's just for me.* Hassan dropped the helicopter down so its undercarriage was almost touching the dinghy's engine. *I want you to say there's a chance . . .*

'Tell the operator that the pilot of the helicopter has taken out a Spanish agent. It is a legitimate target. Repeat. The helicopter is a live and present danger . . .'

Millie steadied herself and, slowly, without emotion, passed on the information to the SVA patrol boat; the words that would bring the life of her captor, her jailer, her rapist – her husband – to its end. Placing the transceiver down again she turned away from McCartney and allowed the tears she'd stemmed to flow.

Zafer showed him, again, how the tracking device worked.

'And this GPS, right . . .' Zafer nodded, eager to get rid of the mad Scouser. He was standing over him, eyes never leaving him, while the other one just stood there, saying nothing. 'It's accurate up to what kind of distance?'

'You can pick them up fifty miles away but, obviously, the closer you are . . .'

'All right . . .' He looked up at Zafer. 'I get you.'

Zafer cleared his throat. 'I'd get going. They were . . .' He hung his head. 'I don't think they're planning on hanging round . . .'

Hamilton planted his hand on Zafer's shoulder. 'Silver scooter, right?'

Zafer nodded. 'Vespa. Chrome . . .'

'Right.' John-John Hamilton nodded to Davey Lane. Davey stepped outside onto the landing. JJ winked at the silent hulk. 'Just one more thing . . .'

'Yes?'

He waited for the lad to look at him and smiled right into his clueless, jellyfish-red face.

'You ain't seen me, right?'

Before Zafer could nod his assent, Hamilton took out his pistol and shot him, once, between the eyes.

'Good lad,' he said, and stepped over him, closing the door on his way out.

Jessika decided it was best all round if she stuck to the A-roads. Many a time she'd idled away a summer's afternoon with girl-friends, laid out on their backs in Regent's Park. J-Flan would jerk her thumb at Park Road on the other side of the railings and tell them: 'See that? A41. Buckingham Palace to Hamilton Square, Birkenhead. Passes right by my Auntie Pat's front door – from one queen to another without turning left or right . . .'

From Stoke Newington they'd ducked and dived all the way through to Brent Cross, using short cuts and side streets through Finsbury Park, Hornsey and Archway until they joined the A1 at Highgate and, from there, hit the North Circular for the last stretch. Far from the exhilaration of her last few rides, Yasmina clung to Jessika out of fear, and a deep-seated dread of what might lie ahead. They chugged on through the night, Yasmina becoming numb to the whining of the little engine, the vibrations of the pillion seat. They passed through Watford and Bushey before pulling over for petrol, and to stretch their legs and backsides, just outside of Berkhamsted. J-Flan went inside to pay. When she came back, Yasmina was perched side-ways on the Vespa's seat, seeking her out with her pale green eyes.

'What?' smiled Jessika – but even on that single, one-syllable word the fear trembled out through her voice.

'Just tell me it's going to be OK . . .'

Jessika strode towards her and took her in her strong, wiry arms. She kissed her forehead, her cheeks, her nose and pulled back to look at her.

'It's all going to be OK, my love. I promise you . . .'

'Really?'

'Abso-fucking-lutely!'

She kissed her again and steered her by the ankles, guiding her back into pillion position.

* * *

'How far ahead now?' asked John-John, leaning through the gap between the two front seats.

'Twenty miles,' shrugged Davey. 'Might be a bit more, could be a little bit less . . .'

'Fuck! We've closed that down all right.'

'Haven't we just? Hasn't moved in a while. Looks like they might've stopped.'

Their young jockey turned towards Davey. 'So I don't suppose I'll be getting any thanks now, will I?'

'For what?'

'For this!' He tapped the Audi's dashboard. 'This . . .' He grinned to himself. '. . . stupid, ostentatious, atrocity of a Garda-magnet!'

Davey Lane just looked at him. For a while he said nothing, then he shook his head. 'Do you know what? If you weren't Eamonn's lad I'd fucking shoot you for that.'

The kid smiled to himself and put his foot down. 'Sorry is the hardest word to say . . .'

'I mean, shut the fuck up, and drive!'

The lad saluted with one finger and burnt on into the night.

Jessika was starting to feel fatigued, but the headlights of the sole car behind them, reflected and refracted in her dozens of mirrors, were starting to bother her. There was something about the way the car was hanging back that seemed ominous. She'd spotted its lights five minutes ago – there was nothing else on the road – so, given the ground he'd covered in getting this close, why didn't he just carry on and overtake? She began looking around for possible escape routes.

Up ahead was a turn-off for a picnic area. She hoped to hell that Yasmina couldn't feel her heartbeat racing out of control. J-Flan checked her mirrors. Without indicating she veered left and followed the brown sign towards Bull's Wood.

If the headlights followed them, they were in trouble. She switched off her own lights, and waited.

'What's happening?' whispered Yasmina.

'Shh! Nothing. I'm just being ultra careful . . .'

She could hear the car's engine out on the A41. It was getting closer. If the car passed them by and continued on into the night then there was nothing to fear. She held her breath and listened out. It got closer. Was it slowing down? No! Thank fuck, no – it had driven right past. She waited a little longer, until the car had gone altogether.

'Where the FUCK have they gone?' shouted John-John. 'They were right there!'

'Must've turned off. Maybe they needed fuel . . .'

'Well, what's the fucking device thing saying?'

Davey checked. 'Saying they're round here somewhere. Not moving though . . .'

'Jesus fucking wept! In front or behind?'

'Would you mind your language please, John-John? We've minors, here . . .'

'Davey. I swear to you, you're my friend and I love you but, please . . .'

Davey grinned to himself. 'Behind.'

John-John slumped back in his seat. 'Right. Let's go back then.'

She'd just started up the Vespa's ignition when she heard the distant engine, heading back their way. It was a thousand to one it'd be the same car – this was one of the busiest A-roads in the country, after all – but some gnawing dread in her guts told her to be on guard. She'd have to tell Yasmina, for starters.

'Listen – don't freak out, right?' Yasmina nodded, eyes wide with fear. 'I think we might be being followed . . . *might*!' She

threw her arms around her girlfriend. 'Might. OK?' Yasmina
nodded again, mute, rigid. 'It's not a chance we can take. So
I want you to ask no questions, yeah? Sit tight and hold tight
while we're on the steed then, when I say, I need you to move
quickly, quietly, and do exactly as I do. OK?'

Yasmina nodded once more. Jessika kissed her on the lips.
'Here we go, then . . .'

She brought up the GPS on her iPhone, checking to see
exactly where they were, and what their options might be.
She heaved the scooter off the main road and into the shelter
of the trees and, with the headlight dipped, set off along the
woodland path, jolting and vibrating with every bump and
pothole. Her brain was spinning like a washing machine,
clutching at theories, rejecting them, instinctively knowing
she was close. The ogre with the face welt. How the fuck had
he known where they lived? Was he just a local oddball – a
stalker who'd spotted them in the street? No. He'd been there
in the Macbeth, the night they met . . . he had some sort of
inside track on them. She pulled over.

'Sorry, love. Get up a mo, will you?'

She lifted the seat up and checked the storage compart-
ment. Nothing. In the near distance, she could hear the
engine getting closer. Shit. She dropped to her knees and
checked the hubs, the fuel tank, anything magnetic . . . The
car was somewhere very near now. Out there on the main
road, he was shadowing them – whoever he was – and he
seemed to know exactly where they were. She ran her fingers
under the back mudguard and there it was: a small, oblong
unit, no bigger than a postage stamp, cunningly attached to
the back wheel's cover. She was about to hurl it in the pond
when her superconscious stopped her. If the signal just stayed
static, they'd know within a mile or two where she and
Yasmina were hiding. And if there were a few of them – if

they had dogs – they'd hunt them down like quarry in no time. But if they could get away; if they could somehow get the bug onto another moving object . . . She checked her GPS and smiled to herself. Well, fuck you, animal men! This was where the fair sex started fighting dirty! She kissed her middle finger and planted it on Yasmina's helmet, straddled the front of the seat and, revving the engine, burst out of the woods at full speed, straight across the A41 at Oddy Hill and on towards Tring.

She parked up in a cul-de-sac a few hundred yards from the train station, removed her crash helmet and crouched to look into Yasmina's eyes.

'Listen, sweetheart – this might just take a minute; it might take half an hour. Longer. But whatever happens, yeah?' Yasmina nodded. 'Do *not* move from here. Nobody knows you're here but me. Nobody will find you, so long as you stay absolutely calm, and absolutely still. *Capiche?* Good girl . . .'

She kissed her on the lips and sprinted off towards Tring station. From now on, whoever was following them would be chasing her, not Yasmina; and soon enough they'd be chasing thin air.

'Whoa, whoa! Hang on, hold your horses . . . just wait there!'

Davey held the tracking device up and peered at it to make sure he wasn't misreading things.

'What is it? What's up?'

'I'm not sure . . .'

'Give that here, will you?!' JJ snatched it from Davey's hands and scrutinised the small screen. 'Where the fuck are they going?'

Davey shrugged. 'Looks like they're doubling back.'

'Why the fuck are they doing that? What's back there?'

'Can I have a look?'

John-John passed the tracker back to him. Davey held it close, checked with the AA atlas that was open on his lap.

'Heathrow,' he nodded. 'Got to be.'

'You sure?' asked JJ.

'Think it through. Where else would she be going?'

John-John Hamilton nodded mutely. Mehmet's slaying would be all over the news by now; possibly the lummock's, too. Maybe the police would link the deaths, maybe not. With all the madness going on between the Turkish gangs, they'd start their search there – but it was only a matter of time before they picked up a different scent. With or without Hassan's daughter, they were going to have to make tracks themselves. He patted Davey on the shoulder.

'Let's go to Heathrow, then.'

He sat back in the rich-smelling leather passenger seat and started to check his pockets to make sure he'd brought the key to his locker. Money, lots of it. New passport. New you. New start – again.

Patty Flannagan tapped gently on the door.

'Did I hear signs of life?'

There was a smile in her voice – a reassurance that here was a woman who had seen life, who knew life and, come what may, would not presume to judge.

'Come on in!' shouted Jessika. 'We're up.'

Patty pushed the door open with her foot and ducked inside, crouching a little so the tray didn't wobble. Jessika and Yasmina were standing at the huge, floor-to-ceiling casement window, looking out over the mudflats of the Mersey, arms around each other's shoulders.

'Ah, love's young dream!' smiled Auntie Pat, placing the tray on the dresser. 'What's your name again, darling?'

Yasmina turned round, smiling meekly. 'I'm Yasmina,' she

croaked, losing her voice on the 'Yas' part. 'Sorry!' She smiled again and shrunk her head into her shoulders, hoping J-Flan would step in. She didn't. She just stood there, looking on proudly as her auntie took in Yasmina's exquisite features. 'Thank you so much for –'

'Oh, turn it in!' she grinned, swatting away her gratitude. 'Jessika knows that she's welcome any time – as are her friends . . .' She took a step back and winked at them. 'Especially one as beautiful as you . . .' She turned to leave. 'Get that down you while it's hot. I'm heading into town shortly, going to watch a film at FACT.'

She pronounced it *fillum*. Yasmina liked her. She wiped the sleep from her eyes and stretched.

'What time is it?'

'It's getting on, my love. It was nearly six when youse got here this morning.'

They smiled at each other, recalling the adventure again. Jessika had got to Tring station, only to be crushed, initially, at the lack of trains at that time of night. Then, just as she'd been about to give it up and return to Yasmina, she heard the clanking trundle of a goods train, heading south. It was perfect. She quickly worked out which platform, sprinted over the footbridge and waited for the heavy locomotive to roll on by. Choosing a big, empty truck with no tarpaulin cover, she flipped the tracking device into its midst and waved it bye-bye as it journeyed on, out of sight.

They'd waited, still wary, and after a while started out on the Vespa – and that's when it came to her. Yasmina had tapped J-Flan, indicated for her to pull over.

'What's up?'

'I think we're too conspicuous . . .'

'Well, there's no trains, darling. You got a better idea?'

Yasmina beamed at her and pulled out her phone. Dialled up the number.

285

'Hi, is that you, Carrie? Sorry this is so late. I'm in some serious trouble. Can you do me one *massive* favour?'

And she came for them. Her burly skinhead taxi saviour drove them all the way to Rock Park on the banks of the Mersey, playing great tunes and telling great stories all the way there. This time she let them pay her.

'Wow! Was it really that late?'

'That *early*!'

'It was indeed. So . . .' She smiled at each of them, individually. 'If youse want to join me to see the film, you are very welcome indeed – but youse'll have to get your skates on. If not – and I suspect not – *mi casa* is yours. Don't make too much mess. I'll see youse when I see youse . . .'

She gave a minimal curtsy and left them to it.

'What do you reckon?' smiled J-Flan. 'You want to see some of Liverpool?'

Yasmina turned to her, her face radiant. 'I'm happy,' she said.

'That's great. I'm happy too. But my auntie –'

Yasmina silenced her with a kiss. 'No. What I mean is – I've never felt like this before. It's just . . . it's amazing. I feel . . . *amazing*.'

Jessika put her arms around her and kissed her on the forehead. 'Good girl,' she whispered. She stepped away and sat on the edge of the bed, watching her fragile lover with all the love in the world. Outside the window, down on the riverbanks, curlew and lapwing skated across the slick and mossy mud, cooing their twilight mating calls. Yasmina stared out in wonder. Everything – everything – was new. She'd had it hard, J-Flan – she was as hard as they came. But sitting there, slowly coming to understand what this was – the enormity of it – she was flooded with a profound enlightenment that, right now, this was something special. She shivered and lay back and let her tears flow freely. No one would ever harm that girl.

They'd checked Millie into St Bernard's immediately they'd landed in Gibraltar and, even though it was a private ward, the RGP had stationed a guard each end of the corridor. She'd been in there nearly two hours, now. The consultant had been excellent. Millie's breathing had become sharp and shallow and they'd radioed ahead for an ambulance, but she was in safe hands now, getting the very best care. Dr Christian was troubled by a shadow the X-rays had picked up on one of Millie's lungs, so he'd ordered an MRI scan. Forty-five minutes maximum, the ward sister had told Mac.

His phone vibrated again. He whipped it out of his pocket to see who was calling. Shanley. The sister gave him the look again and he tried on his smile. She shook her head – again – and jerked her thumb at the little park outside the window. He nodded and, with a quick glance towards the cabin-style clinic they'd wheeled Millie away to, Mac headed off down the corridor and let himself out through the fire doors. Something about the action – the furtive subterfuge – instilled a keen desire to smoke. He ignored it, found a little bench and called Shanley back.

'Sorry about that, sir. Matron's breaking my balls over phone usage on the ward.'

'How is she?'

'Short answer – don't know yet. She's undergoing a full MRI on her chest.'

'Precautionary, one hopes . . .' He was all *rs. Prrrreh-cohrr-shun-rrrree.*

'I'm sure that's all it is . . .' He paused and waited for Shanley to fill him in. Nothing. The silence irked him, yet some childish will to play the game and see who caved first made him sit there and listen to still air. After an eternity, Shanley spoke, gravely.

'You're alone, I take it?'

'I am.'

'Very well. So . . .' Another lengthy pause. 'Hamilton arrived in Ibiza shortly after ten this morning on a flight from Heathrow . . .'

'Interesting . . .'

'It gets better. He was accompanied by one David Lane. This is where it could get tricky, though.'

'Go on.'

'On the simple narcotics matter – the hashish, the El Glaoui connection – we've got him. Hung, drawn and quartered . . .'

'Really?'

'Absolutely. The special-agent fella in Morocco . . .'

'Jawaad? Jo . . .'

'Yep. He's got him. Video, wiretaps, photographs . . .'

'They found Ahmed's stash, I take it?'

'They did. They've got footage and photos and an entire media card filled with the data and details of El Glaoui's rotten life – deals, meetings, drug handovers . . . and Hamilton is there, stage centre, almost every frame. Best supporting actor, I'm telling you. The bastard is done for, when we get him . . .'

'When we get him . . .'

'Precisely. So . . .'

'So – you said it was a tricky one. What's the problem?'

Another silence from Shanley. He never used to be this bad, Mac thought. Worse than bloody Hodge!

'OK. We think – Scotland Yard thinks – he's on the run from at least one murder. There were two killings last night, less than thirty minutes apart. Both Turks.'

'Right . . .'

'But we – they – don't think it's related to the recent troubles. A number of witnesses have come forward, descriptions more or less matching, and at least three of them have referenced a high-performance Audi that was found at Heathrow. Forensics are all over it, as we speak.'

'What about the victims? Any similarities?'

'Well, yeah, I was coming to that. Different weapons used but lots of similarities in the MO. Look, Billy –' He broke off. 'It's Hamilton. Travelling under the name of James Rae . . .'

'So what's the problem?'

'The problem is that the Spanish might claim him as their own. It's their surveillance, their team, their operation, their evidence . . .'

'But this is a murder investigation, now.'

'Precisely. We need you to bring that to bear.'

'Who do I need to speak to? In Madrid –'

'No one. Just the main guy in Ibiza.'

'Who is?'

Shanley hesitated. Cleared his throat. 'Who is Comisario Rodolfo Molina.'

McCartney's arm hung limp. He stood up, paced the little park, looking out over the ice-blue sea. Somewhere, out there, was Ibiza. The White Island. Somewhere, there, was John-John Hamilton, enjoying his last moments of liberty, if he but knew it. Out there, too, was Rodolfo Molina – the man who almost cost Millie her life. He became conscious of Shanley's voice rasping out. He brought the phone back to his ear.

'Molina?'

'Molina.'

'Fuck them,' thought John-John Hamilton. He wasn't going

to turn off at first, but the closer he got to the glass house the angrier he got. The place was his. He'd bought it, with cash; his cash. The authorities may think they'd seized it back under some proceeds of a crime scam they'd cooked up, but whoever was living there . . .

He calmed himself; took long, deep breaths. OK. He'd drive down the dirt track. Park up right outside. But just to take a look – to remind himself how things used to be, and would be once again. It had been a long sabbatical, but these last few days chasing his tail, back in London, asking for favours, for deals, for bits and pieces . . . it wasn't him. JJ was a fucking leader. A doer. Fair enough, Davey liked the simple life – job here, job there, get paid, go to ground; but that had never been him. The Moroccan business had seen him right and served him well for years, but everyone knew it was small beer. Everyone knew where the money was. Those Rozaki boys knew all right. He'd given them their fucking start in this business, and once he'd let the heat die down, sorted his new passport, his persona, his story, he was going to pop along to see those Kurdish wild boys in Walton, and he was going to put forward an irresistible proposition. He felt a tingle of merriment just thinking about it. The boys would soon be back in town.

He slowed up in front of the house and let the engine run as he looked up at the old place – different, now, with so many trees lopped, and what looked like a pool house on the far side of the lawns. He stifled a gust of nostalgia. He'd been king of all this, in his day. People flocked to him – girls frol-icked naked in his pool. It seemed like yesterday. He'd have to make sure it was tomorrow, too.

The front door creaked open and a wary-looking old boy in immaculately creased shorts and a pale blue sweater took a step out, waiting for John-John to declare himself. He pressed the button and dipped an apologetic hand out of the window.

'Wrong house. Sorry . . .'

He backed up and turned the hire car around. The old guy, joined now by his wife, watched until he'd rattled back over the cattle grid and turned right onto the San An road.

The military helicopter landed on a strip at the hippodrome end of the airport. The young private, who had not made eye contact during the short flight from Gibraltar, stationed himself by the hatch and waited for a knock from outside. He popped a code in and hauled the big lever back, causing a loud vacuum-suck as the door opened outwards. Millie, as she had done since they embarked, carried on staring straight ahead. McCartney signalled to the private that it was OK to give them a minute. He saluted, turned and backed down the short flight of steps.

'You OK?' asked Mac. Millie nodded but didn't pull out from her trance. 'You sure you want to do this?'

She turned to him, not quite there in the moment. 'Did we get through to Yas?'

'We're still trying. Her phone is switched off . . .'

'Why?'

Mac shrugged. 'Could honestly be anything. Maybe she didn't take the charger.'

Millie nodded again, her thoughts far away. 'Try and stop me,' she muttered.

'Sorry?'

'You asked if I want to do this. The answer is yes. More than anything – almost anything – I want to get the men who did this.'

Mac took her wrist, stroked the palm of her hand with his thumb.

'OK. That's good. I think that's really –'

She turned back to him sharply, her eyes alert, now. 'What do I have to do?'

Mac gave a resigned cheek-smile and pulled out the phone. 'Recognise it?' She nodded. It was Hassan's phone, retrieved from the helicopter. 'Great . . .' He glanced out onto the tarmac. A line of green uniforms was now waiting to escort them to their appointment with Molina. Mac brought up the contacts list on Hassan's phone. 'Do you think you can –'

She interrupted, not unkindly. 'Billy? Do *you* think you can stop fucking patronising me?'

He smiled, properly this time. 'Sorry. You're right. OK – is John-John Hamilton's number on this phone?'

'I don't think so . . .'

'OK. What about James Rae?'

Her questioning eyes met his. A quick nod. Yes.

'Excellent. Excellent. We're in business. John-John Hamilton, prepare to meet thy Maker . . .'

He went to help Millie up, thought better of it and stood back while she climbed down from the helicopter. For the first time since they'd started out on the mission, Mac experienced the shudder of professional anticipation. For the first time, he fancied his chances of bringing this one in.

What was left of his hair was white, as was the robust moustache. He got out of his chair, smiling broadly.

'Mr McCartney . . .'

'Chief.'

He met him halfway across the floor, reaching for his hand and shaking warmly.

'Good to see you, good to see you . . .' He gestured to a brown leather cup chair and turned back towards his own. 'Last time was not so good . . .'

'No. No, it was not good.'

He stopped, midway through the sitting ritual. The smile disappeared. Eyes fixed on McCartney, he lowered himself into his seat.

'Neither of us was exactly truthful, Mr McCartney . . .'

'It's DCI, these days, sir. Detective Chief Inspector . . .'

'Oh? I was informed that you had retired.'

McCartney smiled icily. This was not going well. 'Not exactly, no. I took some time off.'

'I see. Congratulations . . .'

Mac breathed in through his nose and tried to keep smiling. 'Your English has improved, sir.'

'My English was always excellent, DCI McCartney.'

'Ah. Very good. A master of disguise . . .'

'You too, McCartney. So I hear . . .' He picked up a pen, scribbled a note on his jotter. 'Now, without wishing to be rude – would you care to tell me how I might be of assistance? The truth, this time . . .' He threw Mac a devastating smile. 'In as few words as possible. I have criminals to catch.'

Mac mugged up a cooperative smile and launched into his pre-planned pitch.

'We have a target, sir. Someone we've been after for a while. We believe we know where he's hiding.'

'Here, I presume?'

'Here. And we would very much appreciate your cooperation in –'

'Who is this target you seek?'

'That information is classified, sir.'

'Oh? It is? Huh.' He feigned surprise. 'So I take it you have extradition papers et cetera?'

Mac let out a long, desperate sigh. 'Shall we not play games, sir? You know who we're after. I'm sure you'd love to collar him yourself – God knows, he's given you reason enough . . .'

'He has. And you're right. I have hoped to have this opportunity for many, many years. The chance to make right all the wrong he did. All the bad things he had me do. Yes, I was not innocent. I knew what it was I was doing. But without John-John Hamilton, no. I don't think so. Hamilton is a man who persuades you that wrong is right. Bad is not so bad . . .' He shook his head and looked out of his window. 'Many, many years I want to get this chance. I know you will appreciate this more than anyone, Billy . . .' He stood up and walked the floor until he stood over McCartney. 'I want to look into that bastard's eyes and tell him – Hamilton? You are nicked. Then I die happy.'

Mac stood up himself. 'Sir! Hamilton is wanted in London for murder.'

'Here also.'

'Please. He should face the courts in England.'

'So extradite him. Meanwhile, I shall go about my business –'

The door flew open. DS Camilla Baker stood there, eyes ablaze.

'Are you for fucking real? Both of you! Is this what the job really is? Who gets the catch? Who gets the kill?'

'Madame, I –'

'You don't know who I am, do you?' She strode across the office until she was inches away from Molina, looking up. 'Why should you? Why would you even care?'

'Comisario Molina, this is Millie . . . Camilla Baker –'

'Shush, Mac. I'm talking to Molina. The man who sold me.' Molina went to protest. Millie pushed him hard in the chest. 'That's right, *comisario* – that is *exactly* what you did! You might tell yourself you looked the other way, you took a bung, whatever it is that allows you to carry on coming to work, living your life . . .' Molina was speechless. He sat there, stunned, mouth slightly agape, looking up at the angry golden vision, railing at him with an unhinged fury. 'It must be nice for you, hey? You do your penance. Serve your time. Wipe the slate clean and start again. We all make mistakes, hey? Carry on . . .' She turned to McCartney, cheeks a furious pink, eyes flashing, and jabbed her finger as she spoke. 'Not for me, though. A group of men conspired to take my life away from me . . .' McCartney tried to swallow back the bitter bile rising up. His throat tightened, grief strangling him. 'That's what happened. I went out to work one night, and the girl I was, was stolen from me. That girl never came back, that night. She never will . . .' McCartney choked on the stone in his throat. Millie jerked back to Molina and pointed right in his face. 'That was you. Don't you dare try to fucking deny it. The things you did . . . the deals you cut . . . the situations you tolerated . . . *that* is what took my life.' Her voice had dropped to a whisper now. 'Those men could do whatever they wanted to – and that's down to you.' She crouched down so her nose was almost touching his. 'Mr Molina. Don't even begin to try to tell me that I won't be the person looking into Hamilton's eyes when we get him. When he understands it's over. All of it. That's down to *me*.'

She walked out. McCartney and Molina stayed exactly where they were, in silence.

The call came through on his A phone. Lad called Phil Davies, done a bit in the Dam, Morocco. Apologised for the cold call, said one of the Liverpool boys in Amsterdam recommended he get right onto him. He wouldn't name names – quite right – but it must have been one of the lads for him to have this number. Said he had a cracker – Ibiza seasonal thing, ready to go that summer. Said it couldn't fail, but he needed partners. Didn't want to go to the old guard, heard good things about himself – right again – and wondered if they could meet. Nothing binding – little look at one another, little chat. He sounded all right – bit camp, bit 'jolly-good-show', but that could be exactly what he was looking for, right now. It'd do no harm for JJ to reconnect with life's connoisseurs.

It was just a coffee anyway – what was the worst that could happen? Regardless, he was taking Davey with him whether he liked it or not. On the way out, he ducked back inside for the NAA they'd picked up that morning.

They pulled up in the Jockey Club's car park. Wasn't there, back in the day. He liked the look of it – right on Ses Salines beachfront by the salt pans. Bit close to the airport but fuck it. He was liking this already. Be a good little corner come the summer.

'Sure this is on?' said Davey.

'Not till we get there,' smiled John-John. 'Why?'

Davey shrugged and undid his seat belt. 'Dunno. Feels weird.'

'That's cos it's fucking February, you blert!'

'Suit yourself. Just saying. Davey doesn't like it.'

He checked all round as he shut the car door and followed John-John, doing up his jacket as he crossed the little sand dunes round the back of the cafe.

'James!' shouted the bloke. He got up from his table at the far end of the decked terrace. Older than JJ was expecting. He looked like Our Man in Havana in his white flannel suit. A little too well groomed to be a player, but he knew better than to judge people on how they looked, especially in this game. He stood back until they sat down – proper gentleman.

'This is my partner, David Byrne,' said JJ. Davey held his hand out. The old guy shook.

'David. James. I'm Philip – great to meet you boys. Please . . .'

Nice smile. Looked a bit like Bowie in that comeback video in Berlin. He passed them each a menu.

'I've ordered,' he smiled. JJ was intrigued. What foolproof scheme could this genial professor-type possibly have devised? He looked more suited to a BBC travel programme or *Antiques Roadshow*, something like that. 'It's all very good, but if you're into seafood . . .' His eyes lit up. '. . . the sardines are . . .' He kissed his fingertips. '. . . *magnifico!*'

JJ winked at Davey and placed his menu down. 'Sounds fair enough to me. Sold. David?'

Davey looked away. He still didn't like it. There was no one else around – maybe that was the trouble – but he just could not relax.

'I'll have the Caesar salad.'

'Lovely! That, too, is pretty fucking good. Some wine? Beer?'

Davey shrugged. Davies held three fingers up to no one they could see.

'*Tres cervezas, por favor!*' He sat back and clapped his hands together. 'Fuck knows why I ordered in Spanish. I think she's from New Zealand . . .'

The waitress came out and stood over the table carrying, not a tray of drinks, but a handgun.

'Hi, John-John . . .'

Davey Lane was off over the ranch-style beach fence

straight away, the sand slowing him down as he headed back to the car park. Hamilton sat there staring up at a face he knew well, unable to compute or comprehend what was happening here; that this was the law, and his time was up.

'What . . . what the fuck are *you* doing here?'

'Pleased to see me?'

He stood up, looking from Mac to Millie for a sign, some indication that someone was going to tell him what this was all about.

'Sit down, John-John . . .'

He sat down again, his eyes flickering with questions. 'If this is about your girl –'

'Close, but no. Not that girl. It's about another girl this time. Twenty-five years ago she went to a party of yours in a house not far from here, high on a hill. She was a bright kid . . .' She glanced at McCartney. 'Very good at her job. So good that you never knew her real name. Detective Sergeant Camilla Baker. Want to say hello to her?'

'If I must . . .'

Millie took another step towards the table and leaned her face in close.

'Hello, you cunt.'

Hamilton sprang up, knocking the table over and sprinting off across the beach towards the salt pans.

'May I?' asked Millie.

'All yours,' said Mac.

She didn't run. Keeping Hamilton in sight and her gun in hand, she walked after him, knowing the terrain would slow him down.

He scrambled up to the rough-made road and, exhausted, his head lolling from side to side, tried to drive himself onwards, open up a gap. He snatched a look behind. She was way off; wasn't even running. He could see why. Up ahead, green-and-white police cars sealed off the road. He stopped for a moment, panting for breath, crouched double and leaning his hands on his thighs. He took another look behind. Two, three, four uniformed officers had hold of Davey. The girl – Hassan's wife – was walking calmly, relentlessly towards him with this look on her face. It wasn't as though she was smiling but there was something invincible, something deathly about her. She terrified him; he couldn't move. He felt for his pistol. Fuck! Did he not go back inside for it? He had! Must've left it in the car. He tried to fight back his panic and think clearly, think coolly. This was closing in on him and, whatever he did now, it was going to be definitive. It was John-John Hamilton's last chance.

To his right were the salt pans, as thick and frosty as night-frozen snow. He ducked down and started into another jog, crunching through a field of hard rock salt. The police back on the road started shouting into a loud-hailer, but he could see a way out now. Up ahead was a wooded area and, beyond that, the whitewashed husks of an urbanisation. If he could make it to the trees, he could get into the little housing complex and lose himself. He'd done it before. He broke into a faster sprint, his jacket coming open and swinging from side to side. The weight of his revolver hit him in the ribs. Of course! The double pocket. Supposed to be for a wallet or a mobile phone. He delved inside, prised out the little Guardian – just a light hand pistol for everyday use, but lethal, for its size. He turned to check her progress. She was on the first salt pan – out of range, but he'd fire off a warning, anyway. He knelt down, rested the revolver on his wrist and, screwing his left eye shut, let one rip. He saw it burst a small crater in the salt field's patina, but the bitch just carried on walking. He pocketed the handgun, took one, two, three deep breaths and, exhaling hard, drove himself on towards the woods.

Millie made her mind up not to shoot. Hamilton was panicked, trapped, desperate. He could run all he liked; she'd carry on after him until he could run no more. She wanted to see him fall at her feet. She wanted him to look into her eyes; to know how that felt.

Breathe, blow, breathe, breathe, breathe, blow . . . breathe, blow, breathe, breathe, breathe. He kept his eyes on the trees. Not too far now. His legs were starting to roll as the swamp began to sap his stamina. Still he pushed himself on. If he turned round, he dared not think what he might see. He could hear frantic shouting, dogs barking; the skies were coming down on him.

'John-John. Stop.'

Fuck. He turned round. She was right there, holding her arm out like she was trying to rescue a drowning man. He looked her in the eye, checked the distance to the trees and set off again.

'John-John Hamilton! Stop right there!'

The pans were soggy now, more paddy field than salt drifts at this end of the site. His feet sucked up vacuums of mud as he trudged on, staggering now, slipping as he ran, the woods getting closer. A demented scampering of hooves or paws, splashing through the quagmire. He stopped and turned. Dogs. Alsatians. He groped for his gun and took aim: one, two, three shots. The girl was ten feet away. Twenty at most. He knelt down and took proper aim. He had her in plain sight. Sorry, love. Bang.

She carried on walking towards him. Behind her, it was all a blur, but the girl came closer, and closer, and closer in sharply defined focus, that solemn, avenging look on her face. He fired wildly, his hand shaking, knowing he'd missed, then turned and, screaming out in anguish, ran as fast as his leaden legs would carry him through the salty shallows of the furthest pans. Something snagged his ankle. He twisted and tugged and jerked frantically, trying to shake his foot loose. He hauled his entire leg upwards, dragging a thick, seaweed-strewn rope with it. He let it drop, moving his foot backwards then taking another step forward with his free leg, trying to loosen the rope's grip. He wriggled and jerked, but both feet were snared now, caught in a lattice of nets laid out just below the surface.

'It's over, John-John,' she said. 'It ends here.'

He looked her in the eye and dropped to his knees and hung his head. He stayed like that a moment, his fingers closing around the netting, his knees sinking down in the sludge. Footsteps sloshed towards them. He looked up. The Bowie lookalike came up behind her, hesitated a moment, then put his arm around her. She turned and looked right into his eyes, then buried her face in his chest. He pulled her close and stroked her hair very gently and – strangely, for cops – he kissed her lightly on her scalp.

The icy blast slammed them sideways as they stepped off the plane but, for Millie, nothing could chill the glow that smouldered inside her. She tugged at McCartney's wrist, knowing they were there in arrivals, urging him to quicken his pace. He smiled and squeezed her hand.

'Any minute, Millie,' he laughed. 'Any minute now.'

They were waiting right there, as soon as the customs doors slid back to let the latest flock out. Yasmina with a rangy, cool-looking girl and a handsome older lady and, just behind them, their hands held to their mouths, tears flooding their spectacles, a well-groomed older couple – Millie's mother and father. There were various others grouped around and about – a middle-aged couple with kids, other relatives, friends, probably some ladies and gentlemen of the press mingling in – but Millie only had eyes for one soul. She shrieked loudly, dropped McCartney's hand and ran, arms spread out like a swooping eagle, and gathered up her daughter in a besotted, suffocating bear hug. For an age they stayed like that, speechless, holding each other tight. Mac mugged up a face for the punky girl, who blanked him and carried on smiling down on Yasmina.

Eventually they broke for air and Millie made her way over to her parents, her friends and well-wishers. A good-looking woman in her forties pushed through and came to a standstill right in front of Millie. For a second or two they just stared at each other.

'Hiya, Jen,' Millie whispered.

'I've really missed you,' murmured her sister.

They held one another and stayed like that. Mac sidled away to get a coffee and wait his turn. He was happy. This was good. Queuing up at Costa, he was no nearer knowing if he'd come back; would rejoin the force for good. He knew he was good at it, though – that was for sure. He knew he was born to do this job.

He fingered the little wrap in his pocket. He'd only decided to give it to her, in the toilet, on the plane. Fixing himself, and feeling the rush of exuberant, bristling energy, it was followed by a powerful desire to *do* something – something symbolic, something meaningful. Something lasting. Whatever Millie might be feeling – might think she was feeling – that could never be. He was older, now. He knew how that particular story ended and, for McCartney, it would always end the same way. He'd tell her soon enough – but not now.

He paid for his coffee and stood back and watched Yasmina. Saw the way she looked at the punk girl; the way the girl looked back at her too. It was beautiful. It made him want to cry. Up until then, he was giving the ring to Millie as a farewell. An apology, but also a symbol of something enormous they had survived together; she much more so than himself. But sipping his coffee and watching those girls woke him up to something else. He might never have that again – if he'd ever had it at all – but he was living a life less ordinary in his isolation. In doing this work – and he was going back now, he was certain of it – cops like McCartney, like Millie, were taking small steps towards making a place where Yasmina and the scary punk chick stood a chance. That was not nothing. That was a life worth living. Perhaps, in time, she might come to look upon the ring as a celebration of that.

He took another glug, let the bitter-hot sting sear his throat, then made his way back to the reunion. He whispered into Millie's ear: 'I'm, er . . . can I have you a moment?'

She told the gabbling gang she'd be just a minute, followed McCartney to the bench seat and sat down beside him.

'Hi,' he said.

'Hello,' she smiled.

'I, er . . . I'm going to leave you guys to it. Take your time. There's a bit of catching up to do there, hey?'

Millie nodded, still too heady with the bliss of all this to pick up on any aubade. McCartney took the ring out of his pocket.

'This was my dad's . . .' He held it out on the flat of his palm. 'I'd like you to have it.'

'Me?'

Very carefully she unwrapped it, held it between her fore-finger and thumb, tried it on, took it off. Something caught her eye. She held the ring up to the arrivals lounge strip lighting, and squinted to read the inscription. She lip-synced, just loud enough to hear.

'*For you. Fair Cop.*'

She nodded to let him know she understood, but didn't put the ring on again – not yet. McCartney stood up and smiled down on her and held out his hand to shake.

'Well then,' he said, and turned and headed for the exit. For McCartney, it always ended that way.

ACKNOWLEDGEMENTS

Huge respect and thanks to my editor Beth Coates for her tenacity and sensitivity.

Stanton – warm up. You're going on.

Thanks to Jim Fitz for insights into The Job.

Thanks to Matt Craig, Barry Forshaw, Mike Hodges, Sandra Mangan, Nick Quantrill and the enigmatic Raven for supporting Mac so stoically.

Kate Haldane – thank you.

Big, big thanks to Stephen Parker for always clothing my books in the finest jackets.

And Helen: we are the best.